ALSO BY
MATTHEW STOVER

*Iron Dawn*

*Jericho Moon*

*Heroes Die*

*Blade of Tyshalle*

*Star Wars: The New Jedi Order: Traitor*

*Star Wars: Shatterpoint*

*Star Wars: Episode III: Revenge of the Sith*

# CAINE BLACK KNIFE

# CAINE
# BLACK KNIFE

### THE THIRD OF THE ACTS OF CAINE:
### ACT OF ATONEMENT, BOOK ONE

## MATTHEW STOVER

BALLANTINE BOOKS 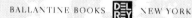 NEW YORK

A Del Rey Books Trade Paperback Original

Copyright © 2008 by Matthew Woodring Stover

All rights reserved.

Published in the United States by Del Rey Books, an imprint of The Random House Publishing Group, a division of Random House, Inc., New York.

DEL REY is a registered trademark and the Del Rey colophon is a trademark of Random House, Inc.

Library of Congress Cataloging-in-Publication Data

Stover, Matthew.
Caine black knife / Matthew Stover.
p.   cm. — (Acts of Caine ; 3}
"A Del Rey Books trade paperback original."
"The third of the Acts of Caine: Act of atonement: book one." — T.p.
ISBN 978-0-345-45587-1 (pbk.)
I. Title.
PS3569.T6743C3 2008
813'.54—dc22        2008027581

www.delreybooks.com

Book design by Liz Cosgrove

*For Robyn, again.*
*And always.*

The future outwits all our certitudes.

—ARTHUR M. SCHLESINGER JR.

"This is my battle wound," he said, and he laid his stump on one of the gangrenous sores on Caine's leg. "This is your battle wound. Our wounds are one. Our blood is one."

"What the fuck are you doing?"

Orbek's lips pulled back from his tusks. "I'm adopting you."

"Are you nuts? I'm the guy that—"

"I know who you are," Orbek said. "You remember who I am. Dishonor you put on the Black Knives. Now that dishonor, you share." He showed Caine his tusks. "Now what honor you win, you share that, too. Good deal for Black Knives, hey?"

"Why would I want to join your fucking clan?"

"What *you* want? Who cares?" Orbek rose, grinning. "You don't choose your clan, Caine. Born Black Knife, you're Black Knife. Born Hooked Arrow, you're Hooked Arrow. Now: say that you are Black Knife, then let's go kill some guards, hey?"

Caine lay on the stone, silent.

Orbek growled, "Say it."

The lamp gave Caine's eyes a feral glitter.

"All right," he said at length. For all his tiny, mostly useless human teeth, he managed a surprisingly good mirror of Orbek's tusk-display. "Like you say: I am Black Knife."

—*Blade of Tyshalle*

# CAINE BLACK KNIFE

The Adventure depicted in this recording has received a rating of

# UV/X

from the

**STUDIO RATINGS ADVISORY BOARD**

for full-sensory experiences of:

**TORTURE**

**SEXUAL PERVERSION**

**EXTREME GRAPHIC VIOLENCE**

and

**ADULT LANGUAGE**

The Viewer's access of the images and sensations contained in this recording constitutes a legal agreement, in which the Viewer fully indemnifies and holds harmless Adventures Unlimited Inc. and all subsidiaries, for any and all damages actually or potentially result-ant to said access, including (but not limited to) emotional trauma, physical injury and mental disability (permanent or temporary).

*introduction*

then: MAXIMUM BAD

now: GIFT

# MAXIMUM BAD

## RETREAT FROM THE BOEDECKEN (partial)

You are **CAINE** (featured Actor: Pfnl. Hari Michaelson)

MASTER: NOT FOR DISTRIBUTION, UNDER PENALTY OF LAW.

The dirt-colored cloud spreads wide, hugging the horizon, draining into hollows of the distant hills. "That's them," I say to no one in particular.

The bloody sun behind my left shoulder stains cloud and hills together, and the shadow of the escarpment overhead spreads like oil across the badlands.

Tizarre stares. Her face goes pinched, and her knuckles whiten on the scabbard of her broadsword. "You're sure? How can you be sure?"

I could quote Sun Tzu at her: *Dust high and sharp will be chariots. Dust low and wide is infantry,* but instead I shrug and hand her the monocular. If Sun Tzu had ever seen infantry like this, he would've crapped his silk fucking pajamas.

Tizarre puts the monocular to her eye, and what's left of her color drains out of her cheeks. "Shapes in the cloud . . ." A whisper. "A *lot* of them."

I nod at Rababàl. "Maybe you want to have a look, huh?"

Platinum flashes in the flick-flick-flick of the coin-size disk that appears, disappears, and appears again between Rababàl's stubby fingers: this is what he does instead of thinking. His jowls, gone slack and sweat-streaked through the grey-coating dust, belie his carelessly nimble hands. "We have only a tendays' supplies. We cannot afford any delay; our backers—"

"Aren't about to get assboned by a couple hundred ogrilloi. Unlike, say, us." I lean on the parapet and look down into the rumpled badlands. "If that band weren't coming here, we could have maybe broken camp and scattered into the wadis. Maybe."

"Get *away*? You mean retreat? Run? *Flee*?" Marade gives me a reproachful stare I can see upside down in her impressively curved cuirass. Must have caught her at prayer: she's in full armor, and I can't pretend I don't like the look. She gives whole new meaning to the word *breastplate*. The twist of scorn on her face favors her—S&M cheesecake on steroids. "I would dislike to use the C-word—"

"My name's a C-word."

Her sudden booming laugh spills blond hair down her back. The hair's almost as shiny as her armor, and I can't help thinking one more time that I could really kinda get into her if she ever gave me look one. Those thighs . . . man. She could crush my pelvis like a biscuit. "But we cannot let them simply drive us like woodcocks, can we? Without a single engagement?"

"You'd know more than me about wood cocks." Her smile slips a little. Sure: dyke jokes. Brilliant. *That*'ll make her like me. "One engagement is all we'll get."

"We have more than two dozen men under arms—"

"Porters with swords."

Pretornio, fumbling within his cassock: "With the Skills of Dal'kannith Wargod, those porters—"

"Sure. Those porters." I make a face. "You think they're looking to fight ogrilloi on five royals a month? They're just hired labor."

The platinum disk suddenly stills. "*Need* I point out—" Rababàl's scowl probably used to really impress teenage apprentice necromancers. "—that you, Caine, are yourself 'just hired labor'?"

"Shit, no. You remind me twelve times a fucking day." This work-for-hire stuff sucks dogshit. The best boss in the world is still only a butt-whisker this side of a collar and a whip. "So if you ignore my advice, you're not exactly getting your money's worth, huh?"

"Perhaps—" Pretornio coughs a wad of dust out of his throat, and wipes sand from his lips with the back of one bloodstained sacramental glove. "Perhaps we should, um, pray. For guidance—?"

"Maybe he's right." Dark swipes underline Tizarre's eyes when she lowers the monocular. She's talking about me, not the Lipkan priest. Out of all of them, she's probably the only one who buys what I've told them. A close-up view—courtesy of Mr. Zeiss—of a few hundred ogrilloi converging on you in that twenty-mile-an-hour grizzly-bear lope can make a believer out of anybody. "Maybe we need to run. Right now."

That gets the partners squabbling again. Everybody's worried about their fucking money.

Shitheads.

I let them argue for a little, then I break it up with a sharp *"Hey.* Nobody said run *now.* We can't run. They're coming *here."*

They stop and stare at me like I just blew tentacles out my nose. I swing an arm over the parapet at the fever-tossed bedsheet of the Boedecken badlands. Wadis spray out from the base of the city in a sagebrush tangle that used to drain off whatever dead river once fed this hellhole. Though a thousand folds cover you from pursuers at ground level, from this high up the cliff wall you can see the bottom of every twist. Probably why those millennium-dead elves built a city here in the first place. "Once they hit these ruins, where are we gonna hide?"

Rababàl's gallowglass Stalton nods toward the dusk-shadowed lip of the plateau that eclipses half our sky. "What about upland?"

"You've seen it. A tabletop for five days' ride. Rising to the mountains. We can't even hide over the horizon."

He nods, understanding. Grim. "At least we'd have a head start."

I could get to like him. We working stiffs oughta stick together. Except I keep wanting to smack the crap out of Rababàl, and if I try it Stalton'll stomp me into a Caine-shaped grease stain. Not personal. Just his job. But it puts a cramp in our friendship.

I give him a shrug. "Nothing outpaces a hunting ogrillo. Especially not us."

"A Cloak." Tizarre's looking a little wild around the eyes. "I can do a Cloak—"

"No, you can't."

"It's just grassland, right? Right? Grassland's *easy.* It all looks alike anyway. Easy. Even all of us. Even the horses. I could—I really *could*—"

"—waste your time," I finish for her. "Ogrilloi are scent hunters. How good's *your* nose?"

"How do you know they're coming here?" The platinum disk vanishes again, and Rababàl heaves himself off the stone-cut bench. He joins me at the parapet. "They could just be—I don't know, following a herd of bison. Migrating. Something."

I open my hand toward Tizarre. She puts the monocular in it, and I pass it to Rababàl. He hefts it appreciatively. "Nice metalwork. Dwarven?"

"Yeah. Dwarven." Like I'd tell you even if I could. "Pick up the vanguard just below that double notch."

He puts the monocular to his eye. He flinches, and has to swallow twice before he can say, "Yes."

I don't blame him for the flinch. "Now track straight down, about halfway from them to here. See the two riders?"

He smothers an indistinct curse. "They look human."

"Yeah."

"*That's* what the ogrilloi are chasing—?"

"Yeah."

"They're leading them straight *here!*"

I spread my hands silently: *quod erat demonstrandum.*

Everybody goes quiet, and their gazes all turn inward while they calculate what that might mean. I flash my teeth at Pretornio. "You want to pray? Pray the grills catch those guys."

He stiffens, and color flares high on his cheekbones. "I will *not!* We should be trying to find a way to *help* them—"

"I'd help them, if I could. I'd help them to a couple arrows through their skulls." I get the monocular back from Rababàl and squint through it again. "But my bow doesn't have the range. And anyhow I'm a crappy shot."

Thunder gathers on Marade's face, and her eyes go colder than her Ice Queen cheekbones. "Caine—" She leans toward me. "I shall decide that was a *joke.*"

The chill in her eyes reminds me that for all her bluff good-natured piety, you don't get ordained a Knight of Khryl unless you really kinda enjoy killing people.

"Decide whatever you want." I can do that *I like to kill* look too. "If those guys make it here, the grills'll come after them. *Here.* Looking around. Searching. Sniffing. Hunting *humans.*"

I let them roll this around their mouths for a second or two. They seem to find the flavor bitter.

"There's two of those guys. There's thirty-eight of us. There's a couple hundred ogrilloi. At least. Do the fucking math."

They turn on each other and everybody starts to talk at once. I shouldn't have mentioned math: they're arguing about their sonofabitching *money* again.

Ever wonder what the gods think of money? Just look at the people they give it to.

I bring up the monocular. One horse is down, struggling, vomiting bloody foam. The other rider has turned back, whipping his horse to reach his partner, but his own horse is stumbling already, barely even carrying itself—it'll never manage a gallop with them riding double—then the horse stumbles again and pitches into a face-first roll, the rider sprawling from the cliff shadow into the bloody sunset, and he comes up limping but still humping ass for his partner who's pinned under his dying horse, and maybe they might get him free before the ogrilloi get there, but even if they do they're on foot now and they don't have a chance of reaching even the scrub-covered fold of dirt that was once the city's ringwall. They don't have anything like a chance, and I have this sinking knot at the bottom of my throat and a cold twist in my guts and I—

I lower the spyglass and stare at it in the palm of my hand: an abstract shape of brushed steel that no longer makes sense to my eye. I looked into the distance and got a twenty-power view of myself. What a sick, sick sonofabitch I am.

I hate that those guys are on foot now . . .

Not that I was rooting for them. No. Not even that I don't really want to see what the ogrilloi will do to them. If I don't want to see it, all I have to do is put away the Zeiss.

No.

I'm *disappointed* . . .

What the fuck is *wrong* with me?

In some shit-rotten depth of my cesspit heart, I *want* the ogrilloi to trap us here.

I want them to hunt us through the ruins. To catch and kill and eat these men and women with whom I have eaten and drunk and joked and slept. To catch and kill and eat even me.

In this stark mirror, I finally recognize my face.

Things just aren't ugly enough yet.

I want this to get all the way worse. To go so dark it erases the memory of day.

It's got nothing to do with balancing on the bubble between Hot Prospect and Never-Was. Nothing to do with slipping backward into the second half of my twenties, trailing three years of hit-challenged Adventures. Those are only surface images. Reflections on a black pool.

A deep one.

I put the monocular to my eye again, unable to believe I actually *want* to see what I want to see—but I do. I do. God help me.

I want maximum bad.

The guy's out from under his dying horse. He's got a rotten leg, limping raggedly, leaning on his partner, shin pouring blood: compound fracture. Poor bastard doesn't have a chance. Now it's just a question of whether the grills'll take them before they can kill themselves.

That sick greasy slime is back in the bottom of my throat, though I *am* relieved. I really am. I know too well what'll happen to us if we're taken by ogrilloi.

But at the same time, y'know . . .

"It's over," I say, glass still to my eye. "This has all become academic."

The discussion behind me breaks off and Rababàl's breath starts to warm the back of my right ear. "They're caught? Let me see."

I don't move. "You really want to?"

I can't help thinking of Dad: he used to tell me praying is only talking to yourself. A useful form of meditation, nothing more. But that was back home. Things are different, here.

So if my prayer is to be granted, I should probably figure out what the hell I'm asking for.

Tyshalle? You listening?

The humans crest a spine in the badlands and go skidding down the slope into a wadi. They sprawl on the sand-dusted rocks; the uninjured one manages to sit by pulling himself up a scrub joshua hand-over-hand. He leans on it for a second or two, watching his friend's blood soak into the thirsty earth. He says something, and his partner casts his arm across his eyes, lies there like he's not going to answer—and a strange light kindles between them, an insubstantial liquid iridescence scattering prismatic splinters that spreads to touch them both, crawling their bodies in a halo of rainbow—

And they are gone.

In the dusty creekbed, only scuffs in the dirt and a black splotch of drying blood shows they were ever there.

Well.

I hear my own voice, dry as that empty creek. "How about that."

"What? What's happening?" Now they all cluster around me, demanding answers that my conditioning won't let me give. Those guys were in my line of work.

They got pulled home.

Funny. I should tell Pretornio: the trick to getting your prayers granted is to ask for something that's gonna happen anyway.

Okay. Not funny.

The ogrilloi are still coming at a gallop, following a trail they're going to lose . . . on a straight line with the ruined city where we're standing right now, which kindles a strange hot black anticipation down somewhere around my balls.

They're coming. Here. They really are.

Hunting humans. Humans they'll never find. Humans who no longer exist in this universe.

They'll have to settle for us.

I raise the lens to take another look at their approach.

On they come: part bear, part gorilla, all predatory leather-skinned di-
nosaur with warthog tusks and fighting claws as long as the knives in my rib
sheaths. They run with spear and shield and bow strapped across their
hogshead-size backs, their long gnarled arms becoming front legs for that
ground-eating lope. It's almost enough to raise a smile.

For a second or two.

Then one big bastard pauses for a second to rear up on his haunches for a
better view of the land ahead, and I get a good look at the blazon, the clan
sign, painted on his chest, and all at once that anticipation in my balls goes ice
cold and my scrotum's clenching hard enough to squeeze tears from my eyes.
Because the blazon's a single swipe of obsidian angled from left shoulder to
right rib, gleaming as though the paint's still wet, curved and wickedly pointed
in the shape of an ogrillo's fighting claw.

I know that design. *Everybody* knows that design.

Okay. I take it back. I take it all back. Fuck *all the way worse.*

Now I'm fucking *scared*, and I want to go *home*, and that's not gonna happen, it's never gonna happen because those guys got pulled exactly there to do
exactly this to exactly us, and my guts dissolve into water chilled by the column of ice that is my spine, and all I can say is—

"Wow."

I shake my head and start to laugh. I can't help myself. Out of all the clans
in the whole fucking Boedecken—

Those are *Black Knives.*

I never even knew what maximum bad *looks* like. That's why I can't stop
laughing.

Because I guess I just found out.

# GIFT

*A*nd you know already it's not a dream.

You know it by the smell of scorched pig fat trailing up from the lamp's smoking wick. You know it by the dirty yellow light leaking in through the veiny grease-smeared parchment that covers the shack's lone window, by the grey splinters in the weathered plank door on trestles that passes for a table, by the mildew-blackened straw humped into a pair of beds back by the earth-wall hearth.

But you know only that this is no dream; you have not yet guessed that this is My Gift to you.

There is the feel of alien muscles, too long and hard for human; your arms are now a double-span longer than your legs. Your pebbled hide slides over ribs too heavy, not flexible enough, guarding a heart that beats too hard and too slow. Pale northern sun barely warms your spinal ridge through the heavy leather of your tunic. Your trifid upper lip parts around your upcurved tusks and you growl, *Kopav Dust Mirror. They tell me he dens here.*

The smaller of the two ogrillo studs inside swivels on his stool till his back is to you. His spinal ridge is bent like a bow: pup rickets, maybe. His skull crest is bald and bleached with age. *You smell human.*

The big one snorts. *Hrk. Human.*

You take a step, clearing the doorway. *I want to find Kopav Dust Mirror. I can pay.*

*Bet you can, citybred.* The small one glances over his twisted shoulder. *Nice boots.*

*Yeah. Hrk. Boots.* The big one snuffles a gust of corruption. Something rotten's stuck in his teeth. Maybe it's just his teeth. *Don't see boots like that in Hell.*

*Or Ignik Dust Mirror. Either one. Ignik 'Tchundiget.*

*Don't know you, citybred.* The little hunchback flips one fighting claw forward over his fist, examining it ostentatiously. *Name your clan.*

*Black Knife.*

Both studs go still. They stare at you so they won't look at each other.

Finally the hunchback says, *Ain't Black Knives. Ain't since the Horror.* His shell of overplayed boredom has dissolved into wary tusk-display.

You shrug. *I can take that up with Kopav.*

*Black Knife? Hrk. Black Knife?* The big one sniggers. *Looks more to me like No Knife.* He looks at the other. *Good one, hey? No Knife.*

Your heart thumps into a heavier cadence that swells your brow ridges with angry blood, and you look down at your arms, at the sleeves of your tunic; sleeves longer than any ogrillo ever wears, sleeves so long they'd foul your fighting claws. If you had fighting claws.

Your wrists are empty as a human's. Blank except for wads of scar tissue.

The stumps of your shame.

You give your shame the answer you carry in a sheath sewn inside your tunic: an SPEF KA-BAR, seven inches of matte-black chrome steel blade so sharp that just its pressure against the side of the big one's neck draws a thin chain of blood-beads gemlike along its edge.

*This enough knife for you?*

*Hey now.* He doesn't move: not as stupid as he looks. *Hey now.*

The hunchback rises, slow, hands up and open, the human gesture of surrender. His fighting claws fold along his forearms. *No need to hook red, hey? Easy now. Just say what you want, hey?*

*I want some eyeball with Kopav Dust Mirror.*

*You might like to tell me what for,* he offers, sidling closer.

*You might like your fuckbitch's head where it is.* You add a little pressure to the knife. Blood spoor pumps your salivary glands. *Keep your teeth off my kill.*

*Hey—hey, fuck!* The big one looks puzzled. Offended. Not frightened. Not hurt. *Hey, I'm cut! He cuts me. Hey—*

The hunchback considers this. *Here's the call, citybred. Come back two league-walks after sundown—*

Your eyes flick toward the window, instinctively, to check the light and gauge the hour, just a flick, less than an eyeblink, but they knew you'd do it and the big one jerks his head back from your blade and one fighting claw jams for your groin while his other slashes for the forearm tendons of your knife hand. You twist sharp enough to knock the groin stab aside, but you feel the tug below your navel and a sudden flood scalds your crotch and thickens the air with sweet hot blood. You flick the KA-BAR in a short arc and the blade sticks in bone; the big one howls and wrenches his arm away into the table and it collapses and he goes with it. The little one lunges fast as a pro but your other hand comes out full of Automag and a single squeeze of burstfire unlaces his belly and blows him spinning backward to crash into the shack wall.

The parchment window rips. Sunlight stabs a curl of gunsmoke.

A continuous clang sings in your ears.

The big one cowers, kneeling, tears painting crimson streaks along his snout. The hunchback sits crumpled against the wall, cursing in a low, steady monotone while he tries to hold his guts in place with both hands. *Fuckbitch. You got a gun. A fucking gun. You never say you got a gun, you fuckbitch.*

You step over to him, Automag leveled on the big one. *Kopav Dust Mirror,* you remind him.

*Fuck my bitch. I never be shot before. Fucking guns. This kills me, hey?*

*Likely.*

*You fuckbitch.*

*Want to go easy? I track that.* You squat beside him and show him the knife. *Want to go hard, I can track that too.*

He stares through you.

You shrug. *Or lie in your shit and hope a Knight comes. Maybe Khryl grants a Healing after you tell him how you try to gut me for my boots, hey?*

His eyes drift shut.

*What you want?*

*It's you, hey? You're Kopav?*

*Yah.*

*You're Kopav 'Jurginget? Kopav Black Knife once?*

His eyes open again. They're the same color as yours. *Once,* he says. *In pup-time. Before the land hates Black Knives. Long gone now. I'm Dust Mirror since the Horror. No more Black Knives.*

Your upper lip curls under and your lower peels down, baring your tusks to the roots. *Except for me.*

His gaze fixes on you, and there's a hint of a spark there before a spasm of pain smudges his face blank. *What you want?*

You stand, knife in one hand, Automag in the other. *Submission.*

*Huh.* His face goes old now, tired and sad. *Just that?*

*Yeah.*

*Fuck my bitch. Dint have to shoot me.*

You cock your head half an inch. *Dint have to rush me.*

*So—submission.* His jaw works. *And?*

*And you go easy.*

He stares at you for a long time. From outside come grunts and distant shouts and shuffle and scuffle, drawn by the shots. Inside there is only blood and bowels and the whimper of the bigger one clutching the spurting gash in his forearm. You can see pain picking up steam by the waves of emptiness that roll through the hunchback's eyes.

Finally he hisses resignation. *Dint have to shoot me.*

You wait.

He rolls himself forward off the wall, kneeling, and lowers his face until his forehead rests on your insteps. You thumb the Automag over to single shot.

He says, *I give myself to you—*

You center the muzzle on the crown of his spinal ridge.

*—fuckbitch.*

The slug splinters a fist-size hole through the floor planks. A wet one. You track the hunchback's brains over to the other.

*Ignik? Ignik Dust Mirror: Tchundiget?*

*Uh.* He lifts eyes like bloody eggs. *Kill me too, you gonna?*

You twitch the Automag and point it between your boots.

*Down.*

Whimpering, he presses his forehead into his sire's gore. *I, I, I give*—he's snuffling so hard he can barely get the words out—*I give myself to you.*

You drop to one knee and tuck the Automag back into its holster by your kidney. Ignik gasps when you grab his wounded arm—bone scrapes together in there: splintered ulna, maybe. You press the gash your knife left on his forearm to the shallow rip his fighting claw gouged in your belly.

*This is my battle wound. This is your battle wound. Our wounds are one. Our blood is one.*

His jaw hangs open like he's trying to draw flies to the rot on his teeth. *I uh I uh I uh—who are you?*

*Use your fucking feet. Black Knives don't kneel.*

*Bu bu bu hrk?* He smears crimson tears off his face with a greasy hand. *Black Knives?*

You palm the KA-BAR and roughly square his shoulders. *You're filthy, little brother. And soft: too long in Hell. Your tusks are grey. Your neck bends easy.*

He slobbers. *And you—you—and you—*

*I am Black Knife.* You flip the KA-BAR pommel-first and hand it to him. *Now, so are you.*

My Gift has now been given, and I release you: you open your all-too-human eyes, stare at the mold-eaten plaster ceiling above your bed, and mutter, "Son of a *bitch.*"

And I imagine that it is the weight of years you shed to rise in that grey dawn. The deep ache in your joints may be the memory of dread: darkness and terror, the cotton-rip of flesh tearing under blunt claws, the icy inevitability of agony and death—

And yet it may be only the scars of half a century at war.

I cannot know. Though I feel the grinding of hip and shoulder and the scrape of hangover-dried eyelid, taste the fewmets of last night's brandy and smell the old sweat that stains your tunic with salt rings—though I can count the pulse in your temples and calculate to a nicety the uneasy pressure in your bladder—I can never know what you're thinking. Perhaps this is why you have fascinated me so. It is as good a reason as any.

Which is to say it means nothing at all.

You limp, stiff with morning, to the dirty bubbled window and rest your forehead against the autumn-cool glass. I fancy you wonder how you came to be so inexplicably old; I fancy you recall yourself facing Black Knives at twenty-five and marvel that as many years have passed from then to now.

You turn aside to the water stand and mop your face with a dripping towel that smells of rot. When you regard your reflection in the silvered glass above the basin, you scowl at the scrapes of white at your temples, at the salt in your once-black beard. You scowl and you shake your head and you scowl some more, and you sigh like a tired old man . . . but we both know it's a pose.

Shall we say: an act?

The dark flame in your eye is as plain to you as it is to me.

Your scowl turns thoughtful, and I know: you're thinking that I could be lying to you.

What My Gift has shown you—is it history? is it news? is it prophecy?

Is it horseshit?

And I watch your scowl settle, and harden, and finally crack toward a grim smile, and I know: you have discovered that you don't care.

I have Called. You will answer.

Have you found in your heart yet a story you can tell your daughter, that sweet half-godling child who dreams of you in her castle bed so many leagues away from this mountain town? Will you share with her guardian a reason? An excuse?

Or when they call for you, will only echoes answer?

Will you say to Lady Faith, ten-year-old Marchioness of Harrakha: "Your Uncle Orbek's getting himself into some trouble. I owe him. He went into the Shaft for me."

Will you say to Lady Avery, the formidable Countess of Lyrissan: "I have to go north for a while; there's news of Black Knives in the Boedecken. You don't want that kind of trouble to your north."

Or will you tell them the truth?

Will you reveal the fresh trip of your pulse? The high sweet song adrenaline hums in your veins, the youth My Gift breathes into your old, tired legs?

Will you tell them that you feel alive again?

This is My Gift to you, My Devil. Come out from your place and walk once more to and fro upon the world and go up and down in it. I give you back your joy. I give you back your passion. Come forth, My Caine. My love.

Come forth and serve Me.

Come out and play.

*part one*

# BELOW HELL

I leaned on the deck rail and silently numbered my dead.

The slow heartbeat of the riverboat's steam-driven pistons pulsed in my bones. The waterfall hush from the sidewheel's rising flukes shuffled the chatter and bustle of passengers and crew into white noise. I preferred it that way.

I've never been exactly social.

I had barely spoken since Thorncleft. I traveled alone. I couldn't have made myself bring companions. Not to the Boedecken.

Not on this river. My river.

Fucking astonishing: how many people I knew who died up here. I couldn't remember all the names. Rababàl, Stalton, that Lipkan supposed-to-be priest of Dal'kannith . . . Pretornio. Hadn't really thought of them, any of them, in maybe twenty years. Lyrrie. Kess Raman. Jashe the Otter. Others. Dozens of others. Thirty-five? Thirty-six?

I couldn't pin down how many. I wasn't sure it was important, but somehow I thought it ought to be.

Back on Earth, it'd have only taken a minute or two to dig the cube out of my library and start to live the whole thing again. I didn't think I would have.

Didn't think I could have.

After I retired—in the bad days, that seven years when my legs never quite worked and the background music of my life was a mental track of the nearest bathroom because I could never tell when I was about to shit myself—I sometimes cubed my old Adventures. Caine's old Adventures. Just on the really bad days. In the bad nights, when the shitswamp I'd made of my life sucked me down and drowned me. But I never cubed this one.

Not that I had to. All I had to do was stop holding it all down.

I still held it all down. Still hold it all down. I didn't even know why. They're fucking *dead*. Every one of them. Dead in the Boedecken Waste.

Nameless corpses in the badlands' dust. Left to the buzzards, the crows and the khoshoi.

Left to the Black Knives.

And if somebody let any of them out of Hell long enough to take a new look at this fucking place, the shock'd probably kill them all over again.

The gravel-scoured folds of the badlands had softened into rolling fields of maize and beans, well-ordered woodlots and neat rows of birch and alder windbreaks. Where the land was too rugged for food crops, the hills were terraced with vineyards: long trellised racks of twisting bark-shagged vines hung with purple and red and green clusters that I could smell even down here on the river. The river was itself new: shallow with youth and careful engineering, its broad slow curves fed the vast network of irrigation ditches and ponds and reservoirs that had brought the Waste to life. And somehow I couldn't make myself believe this was a good thing.

These waves of living green looked like *less* to me.

The old Boedecken had been exactly that: old. Carved by time into its true shape. Harsh, jagged, scarred by existence, grim grey jaws locked onto the ass end of life.

I'd kind of liked it that way.

The river was the only change up here that hadn't surprised me. Whenever I let myself, I could make the river's birth happen inside my head vivid as a lucid dream. Like lots of births, the river's had been ugly. A sea-wrack of pain and terror. A hurricane of blood.

The kind of fun I hadn't had in a long, long time.

I kept my head down while the riverboat churned through the outer sprawl of Purthin's Ford. I wasn't ready to look up at Hell.

I knew it was there. When the light was good and the air was clear, I'd been able to see the Spire for two days.

But I didn't look up now, while neat rows of white brick houses and red tile roofs around well-ordered plazas commanded by greystone Khryllian vigilries drifted south behind the docks and warehouses to either side, while chill black shadows of high-curved bridges wiped the ship from bow to wheel to stern, and the tiled arches were tight enough around the deck that I could smell the soap somebody had used to scrub the stonework clean.

I made a face that cracked the dust on my cheeks. When I licked my lips, they tasted like an open grave.

What was I, superstitious? Didn't feel like fear. Didn't feel like what people used to call post-traumatic stress disorder. Sure, if I let it, every second of *Retreat from the Boedecken* would come alive in my brain just like it was happening all over again. But that shouldn't scare me. Just the opposite.

This place *made* me. I came here a nobody on my way to never-was. I left here the legend I always wanted to be.

Everything I've ever done pursues me. Like a doppleganger, a fetch, my past creeps up behind and strangles me in my sleep. When hunted by a monster in your dreams, you save yourself by facing the monster and demanding its name. In learning the monster's name, you rob it of the power to haunt you. But I was awake. And anyway I already knew my monster's name.

It was Caine.

My father used to tell me that you can't control the consequences of your actions. You can't even predict them. So all you can do is your best, and all that matters is to make sure what you do will let you look in the mirror and like what you see.

I can't remember the last time I liked what I see in the mirror.

There was a writer from Earth's twentieth century who wrote that "sin is what you feel bad after." Of all the things I've done, what I did up here—

Maybe that was the feeling that made my mouth an open grave. That hung a brick around my neck to hold down my head. Maybe it was shame.

Maybe that was why I couldn't put a name to it.

I've never pretended to be a good man. I have done very, very bad things in my life. Anybody who believes in Hell believes that Hell exists for men like me.

Fair enough. I was on my way.

On my way back.

After a while, I pushed myself off the rail and went into my cabin to organize my shit for debarking.

I still hadn't looked up at Hell.


Just so we're clear: I didn't come to the Boedecken to save Orbek. I didn't come to save anybody. Saving people is not among my gifts.

Shit needs to be settled eventually. One way or another. That's the only way I can explain it.

Or even think about it.

There was a novelist on Earth, back around the beginning of the twenty-first century, a guy my dad admired quite a bit. He wrote some books where the basic idea was that since you can't control the consequences of what you do, the only thing that really counts is why you do it. You get it? The measure of right action is righteous intention. This writer was a religious type—a Mormon, don't ask—and I guess he figured that if your heart's right, God takes care of the rest.

Well, y'know . . .

I know some gods. Better than I want to. Not one of them gives a shit about your heart.

A couple of years ago, a friend of mine wrote a book that was supposed to be the story of his lives. Or stories of his life, you pick. Anyway: he wrote that what your life means depends on how you tell the story.

If it makes you feel better to pretend I had some noble purpose, knock yourself out. If you'd rather pretend I was driven by guilt, or by personal obligation, or that I just finally grew up enough to want to clean up my own fucking mess, that's fine too.

This is the story of what happened when I came to the Boedecken. *What* happened. Not why. The only *why* is that I made up my mind. I decided, and I went. That's it. Anybody who needs to know more about *why* should go ahead and fuck off.

Reasons are for peasants.

My dead wife—the one who decided she'd rather go play goddess than be married—she used to like to say that not everything is about me.

Screw that.

Who's telling this story, anyway?

I dragged the travel trunk bouncing down over the ribs of the gangplank. At the foot of the plank I took a couple steps to the side to clear the way for the passengers behind. I stood the trunk on end and sat on it.

*All right, you bastard. I'm here.*

I've been doing the Actor's Soliloquy for so many years it's mostly reflex: whenever my attention starts to wander, I find myself narrating my life in sub-vocal twitches of lips and tongue and glottis. I used to make a good living at it; back in the day, such subvocal twitches had been registered by a tiny device inside my skull behind my left ear and transmitted a universe away to Earth, where a sophisticated computer algorithm had translated them into a quasi-thoughtlike internal monologue for the amusement of tens of thousands of narcotized fans who'd paid obscene amounts of money for the illusion of being me.

My life always played better than it lived.

Those days are long gone, but I still monologue. Now I play for an audience of one.

*Dammit, I'm* here. *How about a hint? A clue? A pillar of cloud? A burning sonofabitching bush?*

I waited, but there was only dockside chatter and the rustling thump of cargo nets, whistles of distant birdsong and the ripple-slap from the river.

God doesn't talk to me anymore.

"Fine," I muttered. "Fuck you anyway."

Maybe He'd decided to hold a grudge for that sword-through-the-brain thing. Which suits me fine, most of the time; I have a grudge or two of my own.

I shoved myself to my feet and dragged the trunk back into the line of passengers filing toward the customs barn.

The queue was minded by spearmen in cheap-looking hauberks, Khryl's sunburst displayed on their chests in scuffed and faded yellow paint. Their helmets and the shields slung on their backs looked like quality work, though, the sunburst design inlaid in polished brass, and the half-meter blades that tipped their spears were conspicuously well tended. Hand labor on the docks was done by teams of ogrilloi, who wore light tunics in various degrees of stained disrepair. The tunics seemed to be some kind of uniform; each of the various work gangs had its own distinctive design.

They also had their fighting claws sawed blunt.

Each gang also had two or three grills in oversized versions of the sunburst hauberks, with helmets that bore flares of steel bars descending from their lower rims, fanning to guard the neck. These supervisors each carried thick hardwood staves maybe five feet long, their ends capped with steel and knobbed with nailheads.

More interesting were four humans who patrolled the dockside on the backs of heavily muscled horses. No cheap chainmail for them; theirs was so fine-linked it rippled like watered silk, and their sunbursts gleamed with gold leaf. Most interesting of all were their weapons: in addition to the traditional seven-bladed morningstar of the Khryllian armsman, each of them carried slung on a shoulder what looked like the most serious kind of riot gun, despite being filigreed with gold on the intaglioed walnut stocks and chased with electrum: under short straight no-choke barrels, their tube-mags terminated in foot-long, no-frills, cold steel bayonets.

Times change.

Some people blame me for that. Go figure.

I gave a sidelong squint to the nearest of the horses until my attention drew its gaze. And got nothing. The horse's stare was bleak: dead as a chip of stone. Curls of foam dripped around the pivots of the curb bit wedged deep into his mouth. A martingale with straps an inch thick locked his head down. And spending all day hauling around two hundred fifty pounds of chainmailed pain-in-the-lumbar wasn't doing the poor fucker any favors either.

It hurt me just to look at, and I don't even like horses all that much. Horses in general. About all I can say for horses in general is they're a hell of a lot better than people in general.

The dockside was eerily quiet, despite the crowd of passengers from the riverboat, despite the teams of sullen hulking dockers cranking donkey-wheel cranes to swing cargo nets off or onto barges, loading or unloading chocked-wheel wagons that stood with yokes and traces empty, despite all the sausage carts, the pastry kiosks and the dozens of little freestanding market stalls thrown up in the shade of high warehouse walls. When the riverboat's steam whistle shrieked noon into the silence, people all over the dockside jerked and jumped and then laughed at themselves—but even the laughter was subdued. Self-conscious. Nervous. People instinctively knew that the quiet here was no accident.

The dockside was quiet because the Khryllians like it that way.

It wasn't a good quiet. It wasn't library quiet, temple quiet, evening-by-the-fire quiet. It was lying in bed without moving because Dad's drunk in the hall and you don't want to give him the idea of coming into your bedroom quiet. When your authority comes straight from God, shit always turns ugly.

And these were the good guys. I've known my share of Khryllians. And they *are* good guys. Honest, upright, true-motherfucking-blue do-or-die parfit gen-til knights of renown. That just makes it worse.

As long as I was just shuffling along in line, it wasn't too bad. A couple of feet every minute or two, dragging the trunk, leaning on it when I had the chance, shading my eyes against the sun to watch the grills work the docks—

I could take it. Being there.

I didn't have to do anything. Didn't have to make any moves. Nobody got hurt. Nobody died. Nothing unlocked the black vault inside my chest. Not even the Spire, a thousand-odd feet of whitestone looming behind my left shoulder. The glare off its facing made a pretty good excuse not to look up at Hell.

The passenger queue snaked to one side of the customs barn; most of the smothering semi-gloom inside was full of cargo crates and livestock and white-shirted human clerks with clipboards, charcoal pencils in stained fingers and behind blackened ears, damp seeping rings below armpits. Autumn sun heated the corrugated steel roof to a medium broil that cooked human sweat, cow and pig farts, machine oil, wood mold and rotting straw into a chewy stench, familiar, suffocating.

Smelled like civilization.

I passed the time reading an enormous poster of fading edge-curled parch-ment that listed in six languages the bewildering variety of items which non-Soldiers of Khryl were forbidden to possess or import into Purthin's Ford. Some were understandable enough: a variety of impedimentia related to com-bat magick, edged weapons with blades longer than two-thirds handbreadth, that kind of thing. But others made me shake my head. Grapevine cuttings? Beverages of greater than 17 percent alcohol? Live mealworms?

The lower margin contained two vividly recent additions painted in double-size brushstrokes of arterial scarlet:

CHEMICAL EXPLOSIVES
FIREARMS

A handful of customs inspectors worked their way among the crates and nets and cargo pallets. They wore circlets of what I guessed might be electrum strapped around their skulls; from those circlets depended an array of individually jointed mechanical arms, each of which supported a lens. The lenses varied in size and color, and the inspectors would squint through each in turn while examining a suspect container. They looked bored, as did the inspector who stood beside the passenger queue, similarly scrutinizing hand luggage.

I smiled bland-friendly as the inspector examined me and my trunk through a succession of six different lenses. All I had with me were clothes, toiletries and gold. The inspector frowned. "You show positive for weapons."

"Can't help that."

"Extend your hands."

I did, palms up. Open. Empty.

The inspector switched lenses, then nodded to himself, muttering as he jotted notes on his clipboard. "Crimson, grade six—arms, legs . . . hmp. And head." He looked up. "Monastic?"

"Used to be."

He nodded. "Very well. Pass along. Be advised that Khryl does not recognize Monastic sovereignty. On the Battleground, you are fully subject to the Laws of Engagement."

"Yeah, whatever."

"Be sure to examine the Laws in your visitor's guide. Monastic training beyond grade four designates you an Armed Combatant at all times. Unarmed Exemption never applies."

"Grade four?"

"Combat grades are detailed in your copy of the Laws. Grades beyond four involve the use of magick. Or, in your case, Esoteric Control Disciplines."

"You seem to know more than most about Monastics."

"I am a Soldier of Khryl. We know more than most about fighting."

"Huh. Fair enough." I leaned a little closer and lowered my voice. "You get a lot of trouble with that stuff?" I nodded toward the poster. "Firearms and explosives?"

"More every day. Ever see what a gun can do to a man?"

"Once or twice."

The inspector shrugged down at the paper on his clipboard. "Bombs are worse."

"I'd rather get blown up than a couple other things I could name."

"Yes." The inspector squinted up. "Know anything about the Smoke Hunt?"

The back of my neck tingled. *Smoke Hunt.* Like an echo of something I almost heard . . . Finally I shrugged. "Fuck all."

"May Khryl grant you keep it that way. Pass along."

I shuffled forward. This trip was turning interesting already. Not in a good way. But I hadn't expected good.

The stamp clerk at the head of the line didn't bother to look up. "Name and nation."

"Dominic Shade." I fished documents out of a worn leather purse that hung from my belt. "Freeman of Ankhana."

The clerk took the documents from his hand and opened them, but instead of reading them he glanced to one side, where a mountain of blond human in glittering plate armor stood at parade rest, visored greathelm under his left arm. The mountain scowled faintly, staring.

I gave the mountain back the ghost of a smile. I learned twenty-five years ago that I can't be read by the truthsense of even the most powerful Khryllian Lord. And nobody better than Knight Attendant—barely out of novitiate— gets stuck with shit duty like checkpoint verification.

Not that it mattered; I was telling the truth. I mostly do.

Dominic's the name I'd gone by when I first came to Home, playing a promising novice at the Abbey of Garthan Hold. In the depths of the gambling hells of Kirisch-Nar, where men fight beasts barehanded in the star-shaped arenas called catpits, I am still remembered as Shade. I was granted the freedom of the Ankhanan Empire some three years ago—not long after I murdered the Empire's god.

But let that part go.

The Knight's lips tightened. The clerk nodded absently. "Welcome to Purthin's Ford, Freeman Shade. I see here you are Armed grade six—impressive for an Incommunicant. Monastic?"

"Retired."

"Ah. Very well." He made a note. "Current occupation?"

"Business traveler."

"Really?" The clerk sniffed and looked up through his brows. "We don't often see Armed Combatants making careers in sales. What's your line?"

"Wholesale weights and measures."

"Indeed."

I tipped a bland wink toward the Knight Attendant. "Prepare, lest ye be weighed and found wanting, know what I mean?"

The Knight Attendant's left eyebrow twitched. Fractionally.

"Yes." The clerk sounded less impressed than the Knight looked. "Duration and purpose of your visit?"

"A few days. Maybe a week or two."

"And you're here on business?"

Maybe it was worth telling the truth here, too. "I'm here to see my brother."

"His name?"

"Orbek."

"Orbek Shade?"

"No." I deadpanned the scowling Knight. "Black Knife. Orbek Black Knife. Sept Taykar."

The Knight's scowl evaporated into blank astonishment. The clerk dropped his pencil, fumbled for it. Charcoal crumbled in his fingers. "Oh, very funny." He brushed at charcoal crumbs, smearing black across his table.

"If you say so."

"What's his *name?*"

I nodded at the Knight. "Ask him."

The clerk turned, mouth opening. The Knight's astonishment had now given way to naked suspicion. "Our Lord hears no lie."

The clerk pointed his gape back my way. "Your brother's an *ogrillo?*"

"Is that a problem?" I turned a palm upward. "Other than for my mother?"

"I, ah, I ah, I—don't know. I suppose not, er—"

The Knight's eyes narrowed over a mouth gone hard. "You claim this so-called Black Knife as brother?"

"How many times do you want me to say it?"

"There are no Black Knives in Purthin's Ford." The Knight turned away, lifting a finger clad in jointed steel. A liveried page scampered toward him, and the Knight spoke in tones too low to be heard through the general bustle.

Couldn't read his lips, either. Call it a wash.

The page headed for the cityside door at a walk with an eager tilt of the torso that hinted it wanted to be a run.

Call it a wash with dirty water.

I pushed a sigh through my teeth. "So all right, let's go, huh?"

The clerk looked blank. "I'm sorry?"

"Is there a law against family visits? Is there some goddamn tax to pay? Do I need a dispensation from the friggin' Justiciar?"

"I, ah, well—no, I don't—"

"Then stamp my fucking papers, huh? It stinks in here."

"Freeman Shade." That mountain of Khryllian steel and meat loomed at my shoulder. "Soldiers of Khryl are treated with courtesy. And deference."

"Yeah?" I showed teeth to eyes as blue and empty as a winter sky while I channeled the ghost of me at twenty-five. "Hey, sorry."

I turned back to the clerk. "*Please* stamp my fucking papers."

There came the metallic rustle that is the only sound well-tended armor makes when its wearer shifts his weight; it didn't quite bury the strangled growl the Knight failed to lock inside his throat. "Soldiers of Khryl are *not* spoken to in this manner—"

"No? Then I guess just now we all must've, what, nodded off and had the same dream?" I showed more teeth. "Does this mean we're in love?"

Cunningly jointed gauntlets creaked with the clench of fists. "Freeman Shade, you are Armed as you stand, and your manner constitutes Lawful Challenge. Must I Answer?"

The second half of my life leaked back into me with a long, slow sigh of old-enough-to-know-better. I jammed the monster back in its vault, but I still had to lower my head before I could speak. Even at fifty, I can't make myself back down while looking a man in the eye.

"No," I said. "I apologize. To both of you."

The Knight glowered into my peripheral vision, waiting for an explanation, an excuse, a *Fatigue from my long journey* or an *I was only joking.*

But I just stared at the floor.

"You apologize."

"Yeah." *What do you want, flowers and a fucking box of candy?* my young ghost snarled, but I fixed my gaze resolutely below the Knight's chin and bit down till my jaw ached.

The Knight took a long, slow breath.

Then another.

"Accepted."

"May I go now? Sir?"

The Knight lifted another finger, and another page scampered up. "Take the freeman's trunk to the lucannixheril."

"Hey—"

"Freeman Shade." The Knight turned an open hand toward a nearby door of iron. It stood open. Down the hall beyond were more iron doors. They were closed. Each iron door had a head-high judas gate. "Wait in there. The page will direct you."

"My papers—"

"You will not need them."

"I *said* I was sorry—"

"And your apology was accepted. Wait in there."

"Am I under arrest?"

The Knight inclined his very young, very blond head. "If you like."

"For what?"

"Because it is my prerogative to declare you so, freeman." His face could have been one of the walls. "As an Armed Combatant grade six, it is your right under the Laws of Engagement to Challenge my authority." He nodded fractionally toward a sunlit opening on the far wall of the customs barn without shifting his expressionless gaze. "Should you wish to make such a Challenge, a sanctified Arena awaits through yonder archway."

"Are you f—? Uh. You're not."

"The matter can also be settled here. You need only strike."

"Strike." I squinted at the Knight. The rules had changed since the last time I was in the Boedecken. Maybe *because* of the last time I was in the Boedecken.

The young Knight offered a bland smile that never rose past the temperate zone south of his arctic eyes. "If I have overstepped, Khryl will favor your cause; Our Lord of Valor is also lord of justice."

"It's a swell theory." I lifted a hand to my face; a headache had begun to chew the backs of my eyes. "Have that page go easy on my trunk, will you? It's new."


The cell was immaculate.

Two doors, both of iron, scoured and freshly oiled; a wide barred window that let in the noonday quiet and a hint of autumn air; walls of whitewashed brick that smelled of clean chalk; comfortable cushions on the built-out brick benches along the walls; a gleaming brass chamberpot in one corner, and in the other, a small table with a pair of fired-clay beakers, an earthenware jug of cool water, a dish of dried fruit, shelled nuts, and a small plate with three different kinds of hard cheese.

Just about the nicest place I'd ever been locked up.

I'd said good-bye to Orbek . . . what was it, four months ago? Had to be. It had been late spring when we made it back to Thorncleft after we settled the thing on the Korish border. Orbek got on the Ankhana train at the Railhead, going home to visit his old friends in the Warrens, he'd said.

To look up some family.

Now with the leaves turning to gold and red we were both on the Battleground, and somehow Orbek had made enough trouble that just mentioning his name bought a quiet afternoon in jail.

I didn't waste time in worry, or energy in pacing. They'd let me out, or they wouldn't.

After a while, I ate.

The sun fell fully on the outer wall of the cell. The brick got pleasantly warm. I stretched out on those comfortable cushions, laced fingers behind my head, and let the headache sew my eyes shut. And for a time I was twenty-five again, young and stupid and vicious, playing *Beau Geste* with the Black Knives in the vertical city . . .

Despite what you've heard, I'm not stupid. I knew already what had been eating me up: that twenty-five-year-old kid. I don't like remembering him. I don't like sharing my life with him. I don't like being reminded I haven't changed all that much.

What's really creepy is that I don't like being reminded how much I *have* changed.

Because, y'know, those black screaming nightmares of blood and terror—

Those aren't nightmares. Not for me. When the scrape of iron on iron wiped away blood and screams and sucked night back inside my head, I was sorry to wake up.

That's the permanent carnival of me.

I rolled onto my side. Slanting sunlight through the barred window loaded my shoulders with an extra quarter century.

The outer door swung open. The first armsman through went left, the next went right, and the third came up the middle: pro style. Each of them had one of those fancy riot guns at slant arms to go along with the morningstars that swung from their belts. Each of them had a forefinger resting lightly on the guard alongside the trigger. Each of them had creases on windburned faces and the lizard eyes of veteran killers.

They wore full-length byrnies and studded steel caps that the afternoon heat must have made resemble walking around with their heads in frying pans. The one in the middle stopped in front of the bench and let the riot gun's business end sag. The muzzle didn't quite cover me. Not quite. "On your feet."

This day was slipping from crummy toward downright fucking grim. "I just woke up."

The armsman stepped back and racked the slide on his riot gun. The muzzle shifted, and the finger slipped through the guard, and I felt a decidedly cold twinge in my testicles. Which was where the muzzle now pointed. "On your feet, *friar*."

"Or what? You'll shoot my nuts off?"

"Or you will insult my office." A new voice, from outside the still-open door: mellow and friendly, traces of a Jheledi lilt making it as deceptively light as the top notes of a pipe organ. "Freeman Shade. Please rise."

A reluctant sigh swung my legs over the edge of the bench. I was too old for this big-dick horseshit anyway. Still, I couldn't help deadpanning the armsman when I stood up. "A boy likes to be asked, dumbass."

Must be something in the Boedecken air. Or something.

Through the door ambled an exceedingly ordinary-looking Knight, below average height—a full hand shorter than me, and I'm not a tall man—well into middle age, thinning hair above a round, kindly face. The Sunburst of Khryl on his cuirass looked shrunken compared with the volume of the chest it didn't manage to cover. A cloak thrown back over his pauldrons was shimmering white only as far as his waist; below, it was splashed the same muddy reddish brown as his greaves and sabatons. A greathelm he carried in one hand was casually passed in the direction of the nearest armsman as he came in. The armsman blanched as he desperately shifted his grip on his riot gun and nearly dropped them both. The Knight didn't appear to notice.

His eyes were warm and brown, and sparkled with some secret amusement as he flicked a finger at the other armsman and waited for him to close the outer door.

The cell felt a good deal smaller.

"Freeman Shade," he said, "I am Tyrkilld, Knight Aeddharr. I would be the Knight Householder for the Riverdock Parish."

"Would you? It's damned swell of you to come personally to welcome me to town. I'm sure you're a busy man."

"Oh, that I am indeed." The Knight chuckled. He blinked as though surprised to find himself standing there. "And to deliver a welcome is exactly why I have come."

"In your Khrylsday-go-to-Tourney armor too."

"Well, that's but to impress the worthy." He crossed his wrists and unfixed the jointed fasteners that clipped his gauntlets to his vambraces. "No one expects to find *your* name numbered upon that gloried roll, freeman."

Knight Aeddharr passed the gauntlets to another of the armsmen. His hands were large and square. The fingers on those hands were short and thick and looked about as nimble as wagon spokes. And about as soft.

This was going to suck.

"So." I let my knees bend a couple degrees, quadriceps and femoral biceps taking the weight that shifted slightly forward, onto the balls of my feet. A breath or two of Control Discipline goosed my adrenals. Everything went bright and slow. "This is where the gloves come off. As it were."

"Of a certainty." Tyrkilld opened those large square hands and spread them

in a man-to-man shrug of regretful necessity. "A mailed hand may well slay before you reveal the truth that God and the Justiciar require."

"You *can* just ask—"

"Oh, that I intend. *Pynhall.*"

I saw it coming: the Control Disciplines had my reflexes hyped enough for
that. I saw it clearly. Not that it mattered.

Just a slap. Open-handed. A wide flat palm that crawled with eldritch blue
witchfire came up from hip level to the corner of my jaw like it had been shot
from a rifle. I didn't even manage to blink before the room whited out and
thunder crashed into the tolling of the vast carillons that call the Beloved
Children to Assumption Day worship at the White Cathedral and I bounced
off something hard and fell on something harder and when the world darkened back into existence and the bells began to fade to distant chimes I was on
hands and knees on a stone floor, staring at a blurred and doubling pair of
jointed steel sabatons caked with brownish-red mud, and *Christ* my head hurt
and I gave it a shake that made it hurt worse and I said—

"Wow."

"Do we understand each other, now?"

I didn't risk another shake of my head. It might fall off. "You have a gift for
expressing yourself."

"You're not the first to notice, freeman." The Knight took a respectful step
back. "You may wish to rise. It's best to be on your feet, and a fair distance from
the nearest wall. I've good control with Khryl's Hand, but there's little help for
you on the secondary impact."

I made it to one knee and looked up into the Knight's kindly round faces:
all three of them. I closed my eyes, opened them, squinted, and there were
only two. "Am I gonna live through this?"

"That remains to be seen. Up you go, then."

My legs'd never make it. "I'm good right here, thanks. How do I get this to
stop?"

"Tell me what I want to know."

"And if I can't?"

"I'm certain you can."

"Then we have a problem."

Armor creaked with Tyrkilld's shrug. "*You* do."

I looked around for something to lean on. The movement threatened to
split my skull. "And if I Challenge?"

"We'll take that as understood, shall we? What are you, grade six?" Tyrkilld
chuckled indulgently. "Strike at your own inclination."

"Oh, sure. Thanks." Leaning with both hands on my bent knee, I let a few more breaths siphon clarity back inside my head. "This is about Orbek?"

"Was that a mystery? The Order of Khryl and the Civility of the Battleground have an interest in the dealings of this ogrillo of yours."

"He's not my ogrillo." A hand to my temple helped squeeze the silent thunderstorm back down inside my skull. "He's my brother."

"So you told Knight Khershaw. And Our Lord of Valor still hears no lie." Tyrkilld shook his head amiably. "With you a Monastic, too. An Esoteric. Likely an assassin."

"I'm retired."

"Not so long ago, you would have been mortal enemies."

"We were. We got over it."

"How this came about must be an interesting tale—"

"A long one, anyway." Too fucking long. "It tells better than it lived."

"—but it concerns me not at all. My first interest lies in what you will tell me about Freedom's Face."

"I'm sure I'd have a snappy comeback if my head didn't hurt so damn much. What the hell is Freedom's Face?"

Tyrkilld sounded honestly regretful. "*Pynhall't.*"

I saw it coming again. Didn't matter this time either. It was the other hand. Which also didn't matter.

I was on my back when my eyes twitched open. The muscles on the right side of my neck were being chewed away by rabid squirrels. I couldn't see them. Or hear them, or touch them when I pawed weakly at the pain. But they were enthusiastic little fuckers. Industrious.

A beige smear that was probably Tyrkilld's face hovered in the middle distance overhead.

"Bodes fair to be a Minor Penance in this for me." His voice had a vaguely oceanic quality, like distant surf. "Freeman Shade, I must tell you that by happenstance—by sad coincidence, for you—my dear father, a Knight of much greater valor and reknown than my poor self, was foully murdered. By a Monastic assassin. Are we becoming still more clear?"

Stone bled into flesh and back out again and my arms and legs spasmed at random; I couldn't even roll over. "Fuck . . . *me* . . ."

"Though I know well it's a dark sin to condemn a man for his brother's crime, I discover I can't help enjoying myself. Just a bit. Hence cometh my expectation of the Minor Penance I lately mentioned; I find myself hoping, in a shadowed corner of my tarnished soul, that you'll play games and be evasive and insist upon this immoral defiance of yours, so that I might deliver Khryl's

Hand unto your sinning head, here, until out from your eye sockets leak the shreds of your vile Monastic brains."

Use leaked back into my body. I made it onto my side and curled around the medicine ball of barbed wire that swelled under my ribs.

"I'd feel bad for you . . . about your dad and your tarnished soul and all—" A trail of blood from my mouth made a tiny fading spiral on the stone floor. "—if you weren't beating the crap out of me right now."

"Can you stand, then?"

"Do I have to?"

"You won't like it if I use the boot."

"I'm no fan of the hand, either." I put out one of my own. "All right, wait. I'm getting up. Give a guy a couple seconds, can you?"

Tyrkilld opened arms to either side of an indulgent smile.

I found one of the built-out brick benches and pushed myself up. The room spun around me and the walls pulsed and my stomach heaved and I staggered past an armsman and made it to the brass chamberpot in the corner in time to decisively lose the cheese and nuts and dried fruit I'd snacked on an hour or two ago.

On my knees again, leaning on the chamberpot, I spat bloody vomit. "Does it matter I'm telling the truth?"

"Each true word scrubs one stain from your filthy heart," Tyrkilld said agreeably.

"I never heard of this Freedom's Face shit until you said the words just now."

"Go to, freeman. Try not my patience."

I got my feet under me and swayed upright. "You're the one with truth-sense, shithead. Am I lying?"

Tyrkilld sighed. "Freeman Shade, are you the man to convince me that Our Lord of Valor's ear for truth cannot be misled by the dark magicks of the elves?"

The vomit-knotted fist in my stomach clenched tighter. "Elves?"

"Next you'll try to tell me that it's pure coincidence that an *Ankhanan* Esoteric has come to visit this *Ankhanan* Orbek Black Knife just *now*."

"Ankhanan . . . ? Oh, fuck." I put a hand to my eyes. "Fuck me like a virgin goat. Freedom's *Face*. Fucking Kierendal."

"Ah, there. There, y'see? Perhaps there is some truth you can share after all. A shy truth, it must be, requiring a bit of encouraging to poke its wee nose out into the light of day." He spread those oak-knot hands invitingly. "Speak to me of this Kierendal."

"Shit, ask me anything. I hate that fucking slag." I wiped my mouth on my sleeve. "So what is it, some kind of Free-the-Poor-Oppressed-Motherfucking-Ogrilloi thing?"

"And behold." Tyrkilld beamed. "Come then; coax your shy truth out from its cranny—" He flexed his right hand meaningfully. "—unless you'd prefer I extend the invitation myself."

"I'm just guessing . . ." I panted harshly, wondering if I might spew again. Probably not.

Dammit.

If I hadn't been so woozy I would've thought to puke down the bastard's breastplate.

"Just . . . guessing. Three years ago the Folk were granted freedom of the Empire. Maybe you heard. They're full citizens now. Full human rights."

Tyrkilld shook his head dolefully. "Ankhanans."

"Don't start. Kierendal is . . . shit, I don't even know what to call her, these days. Call her the Duchess; that's as good a name as any. She's a primal—what you call an elf—who runs some very successful businesses in the capital. Reason they're successful—she also runs a criminal syndicate, a big one . . . grew out of an old-time Warrengang, from a part of the city called the Face. So they were the Faces. Get it? So if someone's running some kind of underground Free-the-Grills shit here out of Ankhana, it's a good bet she's in it somehow. Which is a serious problem for you. Because she is very rich and very powerful, really goddamn smart and completely ruthless. Not to mention connected. Which are the other reasons she's so successful."

"Friends in high places, has she?"

"She used to bone the Emperor. Does that count?"

Tyrkilld accepted this news with a ruefully genial smile and nod. The armsmen didn't even blink.

"Oh, for shit's sake." I shook my aching head and coughed up another wad of sick. "When I get to anything you don't already know, wave a fucking flag or something, huh?"

"Oh, well, yes indeed, there is that. We have a way of uncovering the truth, as you've seen."

"Is this where you start bouncing me off the walls again?"

"Very likely. Now that we've seen you can find it in yourself to be honest with me, when the effort you make—" His hands flexed again. "—is sufficiently *sincere.*"

"Shit."

"Men often do, at certain points in these long afternoons. Let's move on to your, ah . . . *brother* . . . and his friends in the Smoke Hunt."

"The Smoke Hunt?"

"Oh, yes, freeman. You knew we'd come round to this, did you not?"

I took a deep breath, sighed it out. I lifted my head. It weighed a couple tons. "I guess I might have a shy truth about whatever the fuck that is, too."

Tyrkilld nodded an encouraging smile.

I nodded one back. "I think it's hiding up my vile Monastic ass," I said. "See if you can suck it out my butthole."

Tyrkilld's mouth pursed for the labial consonant and this time I didn't see it coming.

The hand took me below the arch of the sternum and shock blasted up and down my spine and out my liver and kidneys and though the top of my head and soles of my feet, then there was only air around me and I tumbled *upward* and crashed into the joining of wall and ceiling and bounced off the bench on the way down, and hitting the brick edge from ten feet wasn't half the blow I just took; I barely felt it. I lay curled around my spasming gut and blood bubbled from my lips while I tried to remember how to breathe.

"Freeman, freeman." Tyrkilld sounded honestly regretful. "You know how the memory of my poor murdered father tasks me."

My diaphragm spasmed and air whooped into my lungs, and I coughed and spat bloody mucus up toward the Sunburst on Tyrkilld's chest.

And missed.

So all I had left was words. I took them slow. Slow and clear and flat. No sense letting him think I was just pissed. "Your father. Was a low-rent. Thug. Piece of shit. Coward." I gagged more bloody phlegm. "Just like you."

I got my breath and steadied it. "He died on his knees."

Tyrkilld's face froze over. "You know *nothing* of my—"

"I know he died—" Slow and clear and flat. "—with a friar's dick in his mouth."

There was stillness then, and silence: only labored breath from both of us, half strangled and harsh, shared now, bound together. Finally our understanding had started to flow both ways.

Into the silence, a winter whisper. "*Get him up.*"

The nearest armsman, florid and glistening and greased with heat, shifted grips on his riot gun uncertainly. "Does the Knight—?"

Tyrkilld's white stare swore murder, and it didn't look picky. "Get him *up.*"

The armsman licked pale sweat from his upper lip and swung his riot gun to hang in a bore-down safari-carry over his shoulder. "As the Knight commands."

From the floor I showed the armsman teeth that tasted like blood. "Touch me—you'll *wish* I'd killed you . . ."

The armsman's face wiped itself blank, and the armsman's foot paused in midstep.

I rolled myself over and let the cool stone flags draw heat and twitching out of my face. "You and your fucking *father . . .*" I spat into the floor. "Let me tell you about *my* father."

I got arms and legs under me and heaved up to hands and knees. My head hung between my shoulders. I didn't have the strength to lift it. "My father," I said, "lived every fucking day of his life with a steel boot on his neck."

There it was, the strength I needed, trickling up my spine from my wounded guts. I could lift my head now. I met Tyrkilld's stare with my own. His was white.

Mine's black.

"My father . . . didn't have armor of proof and the morning fucking star in his hand . . . didn't have a god to heal him, didn't have speed of lightning and power of thunder and the rest of your shit. Only a man. That's all. That's enough. *My* father died a little every fucking day just to—"

I bit down on my breath.

"—just to keep cocksuckers like you from getting comfortable with ruling the world."

Tyrkilld said, "Get him *up*."

The armsman crouched and reached down with his left arm, turning to keep his riot gun slung on the opposite side of his body. For all the good it did him.

I reached up with my right to take the armsman's left bicep in a grip that has been compared favorably to a bulldog's jaws; my thumb dug into the nerve that ran up the inside of his arm along the radial artery. The armsman gasped and twisted instinctively to wrench his arm away from the unexpected pain, which pulled me off the floor and freed my left hand to stab a thumb into his right eye socket while my fingers crushed the armsman's parotid gland in the process of hooking behind the angle of his jaw.

Where the head goes the body will follow, and so when Tyrkilld roared, "*Tashhonall,*" and catapulted himself across the cell in a blurring blue-flamed shoulder-rush, instead of meeting my chest and crushing the life from me in a shower of splintering ribs and shredded lung and spray of blood from a burst heart, he met instead the armored spine of the armsman that I had wrenched between us to absorb the impact.

The armsman never even had a chance to scream.

Tyrkilld hit us like a bullet train on meth and crushed us both against the wall, and though I took it hard—my head blurred into fireworks and something gave in my guts—the poor bastard armsman from kidneys to asshole was just blood fucking pudding.

I couldn't breathe and couldn't stand and could barely focus my eyes, but none of that mattered because while I was sliding half-crushed down the wall in a dogpile with Tyrkilld and the dying armsman, all I had to do was shift my grip from the armsman's face to the trigger guard of the riot gun that was still slung bore-down over his shoulder, because Tyrkilld was yanking the armsman off me and winding up for a killing blow with a fist that smoked arc-welder flame, and because the muzzle of the riot gun was against Tyrkilld's cuisse. It made a sound like *bwank*.

The full charge of buckshot blasted through the armor into Tyrkilld's quadriceps just above his knee.

A spray of blood and meat and bone blew a fist-size hole out of the steel covering the Knight Householder's hamstring and spun him and before he could hit the ground I had my other arm around the dying armsman's chest, hugging him close while we fell together toward the floor; I managed to rack the riot gun's slide and got off another round at one of the armsmen who was jumping to the side for a clear shot.

A couple thumb-size holes burst open on opposite sides of the second armsman's pelvis and sprayed jets of blood as he spun and slammed back against the wall and a ricochet screamed through the cell—slug round. The third armsman's weapon roared and a buckshot charge slammed the dying first armsman against my chest and punched my right side but I had bigger problems right then because blowing most of his fucking leg off just wasn't enough to slow down Tyrkilld, Knight Aeddharr.

The bastard had ahold of the armsman again and even with one hand reaching into the mess of his leg to pinch off his femoral artery the other would be enough to pull the armsman clear one way or another which would be goodnightfuckingirene because killing fire still blazed around that fist. So I let Tyrkilld have the next round in the face. Or tried to.

While I was still pulling the trigger, an impossibly powerful grip latched onto the end of the bore, and Tyrkilld took the whole charge right in the palm of his witchfire hand. Which did not explode in a shower of blood and bone. The blast did no more than knock his hand away. Spent buckshot clattered on stone.

With the twitch of a *what the hell* shrug, I racked the slide and fired again.

Tyrkilld got that undamaged hand of his back in the way . . . but its witchfire was gone. A hole appeared in its palm. And in Tyrkilld's pauldron, beside his neck. And in the hip plate on the opposite side of his chest below his cuirass.

Another slug shrieked around the cell for what seemed like a long time before it stopped in someone's body with a wet-sounding *smack*. Tyrkilld's mouth worked, but no sound came out. Only a wheeze that bubbled with blood. He looked entirely astonished.

I racked the slide again and leveled the bore on Tyrkilld's left eye. "Drop your weapons."

I went on, louder, when I realized that I didn't seem to be hearing anything except a long continuous clang. "By my count the next round's buckshot again so fucking *drop* them or go home wearing his *brains*."

Maybe one of the armsmen—the one standing with weapon shouldered or the ashen-faced one who was sliding down the wall, riot gun rib-ready in hands that were starting to shake—maybe one of them could read lips. They put down their guns.

"Kick them over here. Over by me. Now."

They looked at Tyrkilld, but his eyes had rolled up in his head. Then they could only look at each other. After a second, they complied.

Carefully I shoved the spine-shattered armsman clear. Carefully I stood. My legs seemed to work. Hot syrup rolled down the back of my neck: scalp wound. I kept my elbow against the warm wet that spread down my right side, creeping toward my knee; no way to tell yet how bad I might be hurt.

Right then I felt no pain.

"Combat grades. Yeah, sure." I hooked a toe under Tyrkilld's shoulder and rolled him faceup. I lowered the riot gun's bore to the Knight's forehead. "School's out till your next life, cocksucker."

But instead of pulling the trigger, I stood motionless, head cocked, and listened to the singing silence. A second ticked over. And another.

"All right." I tried a deep breath. It caught against a stab from my side. "You can come in now."

I nodded at the uninjured armsman. "You. Get the door."

The armsman looked blank. "Get the door for . . . ?"

"For whoever's out there listening." Wires of pain ratcheted my ribs tighter over my barbwire guts. "Whoever's not letting a shitload of armsmen bust in here and kill me right now. Fucking let him *in*, will you? If I pass out, I'll fall on this sonofabitch's *corpse*, you get me?"

Light shifted in the cell, and a creak of metal on metal and the rise of dockside noise: the outer cell door had opened.

"Freeman Shade."

This was a new voice: deeper, darker, low, and controlled, oiled and polished as ceremonial armor. "I am Markham, Lord—"

"I don't give a shit. You heard?"

"I heard."

"I made my point?"

"Yes."

"They're your fucking Laws of Engagement, and He's *your* fucking *god*, and if I remember your stupid fucking rules, this means Khryl's Own Motherfucking Self has just declared you cocksuckers had no business starting this shit up with me in the first place—"

"Freeman Shade—"

"And—and—" The cell darkened, and my tongue thickened, and I gritted my teeth and snarled, "And for shit's *sake*, do something for that poor bastard *armsman* . . ."

"We will."

"Fucking *right* . . . cocksuckers . . ." I said, and night rose up within my head and swallowed me whole.

# THE CAINE SHOW

**RETREAT FROM THE BOEDECKEN** (partial)

You are **CAINE** (featured Actor: Pfnl. Hari Michaelson)

MASTER: NOT FOR DISTRIBUTION, UNDER PENALTY OF LAW.

"*B*ut shit, I mean—here we have priests of Lipke's god of war and, and, uh, god of personal *combat*—" Sweat from Stalton's plastered-flat hair trickles past the corner of his mouth, and his tongue unconsciously catches it. "Can't we expect . . . y'know, a miracle or something? I mean, your gods don't just let you guys *die*, do they?"

I look back out at the gathering storm of Black Knives. If I weren't so goddamn gutsick, I'd screw my cover and give the partners the benefit of my Monastic education: the Covenant of Pirichanthe and all the metaphysical Abbey school shit about the Will is a Function of the Body . . . but I just don't have the strength.

"The aid of the Lord of Valor is already here." Marade stares into the badlands, and her mouth has gone hard. "I *am* His miracle."

He rolls his eyes. "I feel better already."

Pretornio chimes in like he memorized this in seminary. "One Skill of Dal'Kannith is to bind men together so that many fight as one; another Skill can give us all the strength to endure the harshest battle: the courage to face suffering squarely, and to stare unblinking into death's eye."

"Hear what they're really saying?" My chuckle's like a stir of rocks in a rusty can. "Same as me. We're on our own."

"But if we can get a rider to the Khryllian outpost at North Rahndhing—" Marade begins, and I have to stop myself from smacking her one.

"Don't play dumb blonde, for shit's sake."

"Caine." Her voice goes severe. "The Order of Khryl has fought ogrilloi for *generations*. Protocols of prisoner exchange are well established—"

"Fuck your protocols. The Order's got nothing to offer these bastards, and you know it."

"Except their lives."

I make a face. "Good luck with that, huh?"

Her voice rises. "No Soldier of Khryl is left in enemy hands. Ever. It is our Law."

"Your Law. My ass."

"Caine." The severity becomes cold threat, and a hand that can crush bone to pudding seizes my shoulder. "The Law is sacred. I will not warn you again."

I shrug out of her grip. "I don't much like being touched that way."

Her brow darkens but before she can open her mouth I plow on. "*Tell* them, Marade. You know this shit. You have to. Tell them what happens to captives of Black Knives. Tell them how many have escaped. How many have been ransomed. Ever. Come on. How *many*?"

Her face goes bleak. She says nothing. Which is an honest answer.

I turn to the others. "Boedecken bitches tell their cubs that if they don't behave, Black Knives'll get 'em. You follow? Black Knives are the grills that give other grills *nightmares*."

Wish I could tell them about Mick Barand. About the bootleg cube of his last Adventure that I smuggled home when I was twelve. Wish I could tell them what the Black Knives did to him.

Wish I could tell them how Barand took it.

One of the toughest bastards in Studio history. How they broke him. How they made him sob and scream and beg. How at the end, he could only shiver. How it took him a week to die.

How he was dead two days, dead inside, before they finally killed him.

"People talk about fates worse than death. Nobody talks about a fate worse than getting caught by Black Knives. Because there fucking *isn't any*."

Do they get it? *Can* they get it?

Marade finally gets up dick enough to step in. "There is truth in what he says," she admits. "Black Knives are feared among all the clans of the Boedecken. Feared and hated. They have abandoned even the debased gods worshipped in the Waste. Our best understanding, based on testimony of the few Black Knives the Order has ever taken—and based on the . . . the . . . the *remains* . . . of their own prisoners that have been recovered—is that Black Knife society centers on sorcery of a . . . primitive . . . and grievously savage kind. Their aim of warfare is capture. Prisoners are . . . ritually tormented, that their anguish might attract demons; their pain—their lives—are exchanged for certain dark powers. The torments of the Black Knives are known to be . . . inventive."

Which pretty well sums it up, but that dry-ass clinical shit won't move anybody. "Are you hearing her?" I ask generally. "Let me translate. We could rape their wives, kill their grandmothers, eat their babies—we could assbone their goddamn *lapdogs*—and nothing they'd do to us would be any worse than it's gonna be *anyway*. Understand? This shit's lip-deep and the tide's coming in."

They look at each other, and they look at me, and after one long shared second of *My, what a colorful turn of phrase he has*, they go back to yapping among themselves like I never even opened my mouth, and I can't make myself listen anymore.

I stare down at the coarse-flecked grain of the parapet's granite and wish I could snarl and howl and bite off a chunk. I'm past the scared. I'm past the depressed. Now I'm *pissed*.

It's not the dying. It's not the torture. It's that these cockknockers don't give a shit what I say.

No.

It's that there's no goddamn reason they *should* give a shit. It's that I haven't done more. That I haven't *been* more. That I have come all this way to get clipped as a fuck-my-bleeding-ass *bit player*.

I deserve better than this. I have *earned* better than this.

I should have been a star.

### >>scanning fwd>>

Rababàl's eyes shift and his lips twitch. "But—if *some* of us can escape, we can send help—even a full rescue; North Rahndhing is not so far away. It might be their best hope—"

"What, they have to work for a living, so they don't even deserve a *warning*?" I lean close enough to bite a hunk out of his jowls. A whisper: "You want to run, you better start right now, you fat fuck. Before I kill you myself."

I bet he tastes like pork.

Stalton shoulders in between us. "That's too close, Caine. Back off. Now."

I look up into his watery shit-colored eyes. "What if I don't want to?"

Marade's gauntlet falls on my shoulder like a steel brick. "Caine, now is not the time—"

"Now *is* the time. Now is the *only* time." I smack her hand away and bare my teeth at the sudden heat this sparks in her eyes. "You pack of fucking *pinheads*—have any of you heard a word I've *said*? These are not animals. You can't buy them off with some hunks of live goddamn *bait*. When they hit the camp, it won't be some kind of mindless goddamn feeding frenzy. The first thing they'll do with anybody they take is *hurt* them till they *give you up*. How long d'you think the porters will stand mute? Shit, why should they? After you've ditched them to be *tortured* to death?"

"Then what do you *suggest*? This is the only way *any* of us has a chance!" Rababàl's venomous glare would be more intimidating without the quiver in his jowls. "Unless you have a better idea?"

And—

Son of a bitch.

It starts way down below my chest, below my stomach, down behind my navel. Somebody just now struck a match under my balls and set my guts on fire.

"Yeah, funny thing." The burn creeps north and ignites a smile. "I *do* have a better idea."

I look from one to the next: Rababàl pale and sweating, Marade glowering glamorously, Stalton going narrow-eyed, Tizarre swiping hair across her brow with a trembling hand, Pretornio twisting his prayer chain between his fingers, and I wonder: Can they see it?

Can they see the flame in my head?

Because all that lumpy grey mush—all the dying here before I ever have a real career, the sinking dread and black despair and the whiny *why-me-god-why-me*—is melting, hissing, and just downright smoking the fuck away. Screw these shit-swallowing bit parts. I never expected to live this long anyway.

But I am for motherfucking sure gonna make a *star-quality exit*.

"Simple . . ." I talk slowly, carefully, so even Pretornio can understand. "Simple: we can't outrun them. We can't hide from them. We can't buy them off. There's only one way any of us will live through this."

Their empty stares wait for me to fill them with hope. Losers.

Fuck hope.

"One way: We have to convince them that hunting *us* is a *bad idea*."

Marade's eyes are the first to spark. "You're saying—"

"I'm saying." I let the flame kindle my voice. "I'm saying we have to *hurt* them."

And it's working. I can see them warm it up, imagining—not in detail, not yet, just tasting the concept—and I can see heat swell inside them to melt that ice-numb dread. I turn from them and lean on the parapet, willing them to follow my gaze out into the badlands. Out at the dust and the Black Knives. Willing them to think with me: *Why not? Let's fuck 'em up.*

"You think—" Tizarre swallows the quaver in her voice and starts over. "You think we can do it?"

A good lie trumps a bad truth. "I know we can."

"And this—" Rababàl's platinum disk flickers faster and faster through his fingers. "This is our best chance?"

"It's our only chance. We have to step up and unleash severe fucking carnage. And we have to do it right."

"What do you mean by *right?*"

I mean bend them in half and assbone them till their eyes bleed, but if I say so Marade'll belt me and Pretornio will probably faint. "My way. No arguments. No committee. No goddamn debate."

"Why *your* way? Marade's order has been fighting ogrilloi for centuries. Pretornio's an experienced infantry commander—"

"Hey, Marade—your people ever teach you what Black Knives do to thaumaturges?"

She half-turns away and sneaks a glance at Tizarre. Then she looks down at her gauntlets. Muscle bulges along her jaw, and she's got nothing to say.

Me, I'm not so squeamish. I hook thumbs behind my belt and lean back to rest elbows on the parapet. "They call it the Black Knife Kiss: they lock lips onto your eye sockets and suck your eyeballs out. One at a time. Bite through your optic nerve. They figure if you can't see, you can't do magick."

Rababàl's mouth works like he wants to say something but can't remember any words.

"And then there's your hands." I look at his; he palms that platinum disk like I caught him scratching his dick. "They twist wire around your wrists tight enough to cut your circulation. Pretty soon your hands turn black. And die. Sometimes they let their khoshoi nibble on them, or strap your arms out wide to attract crows. Sometimes they just leave 'em. Dead. Rotting on your wrists."

"Caine—" His voice quavers, and he swallows. "Still, I—"

"And if you somehow manage to try a spell anyway, they pound these long spikes into your skull. Big steel needles about as long as your forearm, big around as a horseshoe nail. Doesn't kill you. Doesn't even really hurt. But then they take a torch and hold it to the outside end of the spikes. One at a time. The spikes conduct heat pretty well. Still doesn't hurt much; brain's got no pain nerves. But it gives you a hell of a fever, y'know? Worst fucking fever anyone will ever have. Delusions. Hallucinations. A nightmare where you never wake up. You go to Hell while you're still alive. And even through the fever, you can feel chunks of yourself dying. Slowly. Your brain cooks. One piece at a time."

Rababàl's face has gone grey. Guess he's got a vivid imagination.

Vivid enough to keep him from asking me how the hell I know all this, which is a really good thing because I don't have a really good answer.

"But it's not always that bad." I offer a reassuring grin. "Sometimes they get enthusiastic with the torches and your brain boils instead." I shrug. "At least it's quick."

I push myself off the wall and take one step, right into the middle of them. They shift unconsciously, spreading to give me space. That's one good sign. They stand and wait to hear what I'm gonna say next. That's another. "Know how ogrilloi wish each other luck? They say, *Die fighting.* You get it? That's luck for us, too. The only luck we have left."

I give them all a good long slow look at as many of my teeth as I can fit into a smile, and hold out my fist. "Die fighting."

Marade's eyes are the first to clear, and cold determination sharpens the elegant planes of her face. She squeezes a gauntlet into a jointed ball of steel, and extends it to touch my knuckles.

"Yes," she says. "Yes. Die fighting."

Figured I could count on her: Khryllians are suckers for that heroic last-stand shit. And she is so beautiful right now that I better just keep my mouth right the fuck shut.

Stalton squints at me. "You look like you're *enjoying* this."

"Most fun you can have with your clothes on."

Did I really just *say* that? Heat rises in my cheeks. Better not *look* at her either.

He shakes his head. "You're completely insane."

"That a problem for you?"

"Shit, no. I admire it." He suddenly grins and adds his fist to ours. "Die fighting."

Then Tizarre adds hers, and Pretornio, and finally even Rababàl curls his stubby fingers and nods.

Howzafuckinbout that? Forget Marade. This is better.

I can feel it. I can *smell* it. I can roll it around in my mouth and you can fuck my left ear if I don't like the taste. The partners all stand there. Looking. Waiting. Looking at *me*. Waiting for *me* to tell *them* what to do. Who knew it'd be this easy . . . ?

I don't have to say it out loud. It sounds better in my head than it would from my mouth. No more bit-player suckassitude. Now, you yappy fucks, you gutless upcaste bean-counting ass-pirates—

Now, *you're* the bit players.

I just made this into The Caine Show.

**>>scanning fwd>>**

Black Knives resolve out of heatshimmer and dust. They top a fold of the badlands a couple hundred yards away and stop. They can see me now.

I'll never know what the Black Knives were expecting to find outside the gate of the vertical city, but I guarantee it didn't resemble one lone skinny-ass human in black leather, standing on a little rise. Waiting for them.

From where they are, the perimeter wall of the vertical city will frame me in the red-smeared light of the setting sun, leathers stark against the bleached rubble of the ruined gate thirty yards to my rear. My stance contraposto. Relaxed. Careless. My hands open. Loose. Empty. Vivid as a dream.

My dream, anyway.

All they know about humans is hunting us, hurting us, and eating us. They must be thinking, what's that skinny little sonofabitch doing just *standing* there?

Is my face in shadow? I hope not. I hope they can see me smile.

They eye me with predatory wariness. I can almost smell what they want to do: circle me, check me out, get a good sniff, a nice leisurely hyena look-around before they mob me for the kill. But like I told the partners: sure, they're predators, but they're not animals — and they're too goddamn smart to get within easy bowshot of the perimeter wall until they have some idea what's going on.

Which is good. Every second they hesitate is another second for Pretornio to work his wargod juju on the porters. Which is the point of this charade, after all. Well . . .

That's what I told the others, anyway.

Is it so wrong to want one jack-racking balls-to-the-wall setpiece before I die?

That's all I'm after. One good fucking scene.

This better be it. Don't think I'll get another.

Hot. Cold. Numb. Tingling. My heart stutters. My right kneecap jumps like a rat trapped inside my leg. There's a roaring in my ears that makes no sound at all: I can hear my breath going short and smoky, hear the ghost whisper of the bone-dry breeze, hear some kind of prairie chicken scratching at the scrub twenty yards away. My nose feels like it's packed full of sand, but I can still smell sunbaked dust and my own sweat. This could be fear. I can't tell. Can you be so scared that it makes you *happy*?

And not just happy: I've got a hard-on like I could break boards with my dick.

Now one Black Knife starts forward from the vanguard. He struts a little, easy, loose-jointed with exaggerated arrogance. Dominance display: I can almost smell the testosterone. Some of the tension uncoils in my guts. The swagger's overdone.

This'll be an up-and-comer. A bachelor out to rack up style points in front of the big dogs. I've seen better. Shit, I've *done* better.

Y'know, given laboralls and cosmetic surgery, this puppy'd be right at home in my old neighborhood. That must be why I'm turning comfortable out here: the Boedecken badlands aren't all that different from the streets I grew up on. I've spent most of my life surviving pack-hunters more dangerous than these.

Watching him swagger toward me, I know exactly what the rules are.

He stops a little more than halfway here, squints my way, then shrugs and turns his back to me. It's an ogrillo dare, part of his dominance display: dismissing me as a threat.

I keep smiling. My cheeks hurt.

All four of them.

Still giving me his back, he ostentatiously strings his recurved compound bow. A theatrical flourish extracts an arrow; he holds the bow high over his head as he nocks the arrow and draws the string, making sure I get a great view. Then in one smooth motion he turns and fires and I just stand here grinning like somebody stapled my lips to my teeth.

The arrowhead chips sparks off a stone an arm's length in front of my left foot.

Like I said: I know the rules.

His squint turns appreciative, and his trifurcate upper lip draws back from his tusks. Hoots that might be approval come faintly from the pack of Black Knives back at the fold. He paces toward me, nocking another arrow. From seventy yards or so, he lets fly. The arrow hisses past my right ear.

This fucker can shoot.

I open my hands invitingly, beckoning for him to try again. Closer.

Those hoots from the Black Knives are louder now. They're starting to sound derisive. The bowstud's face darkens, and he calls to me: "*Paggnakkid razlim nezz, paggtakkunni.*"

Y'know, it never occurred to me that these cocksmokes might not speak Westerling.

He paces in another twenty yards, and there's nothing theatrical about him now. He draws and fires without aiming and I let breath hiss from my lips and my legs go slack and my arms flop loose and I look at his eyes beyond the arrow's sizzling rush as my right hand flicks up from thigh to face and closes on the arrowshaft, which burns skin as it skids to a stop along my palm. Its steel point stares at me, an inch from my eye.

No speakee? No problem. This is what you call *nonverbal communication.*

I spin the arrow through my fingers like a baton. Should pretty well conceal the electric shiver jolting out of my adrenals. At Garthan Hold, training arrows have sandbag heads.

Hoo.

Live points are . . . a whole different *world*.

Hoo.

All *right*, then.

Now. More nonverbiage—

I balance the arrow, head down, on the tip of my left forefinger, and have an agonizing half second's vision of just how stupid I'm gonna look if I don't pull this off before I shrug a silent *Fuck it anyway* and let fly: leaving the arrow to hang in a blink-long Wile E. Coyote pause in midair, I throw myself into a backspin that whips my right heel through a horizontal arc to strike the middle of the arrowshaft. The shaft snaps around my heel.

The halves tumble away from each other to clatter into the rocks. The prairie chicken thing takes flight with an indignant skrill.

Ogrillo eyes track the pieces' skitter, and when they skip back to me I spread my empty hands—

And take a deep curtain-call bow.

Hot staggering *fuck*. How good did *that* feel?

My grin isn't fake anymore. I've got the flavor now. The scent's in my nose and it's setting my head on fire. This is what it's all about. This right here.

This is Being a Star.

Is anything better?

Huh.

Except—

Where's my goddamn *applause*?

Maybe my applause is the deliberate caution—just short of open reluctance—with which the ogrillo puts down his bow and slips his quiver off his belt. The way he pulls his spear before he starts toward me, like he needs the weight of its shaft in his hands to keep his pecker up. Maybe it's the thick dry slide of his plum-colored tongue around his tusks, and the way he never takes his eyes off me as he approaches.

Applause enough, I guess.

The Black Knives behind him edge closer, working their way down the fold. They spread into a wide arc like an infantry skirmish line, flanks curving toward the city.

If Spearboy here doesn't start the party pretty damn soon, the Black Knife line will envelop the little rise where I stand. Which is gonna suck for me, star or not. Maybe I should have let Marade handle this part after all.

A last stand on a hilltop surrounded by ogrilloi is probably her idea of sex.

As Spearboy stalks up the face of my rise, that whole "should have let Marade" idea starts sounding better and better.

He's *huge.*

Secondhanding a couple Hammets and the Barand have not remotely prepared me for this fucker's sheer immensity. Up close, in the flesh, it's like turning a corner and bumping into something that ought to be extinct.

Seven feet tall. Four feet wide. Wrinkled grey-green hide that covers biceps bigger than my head. Those sun-yellowed tusks. His goddamn *fingernails* . . .

Fighting claws like shortswords. Filed sharp.

Painted black.

That spear of his, more like—what do you call it?—a bill or something: eight or nine feet long, and at least three feet of it is blade as wide as my hand, with a rear-pointed barb on each side, to unhorse riders. Or yank a victim within reach of his fighting claws.

I shouldn't have left my sword with Stalton. And I should have put on my fucking *armor.*

And I should have remembered that despite secondhand memories of being Hammet and Barand from those Adventure cubes, I've never fought an ogrillo before. I should've been thinking more about *living through this* than about how *cool* I was gonna look standing out here with nothing but a fucking *knife* up my *sleeve* . . .

And—most of all—

I really, *really* should have stopped on the way out here to take a piss.

Wetting my pants'll blow that whole Being a Star trip, I'm guessing.

When Spearboy gets about ten feet away, his chest expands and his neck bulges and he unleashes a godawful howl that makes every single hair on my body stand on end. He shakes the spear toward my belly and starts pumping his hips and grunting low in his throat, and I get it.

He's telling me that he's gonna open my guts and fuck me in the wound.

Huh. How about that? I feel better now.

Because if he really thought he could do it, he'd be wet-humping my belly already instead of poncing around like a demented mime.

I feel more than better. I feel *incredible.* Every problem I have ever had has just . . . evaporated. My career. Torture. Death. Dad. All of it.

Everything. Anything. Don't have one single problem in the world except living through the next twenty seconds. And that's not a problem. It's nothing at all.

Live, die, who gives a shit? So I've never fought an ogrillo. So what?

No ogrillo has ever fought me.

I fake a lunge and he flinches, and I laugh out loud.

"Let's go, Fido." I beckon with both empty hands. "Strike up the fucking band."

He makes a tentative thrust. I skip back. He slices at my head and I duck to the side. His eyes are round as plates and piss-yellow, and I bet my left nut that if his whole rumphumping clan weren't watching, he'd be running right now and splashing brown with every step.

His gorilla chest heaves like he can't quite get a breath—

Then he gives his tusks a shake and his head settles into his shoulders. Muscle bunches around the spinal ridge that crowns his skull. He growls something that I don't register as words.

He's found his nerve again.

He starts to circle: three hundred-plus pounds of sentient predator, stalking me. His blade slides through slow, lazy loops, tracing infinity.

Idiots pretending they know something about fighting sometimes say shit like *Other things being equal, advantage lies with the longer weapon* or *Other things being equal, the fighter who strikes first wins.* My favorite is *Other things being equal, a big man beats a small man.*

Know what makes them idiots? Wait. I'll show you.

He finally commits: with a grunt like a rhino's cough he launches a full lunge, jamming that spear straight for my spine by way of my navel. I slap the spear aside with a *clank*, and his eyes go wide at the sparks the knife up my left sleeve strikes off his blade.

Before he has the faintest fucking chance to figure out what just happened, I'm spinning toward him along the spear shaft, left hand grabbing his nearside tusk while my right clears the knife past my left cuff, and when his reflexive sideways yank rips his tusk out of my grip, that same yank shows me the back of his skull. So that's where I put the knife.

The blade's only seven inches. The point doesn't quite come out his mouth. Get it?

"Other things" are *never* equal.

His body convulses: a single giant spasm that rips the knife from my hand and flattens him like he's been hit by lightning. One more wrench slams his head backward into the dirt. His jaws gape around an extra tongue of blood-smeared steel.

His yellow eyes fix on mine with a mournful doggy puzzlement, as though we'd had a deal, as though we'd gone into business together with the mutual understanding that he'd live and I'd die and now he can't quite comprehend how I could double-cross him like this. His eyes cup that canine dismay till the dust he's kicked up settles across them and dulls even the illusion of life.

Wow.

I mean: wow.

Fuck me if I don't really, *really* have to pee.

I look up. Black Knives everywhere. Standing. Staring. Silent as trees.

Which is as raw butt-naked sexual as the kill itself.

Yeah.

I mean: *yeah*.

Now for the curtain call.

*"You see that, you fuckers?"* Ten years of *kiai* have given me a voice that can dent plate armor. *"Did anybody* NOT *see what just happened here? Does anybody need it* EXPLAINED?"

They stand. They stare. Whispers rustle into growls that roll into low thunder.

*"This"*—I sweep a hand behind me toward the vertical city—*"is* MINE. Go *wherever the fuck you want, but you can't come* HERE."

Minor shifts of weight, a general sway like a forest before a storm. I can't tell if I'm getting through.

*"For you, this place is* HELL. You HEAR me? You UNDERSTAND? For *you, here is* PAIN. Here is DEATH."

I turn my hand toward the corpse of Spearboy. "He died EASY. You *will die* HARD. You will die SCREAMING. Your bitches will HOWL. Your pups will STARVE.

*"I will FEED YOU YOUR FUTURE."*

Still they only sway. Their thunder-grumble starts ramping up in rhythm: swell and slack and swell again, like the surf ahead of a typhoon at high tide.

Do they have any fucking clue what I just said?

I look down at the dust in the dead eyes at my feet, and think about predatory carnivores and pack-hunters—

And I start to chuckle. I mean: this *is* about marking territory, right?

So before I turn my back on the massed warriors of the Black Knife clan, before I begin to walk the infinite thirty yards to lead them into the ambush back at the ruined gate, before I even have time to worry about how much extra shitstorm I might've spun up for myself and all of us, I unlace my breeches, open the front, and pull out my dick.

And pee on Spearboy's corpse.

Ahhh, shit. Son of a bitch.

Should have picked up my goddamn knife, first.

# LORD RIGHTEOUS

ight found me on something soft and knobbly that rose along my side and under my head and feet: a brocaded sofa, maybe.

I discovered I could open my eyes.

The plaster ceiling my blank stare found had been painted a tasteful ivory not long ago, and somebody had come by with a feather plume within the last day; the deep curls of the ornate crown molding showed no hint of dust. A cobweb would have died of loneliness.

I tried to sit up, but my gut spasmed and wouldn't lift me. No pain, just weakness: like I'd trained past muscle failure. Way past.

But no bandages. No blood.

Somebody had dressed me in a plain linen tunic and pants. My hand shook a little as I pawed back the right-side hem of the tunic and rolled my head over to find four ragged pink coins of fresh scar pocking my side, neatly bracketing the flattened diamond of age-browned keloid where an Ankhanan Household Knight had put a broadsword through my liver about fifteen years ago.

I fingered the fresh ones. Big enough to be something in the range of 00 buck—maybe 7mm, maybe bigger. Who knows what Khryllians load? Lucky I didn't take it in the face. Lucky old man.

Lucky to be getting older.

There was another new scar, long and thin and curving from my short ribs up toward my nipple, too smooth to be a wound.

Surgery.

Rubber-band muscles shivering with echoes of trauma, I managed to roll myself onto my side. Then I had to rest.

Seated in a severe chair by a severe window was a severe man in severe armor.

The chair was no more than a stool with a back. The window was an arch in the wall, plaster giving way to white stonework open to the westering sun be-

yond. The man was thin, even in armor, with the long narrow head and extrav-
agantly arched nose and cheekbones of Lipkan nobility. His hair was the color
of his armor and cropped to the uniform length of a fingerbreadth. His armor
was starkly brushed and oiled carbon steel, lacking entirely the ostentation of
polish and design that is the hallmark of the Khryllian Knight. Its sole orna-
ment was a stylized hand—the symbol of Dal'Kannith, Lipkan god of war and
father to Khryl—inlaid in electrum upon the upper left of his cuirass, fingers
open and palm facing forward, and on that palm the golden Sunburst of Khryl.

"Freeman Shade." He inclined his head fractionally. "I am Markham,
Lord Tarkanen—Lord Righteous in service to the Champion of Khryl."

"And I am—" I strangled a groan as I forced my legs over the edge of the
sofa and sat up. "—almost impressed. Where are we?"

"This is the invaliddarium of the Riverdock Parish vigilry, freeman."

"Knight Whatsisdick's place? Is that a good idea?"

Markham's lips thinned. "Khryl's Love has Healed your wounds—"

"Yeah, I noticed. Get all the slugs?"

"The single pellet still in your body was successfully extracted, freeman.
And your ribs have been renewed through Khryl's Love."

"Thanks for taking care of it while I was out. Khryl's Love, I recall, feels a
lot like having a handful of red-hot barbwire shoved up my ass."

The Lord Righteous didn't seem to hear. "Your clothing is being laundered
and will be repaired, should you wish; otherwise, it will be destroyed for rags,
and we will replace it without cost to you."

"You do this for everybody you beat the shit out of?"

His eyes were the color of his armor. "Only the innocent."

"So that means mostly yes, huh?"

Those lips thinned more. "Freeman Shade—"

"Y'know, I'm liking the sound of that more and more. Freeman. Free man.
Because that's, y'know, what I am, right? By right of—what do you call it in
Lipkan?—*Terranhidhal zhan Dhalleig*? The Declaration of Valor, something
like that? Khryl Himself has declared you have no right to hold me."

"Yes."

"Then keep my fucking clothes. I'm out of here."

"Your other wounds, freeman—"

"I feel great."

"Khryl's Love treats only wounds taken in battle. There may be internal in-
juries—"

"From what?"

"From the—" Markham's lips went even thinner. "From Knight Aeddharr's
inappropriate, unlawful, and despicable abuse of your person, freeman."

I found myself smiling. "Now, *that* I like. Inappropriate, unlawful, and despicable abuse of my person. Must sting, huh? Just saying that."

Those lips disappeared altogether. "You are owed an apology on behalf of the Order of Khryl, the Civility of the Battleground, the Riverdock Parish, and Tyrkilld, Knight Aeddharr."

"Fucking right."

"Knight Aeddharr is unable to proffer formal apologies at this time—"

"What, did I kill him?" My sigh would have been more convincing without the grin. "Shit, in the old days Knights were tough."

"He lives." Markham's face was stiff as his cuirass. A subtle flick of his finger directed my gaze toward another door. "Your use of the armsman's weapon destroyed a section of his thighbone, which must be reconstructed if he is to walk properly again—"

"So all he gets out of this is a limp? My heart's pumping pisswater for him."

Markham's amazing vanishing lips took with them all the color from his cheekbones and around his eyes. "Should you wish to make another attempt upon his life, Knight Aeddharr has assured me that he will place himself at your convenience as soon as Khryl's Love completes his Healing."

"Huh. Easy to be brave when you've got Khryl to kiss away your boo-boos."

Muscle rippled along the Lord Righteous's jaw. "The apology, freeman—"

"What about that poor bastard armsman? Khryl's Love won't do much for what's left of his spinal cord."

"Armsman Braehew," he ground out around his locked-down jaw, "perished of his wounds."

I stared at the Lord Righteous. The Lord Righteous stared back. Neither of us blinked.

"Braehew." Another name on a damn long list. "Braehew." Hadn't meant to kill him. Didn't even know him. Didn't matter. Wrong place, wrong time, with a shotgun aimed at the wrong guy's balls. End of story.

I have a lot of those stories crowding the back of my head. "What, all the Knights around there had something better to do?"

"The armsman refused Healing."

"He what?"

"Armsman Braehew is survived by a wife and two young daughters. As you said: Khryl's Love would save only his life. He would have required specialized care for the remainder of his days. The pension from the Order will be better spent providing for the comfort of his family than for the care of a cripple."

I carry a scar just below my navel that matches one in the small of my back. I also carry a device implanted along my spine near that scar. That device—along with some specialized powers of concentration, and a bit of magick, that have become habit over the past three years—is the main reason I can now walk. For some years I had done without it; for some years it had worked only intermittently, if at all.

I said, "That's fucked."

Markham sat at attention, as though the Justiciar himself was in the room. "He died with honor. You would not understand."

"Does his *wife* understand? Did anybody ask his daughters whether they'd rather have money than a father?"

"It is not our way to burden a Soldier's loved ones with such decisions."

"And I bet right now they're crying tears of gratitude for your thoughtfulness and consideration."

"I suspect," Markham said, "that they weep only with pride that Armsman Braehew fell in battle, as all Khryllians fondly hope."

"Yeah, all right. Whatever." I looked around for my boots. "Are we done here?"

"There is still the matter of the apology, freeman."

"I'm not much for forgiveness. Let me out of here. I gotta line up a place to sleep."

"Lodgings have been secured for you at the Pratt & Redhorn; it is a small hostelry in this parish."

"Maybe I want to stay somewhere else."

"You will stay in the Pratt & Redhorn."

"Will I?"

"To disobey the lawful order of a Knight of Khryl is a serious offense; it is an offense to Khryl Himself. Am I entirely understood, freeman?"

"Better than you want to be, maybe. Where the fuck are my boots?"

"Freeman, please." Markham looked actively pained. "If we might beg your further indulgence on this one small matter."

"We?"

"I and the Champion."

"You and the Champion?" I shrugged. "What exactly is it you want me to indulge?"

"Since Knight Aeddharr is . . . indisposed, the Order of Khryl, the Justiciar, and the Civility of the Battleground all humbly request that you will deign to accept the aforementioned apology, offered in person by the Champion of Khryl."

I blinked. "What?"

"Since Knight Aeddharr is—"

"No, no, I heard you . . . I mean, I *think* I heard you." I put a hand to my head, but I didn't feel any major lumps, and shaking it didn't bring back any dizziness or blurring. "The *Champion* wants to *apologize*? The Champion of *Khryl*?"

"Yes."

I shook my head again. "It's like getting offered a handjob from the pope."

Markham's brows pulled toward a hint of a grey frown. "What is the pope?"

"Never mind. All right, bring him in."

"I beg your pardon?"

"Let's have it. I'm a busy man."

"Freeman Shade, you misunderstand. The Champion does not come and go at your bidding; I am tasked to deliver you into the Champion's presence."

"I don't think so."

"Freeman?"

"Tell your Champion thanks for the sentiment, but I've got shit to do."

"Freeman, you still misunderstand—"

"One of us does."

"I am tasked to deliver you—"

"And I'm telling you I'm not going." I let my friendly grin go less friendly. "Unless you're also tasked to tie me up and drag me there."

Markham went very still. Still like a lizard that feels the approach of a mouse. "Tie you up, freeman? Not at all. I am tasked only to deliver you; my duty unto the Champion, and to Khryl, requires that I fulfill all lawful tasks. The Champion did not specify that you be willing. Or conscious."

His expression never flickered. "Or alive."

"You're a friendly sonofabitch, aren't you?"

Markham's lips were so far gone it was amazing he had a face at all. "This will be difficult only if you choose to make it so."

I looked at him long enough to remember how old I am.

"What the fuck, huh? Let's go."

A stonefaced armsman brought me my trunk and stood by while I fished out a tunic, vest, and pants and shook traces of bug powder out the window. My boots were damp. Even through the bitter saddle soap, they still smelled of blood.

I wadded up the white linens and underhanded them at the armsman. "Give 'em to the beggars, along with my other stuff."

The armsman let the linens bounce off his chest and didn't even glance at where they fell on the floor. "There are no beggars in Purthin's Ford."

I shrugged. "Then stick 'em up your ass."

Markham was waiting for me under the sally gate of the vigilry. Though my guts still spasmed and my noodle legs were still way overcooked, I dragged the

travel trunk over the courtyard flags in my best imitation of brisk, and I bit
down on my voice to make sure I didn't wheeze when I joined the Lord Righteous at the wide stone archway. "You cocksu—uh, guys—still go everywhere
on foot, right?"

"We bear the weight of Khryl's Armor with our own strength, yes."

"Your own strength, yeah. That's what I meant. But for someone without
Your Own Strength, this trunk isn't exactly a feather pillow, you follow?"

"Of course, freeman." Markham stepped into the street and pointed at a
passing dogcart.

The cartboy—a sweaty grill pushing sixty, barefoot, in a homespun vest and
shapeless pants ragged at the ankle, smelling of ass and cheap booze—
dropped the dogcart's draw shafts and threw himself into submission: knees on
the street, hands behind ankles, forehead into the cobbles alongside the Khryllian's instep. "Will dhe Lord do dhis poor ellie dhe honor'v acceptin' service?"

"The freeman will ride, Eligible," Markham said. "Load the case."

The grill scrambled to his feet and lunged for the travel trunk with as much
alacrity and enthusiasm as arthritis-knobbed joints allowed; I saw the cartboy's
grimace at the trunk's weight and said, "Hey, let me do that—"

"No, no, kwatch—no, I goddid, sure." The cartboy kept his head ducked,
eyes fixed on the cobbles, forcing his spine into an awkward half crouch to
hold his crown ridge below my chin. "You please go climb up, kwatch. Do my
job, I godda, hey?"

I found my lips pulling back and I couldn't unlock my teeth. "Don't call
me that."

The cartboy ducked his head even lower and his shoulders hunched
around his ears. "Hey, don' mean nuddin', kwatch—*kwatch* don' mean nuddin', bud, like—"

"I know what it means." Sudden cords in my neck drew down my head.
"I'm not your fucking *kwatcharr.*"

"Hey, I—hey, I don' . . . I don'—"

"A man has spoken, Eligible." Markham's voice was soft and bland, entirely
matter-of-fact, but it stopped the stammering like he'd cut the grill's throat
with a silken knife. "Freeman Shade? Will you ride?"

I didn't answer. I was staring at scar-puckered stumps, dark and skin-cancer
rippled, on the cartboy's forearms. Stumps of his fighting claws.

Guards in the Ankhanan Donjon had lopped off Orbek's fighting claws at
that same joint. With bolt cutters.

*click clack,* he'd said. *click fuck-me clack.*

For trying to help Caine. That is: me.

Then.

*you understand what they do to me? do you? they do to me what you do to black knives, all those years ago: cut off what makes me* me. *now I never get a bitch. never get pups. what good's being safe? a good death is all i got left. a good death. honor on my clan.*

I found myself trying to swallow around that familiar fist tangled in my guts.

"Eligible? What's that mean, *eligible?*"

"Sure, kwatch—er, boss. Sure. Godda be ellie, hey?" The cartboy swung the travel trunk into the dogcart's cargo cage. He displayed his maimed forearms proudly. "Betcha I am. Don' wanna ged messing wid 'dacks, boss. Sdick to ellies. We dake care a you good."

The cartboy shuffled back between the draw shafts and picked them up. "Good hey, climb up, hey? Where do I run you?"

I looked at Markham. "Eligible for what?"

The face of the Lord Righteous looked harder than the cobbles of the street. "Will you ride?"

I chewed on the inside of my lower lip for a second.

"Shit."

I dug an Ankhanan silver noble out of my purse and flipped it to the astonished cartboy, then stepped to the back of the dogcart and reached for the trunk.

"I'd rather walk."

The Spire gave me the creeps.

It reminded me of the Washington Monument. I posed at the monument once for promo shots, and it's something you never forget: the psychic weight of that monstrously blank neo-stele looming behind your back. A giant white cock, fucking the sky.

Except the Spire was bigger. A *lot* bigger.

I kept my head down. \*Never did things by halves, did you?\*

God, as usual, did not reply.

It wasn't just the illusion of looming threat—the way it leaned over me as though I were about to be crushed by God's Own Hard-On—it was that the Spire really *was*, in a sense, God's own hard-on.

Fucking Ma'elKoth.

A stalagmite of whitestone-faced granite piled on the lowest arc of the vertical city, studded with embrasure-pocked battlements, its bleached immensity commanded the whole of Purthin's Ford and the face of Hell. Six arching sally bridges, staggered in a quarter-spiral, joined it to the tiers of the vertical city. Its uppermost reach overtopped the lip of the escarpment by nearly thirty meters; the five-spired cap caught the sun in a brilliant white-metal blaze that could be seen, on clear days, all the way to the Rymedge Mountains beyond.

And that wasn't enough either. Impossibly huge and impenetrably strong just wouldn't properly demonstrate the big bastard's infinite genius—the god-damn *name* he chose for himself is a phrase in Paquli that translates as *I Am Limitless*—and I guess even in those days he felt the need to prove it with every move he made.

The Spire was also the spillway and control center for Home's original hy-dropower dam.

I'd seen guesstimated specs on it in a Monastic Threat Estimate from about fifteen years ago. The river is the outlet of the Fist of God reservoir, far upland on the plateau. The Fist of God is a vast crater—meteor impact, maybe, or some ancient volcanic hiccup—that went deep enough to penetrate the bedrock water table that fed the river. My river. Now it's a great big pool, be-cause Ma'elKoth corked the entire fucking river down here with this immense goddamn fortress.

Those sally bridges—light and graceful as they looked from down here— were actually immense high-pressure enclosed aqueducts. The highest joined the escarpment where the river used to be a waterfall. The lower five channeled some of the water back to the face of Hell, making five little rivers that spilled down through the vertical city for the grills to drink from and crap in; most of the river's water churned down through the center of the Spire in a series of columns that hydraulically powered all manner of the vast fortress's inner workings, from internal gates and portcullises to water cannon on the sally bridges to elevators big enough to shift entire companies of armored cavalry.

And then the river was graciously allowed to boil out from beneath the fortress and wind its way through the canal system into the city and the estates beyond, and frankly, the whole thing made me a little sick to my stomach.

Because that was where we were going. I knew it from the very steps of the vigilry. "Straight to the Spire, huh?"

"The Eternal Vaunt of the Order of Khryl is our destination," Markham af-firmed stiffly. "Only the vulgar name it the Spire."

"The vulgar name it some other shit too."

Markham's selective deafness still seemed to be working just fine. "It would serve you, as an Ankhanan, to show reverence; you may not be aware that the Eternal Vaunt was created for us by your own patron god Ma'elKoth, after our Glory at Ceraeno—"

"Before he was a god, even. Yeah, I know." I couldn't help but know: the story bubbled to the surface of my mind like a fart in a bathtub. "Toa-

Phelathon had him build it for the Order to keep you out of the Plains War. Biggest bribe in the history of Home."

Markham's nearside eyebrow arched a millimeter. "The Prince-Regent gifted the Order with the Eternal Vaunt out of gratitude for the Order's role in crushing the Khulan Horde—"

"Yeah. Sure. Toa-Phelathon gets Jheled-Kaarn, Harrakha, and Ironhold, and the Order gets the most spectacular fortress on Home. Smartest thing the old bastard ever did; probably won the war for him."

"If so," Markham murmured with a sidelong glance, "it is a pity he did not live to enjoy it."

"Yeah. Pity."

"There is a persistent rumor," he said consideringly, "that the Prince-Regent's death did not come at the hands of agents of the disaffected nobility hoping to control Tel-Tamarantha—that he was, in fact, assassinated by a Monastic Esoteric."

My voice went as empty as Markham's eyes. "I wouldn't know."

"The rumor goes that the First Ankhanan Succession War was actually engineered by the Council of Brothers for the express purpose of placing the Incarnate Ma'elKoth on the Oaken Throne."

Behind my blandly disbelieving smile, I monologued to my audience of one, *Somehow it's always about you and me, huh?*

An edge of uneasiness shaved away the irony. I don't often let myself think about the fractal web of destiny that interweaves my life with Ma'elKoth's. Examining it too closely only makes me queasy. And fucking pissed. There's a reckoning I owe, there.

One of these days . . .

"For my part, I find it an unlikely tale," Markham said. "The Monasteries would hardly be interested in *increasing* the power of a god."

"He wasn't exactly a god at the time." Which is part of what made me a little sick. Still does. He'd built the fucking Spire while he was still human. More or less.

"A god is a god, always and entire, incarnate or no. To the gods, time is a dream."

"It's a swell theory."

Markham sniffed. "I will not debate theogony with an Ankhanan."

"Good thing, too. On this subject I can kick anybody's ass."

The sinking sun cast bloody shadows across half-empty streets. Humans made way for us with inclined heads and tugged forelocks. Ogrilloi crumpled into instant submission and kept to their knees until the regard of the Lord Righteous had passed them by.

The whitestone approach to the Spire's main gate was a maze of interleaved sandbag berms, piled chest-high; every fold of the long winding queue was exposed to the silver-chased barrels of rifles that made sunset flames along the first rung of battlements, and to the black gapes of cannon above. Mounted armsmen paced their snorting horses around sandbag-walled paddocks, long guns propped on hauberked hipbones. Wagons and carts drawn by yoked teams of ogrilloi inched through inspection at a single checkpoint staffed by two Knights and a scurrying crew of examiners who wore metal-framed goggles that looked like simplified versions of the customs officers' loupes. Wagons passed through by the inspectors were walked to a broad parking area. Gangs of ogrilloi unloaded them case by case and barrel by barrel and box by box, hand-carrying each piece into the Spire.

I got it when I finally caught sight of the main gate. What was left of the main gate.

A shattered gape in the Spire's face. Blackened and empty.

Desk-size blocks of dressed stone stood in huge stacks to one side. Some had been fitted already to mend the walls and build again the missing archway. The join of new stone and old was clearly visible, despite what must have been a week or two of scrubbing; the older stone bore brownish ghosts of scorchmarks.

Must have been one serious bomb.

I sidled close to Markham and nodded at the gate. "A wagon, right? Maybe a carriage. No driver. Just horses. A runaway, right up the street—"

"Freeman Shade—"

"That why ogrilloi haul your wagons?" I admired the efficiency: hostages as draft animals. And the reverse.

"Freeman, the Champion awaits."

I was still looking at the shattered gate. "What're you gonna do once they decide it's worth dying to take a chunk out of you?"

The Lord Righteous squinted down at me as though something had unexpectedly come into focus, but he made no reply.

That was answer enough.

Berms and bunkers. Checkpoints and sharpshooters.

More than enough.

Fading echoes, inside my head—

*a good death.*

*honor on my clan.*

"All right, shit. I *am* a dumbass." My wave took in the desperately screwed-down antiterror fortifications. "Orbek figures into this somewhere, doesn't he?"

Markham didn't answer.

My mouth had gone dry, and the fist in my guts had turned to brick. "Markham?"

Markham only kept walking.

"Hey, goddammit, I'm *talking* to you—"

"And I am not answering, Freeman Shade. I am tasked to see to your wounds and deliver your person unto the Champion. And *no more.*" The unsubtle emphasis was accompanied by a quickening of his already brisk pace.

"Come on, give me a hint, huh?"

Markham stopped. His oiled-steel stare followed his long Lipkan nose. "Why should I?"

"Maybe to not be an asshole one day of your life?"

"Freeman, you are rude, disrespectful, and vulgar. Not to mention foul-mouthed. Where in your manner will I find an inclination to do you a *favor*?"

"Shit, if I said something like that to you, we'd have to *fight* now—"

"If you said anything like that to me," the Lord Righteous replied in a tone that could freeze beer, "you would be a liar."

"Ooh, *good* one." I rolled my eyes. "So this is because I haven't sucked enough butt? Shit, why didn't you tell me? Hey, nice armor, Markham. You make that yourself? And I *really* like your fucking *hair* . . ."

I was talking to his retreating back.

"Y'know," I muttered as I dragged the travel trunk clattering after, "maybe there *is* something in the goddamn air."

If there was, it was getting into my head: the headache was ramping up again. A hot swollen mass of hurt gathered behind my eyes, thumping in time with my heart. I winced with its pulse as the Lord Righteous turned away from the berm-baffled gatewalk toward the face of Hell. "What, we're not going in?"

"The Champion awaits on the Purificapex atop the Eternal Vaunt. You will require transport."

The hot throb inside my head when I tried to lift my gaze up the thousand feet of whitestone behind wouldn't let me argue. I shut the hell up and followed the Lord Righteous across the whitewashed flagstones toward the jitney landing.

A thin misting drizzle had ridden into town on the dusk. Watch flames hissed and spat atop single-foot braziers. Lanterns swinging from half a dozen jitneys' overhead lighthooks splashed shadows across the landing. Near the first tier's face stood bulky freight carts, ogrilloi wrestling crates and casks up onto their beds. Heavy-linked chain served the carts for traces, hooked through yokes of eight. Ogrilloi chained in the traces sat quietly, heads down, breath smoking in the evening chill.

The twin thoroughfares that laddered either side of the face of Hell in vast switchbacked zags had been widened and repaved since my time: four lanes of ogrillo-drawn traffic could grind up or down the ten-percent grade without locking wheels. The thoroughfares' long folded slant emptied onto a broad plaza crowded with bundle-laden ogrilloi, returning from jobs or shopping in the city below, waiting to load their burdens onto the jitneys, silent and patient in the rain.

Mounted armsmen made sure they stayed that way.

One of the water wranglers saw us coming. The grill dropped his cask on the flagstones and fell to his knees. "Knight!"

Then another, and another. Water cart drovers jumped down from their seats and cracked urgent whips at the heads of the dray-gangs. Bundles and sacks fell unheeded to the wet stones. Water casks rolled as the wranglers threw themselves down.

And for some reason, this had me thinking about Marade whittling the splinters off a broken shinbone.

I saw her in my mind as if she were doing it right now: planing the shinbone down with a little knife to make a kind of flat toothpick about two fingers wide, then using it to scrape the joints of her sabatons free of black mashed-potato muck. Sticky black mashed-potato muck that smelled like meat—

Rock dust and sand and clotted blood.

I stopped and shook my head, looking up and around to ask the wet twilight what the fuck had reminded me of that right now, and the shape of Hell above and the angle of the lamp-sparked cliff face snatched memory—

And I stopped breathing too. All I could do was blink.

Here. Right here. The Khryllians had built the jitney landing over it. The gateway.

The ambush.

Fire and spears and arrows and screams and the *schannk* of short swords licking along steel rims of linked shields and Marade's morningstar showering shredded flesh—

Whatever the earth remembered of that clotted mush of sand and blood was under these whitestone flags. Right here. Right now. Where these hundreds of ogrilloi knelt in submission to a single Khryllian Lord.

The last of my breath hissed out in a shuddering *Holy crap*, and when I breathed in again, I inhaled more headache.

"Freeman Shade? Are you unwell?" Markham sounded like he hoped so.

"I, uh—no. No. I just—I forgot something, that's all."

"Is there some emergency?"

"What?"

"This matter you recall—does it require attention?"

"I, uh—"

I looked down. My boots shone in the rain, the whitestone flags beneath them grey with damp. In an open joint, a tiny anthill: mounded crumbs of the black earth beneath.

"Yeah. Yeah, it probably does." I scuffed the anthill into a smear of mud. "But it's too fucking late to do anything about it now," I said, and walked on.

My headache got worse when we reached the jitney queue. As near as I could guess, I was standing right on top of where Pretornio had buried the porters. The two who died springing my trap on the Black Knives. I wondered if anyone had ever found the bodies.

I didn't think so. Somehow I didn't think so. Somehow I could feel them down there: tangles of worm-scoured bone an arm's length beneath my soles. Perry? Pivo? Something like that. One of them had started with *P*. I was sure of that much.

Pretty sure.

The other—?

The deepening throb in my head drove off any hope of recall. My eyes drifted closed and I put the heel of a hand to my temple, rubbing in small circular motions that didn't touch the pain, but also didn't make it any worse. I kept doing it. It was something to do.

"Freeman Shade?"

Christ, my head hurt. "What?"

"Please embark, freeman. You are delaying the queue."

I opened my eyes. The five grills in the jitney team knelt against their yokes, traces taut, their breath coming harsh and slow, arms slack and trembling: primly fascist autoerotic asphyxiation. They weren't locked in: not convicts. This was a job. Four grills yoked in tandem, with a bitch single-yoked in the lead. Maybe watching her ass helped keep them trotting. The lead bitch had her forehead pressed to the insteps of Markham's sabatons.

The Lord Righteous didn't seem to notice. "Freeman Shade?"

*i give myself to you.*

I watched drizzle trickle like spit across the back of her grey-leathered skull.

*fuckbitch*

I shook my head and had to look away before I could speak. "Y'know what? I think I'd rather—"

But ogrilloi knelt everywhere, beside and before and behind, and the only direction I could look away was up . . . and up was the third tier, and I followed with my eyes a walkway I had once followed afoot toward wet strangled moans and porcine grunting in a black bloody midnight, and from down here

I could see the angle just above the shattered chamber where I found Black Knives rooting into Stalton's belly . . . bagged in his own armor, hauberk over his face like a rape victim's skirt . . .

"Fuck it anyway." I waved a hand. "Make sure the bitch takes it easy with my trunk."

I rode. Markham walked—well, jogged—alongside, one hand on the cart's bed rail like he belonged in a Social Police LeSec detail. The jitney team trotted around the steep switchbacks of the thoroughfare fast enough that just watching them made me tired. We weaved up the slope, overtaking other weather-splintered grill carts with their sullenly dead-eyed dray teams and ignoring the grills on foot; they'd scatter at the rattle of Markham's sabatons on the stone, dropping their bundles into the drizzle-churned muck to take to their knees and lower their heads.

Off the thoroughfare the levels of Hell slipped down around us, each shabbier and more crowded and more throat-choking with the overpowering stench of grill shit than the one below, as if the ogrilloi had organized themselves into instinctive castes. Down at the first level, they at least had clothes and lanterns and roofs over the ancient walls. Higher, the open gutters were packed with gnawed-down bones and rotten greens and sick yellow turds that melted slowly away in the rain; the only general improvement I could see that the Khryllians had made was to carve drains that emptied the gutters into sluices channeling the solid waste away from the river.

Even all those years ago, I remember being puzzled why the First Folk would have built a city without sewers.

Of course, now I pretty much know.

By the time I stepped off the jitney at the fifth tier vault, I was whipped. Wrung out. The beating was barely half of it. This was worse. This was more. I've been beaten before. This was being beaten down. Beaten down by age, and by memory.

Everything looked too different. Nothing looked different enough.

The switchbacked thoroughfare still threaded high-arched tunnels to end at the vast almost-Gothic vault carved from the escarpment's heartrock, but now, twenty-five years later, there were none of the shadows and dry must and sand, none of the lichen and gnawed-clean bones of small animals. The mica-flecked stone of the vault was scrubbed and spotless and polished to a mirror finish that threw back the light of dozens of lamps. Dual gates of filigreed iron closed both the lower entrance and the arch of the broad ramping tunnel that led to the surface of the escarpment above. The whole place had the air of a busy railhead, full of armsmen, clerks and porters, wagons, and chain gangs.

The last time I'd been in this vault—

I didn't let myself think about it.

"From here you walk," Markham said. "You may safely leave the trunk any-where you like. I will have it sent on to your hostelry."

"Shit. You could've done that back at the vigilry—"

"Yes," Markham said. "I could have."

The jitney bitch had her team backing the cart down the thoroughfare al-most before my feet hit the rock. An attentive page was instantly on hand to take charge of the trunk. Markham directed me toward a new tunnel, broad as the thoroughfares, that had been cut the dozen meters or so through to the face.

It opened onto a cargo aerie: a broad oval cliff of cut-smooth rock, twilight sky, and the creak of oiled hemp as three massive cranes lifted whole wagons and their loads over the lip of the plateau above, swinging them wide over the half-kilometer drop. On my left the escarpment fell away down the levels of Hell to the twilit map of Purthin's Ford and the flat indigo snake of the river, and ahead—

Ahead the Spire jabbed another hundred and thirty feet of swollen white-stone god-cock into the darkening sky.

To my right the world was eclipsed by the buttress wall that supported the final sally bridge. From the city below, those sally bridges looked delicate as rainbows; up close, its arching buttress was a cliff of rain-slick whitestone too vast for comprehension.

The whole thing was just way too fucking big.

I tried to remind myself that I'm not exactly educated—that really, I know a grand total of dick about materials science. I tried to remind myself that for all I knew, maybe granite and whitestone really could support the stress of a fortress fifteen hundred feet tall. Maybe it could hold up open spans of bridge a couple hundred yards long. Not to mention however ungodly many bazillion gallons of water under whatever hellish pressure must be inside. Maybe Ma'elKoth just knew a lot more about engineering than anyone else. Anywhere. Ever.

Maybe it was magick.

Maybe that magick wasn't going to unexpectedly decay while I was way too fucking close to that fucking thing.

Markham led me along the cliff face toward a stone command house that had been built out from the base of the buttress. Like all official Khryllian structures, it was immaculate, all clean white lines and perfect white angles, and looked like it could double as a bunker. The outer room held regimented copying tables staffed by regimented Khryllian clerks making regimented lines of notes on the regimented contents of every wagon going up or down above the aerie; the back office held a pair of standard-issue back office types, distinguished only by their Soldier of Khryl crewcuts and the sunburst blazons on their blouses.

"I require this office," Markham said, and the back-office types gathered their papers and their charcoals and vanished without a word. Without so much as a glance. At either of us. Or each other.

"They don't ask why? Who I am? They don't even ask how long?"

"It is not their duty to know."

The door closed behind them. He moved to the rear wall of the office, which was tiled with the same brilliant whitestone that made the whole Spire shine—probably was the buttress wall itself. He ran the flat of his hand over the stone in a long smooth curve that could almost have been a caress.

He said, *"Phy'nyll tin Pinèsh,"* and the sunset around his hand took on a faint wash of blue that flowed from his outstretched fingers. A rectangular section of wall swung backward into darkness. From within came a subterranean thunder, almost subsonic: a slow permanent earthquake in the absolute black: my river rumbling past.

Oh, for shit's sake. "Is this some kind of joke?"

"Please follow me." Walking through, Markham was instantly swallowed by night.

I squinted into the darkness. "What am I, a fucking bat? How about a lamp?"

"The way is straight and smooth, with hazard to neither head nor foot." Markham's voice echoed with the patience of the stone around us. "If you like, I will carry you."

The way my head felt, I was tempted to take the bastard up on it. Instead I only sighed. "Anybody ever tell you you're a funny guy?"

"No."

"There's a reason for that," I said, and followed into the night-shrouded passage. As soon as I entered, the panel swung shut behind me and the way was dark as a cave.

Even this took me back. Walking along smooth flat stone in absolute black, left hand brushing polished wall cold and dripping with what I hoped was just rock sweat, I was twenty-five again with Marade at my side, walking out cold iron calm from midnight into screaming bloody dawn . . .

I could still feel the spring steel of muscle under the velvet skin of her thigh. I could still smell my blood on her hand, feel her tongue between my lips . . .

Sometime later another panel opened onto lamplight. Markham stepped aside to let me pass first through the doorway.

It was the first place in Purthin's Ford that didn't smell clean. It was also the first Khryllian place that wasn't white. Some kind of Roman-style bath, tiled in brown terra-cotta—a long curving pool of rusty-looking water lay flat and still below a shallow flight of steps. The steps continued into depths invisible in the rusty murk. The room smelled stale and old—far too old for a place built less than twenty years ago—thick with must and decay, lampblack and a meaty butcher-shop funk.

Three steps led up to a narrow walkway that hugged the inner curve of the wall above the pool. The light in the room came from lamps hung on chains above this walkway; there were no windows. The wall near the steps was hung with clothes hooks, the first three holding towels and the rest empty. An array of armor racks stood nearby, all empty save one, and that one was hung not with chain or plate but with ordinary clothing, a tunic and pants that might have been of raw silk.

Markham had stopped in the passageway. "This is the Lavidherrixium. From here," he said from the half light, "you will continue alone."

I shrugged and turned for the walkway stairs.

"No," Markham said from behind me. "You approach the Purificapex of the Lord of Valor."

I looked over my shoulder. The Lord Righteous pointed at the pool.

"Oh, come on."

"You may disrobe here, and hang your clothing. You will find a robe on the far side."

"What am I supposed to do, swim? In *that*?"

"Yes."

"You are batshit insane."

"The taints of Cowardice and Compromise must be washed from you before you may approach." Upper-case emphasis was clear in his tone. "You must be made Clean."

"That's gonna make me *clean*? Are you pulling my dick? It smells like—" I squinted along the curve of the wall and saw the robes hanging on the far side, and the robes weren't white either; they were terra-cotta brown. The same brown as the tiles. The same brown as the rusty tinge of the water.

The butcher-shop funk finally got through to me.

"Oh, for shit's sake." My head pounded. I rubbed my eyes. "I remember this from Abbey school—that fucking Khryllian Sanctified by the Blood of Heroes crap . . . it's supposed to be just a *metaphor*—"

"Freeman, the Champion awaits."

I looked at the water for a long moment. I tried to imagine so much as dipping in a toe. My stomach churned.

I turned for the door. "Tell the Champion I appreciate the sentiment and thanks very much for the Healing and the three-peasant tour, but this is a lit-tle bit way too motherfucking much, and I am out of here like a—"

I came to a sudden stop. The doorway was full of Khryllian. The Khryllian said, "No."

"Markham, get out of my way."

"You may make the attempt to move me."

"I'm telling you I'm not doing this—"

"And I am telling you, Freeman Shade, that you are."

The Lord Righteous's stare was full of cold possibility.

"You pull this swim-in-the-blood shit on everybody who comes up here, or is this something special just for me?"

Something flickered through Markham's eyes then, something I hadn't seen before: something cold and hot together. Something angry, and fright-ened. Wounded.

Dangerous.

"Fuck *me.*" I suddenly had a little trouble getting my breath. "There *is* no 'everybody who comes up here,' is there? That's the going up Hell instead of inside the Spire, the secret passage, the no introductions, all of it. It's so no-body starts running around yelling there's a non-Khryllian desecrating Our Holy Pukinsuckmydick or whateverthefuck you call it. You've never *done* this before—"

"I am tasked to deliver you to the Champion." Markham's voice had gone as dangerous as his eyes.

"*You* don't know what's going on *either.*" I jabbed a finger at the Khryllian's petrifying face. "You don't have a fucking clue."

Markham's jaw worked like he was chewing rocks. "It is not my duty to know."

"And it's killing you. It's eating you alive."

The progress of his self-control could be traced by the slow drain of flush from his cheeks down into his neck. He wrapped himself in supercilious Lip-kan disdain. "It is not my duty to know."

So I turned away and stripped off my tunic. I threw it to the floor under the clothes hooks with a short dark laugh. "Gonna be here on my way out?"

"Perhaps," Markham said warily to my back. "Why?"

"Maybe I'll fill you in," I said as I kicked off my boots and unbuckled my belt, "or maybe—"

I dropped my pants. "Maybe I'll just give you one more chance to kiss my ass."

# LEGEND

They roar toward my back like a tornado on crank.

To hell with the jinking, the juking and the fuck-my-ass serpentine: I take the last ten meters at a dead sprint. A clattering rain of barbed arrows rattles onto the gateway's stone. One of them clips my butt as I dodge around the upright and stumble into the linked shield-wall of a dozen porters. The guy I slammed into doesn't blink. None of them do.

Twelve identical thousand-yard stares: they don't even see me.

Guess I bought Pretornio enough time after all.

Three faces peer over the wall-top. Fuckers. Wish I had something to throw at them. "What happened to my *Cloak*?"

Tizarre grimaces a baffled apology that I'd like to pound into her face with a rock. Stalton hisses, "Come on, they're-right-behind-you come *on*—!"

The hand I grabbed my ass with comes back red. "Fucking *right*."

A few centuries' neglect have chewed back mortar a span deep between the huge dressed-stone blocks of the gateway; I jump, grab on, and scramble up the rest of the eight meters as fast as most guys can climb stairs.

Black Knives boil into the gateway. Shouting. Roaring. Bellows of bloodlust and rage below my feet. I flick a glance down behind me—

Ogrilloi surge and snarl around the twin formations of the porters. The porters stand braced in *kratrio* to either side of the crumbled gate arch: locked shield to shield, the rear rank's shields held flat overhead like a steel-tiled roof, leaving just enough of a slit for their long-bladed stabbing spears to lick outward at any Black Knife stupid enough to stumble into reach.

As I'm clawing over the lip onto the top of the wall, Pretornio lifts his arms as though delivering a benediction. The *kratrii* begin to move.

Leaning into their shields, the porters force their way into the boil of Black Knives in perfect lockstep. Vertical cracks open in their shield wall to pass the short thick hacking-blades each man carries in his right hand. Where they strike, Black Knives bleed.

No wonder Lipke could bitch-hump this whole continent. Half an hour with a priest of Dal'Kannith, and twenty-five surly, untrained, lazy goddamn packbearers are suddenly a Roman fucking legion.

They grind toward each other, pinching off the inflow of Black Knives like a sphincter with razor-blade teeth. On the wall, Stalton leans around the broad curve of the panel shield he's covering Rababàl with. A stack of sword-bladed spears lean in the crenel next to him, and he's got my hauberk in his free hand. "You are one stone batshit son of a bitch."

I flash him a grin and keep moving. He hefts my armor. "Suit up, kid. They'll be climbing—" but I'm already past the shield and in Rababàl's face.

"Now, goddammit! *Now!*"

Rababàl's got a thousand-yard stare of his own: mindview. He reaches out, and the charged buckeyes he scattered in the rocks outside the wall blast flame. The air *shirrs* with stone-shard shrapnel. Burning, bleeding Black Knives howl and claw at each other, trailing meat-scented smoke.

Huh: smells like burnt duck.

Rababàl's expression stays blankly remote and he starts mumbling under his breath. A couple Black Knives leap for the farside wall. Rababàl snaps a smoking buckeye at them like he's flicking a booger, and it erupts into flame that blasts them back to the ground, on fire and howling.

Stalton drops my hauberk and grabs a spear with a *very* stylish one-handed flourish that slashes a hand off the first Black Knife up our wall. The ogrillo roars as it tumbles toward the jagged masonry below. "Caine, your *armor*—"

"Leave it. Pass me one of those spears."

"The arrows—"

"Have you *seen* those arrows?" I may not be the most educated cock-knocker in this city today, but I know the story of Agincourt.

For answer, he hands me his spear and reaches for another. Bright bloody steel jabbing and slicing at their hands and faces convinces the Black Knives to take their chances on the ground.

Good fucking luck. They're about to learn how it feels to be iron.

The porters re-form into a single rectangle that corks the gate mouth, front two ranks facing the smoldering ogrilloi out in the badlands, rear rank facing the broad corridor of the gateway. That's the anvil.

The Black Knives trapped inside—a dozen, maybe fifteen—surge and snarl and roar.

Through the deep-shadowed arch at the inner end of the gateway, jauntily spinning a four-kilo morningstar as lightly as a majorette's baton, strides the unstoppable human battle tank that is Marade.

Already got the hammer part figured, huh?

There is a cheerful abandon in the way she goes to work on the mass of panicked flailing screaming Black Knives, and y'know what?

I think I'm in love.

### >>scanning fwd>>

They stand in little clusters out in the badlands, well beyond bowshot. Watching.

Down below, Marade tosses another dead Black Knife onto the growing pile outside the gate mouth.

That's it, you fuckers. Watch. Not one ogrillo will come back out that gate alive.

Watch, you bastards. You cocksmoking asswhores. Watch.

And think it over.

Tizarre's still babbling about her Cloak. "I don't understand—it doesn't make any *sense* . . . the more power I threw into it, the weaker it got—"

"Yeah, I know. Shut up about it, will you?" She makes a little noise like half a whimper, and I wave a dismissing hand. "Look, forget it. Didn't get hurt, did I?"

Except for the crease on my buttcheek that stings like a bastard every time I take a step, but forget that too. "Go help Marade, huh?"

"Help her do what?"

"I don't give a shit. Just go." Do I have time for her wounded fucking feelings?

I turn away and screw the spyglass back into my eye. Wish I knew enough about ogrilloi to read the expressions on their faces. What bugs me: none of the Black Knives carry packs. Only a few even carry water skins. And there's no koshoi, and there's none of the little sorta-almost-burros Boedecken ogrilloi use to carry supplies and loot. I don't think this is a raiding party. I don't think it ever was. I've got a sinking feeling that it might be a short-range reconnaissance-in-force.

Or worse: like a, y'know, like a *posse* . . .

Now one of them squats. Just drops, right where he is, bouncing down in that Asian peasant-in-the-paddy crouch, balancing comfortably between his knees. And another one. A few more—

And there they go. All of them, dropping in a weirdly beautiful not-quite-random ripple like a crowd settling in after a standing ovation.

Settling in to wait.

No: not all. Three of them peel off and lope away, off into the badlands. Along their backtrail.

Time to go.

My eye socket aches. I need to lay off the Zeiss before I pop an eyeball right the hell out of my face. "Rababàl. We need to get people together. Is Pretornio still dicking around?"

"I wouldn't call it—"

"How long does it take to bury a couple bodies?" Yeah, yeah, respect for the dead, sure. Petro and Lagget were good guys, greater love hath no man, whatever. They're dead, we're not, and I want to keep it that way. "Rababàl?"

No answer. He's staring out at the mass of Black Knives, flicking that fucking coin through his fingers again. "What are they doing? Just sitting there. Staring at us. Did it work? Will they leave, now?"

"If they were leaving, they'd be gone already."

"Your brilliant plan," he mutters. "What are they waiting for?"

I shrug. "Dark."

He squints at me.

"Ogrilloi are—what's the word? You know: twilight hunters."

"Crepuscular."

"Yeah. So they're gonna wait till dark, because their night vision's a lot better than ours. Not to mention their sense of smell. And they won't come in a rush this time. It'll be scouting parties. Little ones, and maybe a lot of them: ogrilloi like to hunt in packs of seven to ten. They'll come in quiet. Infiltrating, if they can. Find out where we are and what we have."

"And how do you expect to stop them?"

"I don't. I expect to be gone."

"*Now* we run?"

"If this had just been about chasing those two guys in the badlands, they'd have left already. There's something here they want."

"Other than us?

I shrug again and poke my chin at the pile of Black Knife dead. "Something worth getting another chunk of their collective dick chopped off. I don't think we qualify."

"I pray you're right."

"You do that."

He makes a face at me. "And now?"

I bite down on a sigh; it comes out a flat hiss between my teeth. "Tell Stalton to have Kess and the grooms start tacking up the horses."

## >>scanning fwd>>

Oh.

Well.

That's it, then.

I take the Zeiss from my eye and hold it balanced on my grimy blood-caked palm. It's a goddamn nifty little thing. Seamlessly linked ovoids of brushed stainless steel. Kidskin-padded eye cup. Laser-ground polarized optics. A little crust of dried blood mars its softly gleaming surface, and I absently rub it clean with my thumb.

Man, I have seen a lot of shit with it today.

Somebody in my line of work must have brought it from back home. Had to be a long time ago. On freemod. One of the old-timers, maybe even one of the guys I grew up watching. The bosses those days were a lot looser about high-tech contraband. This nifty little piece of quality craftsmanship has probably been knocking around this world longer than I've been alive. Getting lost, getting stolen. Traded. Pawned.

Looted.

I remember how startled I was when I first saw it, when Hoppy Spinner pulled it out of his kit bag that afternoon in the God's Teeth. I remember wondering if Hoppy might be another like me: a struggling second-rater nobody ever heard of. I figured he must be in my line of work. I remember how I found out he wasn't.

There were ogrilloi there too.

I remember finding what was left of his body after they let their khoshoi strip his bones. How the shreds and tatters left behind lay quietly decomposing.

I found this monocular in a pool of khoshoi vomit between his fang-scored pelvis and splintered ribs. Khoshoi are as conservative as wolves; whichever one yarked up this hunk of indigestible metal had gone ahead and eaten whatever else had come up with it. All that was left was the Zeiss and a handful of clotted bile.

This little fucking thing is all I still have of old Hoppy. Wonder where he got it.

From the anxious crowd of partners and porters half crouching within the shadowed mouth of the crest passage, Rababàl says hoarsely, "What is it? What do you see?"

I drift away from the passage mouth, through the scrub toward the brink of this vast escarpment. My boots crunch through sand and loose gravel. Below, the vertical city spreads in descending rings like a peeled-open map of the Inferno.

Huh. When I called it Hell, I was just, y'know, riffing. But now I see it with different eyes.

"Come on out if you want," I call. Quiet has outlived its usefulness. "You can see for yourself."

I heft the monocular. "Won't need this."

A long, smooth windup and I pitch the fucking thing high and hard, out over the half-klick drop to the badlands. The sunset picks it up at the top of its arc and makes it shine like a falling star.

It drops out of the light, swallowed by the shadows below. A lifetime passes while I wait for the stillness to give up a faint clatter of metal on stone.

A presence at my shoulder: Stalton. "What'd you do *that* for?"

"I got it off a dead man," I tell him without moving. "I don't want it to pass on the same way."

"Shit, Caine, you didn't want it, you coulda just gave it to *me*—"

I turn just enough for him to see the look in my eyes. "Maybe you don't understand what I just said."

I leave him there to think about it and go back to the other partners.

Far out in the badlands, the vast dust cloud swells wide, one thin arc of its uppermost reach glowing in the last of the sunset. Marade's staring at that cloud like she can read her future in it. And she can.

So can I.

Rababàl and Tizarre stand like they froze solid in the middle of an involuntary flinch. They're staring at a hundred-odd ogrilloi trotting toward us along the escarpment, not more than a mile away. Even as we watch, their gorilla-bear lope fades to a walk, then they start dropping into that wait-until-dark squat.

"How did they get *up* here?" Rababàl fumbles with his platinum disk, drops it, and lets it *chinng* into the rocks at his feet. He doesn't even look down. "How did they get here *ahead* of us?"

"They didn't." I nod back toward the city. "They're still down there. These are new."

"But—but—what are they *doing* up here?"

Marade murmurs the textbook answer. "When marching a large body of troops parallel to a major geographic feature—a mountain range, say, or this rift-cliff—you need a screen of skirmishers on the far side, in case—"

"Marching *troops*?"

Chrome steel creaks as she slowly shakes her head. "Or whatever."

He follows her gaze out to the vast dust cloud now disappearing into the horizon's shadow. "Um. Oh. Um, I see." His nervy voice, finally, has gone calm and quiet. For the first time, he sounds like a grown-up. "I understand. That cloud—that's not a storm."

She nods, still staring at her future. She doesn't seem to like the looks of it.

Yeah, well, me neither.

Tizarre's got that wild look around her eyes again. "Where the hell are the *horses*? Where's Kess and the grooms?"

I wave toward another trail of rising dust, upland toward the sinking sun.

"Bastard," she breathes. "That ratsucking *bastard*—"

"Leave the language to me," I mutter. "You don't have the touch."

That wild look of hers takes on a dangerous calculation. Even money says she's running through all the magicks she knows that can hit them from here. "They haven't gotten very far—"

"They're plenty far. But they won't get a lot farther; that dust isn't theirs. It's from Black Knives on their trail."

Stalton's at my shoulder again. "*More* Black Knives?" he breathes, blinking. Yeah: weak eyes. "Are you pulling my dick? How many?"

A sign that can't unclench the fist in my gut. A shrug that can't shift the weight on my shoulders. That's all the answer he should need.

"Come *on*, Caine. You had the glass. How many are out there?"

So I tell him. "All of them."

## >>scanning fwd>>

I stick out a hand to stop the two thaumaturges in the stair shaft to the escarpment's top. "What d'you got left for Fireballs?"

Tizarre looks at Rababàl. He makes a face. "A, well, a dozen. Or so."

"A dozen. Fuck my ass."

"Had I known how *splendidly* your master plan would work," he says through his teeth, "I would have been more *conservative*—"

"Yeah, whatever." Don't panic. Do *not* panic.

Panic—

Huh. Funny.

What panic?

Y'know, all I'm really getting right now is that hot dark tingle just above my balls. Maybe I really am one stone batshit son of a bitch.

I'm looking *forward* to this . . .

"Okay. Okay, look, can you Reach from mindview?"

"Telekinesis?" He frowns. "Well, yes, a little. I'm not strong."

"Won't have to be. Collect canteens from the porters. Dump the water and fill 'em half full of lamp oil. Drop a buckeye in each, you follow?"

His frown turns appreciative. "I believe I do."

"Tizarre: you can Nightsee, can't you? Can you Whisper?"

She starts to nod, stops. Her feathery brows draw together. "I should be able to. Should. Something's weird in the Flow here. No promises."

"No excuses either. Make it work."

She looks dubious. "The moon's barely past first quarter, and it won't rise till after midnight. Even if I can tell you where they are, you can't fight in the dark."

I nod toward Rababàl. "You'll be with *him.*"

"I don't get it."

"The oil canteens," Rababàl murmurs.

"Yup." She's recon. He's artillery. "We'll fight by the light of burning ogril-loi."

The stubby necromancer stares at me like he's never seen me before. Like I'm some kind of weird-ass animal and he's trying to calculate how dangerous I might be.

He has no fucking idea. "What else you got?"

"For combat?"

"No, shithead. For a bad attack of drizzledick."

"I, uh—Minor Shields. Some. Er, five. Just—y'know. For protection."

"And?"

He glances away. Rising color warms the bottom folds of his jowls. "And, well, I suppose . . ." he says diffidently. Offhand, as if it only just occurred to him. "I mean, y'know, there's my bladewand . . ."

"A bladewand?" I ratchet my dropped jaw back into place and lean so close that when he licks his lips I can smell his spit. "You have a *bladewand*? And you let me walk out that gate with nothing but a motherfucking *knife* up my sleeve?"

"Well, I, ah—it's magick, you see—"

"You don't want to know what I see." I open a hand. "Give it."

"But—but—"

"Give it, or my hand to fucking *God* I will take it off your *body.*"

Behind me, Stalton takes a step back up the crest passage. "Caine, you can't just push him around like—"

I stop him with a look over my shoulder. "Ever see a move like the one I pulled on that fucker outside?"

His answer is a measuring squint.

"You're about to bet your life I don't have another."

Color rises in his face. "That's not—"

I shove my open hand at Rababàl. "Now."

He fumbles the bladewand out from inside his vest. It's all I can do not to snatch it. I've never seen one in person. Not even *secondhand*, not in maybe fifteen years . . . not since I was a kid, playing bootleg cubes of the Lightweaver . . . then he holds it out to me, and I take it.

And I'm *holding* it. In my very own *hand*. I really am.

It's heavy, and warm with the damp heat of his sweat. Almost as long as my forearm, its wine-colored wood is dense as steel, inlaid with an impossibly intricate lattice of fine platinum wire. The butt end swells to an ovoid the size of a hen's egg, rounded and smooth, and it nestles into the hollow of my palm like it grew there. The balance point is a bare fingerbreadth from the butt; the griffinstone inside must be a monster.

A bladewand. I can't fucking believe it.

A breath is all it takes to summon the limpid passionless clarity of the Control Disciplines. They're not so different from mindview. My palm tingles with energy.

Hmm. The Lightweaver used to do it kinda like—

I point the wand at the passage gap and reach into myself, summoning pure concentration, feeling for the trigger point with my mind. Nothing happens.

Shit.

Rababàl's still sputtering. "But—but—but it's *magickal*, don't you understand?"

I do understand. I did a year of Battle Magick at the Conservatory—but if I'd been worth a wet fart at it, I wouldn't be here now . . .

"You're no thaumaturge, Caine. How can you expect to—"

"Shut up."

"Maybe I should take it," Tizarre says uncertainly. "I mean, I'm good with a blade, and—"

"Shut *up*."

Less effort. Just an intention. A feel . . .

A surge inside my right arm: not a tingle, not the electric sizzle that Telukhai always felt, but an actual surge like a tide of hot oil pulsing from my spine to my fingertips—

"Really, Caine, you're only embarrassing yourself. *Years* of training—"

Translucently shimmering blue-white energy licks along the platinum lattice and stretches out from the wand's tip: a plane as wide as my hand and about three meters long that enters the millennial stone of the crest passage wall without resistance. It lasts for only one heart-thumping second, but that's plenty of time for me to give the wand a twitch and carve off a hunk of rock bigger than my head.

Ohhh, yeah.

The hunk slides sideways and crashes down the ramp. The cut is smooth as glass. The bladewand's butt is hot in my hand.

Now Tizarre and Stalton both have that *what-the-fuck-kind-of-animal-is-this* look on their faces too. Rababàl breathes: "Who *are* you?"

I hold up the wand to catch the last rays of sunset. Platinum traceries shine like smears of blood.

I am *really* looking forward to this.

### >>scanning fwd>>

"You know what we're up against now."

They stare at me from their huddles and clusters in the deep vaulted shadows of the immense passage hall, faces pinched and green with dread. Moonrise drips ghost-milk down the crest passage behind me.

"There's no way out. There's no way back. There is no parley. No appeal. They're gonna come, and we're gonna die. All of us. We can't even slow them down. All we've got is a choice. Die tonight, or die from now till next month. Screaming."

Not exactly St. Crispin's Day, but at least I have their attention.

"I am going to die tonight. So is Marade, and Pretornio. Stalton and Rababàl and Tizarre." I nod at the cook, and his lover next to him. "So are you, Nollo. And you, Jashe. And every single one of you. Anybody who doesn't will wish he had. Say it with me: I am going to die tonight."

They look at me like I asked them to do the chicken dance.

"Come on. *Say* it. *I am going to die tonight.*"

Slowly, with a kind of reluctant surly stubbornness, they mumble their way through it.

"Where I come from, there used to be this, like, nation of warriors. When they were going into battle, they'd tell each other, *Today is a good day to die.* And they'd believe it." I nod toward the sunset behind me. "Well, for us it's night. This night. And I don't know how good it is, but it's the only one we've got."

I make a fist and hold it out. "Tonight is a good night to die."

They look at each other, at the niter-scaled walls, at the shadowed vault above. Anywhere but at me.

Christians like to say the truth will make you free. Guess I've got the wrong truth.

"Listen—" I let my fist go slack and rub my forehead. "Listen: I've got my share of problems, y'know? You all know it. I'm an asshole. Nobody likes me. Sometimes I don't like me much either."

I give them a second to disagree. Nobody jumps in. Big goddamn surprise.

"Shit weighs down on me, y'know? Like it does on everybody, I guess. I worry what the fuck I'm doing with my life. I've got a sick dad, and I can't take care of him, and this girl I'm hot for thinks I'm a jerk, and shit, y'know, she's *right*, but somehow I just can't *help* my—" I manage to avoid looking at her. "Ahh, forget all that, it's not important.

"Here's the point: that's all *future* stuff, y'know? Everything you worry about. Everything that keeps you awake at night. All the shitty things the world has waiting for all of us. You know: Failure. Old age. Loneliness. Heartbreak. Cancer. Whatever.

"All that is *gone*, now. You get it? That's all shit to worry about tomorrow— but we won't have to. Not ever again.

"For us, there *is* no tomorrow.

"Think about it. We have *nothing left to worry about*. Nothing. Shit, those Black Knives out there tonight? They're giving us a *gift*. Because all that bad stuff, all the rotten fucking shit that could possibly happen for the rest of our lives . . . won't. Because the only *rest of our lives* we have left is a few minutes to decide how we're gonna die."

"What difference does *that* make?" somebody says. "Dead is dead."

"Don't care how you die? You don't even have to leave this room. Just step over here." I open my arms, offering. "You won't feel a thing."

No takers. No surprise.

"I'll tell you how *I'm* gonna die."

A long, slow look, eye to eye to eye. I let that spark in my balls heat up my voice. "I'm gonna drown in their smoking fucking blood."

A muffled snort from the shadows: sounds like Stalton.

Thought he'd like that one.

"I will choke to death on their raw fucking *brains*. You follow? The cocksmoke that finally kills me will carry the marks of my teeth into his fuck-ing *grave*—and when somebody digs him up a thousand years from now, they'll point to the scar on his throat and they'll say, 'You see that? That was from *Caine*.' "

The passage hall goes quiet, and some of the eyes on me go cold now: the open-behind stare of surrendered hope. Good for them.

Good for me.

"I can't say what happens in the next life. Or if there is a next life. You want that shit, talk to Pretornio, or Marade. I will tell you this, though. There's one afterlife we *know* we can have: we can make the kind of fight here that will become a fucking *legend*."

I come to my feet. "To hell with the next world. Let's be immortal in this one. We're gonna die anyway. Let's do it right."

"Yeah?" Sounds like the same guy, there in the darkness. "But who's gonna know? We'll all be *dead*. Nobody will even know this ever *happened*—"

"We will be remembered." God's own truth: this could be Adventure of the Year. I'll be *famous*. Hell, they'll be famous too. Dying in front of an audience of millions.

Wish I could be there to enjoy it.

"Believe it." I give them a stare like the truth is a nail I can hammer into their heads with my eyes. "Our story will be known."

"Yeah? Who's gonna *tell* it? Who's gonna remember us?"

My conditioning would choke me if I tried tell him, but I have another truth. A better truth. A truth that just might make us free.

"I thought that was obvious." I raise a hand and wave at the black stone of the passage chamber walls, through the stone, out into the infinite night beyond.

Out at the Black Knives.

"*They* will."

# HAND OF PEACE

The robe itched. It smelled like meat.

I padded barefoot up an endless spiral of stairs built out from an inner cylinder of granite; the outer drum curved a good six feet clear of the stairs' empty edge, leaving a long, long drop to the lamplit arc of the Lavidherrixium below.

My hair was drying stiff, and my face felt tight and sticky, and my skin crawled, and I couldn't stop half a grimace that was at least part smile. So many people would be shocked, *shocked*, to find me suddenly fastidious about bathing in blood . . .

Funny thing: most of them were dead. Really funny thing: I killed a lot of them myself.

I'm not known for my sparkling sense of humor.

Eventually the smell of blood and lampblack gave way to clean after-rain and a sunset breeze, and the steps became damp, and I rounded the curve of the cylinder and found myself outside. *Way* outside.

An intricate scale model of Purthin's Ford speckled with pinpricks of fire-light stretched away below, and the sudden shift in perspective from six lamplit feet to six moonlit miles kicked me behind the knees and nearly pitched me headlong over the edge.

I lurched away from the rim, slipping, pressing my back against the white-stone curve of the Spire, bare feet scrabbling for purchase on the damp stair, and I held himself there for a year or two until my vertigo began to pass.

Eventually I could breathe again.

"Holy *crap*." A faded wheeze: that was all I had. "They couldn't post a fucking *sign*? Maybe put up a railing? Holy crap."

The final curve of the stairs looped up to the topmost reach of the Spire. I went up it with my right shoulder brushing the wall and my eyes on the stairs in front of me; even the top of the escarpment, only a hundred feet below, pulled at my balance, dragging my head toward the brink.

I had a feeling that even Khryllians didn't come up here lightly.

The five spires around the top of the Eternal Vaunt curved upward like ten-meter fingers of an upraised hand, plated in lustrous white metal; between them the cap was a steep slant of the same metal, polished and still slick after the rain. The stairs ended where the metal began; the slope of metal curved upward in a convex arc so that its apex was out of view.

I reached down and laid my palm on the metal: smooth and slick and colder than the rain.

Hmm.

I knew enough about the physics of magick to understand that the curve of the finger-spires above would focus Flow on that apex—the cup of the stylized palm—so this metal would be conductive . . . not silver, though. From this height, a slash of sun still burned the horizon, visible through a rent in the slow clouds; in its light the metal showed no hint of tarnish, and I couldn't imagine a legion of Khryllians making the climb up here for a daily polish. Not to mention Ma'elKoth and his friggin' artistic sensibilities . . . which meant this had to be something like, well—

Platinum.

And not leaf, either; though I couldn't guess the thickness, this was clearly designed to be walked on. I frowned up at the vast finger-spires and the plated convex slopes between—could there be this much in the entire world?—but then I shrugged. If your basic Joe Alchemist can turn lead into gold, Ma'elKoth could probably make platinum out of his own turds.

*Figures,* I monologued. *Silver just isn't quite* white *enough, is it?*

"Please join me. The view is better from up here."

My jolt at the unexpected voice didn't quite send me slipping down the platinum slope, tumbling off the rim of the thousand-foot tower and scream-ing down through misting drizzle to shatter some random embrasure far below in a cannonball of meat and bone. Not quite. But it came close enough that I saw the whole thing happen inside my head.

"Yeah?" Panting, I crouched and leaned on the platinum. It felt even colder now, smoother, satin ice. "Then it'll be nice if I live long enough to see it, huh?"

"If Khryl had willed your death for this day, you would have died in the Riverdock customs sequestry. Join me."

The voice was feminine, educated, with the air of effortless Lipkan aristoc-racy that Ankhanan society types so desperately try to emulate; at the same time, it had a full-throated chest resonance belonging more to fields than to drawing rooms. A rasping edge hinted that the woman who belonged to that voice spent a fair amount of her time on those fields shouting orders above the clash of weapons and the drum of steel-shod hooves.

I thought blankly, *a chick?*

I clicked over some decades-old Monastic research on the Order. This'd be the first female Champion of Khryl since, what, Pintelle? Call it eighty-odd years, give or take.

Wow.

Bare feet gave me just enough purchase on the platinum, despite the damp, that if I trusted my weight and didn't lean too far into my balance I could make my way up the slope.

She stood at the focus of the Purificapex, her back to me, hands folded behind her. She wore a robe identical to mine, stained with old blood, raised hood shrouding her head. Her feet were bare, her ankles pale and thick, her calves trim, chiseled white marble; her folded hands were long and hard on thick corded wrists.

Beside her stood a waist-high extrusion of metal sloping up out of the general flooring, smooth on top, gently sloped, maybe ten inches wide and a couple of feet long. On top of it rested a leather bundle, rolled and tied with a thong like a chef's knife wrap.

Good size for an altar, maybe. Or an anvil. Or a chopping block.

On the far side of the altar-block there was some kind of a long handle—like the hilt of a bastard sword wrapped in wire—sticking up at an angle. That handle was the only part of the furnishings that wasn't platinum; it looked old, rusted, eaten by age and exposure.

I padded up behind her. "Think your boy Markham believes this apology crap?"

She didn't move. "It does not matter what he believes."

"Then why the story?"

"It is the truth."

"Oh, come on."

One shoulder lifted a millimeter. "It is part of the truth. The apology is not on behalf of Knight Aeddharr, but on my own."

"Shit, lady, you could've just sent a card."

"You are here," she said, "because it is my wish that you see the Battleground as I see it."

She unclasped her hands and extended one to swing through a long, slow wave out at the darkening downland: the sprawl of city and the gentle swells of plantations and vineyards beyond. "Purthin's Ford. The Knightly Estates of the Order of Khryl."

The gesture turned toward the escarpment, toward distant compounds lit with the glow of coal-gas mantles, and a nearer compound, vast rows upon rows of regimented shacks and cages surrounded by razor wire and guardhouses and greenish beams of roving searchlights. "The Upland Manufactories, and BlackStone Mining, and the Pens."

She returned her hand behind her back, and lowered her shrouded head toward the tiers of the vertical city below. "And of course, the face of Hell."

"Yeah. Pretty. So?"

"Five hundred Knights of Khryl. Ten thousand armsmen. Thirty thousand sworn Soldiers, man, woman, and child. There was a time that the Order of Khryl was so respected—so feared—that the mere chance we might enter battle was enough to end a war. Whole empires bowed before us."

"What's your point?"

"Now we are—" This time her shrug was big enough to hurt. "—jailers. Keepers of the Boedecken ogrilloi."

I nodded a shrug of my own at the platinum spires around us. "But you've got a really nice house."

"Bitter though it may be, this duty has fallen to us, and I shall see it done. For the sake of all that you see around you here. Do you understand this? It is not for mine own sake, nor for Khryl's, nor for the Order's alone—certainly it is not for glory, nor for any hope of the return of bygone days. It is for the lives and hopes and happiness of forty thousand Khryllians, near that many again of the Civility, and near to two hundred thousands of the ogrilloi themselves that I do this. They are each and all my responsibility. My duty. Thus do I fulfill it."

"Thus?" I frowned. "What, you mean by bringing me up here?"

"Yes. By bringing you to the Purificapex of Khryl. By standing you at my side, in a place where only ordained Knights of Khryl have stood till now. By showing you what I see. For we must understand one another, you and I."

Wincing, the pounding in my head telling me I wasn't going to like the answer, I asked, "We must? How come?"

"Because," she said, turning to me finally, pulling back her blood-stained cowl, "I know who you are."

For long enough that the platinum numbed my bare toes, I could only stare.

She missed good-looking by a yard on the hard side: her face might have been shaped from chrome steel by a cutting torch. Her hair hung straight and limp, the color of maple leaves that have lain under snow cover all winter long. Her neck was corded with knife-etched muscle, and her jaw looked to have been modeled on a splitting maul.

But her eyes—

Those eyes . . . damn. I knew that color.

Lifetimes ago, I trained at the Studio Conservatory on Naxos, in Earth's Aegean Sea. At twilight in late summer, as the last arc of the sun slips into the sea and the first stars kindle, the sky goes to indigo velvet: warm, and soft, and impossibly remote. That color.

But in her eyes that remote melancholy was overlaid with cool unselfconscious speculation, a direct and level interest that examined my face, my shoulders. The shape of my hands. The drape of my robe.

I offered another blank mental *Damn . . .*

I played dumb. I've had plenty of practice. "Have we met?"

She spread her hands. "I am Angvasse, Lady Khlaylock, currently the Champion of Khryl."

"Khlaylock?" My stomach lurched. "Any relation?"

"I have the honor to be that great man's niece."

I said, "Uh."

Another Khlaylock was the last thing I needed in my life right now. Or, say, ever. I coughed. "Sorry. I'm supposed to take a fu—a knee or something, right?"

"Formalities need not be observed; I am not in Khryl's Battledress. Here in the Palm of God we are equals. You may stand. You may even call me Angvasse." Faint creases appeared around those startling eyes as though she might be about to smile. "You should understand that these liberties are not taken elsewhere."

"Uh, yeah."

"And you may speak freely here; Khryl is a warrior god. His Sanctum cannot be profaned by mere words, no matter how coarse."

I coughed again. "How do you—who do you think I am?"

She waved a dismissive hand. "Please. An Ankhanan Esoteric enters the Battleground, speaking of Black Knives? I am not ignorant of our history. And now, meeting you in person—I passed my youth in my uncle's house. His portrait of you hangs in his study."

I blinked. "It does?"

"Of a much younger you, of course. Slimmer. Less scarred." Her eyes creased again like she was thinking about smiling but decided against it. "And I thought you'd be taller."

"Everybody does." I scowled at her. "Are you putting me on? A portrait?"

"He is an accomplished painter. When he retires as Justiciar, I have no doubt he will become a noted artist."

I started to monologue, *God save me from the fucking sensitive artistic types,*\* until I remembered that the god to whom I was bitching is Himself one of those fucking sensitive artistic types. "But in his study? I mean, in his study doesn't he want, I don't know, a picture of his father? Or Khryl or something?"

"Such paintings grace other rooms in his manor. You hang on the wall of his study, he has said, as a constant reminder—" Her melancholy took on a curious note of *schadenfreude.* "—of the price of vanity."

"He was never short on that."

"You would find him," she said, "quite changed."

"I'd rather not find him at all."

She nodded. "He does not remember you fondly."

"But still—I mean, I'm supposed to be *defended* against—"

"Not from God. The Lord of Valor directs my attention to threats against His Soldiers and His land."

"I'm a threat?"

"Are you not?"

"I wasn't planning to be." Another shrug. Why lie? "Getting beaten more-or-less to death might have changed my mind."

"And thus I offer my apology. The incident occurred at my command, and I sincerely regret the necessity."

I chewed on that. It tasted like the inside of my lip. "You ordered that bastard to kill me?"

"Not to kill. Never."

"Did you explain that to *him?*"

"We are a young land, freeman; I have not seen thirty years, yet I saw the birth of the Battleground—as you must know, you who had so much a hand in creating it. We are still building the customs and tradition—constructing a society entire—that will fulfill Our Lord's Command to tame His Land and defend the innocents who seek to thrive here."

A wistful undertone hinted that she used to believe it.

I did my best to sound encouraging. "Uh-huh."

"And our circumstance has become desperate. It was necessary to be certain of your intentions."

"What's this got to do with Orbek?"

"Certain . . . elements . . . have begun to interfere in Khryl's society. Violently."

"Yeah, I gathered. So, what, he's hooked in with this Freedom's Face?"

"Freedom's Face is nothing." She turned a hand as though releasing a fly from her fist. "Overprivileged and underexperienced scions of your Ankhanan burghers. Children with too much time on their hands, who have somehow come to believe that the romance of Liberty outweighs skill at arms. Who believe that casual vandalism, minor sabotage, and demonstrations of civil disobedience can bend the Will of God. We *own* Freedom's Face; we can destroy it at a whim. We allow its survival only because we find it a useful beer pot in which to gather your juvenile wasps."

"Has anybody explained that to Tyrkilld?"

"Explained it?" She looked honestly puzzled. "He is Khryl's leading Knight in the control of Freedom's Face. They are no serious threat."

Oh, really? Well.

Well, well, well.

I said, "The rifles and checkpoints looked serious enough."

"We have a problem of our own; they call themselves the Smoke Hunt."

"I gathered that," I said slowly. "What's it got to do with Orbek?"

"This is where the matter becomes . . ." She sighed. ". . . complicated."

I shrugged. "I call it Caine's Law: Everything's more complicated than you think it is."

"Ah."

"There's a corollary," I offered, going for an amiable *keep on chatting, lady* kind of tone. "Whenever somebody tells you shit's simple, they're trying to sell you something."

Again she almost smiled. Almost. "Perhaps. Yet I tell you matters are complex, and I too am . . . selling you something."

"Yeah? What're you selling?"

She fixed me with the infinite melancholy of her twilight eyes. "This Orbek—his claim of being a Black Knife—is this truth?"

"Far as I know." I shrugged and found something to look at in the darkening sky. "That's what his father told him, anyway—Orbek was born after the—after, uh, y'know—"

"And you truly claim him as brother? *You,* of all men living?"

"It's—kind of a longer story than I really want to get into right now."

She shook her head. "You are an interesting man."

"He's pretty interesting too."

"I meet too many interesting people," she said distantly. "Most of them I have to kill."

"Probably just coincidence."

Her voice went sad and cold: autumn winds dropping toward winter. "Not in this case."

The evening damp turned to winter on my neck. "Maybe you want to tell me what you mean by that."

She lifted her face to the heavens and murmured, "*Ammare Khryl Tyrhaalv'Dhalleig, hrereteg yroshallai ti Hammantellentlei av uvranishai ter-*

*ishiin,*" which I somehow knew, without being surprised at the knowledge, in the way you know things in a dream, was Old High Lipkan. Which wasn't a shocker; I have heard Old High Lipkan before. The shocker was that I knew what it meant.

*Beloved Khryl, Lord of Valor, I do this only for the honor of Your Name and the future of Your people.*

This was a shocker because I don't speak Old High Lipkan.

I found myself chewing the inside of my lip again while I waited for her to pull her nerves together. Eventually she lowered her head and took a deep breath. "How much do you know of your—brother's—doings on the Battle-ground?"

"Uh-uh." I folded my arms. "That's not how this works."

"I beg your pardon?"

"This is your party. You lay out the snacks."

Infinite weariness in her nod. "I met him, this Orbek who styles himself *kwatcharr* of the Black Knives."

"He does?"

She went on like I hadn't spoken. "He was sought for questioning in an un-related incident—a murder, in the fourth tier of Hell."

"That wasn't murder," I said.

"Oh?" she said mildly, angling her head toward me.

I met her gaze squarely. She waited for me to elaborate. I waited for her to get tired of waiting.

She sighed. "The killing was done with a firearm—merely to bring such a weapon into Purthin's Ford—"

"How d'you know he didn't get it here?"

Again she waited for me to elaborate. Again I waited for her to get tired of waiting. Eventually she surrendered a nod. "He avoided armsmen and Knights together for some days; he was not taken until I myself joined the hunt. He defied me personally, in Khryl's Battledress, which is an affront to God Himself."

"Ankhanans are like that."

"Yes. You are. While the Empire maintains a pretense of careful neutrality, it is known that some of the Battleground's current difficulties are of Ankhanan origin, and your own relationship with the Empire, and the Em-peror, is known to Khryl's Order. This why you were mistreated; it was neces-sary to ascertain whether you might be associated with these elements. Knight Aeddhar felt he had no better way to prove your innocence. And for this I apol-ogize, on my own behalf, as well as on behalf of Knight Aeddhar, the Order of

Khryl, and the Civility of the Battleground. This apology is profound and sincere, as is my hope that you might accept it."

"I'm not there yet. Get back with Orbek."

"There are no gentle words for this, freeman." Her voice hardened out of that wistful tone, but her eyes were still all melancholy twilight. "Your brother is in the Pens."

"Pens." An empty echo, no meaning behind it.

"Yes. At Shortshadow tomorrow, he will face Khryl's Justice. By my hand."

"Khryl's Justice? Son of a bitch. He's gonna *fight* you?"

"Yes."

"That's not a fight, it's an execution."

She didn't even blink. "It is at his own request: a request that I am, as Khryl's Champion, obliged by custom and by Law to answer."

For a long cold minute, I looked at her. Just looked. She let me. I wasn't really seeing her anyway.

I was seeing Orbek in the Donjon's Pit, walking like he lived only to fight and to fuck and didn't much care which he did to who. I was hearing the trace of a Boedecken burr in his bleak Warrens growl—

*—i am black knife. my dead father is black knife, from before. from when the land likes black knives—*

I was feeling Orbek's fist tangle in my filthy shirt, his hot carnivore breath down the side of my neck—

*—but remember. you win this one? you remember I coulda hurtcha. maybe i be dead, but you be hurt, hey? i want some fuck-me consideration—*

And I was remembering Orbek in the Shaft and Orbek in the Donjon riot and how Orbek had taken care of Faith and all the leagues we'd walked together in the years since Assumption Day, and after a while I turned back to her and my voice came out flat as roadkill. "That's why you set your boy Markham to babysit me."

She picked up the leather bundle and began to unroll it. "Were the Order of Khryl ever to forget the . . . potential hazards . . . presented by Esoterics," she said softly, "my uncle's face would serve as infallible reminder. As might the new scars borne by Knight Aeddhar."

"Huh."

"And you are no ordinary Esoteric. No one wants your hand raised against us."

"I haven't thought that far ahead."

She paused, holding the bundle half closed across the altar-block. "Have you not?"

I scratched idly at the knurls of scar and callus that layer my knuckles. "I guess it depends on what he's in for."

It seemed like a useful lie.

"He was taken," she said, "during a submission violation incident."

"What the hell's that?"

"All Khryl's ogrilloi must make submission when addressed by any Knight. It has to do with how ogrilloi were originally bred; the elves selected for—"

"I know how they were bred. Orbek isn't Khryl's, he's an Ankhanan freeman."

"On the Battleground, all ogrilloi are Khryl's. He refused submission."

"I'll bet he did."

*black knives don't kneel*

A quiet hiss whished on inside my head, like the ignition of an internal pilot light. "I'll bet he did," I repeated.

"Instead, he shouted out his name—as though it might be some sort of battle cry—"

"Yeah."

"—and he attacked." She opened the bundle. "With this."

Inside were Orbek's two KA-BARs—the ones he liked to wear up his sleeves, some kind of half-ass emotional compensation shit for his amputated fighting claws—and a sleek black 10mm Automag.

She picked up the pistol by the barrel and offered it to me.

I went to take it. Slowly. I felt old and stiff. But each step toward her carved ten years off me. I took the pistol and weighed it in my hand. The grip was molded for a hand twice the size of mine—Orbek's size. It felt heavy enough to be loaded. I thumbed the clip release and checked. It *was* loaded.

I slapped the clip back in and racked the slide, then sighted it toward the gleaming floor. "And the Knight survived?"

She said softly, "One of them did."

Her voice caught me. Her eyes held me.

I said, "You?"

In the uncertain light, I could just make out what could have been a pair of new scars like the ones I'd found over my liver: a long ragged smear of pink under her left ear, and a thumbnail-size rippled disk just above her sternal notch. It was a good bet she had an assload more like them under that robe.

Orbek had always been a stellar shot.

I looked down at the gun, then at her, then back at the gun. "Fuck me like a *goat* . . ."

She set the knives aside and spread her hands. "If your desire is for preemptive vengeance, you need seek no further."

I stepped back and leveled the pistol. "I know how Khryllian power works. I know how fast you must be." I took another step back. "I can still put one through your eye before you can move."

"I am certain of it."

Moisture trickled down my spine. I licked my lips and found sweat there. "What the fuck are you *doing?*"

"I am waiting for you to decide."

I stared at her over the sights. "Even if I decide to shoot you."

"Yes."

I flicked a glance toward the stairs. If my hand twitched when I squeezed the trigger, I'd need all the head start I could get.

Her stare remained steady. Calm. Empty.

Waiting.

It'd been a long time since I killed a woman.

A shimmer of memory, a quarter-century old: her uncle's broken face, left eye dangling from the optic nerve below its shattered socket, punctured and leaking vitreous humor down his nasolabial fold past the corner of his mouth. *Christ,* I thought, *tangling in my life is pretty fucking hard on this family.*

I gave my head a quick irritated shake. This was the wrong time for *that* shit.

Besides, tangling in my life is hard on everybody.

"This has to be," I ground out through my teeth, "just about the most fucked-in-the-ass stunt anybody's ever pulled with me."

"And?"

"Shit." The pistol got heavy: like straight-arming an anvil. "Oughta shoot you just for creeping me out."

"Is your brother a blooded warrior, freeman?"

"What's that got to do with anything?"

"I was flanked by two Knights Venturer." The sad distance in her eyes became somehow less distant but more sad. "He shot them first."

I stared. She stared back. After a minute, I blinked. She didn't.

"What?"

"Need I rephrase?"

The pistol sank. It didn't matter. I'd forgotten the pistol. "You had your back to him. Or something. He never saw your blazon."

"No."

"He didn't know who you are."

"He knew."

"No goddamn way. Not a chance in Hell, and that's not a fucking pun, either. No way."

"And yet it is so."

"If he *wanted* to die, he could have just blown his own bloody head off—"

"Yes."

"Then *why*?"

"This is a question which has troubled me for three days now. Can he have been enchanted? Pixilated in some way? Has his reason been driven from him, or is it simple despair and a desire for a memorable end?—for it is no small thing to be slain by Khryl's Own Fist."

She put out a hand to the altar-block as though she needed some strength she could draw there. "When I learned of your arrival, it struck me that you might become interested in answers to these questions."

I looked at her for a while again. Again she let me.

Pretty soon I shrugged down at the gun, then tossed it back on the leather wrap. I stared off over the city to hide the look on my face. "I want to see him. Tonight."

"Freeman, civilian access to the Pens—"

My neck clamped down on my voice, making it scrape like a red-hot rasp. "I'm his next of goddamned kin."

"You truly claim this?"

I looked down at the bracelet of scar around my right wrist. I traced its wrinkled surface with my left index finger, remembering—

Remembering dragging myself on my belly up the Shaft in the Ankhanan Donjon, half-dead legs twitching and useless, lantern in one hand and ring of keys in the other. Remembering finding Orbek chained to the wall.

Remembering what they'd done to him.

"Yeah. I do."

"As a member of his immediate family, you have the right to visit your ogrillo on this, his final night of life. Say to Lord Tarkanen that such is my will."

"He's not my—ah, fuck it anyway." I stared down at the cloudy smear of sunset gleaming from the platinum floor. "Thanks."

"It is our way."

"Are we done here? I better leave before I blow past sad and show up at angry."

"Angry at whom?" Her eyes said that for her, sad was the edge of the world; angry was a mythical monster somewhere beyond. "Would you punish a sword for the acts of its wielder?"

"I've done it before." I looked away again. "That's another story I don't want to get into right now."

"Would you not prefer to strike at those truly responsible?"

I thought it over. No, really: I did. I'm no great believer in justice, and—
like Ma'elKoth used to say—revenge is the shibboleth of spiritual poverty.
But—

This was *Orbek*.

I sighed. "I'm listening."

So here's yet one more way this whole shitstorm's my fault.

That book-writing friend of mine would say you can arrange any story
you're in to make anything your fault, and maybe that's true. But I *knew* it
then. I could feel it.

We were standing in a boundary condition: on one of those infinitely complex fractal positions where the smallest gesture might trigger the slide toward
an infinitely unpredictable resting state. We were the butterfly in Hong Kong,
and the whisper from our wings was going to alter the path of the category 5
hurricane in the Atlantic.

I could feel it because that's what I do. When I breathe myself into mindview, I can even see it: black Flow, the energy of change itself. The cosmic
web of causation. Quantum smears of probability, and the islands of order that
are the heartbeat of chaos.

Hell, it's more than what I do. According to a certain pack of demented
clusterhumps who are a chronic hornet's nest in my buttcrack, it's what I *am*.

But fuck them, anyway. This story isn't about them.

She took a deep breath, and her hand tightened on the altar-block. "Your
brother had fallen among bad company, here on the Battleground. The truth,
I fear, is in fact darker: that he had become part of the Smoke Hunt."

"If you really want to know what's going on, why aren't you just sending
down some Knights with a list of questions? With that truthsense of yours—"

"It is not ours, freeman, but Khryl's. And even so, it has its . . . limits." Her
indigo gaze darkened. "Are the Monasteries unaware of this?"

I met that squarely. "Still, though. What do you think I can do that you
can't?"

"I'm sure I couldn't say, freeman." That wistfulness had slipped back under
her voice, and I realized it had been always there, deepening subtly every time
she called me *freeman*. "I suppose that would be between you and your conscience."

"Yeah. Conscience. Sure." I sighed. "What do I have to do?"

"You will pledge yourself to a Call of Duty, sealed and sanctified by the
Witness of Our Lord of Valor."

"You want me to work for you." I squinted at her. "That's not as good an
idea as it sounds."

"You would . . . work . . . not for me, but for Khryl."

"He might not like it either."

"Nothing in the Battleground is a question of what we *like*, freeman. It is necessary that the enemies of Our Lord meet His Justice."

"You mean *your* justice," I said, nodding down at the pistol.

Her eyes went bleak as winter dusk. "It is the same."

"The coincidence's kinda funny, huh?"

"Not to me."

"Not much is, I bet. What's involved in this Call of Duty shit?"

"Through me, you will pledge yourself to Khryl's Service in this matter. Your pledge will be Witnessed by the Lord of Battles Himself, and your compliance will be enforced by His Will until He is satisfied that you have completed your task. Once invested, the Call of Duty is absolute; you will faithfully comply with the terms of His Call and pursue its resolution to the exclusion of all other concerns."

My teeth found the inside of my lower lip again. It was starting to swell. "What if I don't want to?"

"Freeman, you *will* want to. Taken freely, His Call becomes your own most potent desire. For the duration of His Call, you will burn for its completion."

"You sound awful damn sure I'm going to do this."

"Your alternative . . ." One finger twitched at the Automag. ". . . remains."

"What if I don't like that one either?"

"The ogrilloi of the Smoke Hunt," she said tonelessly, "bear marks at the bases of their spines. The mark is a simple curve of black, shaped like a fighting claw."

I found myself dropping my gaze toward the red-smeared streets, but I didn't see them because I wasn't looking down a thousand feet at the city. I was looking down twenty-five years at lean, stringy, desert-hard Black Knife bitches. Dancing in the firelight below my cross.

"And now, today, to my city, comes the legendary Bane of the Black Knives. The Skinwalker himself. I cannot believe this is coincidence."

I shook the flashback out of my head. "It's not. Not even a little."

"Thus it is that I have brought you to my side."

"You want me to stop the Smoke Hunt."

She said, "Yes."

"And you think I'm gonna jump at the chance because they're playing at being Black Knives."

"Yes."

"And you're willing to turn me loose in Purthin's Ford because you're afraid that Justice and Truth aren't gonna cut it this time. Because Khryl makes you play by too many rules."

"I told you it was . . . complicated."

"Lady, that's not complicated at all. Think about who I am." An effort of
will unknotted fists I did not remember clenching. "That's what I came here
for."

"Yes," she said. "I believe that of all living creatures, perhaps you alone truly
understand what it is that Khryl's land faces: the doom that lours upon His
people. Perhaps you alone truly understand what the Black Knives were, and
would be once more."

"Screw Khryl's land. And his people." I stared into the clouds. "Even
Orbek. It's not like he'll thank me."

"Yes," she said. "You still hate them. The Black Knives. Even after so many
years. It burns in you. I can feel it."

"Some things," I said slowly, "you don't get over."

"Yes." Starfire kindled in her eyes. "Yes."

She thought she knew what I was talking about. I could read in those eyes
that she did know something about hate. Something. Not everything. I remember being that young. I remember thinking I knew what it is to hate.

"I believe it is Khryl Himself who has brought us together," she said. "That
Khryl Himself has decided that you are the last best hope of His people."

"I'm just a guy. A guy who's gotten lucky a couple times, that's all."

The creases around her eyes squeezed toward a smile. "And many who believed so now moulder in the dirt."

I couldn't exactly argue the point.

Her face hardened. "Thus it is that I have brought you to my side. Thus it
is that Khryl excuses my defiling His Purificapex with your presence—you,
the disrespecter. The blasphemer." Her voice could have cut glass. "The
Enemy of God."

I shrugged. "Not your god."

"Prince of Chaos. Blade of Tyshalle."

"I always heard Tyshalle and Khryl were on pretty good terms."

"Not even human."

I blinked. "Excuse me?"

"It is known to the Order that you are of the *Aktiri*. That you escaped from
the True Hell—not this pale irony below us—along with your demon Artan
brethren, on what has become known in Ankhana as Assumption Day."

"My demon brethren. Oh, sure." I made a face. "Y'know, one of your
Order's greatest Knights was one of my 'demon brethren'—"

"You speak of Jhubbar Tekkanal." Now the smile did break through her
weary mask, but it was a smile without joy or humor. "Did you think his ori-
gins unknown? Did you think his true nature could be concealed from

Khryl?" She tossed her head like an offended mare. "Why do you think his epithet was *the Devil Knight*? It was his purity of heart—the power of his faith—that enabled him to transcend his demon heritage. You—"

Her stare was bleak. "You are known to be without purity, and without faith."

"Yeah, okay, whatever." Though truth is a fine thing, it's still not much fun to have everybody I meet shove it in my face. "We're demons, sure. Fine. Must not bother you too much having us around, though, right?"

The corners of her mouth turned down. "We are not here to speak of these things."

"Yeah. Fancy guns your armsmen carry. And that razor wire. And the searchlights and those coal-gas lamps at the Pens down there. How many Artans you got living in Purthin's Ford, anyway?"

"In Purthin's Ford?" Her eyes glinted. "None."

"Sure, all right. Where do you keep 'em, then?"

"They have nothing to do with you."

"Where I come from—what you call Hell, I guess; we just called it Earth—a lot of people wanted to work for the Company. The Overworld Company. I mean a *lot*. A lot more wanted to be *Aktiri*. Only the smartest, toughest, most ruthless bastards made the cut in the first place, and the ones who have survived here since Assumption Day aren't just smart, tough, and ruthless, they're goddamned *lucky*, too. Which makes them just about the most dangerous sonsofbitches you ever didn't want to meet in a dark alley. I've spent three years making sure these rimjobs behave themselves. Or making them dead."

Her eyes were cold as the space between stars. "They have nothing to do with you."

I stopped myself from spitting on the floor. If I did, she'd probably belt me so hard I'd land in Thorncleft.

Maybe she didn't understand what they were after. Hell, maybe I didn't either; I could be wrong. After all, anybody Earthside would know *Retreat from the Boedecken*; they'd know better than to fuck around with Black Knives. Or with me. "All right. Let's have it, then."

"It?"

"Your pitch." I rolled a hand. "Your offer. The deal."

The starfire in her eyes smoked over. "You said this is why you came to Purthin's Ford."

"Yeah."

"Yet now you require a fee?"

"I came here to dope-slap some sense into my brother. I sure as fuck didn't come here to get the snot stomped out of me by Right Arm of God theofascists in the middle of some butt-raping terrorist insurgency. And I'm not real interested in having it happen again."

The smoke in her eyes thickened. "Not money, then, nor land; you seek no reward."

"Two. Well, one reward. One tool."

She lifted her head. "The reward?"

"Orbek's life."

"It cannot be."

"Then no deal."

"Ask anything else. The Justice is ordained by Khryl Himself, and I have no authority to alter, gainsay, or refuse to answer. Orbek Black Knife made this Challenge; he has placed his fate under the Regard of Khryl, and that is where it lies."

"What if he withdraws?"

She turned toward me. "Then he must make submission."

"Let's say that's not a problem."

"There is still the murder in Hell."

"Let's say that's not a problem either."

She offered a reluctant shrug. "Perhaps the Lord of Justice might be satisfied with exile, upon pain of death, from all His lands forever."

"Done."

"Then—granted your assertions—done. What tool do you require?"

I tried to look casual. "Authority."

Her stare said she was pretty sure I was about to sprout horns and a tail and come after her with a red-hot pitchfork.

"Your authority comes straight from Khryl, right? That's what I want. I want freedom of action. The next time some asswipe Tyrkilld takes a swing at me, I want to flip out the Holy Foreskin and tell him to suck it, I'm working for God's Own Motherfucking Self."

She gave me that pitchfork stare for a long time. When she finally decided to talk, her expression hadn't changed. "It is said that you are a man without limits."

"That was Ma'elKoth."

"Boundaries, then. That there is no line you will not cross."

"People say lots of shit about me."

Sunset began to burn through the smoke that hooded her eyes. "You must understand that I am the same."

"Yeah, all right."

"In service to my Lord—in the defense of His Land and His Soldiers—I have no boundary."

"I believe you."

She idled back to the altar-block pedestal that protruded seamlessly from the cool smooth platinum on which we stood. She reached to lay her hand lightly on that angled handle, fingers curling gently around it in what was almost a caress.

The universe snapped into focus.

*—the soft prickle of blood-rusted wool against skin drying tight and stretched—*

*—the damp-glazed chill of the platinum under feet colder than the breeze that smelled of coal smoke and rain—*

*—eyes shrouded with limp wet hair the same bleak brown as the robes—*

*—the swell of breath bringing small hard breasts up along the inner curve of fabric—*

*—both hands buzzing with the memory of knives—*

Words came from me without volition—

"What the fuck did you just *do?*"

*—because these were the words I always said now.*

These were the words I'd been planning to say at this moment since the birth of the universe.

And by the time she spoke, I already *knew*—

"This," she said softly, "is the second most sacred relic of our Order. It is all that remains of the Accursèd Blade that struck off the Peaceful Hand of Our Lord of Valor."

And it happened—

*—the flash of grey steel and the jewel-spray of blood in firelight blossomed inside my head blazing the silent anguish of a wounded god—*

*—as it was going to happen five hundred years ago.*

Again.

And again from my mouth came the words I *always* said now—

"What's happening—? This is—this is—I've felt this before . . ."

I knew her answer.

"You have not. It is the Regard of Khryl."

The words echoed within me endlessly, as though she still had yet to say them, but they had been said long ago but were forever speaking now.

"The Gods exist beyond the grip of time. When we draw Their Eyes, They brush us with Their Power."

"No," I insisted forever. "No, I know this feeling . . ."

She always said, "It is the echo of the future."

"No . . . no, I really *have* . . ."

*I have always been here because there is no past: all that exists of the past is*

*the web of Flow whose black knots are the structure of the present. I will always
be here because there is no future: everything that is about to happen never will.*

*Now is all there is.*

*I have always sat in the rubble of the Financial Block, facing down the length
of God's Way over the carnage and ruin of Old Town, perched on a blast-folded
curve of assault-car hull with Kosall's cold steel across my lap. The rumpled and
torn titanium wreckage permanently ticks and pings as it eternally cools under
my ass. A few hundred yards to my left, there has always been a smoldering gap
where the Courthouse once stood, surrounded by a toothed meteor-crater slag of
melted buildings; even the millenial Cyclopean stone of the Old Town wall sags
and bows outward over the river, a thermal catenary like the softened rim of a
wax block-candle.*

*I face the god in the infinite now . . .*

I said again forever, "It's an echo of my past. Or something. Let the fucking
thing go, will you?"

She released it, and time leaked back into the universe.

I stared. "So that's what's left of the Godslaughterer's sword? For real?"

"Do you not know it so?"

I nodded thoughtfully, scratching at my beard. Threads of dried blood
wormed across my fingertips. "The Peaceful Hand?"

"The hand He extended in friendship to Jereth of Tyrnall, when Our Lord-
Father Dal'Kannith sent Him to offer truce in the Deomachy. The hand that
Jereth treacherously struck from his wrist. With this very blade."

"Huh. That's not the version we learn in the Monasteries."

Her forefinger tapped the plain age-eaten knob that once must have been
the pommel; even this was enough to claw my brain with déjà vu.

*—I squeeze its hilt until its hum matches my memory: it buzzes in my teeth—*

"Shit, don't *do* that, huh?"

She took her hand away and turned her palm upward. "And do you have
reason to believe your version of the tale true and ours false?"

I shrugged, opening my own hand toward her. "History depends on who's
telling the story."

"The power of Justice that runs in the very Blood of Our Lord destroyed the
Accursèd Blade," she said, "but His Peaceful Hand was severed, and Our Lord
maimed, by treachery; so it was that Dal'Kannith decreed on that black day
the birth of the Knights, that we should become the Hands of Our Lord. As
Champion, I am His Living Fist. In His service, what I do is His Will. Whatever I do. That is how I can bring you—even you—to this holy place."

My smile of understanding wasn't a smile. "All your sins are forgiven in advance."

"I am righteous by *definition*. Until He proclaims by *Terranhidhal zhan Dhalleig* that I am no longer his chosen Champion, I am incapable of sin."

"Not exactly peaceful hands."

"No. The Hand of Peace was struck from him. We are Hands of War. The Hand of Peace is—" She gave a negligent flip of the head that spun blood-damp hair around her eyes. "—where we stand."

I looked around. Those spires resembled fingers for a reason . . . *You and your candy-ass artistic metaphors,* I monologued.

God did not reply.

"So what's the point of all this?"

"You must understand," she said, "that I treat with you only because you are a lesser evil than the darkness we face. You must understand—though we stand upon the holiest sanctum of our Order, though we are on Khryl's Own Palm of the Peaceful Hand itself, despite the lineage of the Accursèd Blade, its sanctity so vast that a lesser being might be struck dead for merely daring to gaze upon it—you must understand that if I ever even *suspect* you might be a more immediate threat—"

She wheeled on me. Her lips had peeled off her teeth and her eyelids had vanished, and there was nothing human in her chrome-steel face. She seized the naked hilt of the Accursèd Blade and banished time and sense from the universe. She said forever, "Here under the Eyes of God Himself, I swear upon Mine Own Legend of Honor that I will pull this hilt from its resting place and *fuck you to death with it.*"

She let her echo die at the end of all things.

When, after several cosmic ages, she finally let go and the world started to turn again, I said, "I take it that's a yes."

# *HERO*

## RETREAT FROM THE BOEDECKEN (partial)
### You are **CAINE** (featured Actor: Pfnl. Hari Michaelson)
MASTER: NOT FOR DISTRIBUTION, UNDER PENALTY OF LAW.

Screams of burning ogrilloi echo off the stone. Eight or nine of them—a swell bonfire down there.

The light they cast gleams on steel teeth of two *kratrioi* closing in on them from either end of the alley, and from up here it looks clean, precise, even elegant: close-order drill on a parade ground.

Y'know, for a weaselly little twitch, that Pretornio swings serious dick.

*Caine.*

I look up and give a wave toward the impenetrable night-shadow that shrouds the distant parapet where Tizarre and Rababàl stand.

*Two packs converging on your position. Get ready.*

Yeah: they've heard the screams. Running to get a look. And they're gonna die for it.

I turn toward the featureless shadow-shapes of Marade and Stalton. "Here they come. Fade."

*They're right on top of you—*

I wave a second acknowledgment and swing through the window gap in the crumbling wall, get low, and squeeze some heat into the butt of the bladewand. The thumping of bare feet and clicking of toeclaws on stone has my balls sucking themselves up to my rib cage. Huge blacker shadows hurtle into the shadows in front of me and I stick the bladewand through the window and a pulse of blue energy licks from its end, casting enough light that I can see three or four of them begin to just come apart.

They grunt and gasp as they fall and one starts to howl and I duck below the sill and press against the night-chilled stone as the canteen full of oil that Rababàl has Reached down to just above their heads ignites with a metallic *whang.*

When I look back out the little window, everything's on fire.

Including about fifteen Black Knives.

### >>scanning fwd>>

Fucking *stuck*—goddamn crest ridge's like a bench vise—

Good thing the fight's over. This could've been terminally embarrassing.

I step on his face—my boot heel squelches in his open eye—and stick the bladewand back behind my belt so I can use both hands.

Ghost-blue flickers from oil flames guttering in the cracks of the flagstones. The last two Black Knives wheeze and gurgle against the wall, sagging. Marade rips the smashed visor off her helm with a squeal of tortured metal, then limps painfully over their smoldering throw nets, slaps aside the hammer one raises in feeble defense, and lifts her morningstar.

"Leave them," I pant at her. "Inhaled flame . . . dead already."

She turns a blood-smeared face toward me: the smashed visor must've crumpled in enough to break her nose. "We can't just let them suffer—"

Stalton sags against the crumbled wall, cradling the pudding that used to be his left wrist. "Sure we can."

He nudges one of the throw nets with his foot. "It was a pretty good speech, Caine," he says with a shaky, shocky laugh. "But that don't-let-'em-take-you-alive thing is starting to look like a problem."

With the dead ogrillo's head braced between my boot and the oil-scorched flags, a twisting wrench yanks my sword free of his skull. The effort unfolds a scarlet bloom under my short ribs where his hammer caught me, and I wheeze a little as I lift the sword.

"Oh, for shit's sake. *Look* at this."

Right at the mess of brains and bone splinters, the blade takes a thirty-degree bend and almost a quarter fuck-my-bleeding-ass *twist.* "You spend like half your motherfucking life learning how to get a sword *into* somebody's skull—how come nobody teaches you how to take it *out?*"

They're not listening; Stalton's trying to tighten the straps of his battered shield one-handed, and Marade's looking down at the mess those warhammers made of her right thigh.

"Screw this piece of shit." I drop it. Swords suck, anyway.

Wouldn't happen with a knife.

I pick up the warhammer he hit me with, hefting it for weight and balance, and the bloom of pain below my short ribs spiders into a spreading numbness that buckles my knees.

Oh, damn.

I lean on the warhammer and palpate my liver through the cool slick chainmail and my padded surcoat. It doesn't exactly hurt; the sensation is too vast, too oceanic. My gut's bloating already, and pressing on it opens a black pit that sucks away my strength. Dunno how bad it really is, but the night darkens and goes liquid around me, and sounds stop making sense. Bad enough.

Shock, though, I am trained for. Breathe.

And.

Breathe.

And—

Breathe, and—

And a few seconds' focused concentration on my Control Disciplines pumps my blood pressure high enough to swim the world back into focus.

Breathe.

And breathe.

A shift of attention within the Disciplines amps my stress hormones; the pain fades and strength leaks back into my legs and arms, and my head clears.

Forget love and money, baby: adrenocortical steroids make the world go round.

After most of a minute I can stand up straight and finally get a decent look at this hammer. The haft's longer than my arm and the iron head runs about three kilos, but two-handed, I can swing it well enough. My gut and Stalton's wrist can both vouch for the impact the bone-shattering peen can deliver; the spike on the back side has the same shallow curve as an ogrillo fighting claw and can punch through steel plate—Marade's right cuisse looks like the surface of the moon, and at least three of those craters are deep leaking punctures.

Should work well enough on ogrillo skulls.

Marade shakes her head distractedly, sprinkling her legs with blood from her nose. "Caine. I'll need your help—"

A surge of motion behind her, and she interrupts herself with a *shirring* backhand of her morningstar that meets the clumsy lunge of the dying Black Knife and splatters the wall with his brains.

That girl can *hit*.

His corpse flips against the other Black Knife. The live one gives a snarl, but he's got nothing left—the snarl's mostly groan and he collapses beneath his dead clanmate's body, still staring murder up at Marade as he strangles on the fluid filling his burnt lungs.

Y'know, if she and I could find some way to live through this—I mean, y'know, if she likes me at *all* . . .

She staggers toward me, fumbling at the upper curve of her perforated cuisse. "Help me get this off, will you?"

I drop to one knee and slip my hands up under her tasset to feel for the top buckle, and I must truly be a sick fucking puppy, because the feel of her warm flesh through the sticky cloth of her breeches has my breath going even shorter than that body-shot from the hammer did.

"I, uh—" I have to cough my throat clear. "We don't have much for bandages—I mean, my shirt, I guess—"

"No need," she tells me. "Soft-tissue wounds aren't serious for me. I just need this off. The ripped edges are cutting into muscle—I can't walk and I can't Heal. And I need to see what I can do for Stalton's arm."

My gut could use some attention too, but—

The way she's *talking* . . .

I stop and squint up at her. "Kinda lost that whole *Ivanhoe* cadence all of a sudden, haven't you?"

"What?" She looks startled, and a guilty flash shifts her eyes. "I, uh—"

*Caine.* The ghost-hiss of Tizarre's Whisper shushes from just behind my left shoulder. I raise my arm to signal I've heard her. *Two more packs, and another's linking up. About two bowshots south and closing.*

I nod to myself and pull my right-hand boot knife. Marade scowls down as I start sawing through her cuisse's retaining straps.

"Caine?"

"That was Tizarre. We have company."

She bares her teeth and looks over her shoulder. "Stalton?"

"I'm mobile," he says thinly. He doesn't sound too sure of it. "Which way?"

"Fuck it." The last strap parts and her cuisse comes off in my hand. "Just get out of sight. We'll hit 'em right here."

### >>scanning fwd>>

The ogrillo hesitates for one frozen second when I point the bladewand at his eye. I summon the surge of intention that will slice off the top of his head but all I get is a bluish static discharge and enough heat from the bladewand's eggbutt to scorch my palm and *shit* how long does this fucking thing *take* to repower *anyway*—

He grunts and spreads a huge wicked grin and lunges, swinging, and I duck inside the dark whirr of his warhammer and spike that wicked grin of his with the business end of the bladewand.

Its mithondion wood is dense as steel and it punctures skin and rips muscle and splinters bone; it grates into the hinge of his jaw and sticks fast and rips from my fingers as he rears back, bellowing the nerve-numbing shock of the bone-shot. His hands go loose on his hammer's haft, while mine find it below the head. A hard twist of the haft and a sidekick to his gut don't move him at all but shove me away and leave me on my feet in front of him with his hammer in my hands. And the bastard turns and bolts like a startled cat.

With my *bladewand* still sticking out of his motherfucking *face*—

"Cocksucker!" I spring after him but something tears in my belly and ogrilloi can do forty at a sprint and I couldn't catch him on a motorcycle. "Shitlicking cunthole come back and *fight*!"

I throw the warhammer as hard as I can. It spins along the street and slams him across the kidneys and he staggers, but he keeps his feet and never even looks back.

He vanishes into the hot dry midnight, and all I can do is cuss and snarl and look around for somebody else to kill.

I find only smoking corpses and the clitclat of toeclaws moving away into the darkness and Marade in her battered armor springing onto the back of one huge buck who's not quite fast or smart enough to have bolted with the others. She's lost her morningstar somewhere, but it doesn't matter; with one hand sliding around his bull neck to grip her opposite rerebrace, her other hand finds the back of his crest ridge, and with Khryl's Strength, she doesn't have to settle for the strangle. One grunting flex practically pops his head off.

He's dead before they hit the ground.

She lies across him, panting. By the time I get there, she's rolled onto her back, still gasping shallowly, and it's easy to see why: her breastplate's a mess. Must be like trying to breathe inside an iron maiden. The kind with spikes. "Here, let me help—"

"No—no, I can—" she wheezes, pulling off her gauntlets. Blood bubbles from her smashed mouth. "Where—?"

I shake my head. "Fuckers ran off. Not that I blame them. And I—I—"
"What?"

I can barely make myself say it. "I lost the bladewand."

She nods exhaustedly. Her eyes drift briefly closed. "All right. All right. We can—we still can—"

"Still can what? Die ugly?"

She fumbles under her gorget for the cuirass buckles. "Khryl loves me—once I can breathe, I can pray. He'll Heal me. Us. Fight *on*."

"Yeah, okay." I reach down and smooth blood-soaked hair out of her eyes.

"That was a real pretty neckbreak, Marade. Since when do Khryllians teach the sleeper?"

Her fingers slip on the buckles, and that guilty flash crosses her face again. "Caine, I—I mean—"

"Forget it." A few of the downed Black Knives are still twitching. One drags himself painfully toward the shadows. The flames of oil clinging to the crumbling walls and across the sand-packed street gutter and fade; we're about to lose the light. Much as I'd enjoy watching Marade remove her breastplate, I better get with business.

Her last kill had dropped his warhammer; I pick it up. "If you're okay with getting that plate off, I'll go smoke the wounded."

She gets the straps unbuckled and slips the cuirass enough that she can sit up, then freezes, her head cocked.

"What?"

"Tizarre." She lifts one arm in the *I hear you* wave at the night-black parapet far above. Her face goes blank, then grim. "Pretornio's in trouble."

"Worse than us?"

She yanks at her breastplate. It comes off with a squeal of ripping metal. "Yes. The porters broke. They've been overrun. Some of them have already been taken."

"Taken? Taken *alive?*"

A single nod. "We have to—have to get to them—" She heaves herself to her feet, swaying. Her surcoat gleams red-black, soaked through with gore. She takes an unsteady step, and another, and stumbles against a wall. She leans there, retching blood.

"You're in no shape to go anywhere. You shouldn't even be upright."

"Have to," she says. She pulls the collar of her surcoat up to mop her mouth and chin. "We stand to pray. By the time we all get down to Pretornio, I'll be able—"

She stops and looks around, blinking stupidly. "Where's Stalton?"

I ape her, feeling stupider than she looks. "Fuck me. He was right over—"

Right over where there is now only fading flames and Black Knives in various states of disrepair.

"Stalton! Hey, Stalton!"

"*Caine*—!" she hisses, making shushing motions with her hand.

I ignore her; anybody who can hear me already knows where we are. "Stalton! Come on, man, link up! We gotta move!"

I stand for a while in the quiet wind, listening to the whuff of dying flames. A stir in the sand looks like it might be tracks.

"Stay here and pray," I tell her. "I'll find him."

Blood streaks and scuffled sand lead me beyond the firelight. Another dip into the Control Disciplines fully dilates my irises and floods my retinal rods with rhodopsin. It's not quite Nightsight, but I am trained to see things clearly without looking straight at them; in the starlight, the fringes of my meditation-enhanced peripheral vision are sufficient to find a spot in a right-of-way between two crumbled dwellings where Stalton's boot tracks disappear into the prints of bare ogrillo feet.

My hauberk suddenly gains a couple hundred pounds and I really, really need to sit down. Better not. Don't know if I'll get up again.

This glorious death thing could be going a hell of a lot better.

"Caine? Where are you?" Her voice is stronger already. "What happened to the lantern?"

"I don't know. Lost."

"Stalton?"

"Him too."

She comes stumbling toward me, blundering through what is to her impenetrable darkness. "What do you mean? Is he dead?"

"I don't know. Maybe. His tracks stop here. Theirs go on. There's no body."

"How can you—" She stops herself, and the night goes silent around her. "You can see."

"Sort of." Why bother to lie? "A little."

For what feels like a long time, she stands perfectly still. I can hear her breathe.

"What are you?" Her voice is quiet. Slow. Fatal. "Monastic?"

In the distance: fading human screams.

"What difference does it make now?"

"Some kind of Esoteric. You must be. Why did you not tell anyone?"

"We all have secrets," I remind her.

"An assassin," she murmurs, a bleak dropping half-whisper, as though discovering what I am has broken something precious inside her. An inexplicable hint of tears. "Who is your target? Is it me?"

Given the history between the Monasteries and the Order of Khryl, there is some justification for paranoia. "It's not like that."

"What, then? All of us? This is what you've been pushing for, is it not? We all die. A brilliant strategem—"

"Marade, cut it out. Pull yourself together." I need to do the same. "We're not done yet."

Her silhouette gives a silent nod. A sniffle in the darkness. "Yes. Yes. Pretornio, his men. Stalton. They need us."

"That's right." I unbuckle my belt and let it drop, then shuck my hauberk and surcoat off over my head. Finally. Just the leather tunic and pants. I can move again. "You go for the priest and the porters. Do what you can."

"And you?"

"I'll find Stalton." One way or another.

"If he is dead—"

"Then no problem. Tizarre can link us up." I breathe adrenalized strength back into my legs. Some, anyway; there's a limit to the Disciplines, and I'm not far from it.

I'm as ready to go as I'll ever be.

"Caine, I—this is—" The outline of one hand, reaching. "We'll not see each other alive again, I think."

"I guess probably not."

That shadowed hand gropes in the darkness. I let it find me, and she gathers me into a bearhug, lifting me effortlessly from the ground with steel-sleeved arms that could crush my spine with a shrug, but through her sodden surcoat her breasts are soft and round and instead of crushing death I get her bloody lips on mine in one copper-salted kiss.

Before I can even clearly think *What the fuck?* she sets me on my feet again.

"Die fighting, Caine," she says, and stumbles off toward the guttering flames beyond.

I watch her go for a second, and two, and three and four, and I am such a useless sack of shit coward that I can't say a word. Not a word even now.

And she's gone.

Shit.

My good-byes go only to the night and to the dead.

The last of the flames flutter out. All that's left is to breathe back my night-vision, find a warhammer, and trot off on the Black Knives' trail.

### >>scanning fwd>>

So these two decided on a snack. Easier than lugging his body all the way back to their camp, I guess. Just goes to show: your average Black Knife can be every bit as selfish, undisciplined, and lazy as your average human.

Somehow that should be more comforting than it is.

I should blow. Leave them to their dinner and go see if I can find Marade, because there's really fuck-all anyone can do for him now, and I would go, I would, but the moon's finally coming up and in that strengthening silver-bleached glow, there's something weird about how they're kneeling over his belly.

One keeps a hand on the bunched hauberk where it's pulled up over Stalton's face, and the other is half turned on all fours so that his legs pin Stalton's to the sand, and while the meaning of this is still seeping through my mental wall of *no fucking way* his body twists and bucks and the tangled mess of guts twitches and—

And fuck me *fuck* me fuck me *God* he's *still alive*—

With all their grunting and slurping they can't hear me as I slip over the sill of what must have been, a thousand years ago, somebody's bay window, hammer over my shoulder, and with a big slow backswing, I step up and golf the head-end one right in front of the ear.

The impact straightens him upright on his knees, eyes blank and staring over his shattered cheekbone, and the one kneeling on Stalton's legs manages to lift his head in time to catch my downstroke between his eyes like a steer in a slaughterhouse. The peen leaves a fist-size dent in his skull and his eyeballs splatter and he topples sideways and before his corpse can even hit the ground I spin and let the first one have the back-spike through the nape of his neck. It punches though bone and I use it like a gaff to drag the bastard backward off Stalton's chest and out of the mess of guts and black soggy sand.

The two Black Knives flop and twitch and kick and grunt as their autonomic nervous systems refuse to believe they're actually dead, but after a while their *hukk-hukk-huhhkkkkk* becomes fading hisses of escaping breath, and the only sound in the broken chamber is thick hitching gasps that could be sobs, and I can't tell if it's Stalton or if it's me.

The chainmail over his face twists side to side. His hands are still bound under his back. I drop to my knees beside him, just where that ogrillo had been, and gently pull the hauberk down to his shoulders.

His eyes are squeezed shut like he's afraid they'll burst, and his mouth and chin and cheeks are thick with tear-streaked blood. He's sobbing like a heart-broken teenager. I slide one hand under his head and stroke his hair with the other and say some stupid meaningless shit about how he can quiet down now because everything's okay, it's all over and it's okay, and somehow that stupid meaningless shit must not sound stupid to him, because his breathing starts to even out, and pretty soon he lets himself open his eyes. "Who—?"

"It's Caine, Stalton."

"C-Caine? Caine, I . . . hurt. It hurts, Caine."

"Yeah, I know." Fuck. Better if he dies now. Better if he died twenty minutes ago. Fuck. "Shh. Hush now. Let it go."

"It's not . . . I've had worse . . . it's not too bad. The pain." His voice is blurred. Shaky. "Like a little—little food . . . *food* poisoning . . . that's all. Caine?"

I'd tell him to save his strength, but, y'know, for what? "Yeah."

"Got . . . water? Thirsty. Mmm, really thirsty."

Me too. I don't remind him what we did with our canteens. "Yeah. Yeah, sure. I'll get you some water. In a minute."

"Wasn't supposed to *be* like this . . ."

Tears roll out from the corners of his eyes and trail down his temples. "Just a j-j-*job*, that's all. Little . . . bodyguarding. Lead to something better, you know? Nobody said it'd be like *this*. It's not—it's not supposed to end *here* . . ."

"Yeah." I lower his head back down to the sand-packed floor. The moon glows in over my shoulder. "I'd make it different if I could."

"I, uh—I . . . ahhh, fuck." His back arches. "Can't—can't even sit up . . ."

Not with his abdominals chewed away. "I know. Don't try."

"Can you—? Can you help me see—?"

"You don't want to."

"It's really bad . . . ? I can't see. It is. It's really bad."

"Trust me."

I get to my feet and pick up the warhammer. It's gained a ton or so; I have to rest it on my shoulder, and the weight still buckles my knees. I've killed men before. But I've never killed a man who's *real* to me. Who's a person. A guy I like.

A man I wish could have been my friend.

"Yeah. Yeah, okay. Caine, don't—don't—"

"It's better like this. Quick."

"No. No, not that. It's okay. Just don't—" Fresher tears roll along the streaks down his face. "—don't *tell* anybody, okay?"

"Tell—?"

His raw streaming stare begs me to promise. "Don't tell them I went out like a . . . like a *punk*. Tell them I . . . died *fighting*. *Tell* them. Okay?"

Like there's anybody I can tell who'd care. But I guess that's not the point.

"Yeah." I shift my grip on the hammer. My arms tremble. My hands prickle sweat inside my gloves. "Ready?"

"Does it have to be—is there . . . is there any way—? Marade or Pretornio or—"

"No. It's just me. And I don't know anything about Healing." I show him the hammer. "This is what I know."

His eyes fix on mine. "Don't tell them I went out like a punk."

"You won't."

The hammer goes up over my head and I bring it down like it's an axe and his skull's a log, and there is a crunch and a splatter and y'know in the end, I told him the truth. He didn't go out like a punk at all.

Didn't even close his eyes.

Tougher than me . . .

What I just did bitches my candy ass before I get back out the window.

Reaction buckles my knees and throws me retching against the sill. I crumple just beyond the mess of corpses and skid myself into a corner. And all I can do is sit and shake.

Because I'm looking at my future. What's left of it.

It's here. It's this.

Fighting them is pointless. I don't really give a rat's butthole about that glorious-last-stand crap I sold everybody on. Sounded good coming out of my mouth, but it was dogshit and I can taste it now.

This is a hell of a time to find out I'm no hero.

Only one thing I can still do for them. One thing. For these people I conned into dying ugly. I hope the next one is easier. No, I don't.

Shit, I don't know. Can it get easy to kill your friends?

What if it does? What does that make me?

Huh.

Guess I'll be finding out.

# HALF ELIGIBLE

*I* don't have a clear memory of the Rite of Investment, which is probably a good thing. Like nearly everything else Khryllian—once you get past the pretty armor and nice white buildings and the defend-the-innocent-and-be-kind-to-peasants crap—what I do recall is flat-out nasty.

It all took place under the Regard of Khryl, which makes it bleed together in my head, but there was some bare-fingered ripping of flesh involved, hers or mine or both, and a lot of precious bodily fluid likewise, and at one point I'm pretty sure I had my hand inside her rib cage.

With my fingers wrapped around her beating heart.

Get what I mean about flat-out nasty?

Or maybe it was her hand and my heart. Like I said, I'm not real clear on the details. Somebody's hand was inside somebody's chest. Khryllians are big on sticking their hands into people. Penetration of flesh and shit. It's that god-damn Healing of His. Once you sand the corners off consequences, people start to get really fucking weird.

Some people say that's what happened to me. But screw them anyway. None of them could have lived through my consequences.

Anyway, I came walking down out of there with my right fist full of metaphoric Holy Foreskin, and it was not the most comfortable thing I've ever held.

But I was fucking right going to get my handjob's worth.

Rounding the last curve of stair down into the Lavidherrixium, rubbing worm-threads of dried blood from my skin and hoping these sick bastards at least had a goddamn shower I could use before I had to go out in public, I didn't notice how the murmur of breeze above became the murmur of voices below until the voices took on actual words.

". . . and that, my Lord, is a matter to offer up unto the Regard of the Lord of Valor. Which is none other than my full intention here, and which you, my Lord, have a truly astonishing lack of authority to prevent."

I could clearly hear the nailed-shut clamp of Markham's Lipkan jaw. "I repeat: You may not ascend. You must depart immediately. That is an order."

"The Love of Our Lord of Valor has cleared the clamor from my ears, my Lord; I kenned you well at first breath. And every time since. What I have *not* heard is by what authority you propose to stand between a Knight of Khryl and the Regard of God, nor yet, precisely, how you propose to enforce this preposterous tyranny upon my person."

"I am Lord Righteous in service to the Champion of—"

"Oh, aye, there is that, and the trifle of authority you wield is held in fief from her, true enough. But even Herself can stand between a Knight and Our Lord only if the unfortunate Knight in question is proven Recreant, Craven, or Base. Is one or more of these a charge you'd care to offer a poor half-crippled Knight the barest glimpse of a wink to Answer? For the dispute can be settled between us right now, my Lord Righteous in Et Cetera. Assuredly it can; we need only step out where we will not defile—"

"I *repeat.* You may *not* ascend. You must depart *immediately.*"

I could imagine the look on Markham's face. It made me smile as I followed the curving walkway above the long pool. Despite recognizing the other voice.

"This unlawful, sacrilegious—one might even say blasphemous, were one of a more judgmental temper than my poor self—insistence of yours could, within the bounds of reasonable possibility, lead a Knight of suspicious nature to wonder if there might be something, above in the Purificapex, that you'd mislike him to encounter. And to speculate what this mysterious something might, in fact, turn out to be."

"Yeah, Markham, tell the man." I ducked under the last of the hanging lanterns above the walkway. "What is it you don't want him to see?"

In the meat-smelling damp, Markham stood blankly still, pale as a Lipkan corpse. Trickles of condensation rolled down his armor.

One of the racks now held an impressively polished set of Khryllian plate that could have been made for a short bear. From one of the wall hooks, an arm's length from where my clothes lay in a wadded pile, hung a padded surcoat and leggings, and bleached linen underclothes. From another hook hung a long white cloak.

Standing facing the armored Lord Righteous, buck naked as the day he was born but with a shitload more hair, arms akimbo, the white-shot thatch that

covered his vast chest and asscheeks and tree-trunk legs not managing to conceal an impressive array of scarring that included an angry red knot on a scarlet rope around his right thigh, stood Tyrkilld, Knight Aeddharr.

This worthy's jaw hung slack, and his face rapidly drained bright red into
killing white.

"How's the leg, shitheel?"

Tyrkilld's mouth closed with a snap so loud he should have cracked a couple teeth. He took a breath, then another, and by the time he finally spoke, his
voice was nearly human.

"It gives considerable pain. But against finding your vile self in this holy
place, it bears comparison to casting a taper upon a house afire."

"Thanks." I turned toward the pale steel outrage that was Markham's face.
"Angvasse wants you to take me to the Pens. To take me to see Orbek."

His expression didn't so much as flicker. "The way lies back along our
path," he said. "As soon as you dress—"

"Through that office?" I nodded judiciously. "Go wait for me there."

He looked blank. I flicked a couple back-of-the-hand *shoo*s at him.

Markham's face had gone beyond red. It was the color now of the robes. "I
am tasked only—"

"Shut up about your tasks." Maybe I could give the bastard an aneurysm
and drop him right here. "Take a fucking hike. I'm sick of having you stare at
my ass."

"I—" Markham's mouth snapped shut, then swung open again. "I—"

"Go on, fuck off."

"My duty is to the Champion—"

"I got your doody right here." I lifted my handful of metaphoric Holy Foreskin. "*Ch'syavallanaig Khryllan'tai.*"

It got real bright in there.

I had to squint against the blaze that sprang from my upraised palm, even
though I knew enough to point it away from my eyes; it lit up Markham like
he'd stuck his face in an arc welder. Tyrkilld smothered what would have
been, from anyone other than a Khryllian, a blasphemous obscenity, and
shielded his eyes with one bull-shank arm.

It's not for nothing that one of Khryl's epithets is "the Brilliant." Maybe it's
a sungod thing.

It also felt like the palm of my hand was being burned to ash and cinders
while being continuously Healed, which is no coincidence, because that's basically what was happening. Also a sungod thing.

I guess Khryl doesn't want His Invested Agents throwing His Authority
around casually. Like, for example, just to piss off Lipkan ass-cobs. But,

y'know, that's one of those Covenant of Pirichanthe things. The gods can only grant power or take it away; what you do with it is up to you.

Which is why I could stand there with a mouthful of grin, even while I was shaking steam off the new pink skin on my palm and patting out the line of smolder that was climbing the cuff of the blood-robe.

"You know what that means?" I waved the hand a little more. It still stung like a bastard. "It means you have to fuck off. Now."

Markham's only reply was a flickering glance of pure cold revulsion before he executed a crisp quarter-face and marched into the night-black corridor. Tyrkilld and I listened to his footsteps fade away.

We looked at each other.

"That," Tyrkilld said slowly, "was entertainment near sufficing to counter the obscenity of your presence."

I couldn't help grinning at him. "Yeah, I can't stand the sonofabitch either."

He paced slowly toward the pool. "So Our Lady Champion's . . . *apology* . . . took an unusual form."

I went over to my clothes and peered around. "You guys have a shower or something?"

"I made no request for an apology to be made. Of any kind."

"Shower," I said. "Sh. Ow. Er. You have one? I itch like a whore in a haystack."

"The sole apology I owe is the one I go to offer unto Khryl."

"For trying to kill me?" I said to his back. "Or for failing?"

He glowered down at the bloody water. "We are at war. I did nothing wrong. Nothing."

"Tell it to Khryl."

"I intend to."

To hell with the shower. I peeled off the robe and let it drop, then picked up my pants. "Is that what this is about? You want me to tell you all's fair because you think you're at war? Fuck you, shitheel."

"Like that, is it?"

"And it always will be." I shook out my pants. "I'm not much for forgiveness."

"Has any been requested?"

"Not by you." I lowered the pants to the floor. "You're walking pretty good for somebody who had about two fingers' worth of thighbone shot off."

Tyrkilld looked down. His right hand made a fist. On its back was a disk of new scar, big around as a gold Ankhanan royal.

After a moment, he said softly, "The armsman —"

"Braehew. Yeah, I heard."

Tyrkilld nodded distantly. "When a Soldier gives himself to Khryl, there are ways in which he might . . . continue to serve."

I stared, my pants forgotten. "What, a bone graft? You're walking on a piece of that poor bastard's *leg?*"

"I am. My hand shares several of his bones, as well—as does your side."

I pressed my bright-pink palm to the quadrangle of new scars over my liver. "No fucking way."

"Your ribs were shattered. Did no one tell you this?"

"No." I felt suddenly ill. More ill. "Nobody bothered to explain."

"I will be calling upon his widow and orphaned daughters later tonight. Perhaps you'd be gracious enough to accompany me."

I shook my head in blank astonishment. "Every one of you bastards is completely bugnuts. Every single one."

"He fell in honorable battle—"

"My ass."

"—in service to the Lord of Valor. It is my duty to offer whatever consolation his widow may require."

"*Whatever* consolation?" I shook my head again. "I don't want to know."

Tyrkilld's voice was hoarse. And bleak. "Braehew died without sons."

"Didn't I just say I don't want to know?" I waved him off like somebody else's fart. "The more I find out about Khryllians, the less I like any of you."

Tyrkilld spoke from under his lowered brows. His face could not be seen. "House Aeddharr has been the flower of Jheledi knighthood since before the grand Lipkan Empire was even a ring of dog's piss. Since before Our Lord of Valor was more than a simpleminded goatherd with a gift for the sling. I have some knowledge of the obligations of nobility. Which knowledge a person of generous nature might forgive me for suspecting you *lack*."

"I'll take that as a compliment."

Tyrkilld turned a sidelong eye upon me. "If it's no forward remark from one who was lately engaged in damaging your health, you seem well."

"I'm all right."

"Which is a point of curiosity to me, as Khryl's Healing extends only to hurts taken upon the field of battle."

"So?"

"So it is a curious happenstance that the hurts Khryl's Hand delivered unto your person through mine own seem Healed as well. Seeing as how they were delivered before the fighting began."

I shrugged as I finally stepped into my pants. "There's fighting and there's fighting."

"Ah?"

I pulled my pants up. "That fight started when your poor bastard Braehew pointed his shotgun at my balls."

"Oh, did it now?" Tyrkilld frowned thoughtfully. "I would not have regarded it so."

"That's why you lost."

"We *lost,*" Tyrkilld said, drawing himself up with an impressive display of dignity for a naked man, "because such was the Judgment of Our Lord of Valor."

"Ever occur to you," I said as I fastened the row of buttons up the side of the pants, "that maybe you just got beat?"

"Hnhn?"

"Don't you wonder? Maybe I just kicked your ass. Maybe I got lucky."

Tyrkilld's eyes went dreamy and his voice gentled. "Might this be, to my unworthy ear, the music of a confession?"

I snorted. "It's just that your Utterance of Valor shit is kind of, well . . ."

"Primitive? Unreliable? Childish? Stupid?" Tyrkilld shrugged a couple yards of hairy shoulders. "Only to Incommunicants. To distinguish between simple defeat and the Judgment of God is not difficult in most cases, and in this one it's clear as Trahammeth's Glass. At the critical moment, Khryl withdrew from me His Love."

"Oh, I get it." I favored him with a bland smile. "You're saying Khryl Himself affirmed what I said about your father."

Muscle rippled along his wide jaw. "That's not what we were fighting about."

"The hell it wasn't."

Streaks of flush like claw marks surfaced across his chest, and the skin over the knuckles on those oak-knot hands went white. "You . . . are a very, very bad man."

"Do you know that when you get *really* angry, even your nuts blush?"

Tyrkilld spun and stomped toward the pool hard enough to shake the stone floor—but he stopped at the edge. "What you said . . . about *your* father . . ."

The view wasn't any better from behind. "What about him?"

"You made him sound a fine man—a man of great courage and conviction," Tyrkilld said quietly. "A far better man than your vile self."

"Maybe we have that in common."

"Possibly we do. May I express my regret that I can never make his acquaintance?"

"Don't." I picked up my tunic. It was inside out. "He would've spit in your fucking face."

When I looked up, Tyrkilld had turned away and was silently wading into the blood-tainted water, and somehow, unaccountably, I felt like an asshole. More of an asshole.

"Don't take it too hard." I tried to swallow it, but the truth came up my throat like vomit. "He'd spit in my face, too."

Tyrkilld stopped. "We *are* at war."

"Sure you are."

"You can have no faint idea—"

"You think you're at war."

"And what, if you'll again indulge the curiosity of a poor ignorant parish Knight, is *that* intended to mean?"

"When you go upstairs to see Khryl," I said, "stand there with your bloody cock and balls in hand and pray to Him that you never find out."

Tyrkilld shook his head grimly. "There is not a gracious bone among your double hundred, is there? Not a one."

"I had a gracious bone once. Some Khryllian ass-bandit beat it to paste."

He was silent for a moment, staring into the slow thick ripple of the bloody water around his thighs.

"What you said this afternoon—about men like me ruling the world . . ." Tyrkilld looked over one shoulder. "Men don't rule the world, you might know. We scarcely rule the Battleground."

"I wasn't talking about this world." I got my tunic straightened out and began to shrug my way into it, and so it was from the inside of my tunic, half-muffled and blindfolded, that I heard Tyrkilld's reply.

"*That* I know well enough."

I said, "Fuck me like a goat."

"I'll pass, if it means no particular offense."

"Oh, for shit's sake." I managed to get my head out and pulled the tunic down. I got one of my boots and began trying to pull it on, snarling under my breath, "Should've just drove into town on a circus wagon with a motherfuck-ing brass band playing 'Send in the Clowns.' "

"Your pardon? My ears are less than—"

"How'd *you* know me?"

"Ah. Well, there's little to it, at that. We've met before, is the sum of the tale. I was with Lord Khlaylock, back in the day. Back in the day in question, one might say."

"I don't remember you."

"I was one among several, and you were . . . well, you."

"I still am. More or less. Maybe you noticed." I stomped my boots the rest of the way on. "All right, I'm dressed. Markham's gone. Let's drop the fucking games."

"Your pardon?"

"You're going to do me a favor."

He wheeled on me, slowly, head back, eyes half slitted, two-thirds of a disbelieving smile crawling across his lips. "And how does one arrive at this improbable conviction?"

"You owe me, Tyrkilld. You owe me your life twice over already today."

Those oak-knot hands went to his vast hairy hips. "Indeed?"

"At the Riverdock customs sequestry, your life was forfeit by your own Laws of Engagement."

"Not my Laws. Khryl's. And my gratitude for your unexpected mercy is unbounded, never doubt. But a second time? When could this have occurred?"

"About fifteen minutes ago. Call it a tenth of a watch."

"Ah? You spared my life when I was not even present to appreciate your mercy? How virtuous."

"If you say so."

"And how, precisely, did you perform this extraordinary act?"

"I didn't tell Angvasse Khlaylock that you're an Ankhanan agent."

The smile vanished. His head rolled forward, and his hands came off his hips, and his weight shifted and he took the beginning of a breath, and I said, "Better not."

He stopped at full poise.

"Think about it," I said. "She's right upstairs. She just Invested me with the Authority of Khryl. I don't care what magick you've got to fuck with her truthsense. She'll never believe you. Never."

He subsided into a kind of relaxation—the kind you see on lions who are trying to decide whether they're hungry—and forced another of those disbelieving smiles onto his face. "And here we've arrived at another improbable conviction. Preposterous, one might even—"

"Don't."

"I am a Knight ordained and—"

"Yeah. A Knight ordained and whatever who's working for Kierendal. Let's not argue, huh?"

"It's so entirely ridiculous—"

"Shit, Tyrkilld, what do I care? But you're gonna do this thing for me. Nothing serious. Just deliver a message to her."

"To your Ankhanan elf gangster-queen?"

"Tell her I know she's in Purthin's Ford, and I know why. Tell her we don't have to be enemies. We have interests in common here. We should meet, and we should talk. I'll even let the whole ordering-you-to-beat-me-to-death thing go. As a courtesy."

He gave me a pretty credible snort. "Uncommonly magnanimous—or might it be your habit to extend amnesty for imaginary crimes?"

I gave him back a shrug. "Kierendal and I have an unusual relationship. She gets nothing but good from me, but every so often anyway she decides to have me killed. I guess I'm used to it."

"Custom gives ease to many a queer fashion."

"Something like that. Unless she didn't tell you to do anything about me at all."

"I'm sure I couldn't say."

"Because that'd mean she's decided to have *you* killed."

Tyrkilld looked suddenly thoughtful.

"She knows Orbek, and she knows me, and she knows I'd be here as soon as I got a hint Orbek might be in trouble. If she wanted you to live, she'd have warned you to expect me. And reminded you that I've killed men for a hell of a lot less than slapping my head into next fucking year."

He shrugged. "Nor would any such warning have signified overmuch, even had your hypothetical elf-queen managed to impress upon me quite how entirely skilled you are at it."

"Have it your way. But tell her what I said, huh? I don't want to piss in her soup. And she won't want to piss in mine."

"And so, perchance—" Tyrkilld squinted past me, like he was looking for something in the darkness of the passageway down which Markham had vanished. "—were a man to unexpectedly find himself in a position to do such a service for your estimable self, whence cometh recompense, and in what manner?"

"I'll tell you how I knew. What gave you away."

"Oh?"

"Think about it, Tyrkilld. Khryllians aren't as easygoing as I am. Knowing where you fucked up could save your life. Could save lots of lives. Like, say, the lives of everyone in Freedom's Face, y'know?"

He looked down into the slow roil of bloody water around his thighs.

"I suppose . . ." Even in the dead silence of the Lavidherrixium, I could barely hear him. "I suppose there would be value in that. To learn how you could be so certain."

Dumbass. "I wasn't. Not certain."

His head snapped up. His mouth dropped open.

"Fucking amateur," I said, and turned for the darkness.

From the outside, the Pens was Mid-Period Gulag: barbed wire and bright lights and guard towers posted with sharpshooters. I automatically noted shadows, fields of fire, available hard and soft cover, and shook my head silently. Somebody knew what they were doing.

Somebody Artan: the wire fencing looked galvanized, and the searchlights had a moon-greenish glow I recognized. The limelights at the Railhead in Transdeia are exactly that color.

This Faller character . . . Back in the day, I used to run Earthside transit operations for the Overworld Company out of the San Francisco Studio; I knew most of the techs and OC operatives by sight, and all of them by name. How could Faller have come out of Transdeia and I didn't know him?

Maybe tomorrow I'd pay a visit, and ask.

Tonight I had to save Orbek's life.

Getting in to see Orbek wasn't a problem. I didn't even need to whip out the Holy Foreskin. With Markham to hold my hand, we walked right through the gates and nobody looked like they were even thinking about stopping us.

From the inside, the Pens looked less like a prison camp than a kennel. Banks of eight-by-five strap-iron cages sat on legs a meter off the scraped-bare stone of the escarpment. No plumbing, just eligible trusties with rakes and buckets and wheelbarrows and a vast manure pile at the cliffside fence.

The dusk clogged up with misting drizzle again. I was starting to hate the weather in this town.

Some stretches of cages stood open and empty, waiting for convicts who stood in chains of eight in the mustering pen. Some stretches of cages were full of indistinct shapes, huddled against the damp. Trusties fanned out among the rows, tossing tarpaulins over cage tops to keep out the rain. Chill white flames burned steady in some cage-irons' lattice gaps: cold greenish-yellow gaslight erasing color in cold greenish-yellow eyes.

The drizzle thickened toward rain. Head down, arms crossed over my chest, I walked behind the Lord Righteous. An icy trickle traced my spine from my plastered-flat hair to the crack of my ass. Shivers started below my ribs and rippled out into my legs and up to my neck.

At least it was rinsing off the old blood. That was some consolation.

Sure it was.

Markham walked with a long swinging confident stride. He didn't seem to notice the rain running inside his collarpiece. Maybe the armor had drains in its heels.

I might start to hate the bastard.

I stared up under dripping eyebrows at his back, cataloguing every joint in that rain-beaded armor where a fighting knife's spearpoint might drive through into flesh. Not from any ill intent. Just on general principle.

Mostly.

He led me past the kennels toward a broad, flat field that steamed gently in the rain. Closer, I could see that the field was checkered with square panels of iron grillework though which the vapor leaked. At the edge, the grilles were set into stone over the mouths of ten-by-ten pits cut fifteen feet deep into the escarpment's bedrock. The vapor—

Breath and body heat.

"Um," I said, "you got some kind of ladder or something? Or do I just jump?"

"No need." Markham waved a gauntlet ahead. "Your ogrillo has a visitor already."

Out in the middle of the iron and stone field stood a pair of hulking trusties, immense shoulders hunched to their ears, and an uncomfortable-looking Knight Attendant. One of the trusties held what looked like a short siege ladder: a metal pole that sprouted rows of pegs a couple of spans apart along opposite sides.

Markham stopped at the edge of the field. "I leave you here, Freeman. Put yourself in the care of yonder Knight Attendant."

"What, you're not gonna walk me home?"

"Your possessions will be delivered to the Pratt & Redhorn hostelry. Any page can direct you. Good evening." He executed a crisp about-face and marched off into the rain.

I shrugged and set out across the field.

Some of the grilles had tarps draped across them. Most did not.

Orbek's didn't.

The trusties and the other Knight Attendant were staring down into Orbek's pit. The rain half-muffled growls and grunts and low-throated snarling howls. Helm tucked under his right arm, the Knight watched with the grimly blank look of a man refusing to flinch from a distasteful obligation. The trusties both had trifurcate lips drawn back from filed-blunt tusks: grins or sneers, I couldn't tell. Yellow eyes slitted, steam curling from snouts, one massaged the stump of a fighting claw with his opposite hand. The other rubbed his own crotch through his burlap pants, unself-conscious as a dog licking its balls.

The howls rose into yelping. Sounded like pain. Didn't sound like Orbek. "What, you make him kill his own dinner?"

"Not exactly, Freeman." The Knight stepped to one side to let me pass.

"Then what's that fucking noise?"

A faint crinkle twitched at the corners of the Knight's eyes. "Exactly."

It wasn't until I got to the edge of the pit that I suspected a Lipkan Knight of Khryl could actually have a sense of humor.

"Oh, for shit's sake." I rubbed my eyes. Headache thundered in my skull. "I didn't need to see this."

What I didn't need to see was Orbek and his other visitor.

Fucking.

A middle-aged ogrillo bitch, naked but for a pair of battered boots, stood braced wide-legged, facing the near corner like a boxer leaning on the ropes between rounds, while Orbek pounded her from behind.

Orbek was on another planet: eyes squeezed shut, spasms in his massive neck jerking his tusks ripping at the rain. The bitch's dugs swung and bounced like wattles on a spastic turkey. Another spasm of yelping brought her head up and she met the eyes above and she howled even louder: performing, exaggerating, a sardonic lip-curling mockery of passion, thick purple tongue lolling between her tusks, green-yellow eyes wide, fierce, challenging—

Like she was daring us all to jump in and have a whack at her too.

I looked over my shoulder at the Knight Attendant, whose expressionlessly polite stare somehow managed to look like a smirk. "Let me guess. You asked what he wanted for his last meal. He said, 'Cooze.' "

The Knight snuffled something close to a laugh without cracking his deadpan. "The Pens is a jail, not a brothel. This is a conjugal visit." He nodded down at them and offered an apologetic rattle of a shrug. "Likely their last."

"Conju—that's his *wife*?"

"I take it you and your—mmm . . . brother—aren't close?"

"Son of a bitch." I shot the Knight a baffled look. "Since when do ogrilloi get married?"

"I'm sure I cannot say. Some new Ankhanan silliness, I'd wager." The Knight inclined his head in a sketch of a bow. "With apologies in advance for any offense, it's well known that Ankhanans are mad."

"Yeah." I waved at the trusties. "All right. Open the lid. I'm going in."

The Knight inclined his head an inch farther. "Now?"

"Unless you're enjoying the show."

"Erm. Please, Freeman. As you will."

"Yeah, me neither." I leaned over the grille. "Orbek!"

Ogrillo eyes popped open, met mine, and bugged wide. "You."

"Me. Get off her. And for shit's sake put your pants on."

A long stare, fading from angry to mournful, eventually turned into a shrug. The young ogrillo's beer-barrel chest swelled and sank: a resigned sigh. "Might as well. One big fuck-me bucket of icewater, you are."

"I'd say I was sorry if I, y'know, was."

"Yeah." He grinned back his lips to expose the ivory curve of his tusks. "Shoulda figured you'd show up, little brother."

"Yeah. You shoulda."

The Knight murmured, "He doesn't seem entirely happy to see you."

I shrugged. "I'm used to it."

Going down the ladder made my head hurt worse. The gaslight from outside reached only halfway down, and the gloom below had a reddish tinge. The stone walls of the pit were gray-green with old damp. The drizzle had slackened again, but the iron grille condensed moisture from the thick foggy air; every second or two I'd get a plash from fat rusty raindrops.

The cover of the shit bucket standing in the corner didn't quite fit, but that stink drowned in the acid reek of unwashed ogrillo: a chewy funk of sweat and pheromones and animal sex. By the time the trusties had withdrawn the siege ladder and clanged the grille back into place over his head, I was half blind with pain. I sagged against a slimy wall and tried to sort through the thousands of things I probably shouldn't say.

Orbek was still lacing up the side of his breeches. He'd let his bristly spine ruff grow: he now had a reddish Trojan-helmet brush sticking straight up from his crest ridge. He'd gained weight, too: massive curves of new muscle rippled under the grey skin of his bare chest and shoulders, though he had still another five years or so before he'd hit full mature size.

Not much chance of that now.

When we'd met, in the Ankhanan Donjon, Orbek had been only seventeen. Three years? Was that all? Christ, we'd been through a lot since then.

I had to say something. I thought about seeing Orbek off at the Palatine station three months ago. On his way home, he'd said. Back to the Warrens for a while. Look up old friends. Take a vacation.

Visit family.

"Aren't you supposed to be in Ankhana?"

The young ogrillo pulled his side laces tight and tied them off. "Aren't you supposed to be dead?"

"I'd have a wiseass answer for that if my head didn't hurt so bad." I gazed up into the green-glowing drizzle through the grille. "I have this dream, y'know? More like a fantasy. That once, just *once*, somebody I care about is in trouble, and when I show up to help, they're actually happy to see me."

"That why you're here?" Orbek's voice was dark as coffee. "To *help*?"

Drizzle condensed to rain and dropped from the grille into the silence between us. The fist in my head thumped the inside of my skull once. And again.

I sighed. "Yeah, well, it's a dream I have. That's all."

Orbek spat into his hands and slickened his spine ruff; it sprang back to vertical, wet and gleaming. "Pull up a floor, hey? Don't look so good, little brother. Better sit before you fall."

In those yellow eyes was a wariness that could instantly trip hostile; this somehow made everything easier. I can always fall back on being an asshole.

I squinted at the ogrillo bitch. "Kinda old for you, isn't she?"

The bitch had slagged her way over to a bundle of soggy blankets that seemed to be the pit's closest thing to a bed, and she lay on them now, watching incuriously, one big-knuckled hand rubbing idly between her legs. "Call her Kaiggez," Orbek said softly. "I'd introduce you, but I dunno who you are today."

I could feel the Knight Attendant watching through the dripping grille above. I nodded to the bitch. "Dominic Shade. Don't get up. I don't like hugs and there's no fucking way I'm gonna shake that hand."

Her expression was unreadable. "*Korloggil nas paggarnik, paggtakkunni?*" she said softly. "*Perrlag Nazutakkaarik rint diz Etk Perrog'k?*"

The wet trickle down my spine got colder. I do know a few words of Etk Dag, nowadays. One of them is *Nazutakkaarik*. It's a nickname. A title. The Black Knives had called me that. A few of them. Toward the end. When only a few were left.

I shifted my weight, sliding my back along the wall toward the corner. "He told you who I am."

Orbek smirked around his tusks. "She don't talk Westerling, little brother. Says she's happy to meet her brother-in-law."

"Brother-in-law my ass." A creeping flush of anger drove off some of the chill. I squeezed my voice down to a blurred snarl, mindful of ears above. "What did she really say? 'Tell the Skinwalker he's welcome in the Boedecken'?"

"Hnh." Orbek's smirk never flickered. "We don't call it Boedecken. We call it Our Place."

"You got a hell of an attitude for somebody who's gonna die tomorrow."

"Maybe I should snivel like a human, hey? That make you happy? Because you being happy, that's what I live for."

"I didn't come all this way to be fucked with, big dog."

"Rather fuck with *her*, little brother." The young ogrillo spread hands the size of frying pans. "Wanna watch some more?"

"Oh, sure. Like that horse cock of yours won't give me nightmares already." I shook my head. "You got nothing better to talk about than the old days? About the—what do you call it? The Horror?"

"Talk? Haven't been talking." White flame glowed in the back of his eyes: nighthunter retinas catching and concentrating the dim gaslight that reflected down off the rain-shined walls. "Been *listening*."

"Uh." Like any sucker punch, it didn't really hurt. But it rocked me. It knocked me to pieces and stirred up the chunks.

Orbek lowered himself to the blankets beside her, his back against the wall, one huge arm curling protectively around her shoulders. She snuggled down into his lap and kissed the inside of his forearm.

He twitched his tusks. "Back then, she's *terkullik*. Crèche-maid. First bred and nursing. See this?" With his free hand, he stroked a rumpled sheet of black scar that spread up her left thigh to her flank. Where her left hind dug should have been was only a dark knot. "Know where she gets it?"

"I can guess."

"Don't have to. She gets it carrying pups out of the fire, little brother. You know which fire. Dead pups."

The light in the back of his eyes shimmered like moonlit ice. "Her dead pups."

She reached up and caressed his arm, drawing it around her face. Her thick purple tongue oozed out and licked fog-beads from the stump of his fighting claw. Her gaze held no anger. No hostility. Only a fiercely concentrated watchfulness: one predator staring down another.

Over the body of our prey.

Those stirred-up chunks suddenly clicked together into a new shape. "Oh," I said. "I get it now."

"Do you?"

"Sure. Got yourself a Black Knife bitch." I lowered myself into a somewhat hip-creaking version of an ogrillo squat. "She's up the pipe, huh?"

His tusk-display went fierce. "I'm only *half* eligible."

"How many? You know yet?"

"Four. We go to a *norulaggik* for a sniffie before I get bagged. She says three bucks and a bitch."

I let myself smile, really smile, for the first time since I boarded the steam-boat below Thorncleft. "Orbek. Stud-daddy Black Knife."

The hairless meat of the ogrillo's brows drew together. "How come you go happy all the sudden?"

"You fucking knucklehead. Ever stop to think I might have something to say about Black Knives coming back to the Boedecken? Think about who I *am*, for shit's sake. What'd you think I was gonna do when I found out? Throw you a party?"

The young ogrillo seemed to draw in upon himself: a smaller target. "Guess what? Don't think about you."

I inclined my head toward the steady stare of his bitch. "*She* does."

"Yeah, well," he said, "she's got reason."

"Shit, Orbek, I came all this way worrying I might have to kill you."

The wary cold distance started to drain out of Orbek's eyes, and he half-relaxed with a friendly snort. "No worry there. Champion's got the killing part handled, hey?"

"Easy enough to fix."

"You think so?"

"Sure. Walk into that arena and kiss her feet."

Orbek's head lowered like a boar's. "Can't do that."

"Sure you can."

Tusks swung side to side. "Black Knives don't kneel."

"My ass. That's what knees are *for*."

His head ratcheted lower. "Can't."

"What are you afraid of? The shit with Kopav? It's handled, Orbek. I've squared it already."

Orbek's head jerked back up, and that wary light flicked back into his eyes. "You know about Kopav?"

"Everything I need to." I cast a significant glance up toward the fog and the night. "I have a highly placed source."

"Him?" Orbek's nod was slow, understanding. His gaze still teetered on the edge of hostile. "Huh. What's He want with me?"

"I don't know. And I don't give a shit. We'll worry about Him after you live through this, huh?"

"I take a shot at Him once. You know that? Well, almost. On Assumption Day. Maybe He holds a grudge."

"Maybe He thinks He's doing you a favor."

"And maybe khoshoi fly out of my butt. Needs to mind His own business, hey?" The young ogrillo's arm tightened around the bitch's meaty shoulders. "So do you."

"You *are* my business, knucklehead. Give the cocksuckers what they want, then take your wife home and live happily ever goddamn after, will you?"

"*Terlukk pagganik rez haggallo, paggtakunni,*" the bitch murmured with an air of lazy malice. "*Utoppik negge tesslent jeroppik* Black Knife? *Pok ler* Limp Dick?"

"Black Knife *ekk*," Orbek growled under his breath. "*Paggano rez hagallo* Black Knife. *Keptarrol* Black Knife."

"What's *that* about?"

He muttered, "She asks what she should tell my boys when they're born. Is their clan Black Knife? Or Limp Dick?"

I scowled. "Doesn't speak Westerling, huh?"

"*Don't* ain't same as *can't*, little brother."

"I get that. So what's with Lady Macbitch? Why's she busting what's left of your balls?"

"She wants Black Knives to live free. So do I."

"Free. Right." I jabbed a finger at Orbek's huge chest. "I *know* you, big dog."

"You know shit."

"Come on, kid, you've been talking about how you'll never have pups since the day you adopted me. It was the *reason* you adopted me. Remember?"

"I remember lots of things."

"What did she tell you? No fight, no fuck? Shit, Orbek. You don't think this is a little extreme?"

He snorted. "Are you the right guy to jab somebody on going too far—" Lips curled back from long hooked tusks. "—for his *wife*?"

I had to look away. A second or two passed before I could squeeze the bloom of pain in my chest down into its usual fist-size ball of barbed wire. When I could talk again, I said, "You think she loves you? She doesn't give a damn for you, Orbek. She's playing some game of her own."

"Love? She loves what *I* love. She dreams what *I* dream. That's her game. Mine too, hey? That's why we marry. She loves Black Knives. She dreams being free. Together, we dream Black Knife freedom. Together we make our dreams true. Forever."

My headache came dripping back with each splash from the grille. "Maybe you'd better explain this to me. Small words, okay?"

Orbek disentangled himself from the bitch and rose. Suddenly the pit felt a lot smaller. "My fight with the Champion ain't cause I don't submit. It's cause I don't *have* to. We fight over whether *Black Knives* have to submit. To Khryl. To His Law. Get it? To say Kopav was self-defense, I gotta get down and kneel. Give my life to Khryl. Gotta say I live or die by *your* law."

He shook his head, lips curling in a snarl of revulsion. "Kopav's submission makes me Black Knife *kwatcharr*. If I submit, so does my clan. We belong to Khryl, then."

"That's idiotic."

"You think so? When the Khulan Horde falls at Ceraeno, what happens to Boedecken ogrilloi? They got my same choice: submit or fight. They submit. And now here they are, hey? You see much of how Khryl's ogrilloi live? It's no fuck-me *joke*, little brother."

"I haven't been laughing."

"But I am Black Knife. Now *kwatcharr*. Black Knives never make submission. Not then. Not ever."

"Only because there *weren't* any—"

"Yeah." Orbek leaned toward me, lowering his voice. "Yeah. You do that for us, little brother. After the Horror we scatter to cities. Submit to other clans. By the time the Khulan Horde loses at Ceraeno, Black Knives aren't Black Knives anymore. Kopav Crookback ain't Black Knife back then; his sire gives him to Dust Mirrors. Kopav's sire and his bitches' other get die without submission. So my clan is free. Of all the Boedecken ogrilloi, *only* Black Knives are free. And they will be always, unless I hang chains on them myself."

"What, you're gonna die over a fucking legal technicality?"

"No technifucking*anything*. The Champion is the Fist of Khryl. Stand against her, and I stand against the god. So I fight her, and I die. But I die *fighting*. I die *free*. Honor on me. Honor on my clan. Next year in Ankhana, there is my oldest boy, Orbek Black Knife: Kaiggezget, to be Black Knife *kwatcharr*. Black Knives live free forever."

I shook my head. "Ever think it might be better for these pups of yours to grow up knowing *you*? Being *with* you?"

"Better than being free? Who am I talking to here?"

Somehow that's always the question with me. I brought a hand to my eyes, trying again to massage the headache away. It didn't work any better than it had before.

"My father runs to the city," he said. "This is his shame: that he runs from the Boedecken. Those days, my father's younger than me when you and me meet in the Pit. My mother dies in Alientown. Killed by a drunk headpounder. My father fever-chokes in the Warrens. My brothers die in the Caverns War. None ever sees the Boedecken. Until me. All we ever know of Our Place—all we know of Black Knives—is what my father remembers, from cub-time. Before the Horror. Before *you*. When Black Knives rule Our Place. When other ogrilloi circle from our track. When their bitches use magick to scuff out their scent because they nose ours. When men run from just our *name*."

"People run from some of my names too, kid. It's not something to be proud of."

"*You* say. Easy for you. You walk like a king. More than a king—kings *hide* when you come to town. When you talk, *God* listens."

"It's not all it's cracked up to be."

"Now God listens to *me*!" One ham-size fist struck his barrel chest. "*Our* god. Black Knife god. She hears my prayer: bring Black Knives back to Our Place. Bring back men's *fear*."

I could feel a black knife of my own twisting in my guts. "You don't know what you were asking for."

"I do. Our god is no Ma'elKoth, little brother. She makes her bargains up front. She tells me my life is Hers now, and She spends it how She chooses."

"She chooses my ass." I jerked my chin toward the bitch in the corner. "*They* choose, Orbek. That's what your father never told you. Black Knives were never kings. They were *always* slaves. Slaves to the *bitches*."

He just grinned at me. "I stand with God, little brother. You know nothing."

"I was *there*—"

"And I am here."

"*Terggol pettikaar homunn horrillterazz*," the bitch murmured. "*Rummattagarr yas burratt net?*"

I looked at Orbek. He showed me more tusk. "She says she knows humans are born half-eligible, but she wonders where you lost your balls."

"Tell her—" I stopped and shook my head, disgusted. "Forget it. I got nothing to say to you, you fucking slag."

"Hey." Orbek's grin dissolved. He pushed himself to his feet. He practically filled the pit. "Watch your mouth with my wife."

I looked up into my brother's cold yellow eyes. "She wants you *dead*, dickhead. I'm on *your* side."

"My side is the Black Knife side."

"I'm trying to save your *life*."

"Nobody asked you."

"All you have to do is tell that guy up there that you'll submit." I waved a hand at the gaslit face of the Knight Attendant peering down through the grille. "That's him. Right up there. Just say it, and I'll get you out of this."

Orbek wouldn't even look up. "Don't need your help. Don't want your help." He took a single step that brought him looming over me. "Nobody asks you to come here. I'm asking you to go."

I went perfectly still. For a long time I stared up at the red-streaked silhouette of this ogrillo I called brother. I remembered that if not for Orbek, I'd be dead now. I remembered meeting Orbek in the Ankhanan Donjon; I remembered our fight, and the birth of our friendship. I remembered how Orbek had single-handedly won the Donjon riot that had freed us all. I remembered thinking, back when we'd met in the Donjon's reeking Pit, that Orbek was a lot like I'd been at that age. Now I could only wonder at how wrong I'd been. Had I *ever* been this young?

No, of course not.

Neither had Orbek.

Slowly, I hoisted himself back to my feet. "Gonna tell me what's really going on?"

"I don't know what you mean."

"Good story, Orbek. Real good. I almost bought it." I waved at the Knight Attendant above. "Let's have that ladder, huh?"

I took Orbek's massive wrist in an ogrillo handclasp and pulled myself close, my mouth a handspan from his ear. "Want to tell me the truth?" I murmured, barely above a whisper. "Dying won't help your friends in the Smoke Hunt."

"Don't *touch* me!" Orbek yanked out of my grip, and a huge hand slammed the middle of my chest so hard I bounced into the wall. "*Never* touch me. Never again."

My head rang. I leaned on the wall, breathing strength back into my legs. "Like that, is it?"

There was sudden anger in his eyes, and revulsion, and naked loathing. Those ham-size fists twitched up by his face. "You think I *want* to get out of this, little fucker? You think I *want* to live?"

"Orbek—"

A fist rose, but it didn't fall on me. It fell on him. On the side of his head. Next to the black-streaked track that led down from his eye.

Ogrilloi cry tears of blood.

"After what I do? Think I want to live? After being bitch to *you?*"

He hit himself again.

*Oh,* I thought, blank as cut stone. *Oh, I get it. Oh, Christ.*

I could still look him in the eye, though. I'm tough enough for that. "You knew who I was. You knew what I did."

His chin lifted until he was looking at me between his tusks. "Knowing's one thing. But being *with* her—being with someone who's *there,* who lives *through* it . . ."

He lost the words in a throat-deep snarl. I've heard that snarl before. Here in the Boedecken. I heard it from bucks tripping on tangles of their own intestines. I heard it from bitches cradling corpses of their cubs. "Orbek, listen—"

Cables in his neck wrenched his head around. "You never understand my dishonor. You never understand my *shame.*"

"Orbek—" My eyes burned. My chest felt like I was trying to breathe under a pile of Black Knife dead. "In the Shaft, you told me that now I share the dishonor I put on the Black Knives. That now what honor I win, I share that too."

His yellow stare was raw with pain and loathing. For me or for himself, I couldn't tell. "I'm younger then. Younger and stupider. Stupid enough to think you know something about honor."

And in the end, I'm never quite as tough as I want to be. I found myself looking down at my hands. As usual. "Everybody does shit when they're young and stupid, Orbek. You just have to fucking live with it."

"I don't."

"It's not that easy."

"Is for me. You should go home."

"Or what?"

Lips peeled back around his tusks. "Something could happen to you."

"It usually does."

He flicked a glance at Kaiggez. "Ain't you got a family now?"

"Yeah. And you're part of it."

The trusties pried up the grille, and the siege ladder slid down into the pit. I put a hand on a spoke-rung, and a much larger hand fell on my shoulder and turned me around with irresistible strength. "What you think you're gonna do?"

I answered with a smile that was as friendly and relaxed as I could manage. "Whatever I think I should."

"Not asking now. Telling. Stay out of this."

"You might want to take that hand off me, big dog."

"*Listen*, little fucker—"

"Last time you jumped me I was crippled." I showed some teeth to those fierce yellow eyes. "Think it's gonna work out better for you today?"

"You better—"

"*You* better do what you're fucking *told*."

He froze.

"You hear me? When Angvasse Khlaylock comes around for her Challenge, you get down on your knees. You've been told. Do it."

"You tell me *nothing*. I am Black Knife *kwatcharr*—"

"You're not shit."

That powerful hand switched from my shoulder to my chest and pinned me to the wall. Orbek bent over me, tusks inches from my jaw. Behind him, Kaiggez sat up, her eyes catching witchfire highlights. Orbek's breath smelled like roadkill. "Want to try me, little fucker?"

"You got it backward." I went completely boneless, letting him support my whole weight; if this went bad, I'd need both legs to kick. "I took your submission in the Donjon, shithead. You're *mine*."

His hairless brows drew together in a rumple of meat.

"Yeah," I said. "That's right."

I leaned around him so I could get a good look at the cold calculation growing in Kaiggez's eyes. I blurred my voice low to keep this from Khryllian ears above. "You getting this, Lady Macbitch? Orbek's nobody special. He's sure as fuck not Black Knife *kwatcharr*."

I grinned right into his blankly wounded face. "*I am.*"

His face went from wounded to dead. I hadn't just hurt him this time. Something was dying inside him. Dying right in front of me. "You—you can't just—"

"I didn't. You did. Now take your fucking hand off me before I kill you myself."

I'd worry about his goddamn feelings after I didn't have to worry about his life.

His hand only tightened, and I'd had enough of this shit. I popped the nerve cluster on the inside of his bicep; he grunted and his hand spasmed open. I stepped up close and gave him a couple seconds to decide if he had a move to make.

He leaned down close enough that a twitch of his head would hook a tusk into my eye. "Don't want you in my business, little fucker. Don't want your teeth in my kill. Fucking *human*—"

Just talk. I turned my back on him and started up the ladder.

"Everything you do makes trouble," he snarled after me. "Everything you touch fucks up. You come around and everybody *dies.*"

"Should have thought of that before you adopted me," I said, and slipped over the rim of the pit into the night and the rain.

# THE MEMORY OF DAY

## RETREAT FROM THE BOEDECKEN (partial)

You are **CAINE** (featured Actor: Pfnl. Hari Michaelson)

MASTER: NOT FOR DISTRIBUTION, UNDER PENALTY OF LAW.

The middle distance hums with echoes of roars and bellowing: somebody's still fighting, a tier or two below, close enough that I can hear them over the rising wind. But it's not them I have to find. As long as they're fighting, they don't need me.

Hello? Goddammit. Hey! Over here!

Come on, come *on*—

Nothing.

Standing in open moonlight waving at shadows on the parapet is only making me feel like an idiot. Tizarre must be busy with the others. Or she's just not there. Or—

Flame explodes in a brilliant surging tidal bore along the face of the vertical city. Above flat black stone, ragged billows of sunfire claw against the wind.

Shit.

That's not the *or* I was hoping for.

### >>scanning fwd>>

His Minor Shield is warm as flesh, a curve of softly shimmering almost-glass that gives a little under my hand. I'd lean on it while I get my breath but if he passes out it'll dump me on my face, so I settle against the age-rounded stone of the narrow alleyway instead. But even leaning is too much: my eyelids go heavy and my knees go to cloth and fuck me stand up fuck my ass stand *up*—

Balancing precariously on someone else's legs, I try again. "Come on, god-dammit, *talk* to me. Which way did they *take* her?"

On the Shield's far side, Rababàl's still fumbling inside the bloody tangle of his cape. The arrow shaft sticking out from his shattered collarbone twitches in a different rhythm from the hitching pulse of the one through his lung.

"Bastard . . . *stay* there, you . . . *bastard*," he gasps. He tries to push himself up the wall of the little cul-de-sac, but his legs are worse than mine and he sags back down onto the sand drift in the corner.

"Just stay there. . . . They'll be back, be back any second now. Just—I just . . . fucker. You *fucker*."

He says it like it's the worst word he knows.

"Before—before I do it . . . all I want—I want is—I want to watch them kill *you*. I hope they . . . uh. Uh. I hope it *hurts*."

So he's the kind who needs to blame somebody. Maybe he's got reason.

"Look, forget me, huh? Think about Tizarre. You want to leave her *with* them?"

"I don't . . . don't *care*," he wheezes. "Ahhh . . . hkk. There it is." One of his hands comes out of his cape holding a buckeye. "My last . . . I've been saving . . ."

"*Listen*, goddammit!" I give his Shield a solid whack with the toe of my boot, and the impact feeds back enough through his Flow-link to make him grunt. "You sack of yellow shit—sure, *you* get to go clean. What about Ti-zarre?"

"Fucker." Bloody froth trails black from his mouth in the moonlight, and he finally meets my eye, and I have never seen such naked loathing on a human face. "This was *mine*, you fucker. It was mine. My *shot*. All these years . . . working—*waiting* . . . you *fucker*."

What the hell's he talking about? "Come *on*, Rababàl—this is your last chance to not be a pissy bitch—"

"It was *mine*!" His shriek sprays black froth into the sand between us. "*My* idea. *My* plan. Mine, you fucker! And then you . . . *you* . . . now it's all about *you* . . ."

His voice breaks down into harsh hollow gasps, and—

Is he crying?

"Who are *you* anyway? Huh? *Who the fuck are you?* You're *fucking nobody*! What gives you the right to . . . the right . . ."

The alley mouth behind me begins to whisper with the clicking of toeclaws on stone. Lots of them. Not too far away and getting closer.

He's sobbing openly now. The buckeye lies forgotten on his limp, nerveless palm. "What gives you the *right* . . . ?"

"Right's got nothing to do with it. Maybe you haven't noticed."

His sobs hiccup to a sudden stop. He blinks once. And again.

He says quietly, "East."

He leans to one side and gathers the last two canteens into the curve of his working arm. "Away from the central ramps."

"All right." The clicking's getting louder. "Rababàl—"

"You should go."

"Yeah."

"Caine."

"Yeah?"

"I don't forgive you."

I look back. His stare is colder than the moon.

"Do you hear me? You are not forgiven."

I give him a nod. "I hear you."

It seems to mean something to him.

"Go."

I find handholds on the wall and search for the first foothold with the toe of my boot and find it and up I go. I make the top of the wall a second or two before the alley fills with Black Knives. They move cautiously toward the curve of force that seals the cul-de-sac. From beyond the curve, one tiny motion: Rababàl's fist closing around that buckeye—

And I decide to get the hell out.

Around the black-gapped wells of collapsed rooftops, the walls are thick enough to run on. Black Knives shout behind me and arrows hiss into the night, but they can't pursue without climbing the wall or breaking the Shield, and I'm already fifty yards away when the night roars flame behind me.

I don't look back. At least I didn't have to kill him myself.

I keep running.

East.


## >>scanning fwd>>


The ground he's carrying me over—what I can see of it past his huge gorilla ass—is still the city's sand-dusted stone, bleached by moonlight. Must have been unconscious no more than a minute or two.

He swings along at a leisurely walk. Sure. Why hurry?

Twisting enough to get a look behind us scrapes the throw net across my face. The rough prickly hemp is wet with blood. Probably mine. Head wound, I bet. Which explains why I can't remember how he caught me.

No way to tell how bad I'm hurt. The strings of puke on the hemp are probably mine too. This fucker's shoulder is broad as a saddle, but playing sack-of-potatoes over it isn't doing my guts any favors.

But it was worth taking the look; we seem to be Ass-End Charlie in this little parade.

All right. All right because he's no expert at the frisk. There's one he missed.

Pressure of the steel: hard against the curve of my spine between my shoulder blades—

All right. I can do this.

Slowly. Slowly. I rotate my wrists, turning my hands within the—ropes? strips of leather?—that bind them behind my kidneys.

Slowly. If he tumbles I'm awake, I'm fucked.

Uh: more fucked.

Half-numb fingers grope for the point of the sheath . . .

There. There. Yeah.

All right.

Better use my left. Might cut a tendon.

I get a grip on the sheath and squeeze. The razor edge of the thrower slices through the sheath's stitching almost without effort and goes through the leather of my tunic even easier. A line of ice bites into my fingers, but the tendons seem okay: I can pinch the sheath and work the exposed edge against the bindings on my wrists and it's too much movement but he's jogging along oblivious beneath me and I bounce on his shoulder limp as a corpse and now my hands are free.

Slowly. Slowly. Fingers working down the back of my collar find the thrower's hilt—

I draw the knife.

So.

This is it. My chance. My last chance.

Won't even have to take my hands from behind my neck. Point against my jugular. One hard shove into my carotid. Unconsciousness in seconds. Death in a minute or two. Quick. Painless.

Over.

It's worth doing. Shit—if any of them saw me with the bladewand—the Black Knife Kiss—

It's worth doing. It is. Right now, right here, I can opt out of an infinite festival of hurt. And maybe I will. Maybe I—

Huh.

Nahhh.

I really am a stone batshit sonofabitch. I must be. Or just a plain fucking idiot. It's not like I don't know what they're going to do to me. Of all human beings within a hundred miles, a thousand, I'm the one who *does* know. Who *really* knows. It's like—

It's like I *want* it.

I want to go all the way down.

Whoo.

It's a goddamn shame you only learn the really interesting shit about yourself when it's too late to be useful.

But—

If that's what I really want, if that's what's really driving me, I can just lie here over his shoulder. Hellbound Express. No lines, no waiting.

But, y'know—

There's this knife in my hand.

And my ankles are tied, and I'm bagged in this net and bleeding and wounded and shaking weak, and I don't even know how many of them are here and I'm probably going to start retching again any second, and I know already I'm gonna be sorry for this. Of all the fucking idiotic things I have done in my fucking idiotic life—

And somehow anyway, it still seems like a really good idea.

So gently, delicately, I slide the point of the knife through a gap in the net, just to one side of the bony knobs of vertebral ridge between his kidneys, and angle it in toward his spinal cord and hold it tight as I can with my left while I make a fist with my right.

And pound the knife into his spine.

The blade scrapes on bone, and he makes one thin grunt—more puzzled dizziness than pain—and the point skids off the bone into the disk and I pound the knife again and it shears through cartilage into his spinal cord and he huffs a muffled interrogatory snort when his legs stop working.

He slams to his knees, and my weight over his shoulder shifts his balance and he topples backward. Onto me.

Pinned, face smashed into his sweaty goat-smelling skin, his impossible weight crushing breath from my chest—

No hope in hell of shifting however many hundred pounds of twitching, writhing ogrillo who now begins to howl his uncomprehending distress—

On the whole, this could be going better.

But through the sudden shouting of other ogrilloi, there rings another voice, a human voice, and into one of those fractional pauses where everybody seems to be drawing breath at the same time slides a familiar *shrrr-splat* and the meaty *flr-thmp* of a falling body—

I really, really love that girl.

His weight vanishes. I open my eyes.

Marade has him up over her head one-handed like he's just a half-stuffed scarecrow.

His talons gouge black furrows in her skin as he scrabbles at her arm, but her other hand is full of morningstar and the blades whistle and his brains splash around me in a bloody rain.

She tosses his corpse aside and looks down at me, and she's not even wearing her armor anymore. Her surcoat and leggings are ripped and plastered flat with blood, and even through the muck of gore and sand that paints her face, I can see disappointment so bitter it blows out her knees and drops her to the stone beside me. "Oh," she says. "Oh. It's you."

I should probably make some kind of snappy comeback, but my mouth isn't working and neither are my lungs. Her face, the moon, the city, the universe itself contracts to a single point of light.

And winks out.

## >>scanning fwd>>

I know I'm awake because no dream hurts this much.

A lifetime's practice holds me still, keeps my eyes closed and my breathing steady. Moving feels like a bad idea anyway; just breathing ignites enough fire from my guts that I'd stop if I could. Under my head: rounded, firm but softly yielding, structural, warm as flesh—

It *is* flesh. I'm naked on somebody's lap.

Somebody with no pants on.

Um. Yow.

"I know you're awake."

Marade's voice, just above a whisper. A hand strong and hot and smelling of vomit and old sweat cups my cheek. "Caine? Khryl's Love can Heal your remaining wounds, but you must be silent, do you understand? You must control yourself; I cannot do it for you."

I summon a hoarse whisper. "Control?"

"You were screaming."

"Uh. This isn't—" My voice scrapes into a cough that blooms scarlet from my ribs through the top of my head. "Oh, crap. That really hurts."

It hurts so bad I can only laugh. Laughing hurts worse.

"Softly, Caine. I cannot guess how near they may be."

They who? "I was just gonna say: this isn't exactly how I pictured waking up across your thighs."

The hand moves up to stroke my hair, and her voice is soft and sad. "Do you never stop?"

I open my eyes and see only the same Mandelbrot blooms of color that I'd seen with them closed. "Um, I can't see. I can't see a damn thing."

Fuck. Fuck fuck fuck. Blind? So much for my fucking career—

"It's all right, Caine. It's all right. It's dark, that's all."

"What happened? What's going—wait. I remember—"

The vertical city. Black Knives in the badlands. The ambush . . . ogrilloi screaming as they burned . . . the fight at the gate, the fight on the third tier . . . Rababàl.

Stalton.

Breathe—breathe—find Control. It's only pain.

Yeah, shit, huh—only pain, yeah, sure, fucking right. Hard to meditate with splinters of rib scraping around your lung.

"What—*hrrr*—what happened to your armor?"

"So dented and rent that I can no longer wear it. And . . . I'd rather do without. From what can it now protect me?"

Slowly, incrementally, I push the pain outside myself. "Our clothes?"

"Khryl's Love is swift; in the dark, wounds may close with cloth inside—"

"Okay, I get it."

How much does my life suck? Finally naked with Marade, and I'm too busted up to do anything about it.

Huh. Not entirely naked—my exploring hands find wet sticky cloth tied around my belly, and more around my right thigh. Sticky and crusty with the texture of burnt-on coffee grounds where it isn't wet.

Clotting blood. A lot of it. I can't find any dry cloth. Under the sticky cloth around my thigh, something hard and raggedly sharp like splintered bone sticking up—oh yeah—

I remember snapping off the head and flights but leaving the shaft in. No way to tell if it nicked my femoral artery; if it did, pulling the shaft could bleed me out in minutes.

I seem to be severely fucking broken, here. Which somehow doesn't really bother me. Not really at all.

Huh.

If I didn't hurt so goddamn much, that'd be kind of interesting.

"So these bandages have to come off, huh?"

"Yes. Khryl's Love has Healed your skull fracture, but He will need both my hands for your belly and your leg, if you are not to bleed to death."

Breathe.

And . . . *breathe* . . .

"I must ask you, Caine, and you must tell me truly: do you wish to be Healed?"

"Are you kidding?" Right now I'd trade my balls for a fucking aspirin. "Yeah," I tell her. "Yeah, I want it."

"Because you must know what we face. I can remove the shaft from your leg, and . . . you understand. Bleeding out is a gentle way to die."

I've already made that choice. "And leave you here alone? What kind of guy do you think I am?"

"I have discovered, tonight, that I do not know. And so I ask."

Uh. I'm not ready for this. "Where are we?"

"Still in the vertical city. Deep in one of the chambers. A storm cellar, perhaps; there is only one door."

"How many of us? Who's here?"

"Just us. You and me."

"Yeah, okay. Okay."

Another few seconds of measured breath. I find that I have to ask. I have to know. It doesn't matter that I don't like them, or that they don't like me. *Like* doesn't matter anymore. If it ever did.

"Pretornio?"

"The porters' formations were—not mobile. Seven dead. The rest—"

She doesn't want to say *taken.*

"Yeah, okay."

"Stalton?"

I know what she really wants to ask. She doesn't want to know: she *needs* to know. She can't stop herself. "Did you . . . did you find him?"

Maybe she needs to work her way up. To talk around the question.

"He's—"

Maybe she's not the only one. Why is this so hard to say? "He's dead."

"You're sure?"

"Yeah. Real sure."

She waits for me to elaborate.

Finally: "What about Rababàl—Rababàl and, and . . . Did you—I, ah, I saw a flash . . . ?"

"Yeah."

The pain's leaking back in through my wall of Control. I shift, trying to find a position where the cold burn in my guts doesn't make my head swim. There isn't one. "The last explosion—? The big one?"

"Yes."

I shrug against her thighs. "That was Rababàl. That's why it was the last."

Silence. I feel her breathe.

"Did he—?"

"He had three or four arrows in him. Couldn't even stand up."

Don't think I'll tell her how he cursed me as he lay bleeding into the dead weeds. "He decided to go clean."

"Clean." Her echo is tiny: comprehending. "The explosion was . . . bits and pieces of bodies—a waterfall of fire—they rained all over the lower levels. I've never seen anything like it."

I'd tell her he went out with a bang, but she wouldn't think it's funny. "Some of those pieces were his."

"Yes." Her warm soft flesh rises and ebbs under me in a long sigh. "We may live to regret that we haven't joined him."

"Pretty likely." Pain surges like vomit climbing my throat—

—oh, crap—shouldn't have thought *vomit*—

"Marade?" My voice has gone thick. "Better move. Think I'm gonna puke."

"You already have. Several times."

Must be true: a spasm of retching that rips unnamable things inside my belly spills only thin acidic drool from my lips.

"Caine—" she says as I go quiet again. Her voice is thin, tight, hesitant, like she's working herself up to ask something she doesn't want to know the answer to. "Caine, I couldn't find . . . what about—what about—"

Yeah. Wish I had a better answer. "It's not good news."

Her breathing hitches. "They have her. That's what you think. They have her, and, and—"

A bare whisper, half a breath from silence. "—and she's alive . . ."

"I don't know. Probably." I shrug helplessness against her thighs. "I was going after her when they took me."

"Caine—what you said—what they do to thaumaturges—"

Her voice fails, and the hitch in her breath becomes faint gasping, and her arms tighten around me: begging me with her body to tell her I was exaggerating, that I just made that shit up, that it isn't true and it's not going to happen to Tizarre.

But I wasn't exaggerating, and it is true.

"They might not know. She was armed. If she fought them blade and shield—if she didn't use any magick—they might think she was there only to cover Rababàl's back."

Best I can do.

A couple wet sniffles. "I was—I wasn't—" I can hear her swallow. "You weren't who I was looking for."

Her voice goes solid again. Soft and flat and brutal. "I was looking for her. Finding you was an accident."

"It's all right, Marade. I know. It's all right."

"She and I—she's my *partner*, Caine. You wouldn't understand. You don't . . . you don't *need* anybody—"

That's what I keep telling myself, anyway.

"We've been partners—forever. Even in school. Marade and Tizarre. We're a *team*. Halves of a greater hero. That's how we pitched it. To the bosses. We were going to be like, you know, like the female Fafhrd and the Gray Mouser."

She's not giving away anything I haven't figured already. But still, she should know better. "Marade, don't—"

"*Fuck* it," she says, harsh, freighted with loathing: the stinging emphasis you get from someone who never uses obscenity. "Fuck *it* and fuck *them*. What does it matter now? If they have a problem, they can edit this out."

"Yeah. I guess they can." I close my eyes against the darkness, open them again. "Anyone else? Do you know?"

"I'm not sure. Tizarre and I . . . we used to talk about it, late at night. Trying to guess. Kess, maybe. And I think Stalton . . . was. I think. Probably."

Wow.

A sawtooth knife scrapes inside my ribs: everyone who ever rents Stalton's last cube will watch that hammer come down at their own eyes. Be able to *feel* it. If I weren't going to die here, I could do it myself.

Wow.

"And you, of course," she says. "Finding you working for Rababàl is what made us realize we weren't the only ones."

"Why me of course?"

"Because we recognized you. From, uh, you know—from school."

Holy crap. "For real?"

"Oh yes. We knew all about you. We came in the quarter before you graduated. We were—I guess you could call us fans. Your first fans."

Huh. So far, my only.

"I don't—" Why do I feel like I should apologize? "I don't remember you."

"A couple of first-quarter girls? Why should you? You were the campus stars—you and your friend. You know, the elf—?"

Yeah. Conditioning won't allow us to speak his name, but we don't have to. And, y'know, thinking about school gives me a weird warm feeling. Even the pain in my gut fades a little. Much as I hated the place, I like remembering it.

Talking there and then beats the shit out of living here and now.

"We always—we kind of thought you must be dead, or something."

"Or something?"

I can feel her shrug in the shift of her breasts. "Everyone thought you'd be a big star. I mean, it's been, what, six years? Seven? We thought we would have heard of you by now."

"Yeah, well, my life hasn't been going exactly to plan. Maybe you've noticed."

Her sigh is silent, but I can feel it. "And—that friend of yours. He was so gifted. Best in the school. Whatever happened to him?"

I shrug against her thighs. "Nobody knows. Dead, probably. He never came back from—" Can't say the word. "Never came back from, y'know, his, uh, training. You know."

"Being the best . . . it doesn't really count for much, does it?"

"Not unless *best* means *luckiest.*" It comes out pretty well, but the cold twist above my wounded guts reminds me how much I still miss him. Not that it matters now. If you believe the religious types, I might see him soon enough.

"Tizarre . . ." Her voice has gone to hush. A drop of moisture splashes on my chest. "Tizarre had such a crush on him . . ."

Another drop. I resist the urge to taste it.

"She used to write about him. Poetry. Sometimes *to* him. In her diary."

"Yeah?" I have had as much as I can take of this maudlin crap. "She'd have been disappointed. He was queer."

"He . . . what? He was?"

"Most likely. We never talked about it. But I'm pretty sure. Only way she would have gotten anywhere with him is if she suddenly grew a dick."

"Caine, you—" I can feel her shift in the darkness. Maybe shaking her head. "Why do you have to be such a . . . an *asshole* all the time?"

Oh, for shit's sake. Here we go. "I wonder that myself."

"You're so . . . hostile. So *angry.* Are you always like this?"

"Sometimes I'm worse."

"That's what I mean. You say it like a joke, but it's not. Not really. You always have something rotten to say about everything. Even yourself."

"Hey, I've got an idea for a good time—why don't I bleed to death on your lap while you outline my defects of character?"

"Hnh. And to think I—I thought—"

"What? You thought what?" It comes out harsh: a lot colder than I meant to sound. Because I really want to know.

Because she and Tizarre—Tizarre and her crush on my friend . . . I mean, what about Marade? Did she ever have a crush of her own?

From balls to brain I ache with hope that she's always had a thing for bad boys . . .

Because my body doesn't care where we are. My body doesn't care how broken I am. How much I hurt. My body doesn't care about anything except the smooth warmth of her skin. The soft full arc of breast against my arm. Because right now all I can think about is that one mind-bending kiss.

But all she has for me is a resigned sigh as she shifts her grip so that she can cradle me in her arms like a baby. "Are you ready now?"

Ahhh, shit. "Yeah. I guess I am."

Without apparent effort, she lifts me off the floor and stands.

"Khryl's Healing is a power of Love." Her voice has recovered that *Ivanhoe* swing: she's got her Knight on now. "It is His Love for those wounded in the service of Valor that knits flesh and bone. But because my flesh is Its channel, His Love can only follow my own."

Really? My breath goes short, and not from pain. "Marade, I—"

"Shut up." Her real voice, with a snap to it. A fresh sigh brings on her Knight again. "You must be silent, Caine. You must. To find love for you in my heart is . . . difficult. At best. And when you speak—"

One more sigh, short and bitter. "When you speak, it is *impossible*."

### >>scanning fwd>>

Years pass in a thermite blaze.

Sticking her fingers into the holes on either side of my thigh was bad enough; when her whole hand goes into the wound in my gut, my control breaks.

It's so *wrong*—her fingers wriggle and slide and I can feel them, I can feel *every one of them* and I *reject*, I *deny*, I *refuse to feel* but there is a savage intimacy to it, beyond extreme, a secret sharing profound and profoundly wrong that surges up my throat like vomit and I shudder and moan—

She's reaching inside, pushing through the torn viscera, groping into the hole that fucker's fighting claw ripped in whatever the hell the organ might be—liver, stomach, large intestine, I don't know, it hurts so much I can't remember which is what—and when her attention turns to Khryl's Love, the white phosphorus it ignites inside me burns spastic jerks through my arms and legs and bangs my head on the floor.

Faint pearly iridescence like faerie fire crawls her skin again, and when the screams start to rip upward from my gut to the top of my head, she brings her shimmering arm to my lips.

"Bite down," she says, distant. Clinical. "Go on."

I take her salt-sweet skin into my mouth and latch onto her ulna and taste dust and sand and sweat and muffle my screams on her flesh as every twinge and pang and ache that would make a misery of the weeks of healing this wound would require is crammed into five shattering minutes that transcend agony.

When my knitting belly has finally pushed her hand back out, she lays it along my flank; the iridescence fades from her skin and we collapse together into the absolute darkness, gasping exhaustion in each other's arms. "Y'know . . ." I wheeze out the words. "No matter how . . . well it works . . . that shit is *never* gonna be popular."

"Nor should it be." Her voice is faint, but her breathing is already regularizing: she's in a lot better condition than I am. "Khryl's Healing is for heroes. His Love does not spare your pain, but requires that you embrace it. Even love it: the badge of valor."

"Yeah . . . sure. But . . . I don't think the pain loves me back . . ."

I swear if I'd lived through this, I would've finally quit smoking. I really would.

We lie together in silence for a while. The darkness is a comfort now.

I remember once my dad saying, on one of his bad days—I think it was a belt he beat me with that time, but I'm not sure; the beatings all kind of blend together—but I remember lying curled up on my cot, bleeding, shivering with hurt and shame, and I remember him saying in that thick dripping lunatic's voice: *Just think about how good you'll feel once you stop hurting.*

I thought it was a joke—one of those harsh psycho attempts at humor that were the way his love for me would try to punch through the walls of his bad craziness—but, y'know, right now I wonder if he knew something I've never figured out until just now. Because now that I've stopped hurting, I feel *great*.

More than great.

Because I'm still naked with Marade, and her skin is infinitely soft over spring-steel muscle, and her taste is still on my lips and I'm not busted up anymore.

And I *felt* it—felt it through the Healing. Felt it like an arc of lightning through her hands into my heart. She somehow managed to find a way to love me.

Oh, lord. Holy stinking crap on a stick. *That* didn't take long. Better roll over. If she touches my dick by accident, she'll think I pulled a knife.

She's shivering. It's not cold here.

Her shivers grow into trembling, then to shaking, and her breath hitches into quiet, half-stifled sobs, which gives me a soft-on faster than naked pictures of my grandfather.

I've heard some guys get hot for women in tears. To each his own, I guess, but I think that's kinda sick. Something about Marade sobbing like a little girl is as wrong as the feeling of her hand inside my belly.

"Hey—hey, Marade, come on . . ." I scoot around her—leaving some ass skin on the rough stone of the floor, but forget that—and slip my arm around her shoulders. She buries her face in the hollow of my neck. Tears trickle down my chest. I hold her and stroke the long dusty cascade of her invisible hair, murmuring the same kind of meaningless shit I used on Stalton.

And it works this time, too.

"I just . . ." she murmurs against my throat as her shaking slowly quietens, "I just keep thinking—hoping—*dreaming* that they might somehow take pity on us . . . that they might bring us *home*."

I know which *they* she's talking about: the bosses. Our bosses. "They don't do that. Not for us. Not ever."

"But they—sometimes, sometimes they *do*. Emergency transfer. You know they do. We've all heard—"

"Only for stars. Big stars. Bigger than any of us will ever be."

"You don't know that. They could—they might—"

"Marade—" I hold her closer. Even through the dust and sweat, the scent of her hair—

I better forget that shit before I turn into one of those kinda sick guys I was ripping on a minute ago. "Marade, listen. I didn't tell you this before—or anyone—because, y'know, I didn't know for sure that any of you were . . . in our line of work. But those guys—those two guys the Black Knives were chasing? The ones who led them here? What did you think happened to them?"

"I—I don't know. I didn't really think about it. I suppose I thought the Black Knives caught them."

"No. They were pulled. Transferred home."

She stiffens against my chest. "Pulled? They were—"

"Yeah. They were—like us. In our line. Sort of."

"But—see? Don't you *see*? That's what I was *talking* about—"

"No. It wasn't an emergency transfer. I'm pretty sure it was planned."

"Planned—?" She's gone breathless. I'm not having an easy time of it myself.

"I'm pretty sure they were bird-dogging us. That they led the Black Knives here. On purpose. For the bosses. Because *we* were here."

"That's—that's not *possible*. They don't do that kind of—they *wouldn't*."

"You sure? Think about it: at least three, maybe four or five of us. Or more. Nobody major. Nobody even big enough that we'd ever heard of each other. It costs a lot of fucking money to train and transfer us. How can they—the bosses, our sponsors, whatever—how do they recover their investment, when none of us'll ever be big enough to generate our own audience?"

"You're saying—you think—"

"I'm pretty sure."

"Oh, great Khryl—oh my fierce courageous *God*—"

"Yeah. This Adventure . . . *our* Adventure—" I shake my head, helpless to soften this much.

Or at all.

So I just say it. "It's a snuffer."

"You can't—you can't *know* this—"

"Know it? I can *feel* it. So can you." And something about this strikes me funny, in a frostbite-on-the-balls sort of way. My laugh comes out bleak as our future.

"There are people back home who'll pay a lot to be us while we're tortured to death. That's what we are. All we are. Victims in a snuffer."

Now I get Stalton. Really get him. I understand about not going out like a punk.

"Then—" She pulls away, just a little; her impossibly powerful hands still rest lightly upon my collarbone and my pectoral. From the shift in the soft timbre of her voice I can hear she's turned her face from mine. "Then we shouldn't give them the satisfaction. We should just . . . die. Die *here*. Like Rababàl. Right here in this room. In the darkness. My weapon is on the floor; your clothes and that last knife of yours are beside them. You are an assassin. I know you are. If I asked you, Caine—if I asked, would you—?"

"No."

"Caine—"

"No."

Through the palms of her hands I feel her tremors flickering back to life. "Must I—if I beg—"

"Not a chance. Not you. Not ever."

And please God don't let her ask what she could do to persuade me. I'm afraid I might tell her.

So before she can get around to it, I pull her close. This isn't my Comfort the Sobbing Chick hug.

This is my Can You Feel My Heart Beating hug.

Her breasts spread softness across my chest, and I put my cheek to hers and I whisper, "I have a better idea."

"Caine—I don't—"

"Remember what I said, back when this started?" I turn into her just enough that she can feel the motion of my lips against her skin. "I always have a better idea."

"But—"

"No. Listen to me. If we die here, here in this room—shit, that'll just prove they were *right* about us. Don't you get it? Why should we do those fuckers the favor of confirming their shit-ass opinions?"

Now her arms go around me and they tighten like a playful anaconda. A trace of awe colors her murmur. "Wait—I *understand*. That's it—what you've been after. This whole night. Ever since you saw them in the badlands. Your insane boldness. The lunatic confidence, the screw-you attitude. The speeches. Walking out to face the Black Knives alone . . ."

"Goddamn right. That's the best revenge we *have*, you get it? The *only* one we have. People used to say the best revenge is living well. Dying well is almost as good."

I put my lips to her neck just behind her ear and whisper, "We can make them *sorry they did this to us*. We can make them weep for all the money we would have earned them—"

I slide my lips down her long smooth throat, and she lifts her chin to let me taste her to the collarbone. "And to do that we have to *fight*. We have to *keep* fighting. No matter what. Even when the Black Knives take us. Even when they torture us. We have to *not quit*. That's our revenge: we'll make those bean-counting shit-lickers mourn the stars we *would have been*."

"Yes." Her arms squeeze some more, and she better let up before I pass out. "Yes—I *see* it . . ."

But now she goes gentle again and pulls away, and one of her hands goes back to my chest, her palm a wall of muscle and bone. "Caine . . . do you really mean *we*?"

A tiny whisper, young and lost but still thinking it might be found: "Do you really think . . . I mean, we knew—you know, about you. Everyone *expected* you to be a star. But do you—do you think . . . ?"

Her whisper trails away, but I know what she's asking. "Yes. Absolutely. No doubt about it."

"Really?"

The breath of hope in her voice is so faint it's breaking my heart.

"Don't lie to me, Caine. Not now. You really think I could have . . . have been a star? That we could? Tizarre and I?"

"Marade—" If only she could know how much I mean this. "Marade, you *are* a star."

Her hand is trembling again, and my heart is going with it. Better not stop now. Dunno if I'll have the guts to start again. "I can't say about Tizarre. She's—nervous, y'know? Self-conscious. But you—the first time I ever saw you, I knew. I didn't know you're in the business, but I can tell a natural on sight. You're already a bigger star than I'll ever be."

"Really?" Her voice is hushed. "You believe that?"

Here, safe in the dark, I don't mind saying it. "Sure. What am I? A ghetto throat-cutter with a shitty attitude. But you? You're . . . *magnificent*. An honest-to-shit Knight in Shining Armor. You walk into a room and people forget what they were talking about. You are all presence. Confidence and power. Grace in motion. You make people want to get on their knees and hope you might notice them."

I take her hand from my chest and lift it to my face. Even blind, she might feel my conviction. "You're a hero. A *real* hero. The best kind. Upright. Virtuous. Loyal. Defend-the-weak and your-strength-is-the-strength-of-ten-because-your-heart-is-pure, and everything that makes people love heroes in the first place. What makes people wish *they* could be heroes, too. The best in all of us, you know? Lancelot and Percival and Arthur all in one. And to top it all off—" I give her a come-on-laugh-with-me chuckle. "—you whip *mountains* of ass."

"Caine, that's—if only I was really like that . . ."

"You are."

"But I don't feel like—inside, I'm not . . . not—it's all an *act*, Caine. Don't you see? It's an act, that's all."

"So what?" I shrug. "Why shouldn't it be? That's what we *are*."

Has this never occurred to her? "What we are is whatever we can make people *think* we are. That's what we *do*. It's our *job*. And what I said—everything I said—that's what I think of *you*. Which only means you're really, really *good* at it. Not to mention that you . . . you are—"

Fucking sack-of-shit coward. Say it.

*Say* it.

"That you are, without question, the most stunningly beautiful woman it has ever been my privilege to meet."

Got it out. And I didn't even sound like an idiot. I hope.

"Do you really think so?" The hand at my face comes alive, warm, sliding behind my neck. Another hand finds my collarbone, then slowly traces my chest down to the ribs of muscle below my ribs of bone. It lingers briefly on the fresh young scar there. Then heads south.

I guess sometimes I say the right thing after all.

"You really think I'm beautiful?"

And her lips are close enough to mine that her breath warms my beard. Her fingers find my pubic hair and my hard-on is back like a hurricane and I don't think I can talk right now.

Her hand closes around me like I'm the steel haft of her morningstar.

"I understand now. I finally understand. You're trying to *save* me."

All I have is a breathless stammer. "Marade—Marade, I can't—I can't—"

"*Stars*. That's the answer. We can be stars—we can make them *believe* in us. Believe we'll be profitable. Believe we'll be *big*. Then they'll bring us home. All we have to do is *convince* them."

Never gonna happen. Not to us. I should tell her.

I should.

Instead I just find her lips with my own and let her tongue slide into my mouth and shut me right the fuck up. She shivers and pulls my hand to her, into the warm slick wet between her legs.

Maybe false hope is her only hope. Maybe she needs to believe it. One of my dad's favorite writers said, *We must grant each other the illusions we need to live.*

Or maybe that's *grant ourselves.*

"You are not what you pretend, Caine. I know it. I can *feel* it." She lowers herself to the hard stone floor supine and draws me down along her, my spring-steel cock against her iron-within-velvet thigh. "There is a hero inside you. A star. We can *live*, Caine."

And I am shivering too hard to answer her, and she reaches around me and pulls me into her, and my shiver becomes a shudder. She locks her legs around my hips and gives a little cry, a tiny yip, and lifts me from the floor with a hungry surge of her hips —

"We *will* live, Caine. That's our promise. To live. To be the stars we know we can be."

"Yes," I tell her. "Yes."

What else can I say? What else do I *want* to say?

"And if they take me home — if they *take* me —"

Her voice gathers power in the rhythm of her hips.

"I *will not* leave you *here*. I will *not* leave you in their *hands*. I swear, I swear, I *swear* it. I *will* come for you."

"I know . . ." Breathless. Gasping. "I nnnn — nnnn —"

"And you will come for me."

"Yes."

"Say you *will* —"

"Yes —"

"*Say* it —"

"Yes, Marade, *yes*. Yes, I will come for you —"

"You will. You will come for me, Caine — you *will* — you *will* —"

She spasms around me and her legs clench, and she could crush my spine to powder and I don't care now. It doesn't matter and it will never, *can* never matter, for there is only her flesh and mine and the vast wave we make to-gether that stretches forever toward a crest in an infinite white glare that dissolves away all the dread and hurt and regret and anger and everything that could ever be wrong with the world.

And—

## >>scanning fwd>>

We lie in each other's arms, tremulous and gasping.

After a time I pull out of her, and she gives a little moan, brief, fading, and she clutches me against her, and I hold her twice as hard.

So we're the ones going out with a bang.

Yeah. Still not funny.

I give her a final kiss, one last lingering meeting of intimate flesh, trying to say with my lips and my arms what I don't think I can say with my voice: that this wasn't a mistake. That it wasn't hormones and extremity. That we weren't just fucking.

At least, I don't think we were.

And sometime later we part, and begin to search out the tatters of our clothing.

Oddly shy now . . .

I should say something.

I should say—"Marade . . . Marade, I—"

"Don't."

"But—"

"Just don't."

So I don't.

It's a long dark silence.

My hand falls on my knife by instinct. A heavy metal-on-stone scrape tells me she's found her morningstar.

I come to my feet in the black. "Must be getting light."

Faint rustlings of cloth as she stands beside me. "Yes."

"Are you ready for this?"

"Yes, Caine. Finally, yes." Her voice is strong now. Solid and sure. "I am."

"Then let's go."

Shoulder to shoulder, we walk from blind dark into rose-steel dawn.

They're waiting for us outside.

# Eyes of God

"I must *say*, Freeman Shade, I am, ha-ha, hrm, favorably impressed by your *piety*—"

Ule-Tourann, the Family Bishop of Purthin's Ford, moved up one of the sanctum's ramped aisles in a loose-jointed shamble. From under the Bishop's biretta straggled curls of oiled hair the same color as the grease spot on his surplice. He moved like a man who'd heard of exercise but had never actually seen it done. And he yapped. Ruthlessly. Yap yap yap yap: a stupefyingly endless river of content-free noise.

". . . if only *more* Beloved Children would make Atonement *their* first order of business when they arrive in a new city. If only. Though the final boat came in, er, well, I would suppose—that is to say, usually the last of the steamers arrives no later than the end of fourth watch—"

"I got held up in customs."

"Ah." He blinked and nodded like he actually understood. "Well then, it's as it may be, eh? If it is Willed, it Shall be So. Ma'elKoth is Supreme, yes?"

"So they tell me."

The sanctum resembled that of the Cathedral of the Assumption in Ankhana: a bowl of benches surrounding a walled expanse of floor, like stadium seating around an arena. But here the sanctum was floored with rose-veined marble, and lovely runners of scarlet and gold led from each radial aisle to the broad altar in the center. Astride the altar stood a colossal bronze nude of God Himself, resembling the one that stood in the Great Hall of the Colhari Palace—double-sided, so that the face of Ma'elKoth looked out before and behind, and bearing stylized representations of both male and female genitals—though where the original stood with arms akimbo, this Ma'elKoth had arms outstretched above, forming pillars that supported a domed ceiling of colored glass. All the dazzling blues of a clear noonday sky at its apex, the dome shaded into cloud-swirls of sunset reds and golds near its base.

The Bishop continued to chatter in an amiably mindless way as we threaded among the acolytes and underpriests who roamed the sanctum brushing carpets, polishing the altar, clambering up and down the cunning collapsible scaffold that let them burnish the bronze Ma'elKoth. The current of his yap-river carried us beyond the sanctum, through the administrative wing, and all the way to his office.

The Bishop installed himself in an immense cowhide swivel chair that he spun away from a writing hutch the size of a meat locker. He added some wrist-size logs to the grate and waved them alight, then gestured toward a horseshoe chair upholstered in knobby green brocade. "Please, Freeman Shade, be comfortable, ha-ha—hrm, yes. Before we *proceed* to the, er, the Atonement cells, there was that small *matter* . . . ? That is, I was informed that you, ha-ha, wish to make an *offering*, yes?"

I barely heard him. The shutters were open. I drifted across the room to stand at the window, and I looked up into Hell.

Watchfires on the battlements cast orange smears up the sides of the Spire, pocked with yellow crosses where lamplight shone through arbalestinas. The light on the face of Hell was redder, just enough to make out ghosts of structure; cookfires and lamps and window-leaked hearth glow scattered sparks across its face. There, off to the right, just above the third bridge—hung now with age-greyed blankets and stained tunics, a sloppy-fat ogrillo bitch dozing beside a fire can on the ledge, while a couple pups sat naked, giving each other the occasional listless punch on the arm, near a gap where the retaining wall had collapsed—that was it.

That was the parapet. Right there. Where I had stood with the partners half my life ago, watching Black Knives run the badlands. Now it was ogrilloi in the vertical city and humanity below. I wondered if any of them had looked out over the river today. If any of them had watched the riverboat.

If any of them had seen me coming.

"Erm, ha-ha, Freeman Shade—? There was, erm, an *amount* discussed, yes? A hundred—?"

Hell above me. Hell behind and Hell ahead.

I turned aside from the window. "The vessel with the pestle," I said in English, heavily, because this was Ma'elKoth's sense of fucking humor and frankly it was just goddamn embarrassing, "has the brew that is true."

The bishop's face went blank and slack, shapeless as a mask carved in pudding.

I snapped my fingers. Bone structure developed within the bishop's cheeks like a telescopic image being twisted into focus; his jaw firmed, and keen purpose drove the genial glaze from his eyes. He sat forward in the swivel chair and pushed his face sideways with one hand until a string of audible joint pops shot down his spine.

"Knowing how to do that buys you ten seconds to explain why I shouldn't have you killed."

I said, "You know me."

A wave of clarity passed over the bishop's face.

"Lord Caine." He rose and extended a hand. "You're expected. I have your equipment right here."

I took the offered hand. "Caine."

"Pardon?"

"Just Caine. Freeman Caine, if you want. I'm not Lord anything. Better you just call me Dominic Shade."

The bishop shrugged. "I'd be honored if you'd call me Tourann."

He dug a ring of keys out of his robe and unlocked one of the cupboards on his writing hutch, then muttered briefly under his breath and made a series of circular gestures with his left hand while with his right he reached in farther than the hutch was deep, and began briskly pulling out more objects than could have fit within it. "Sorry I can't show you the rest of the station. Security. You understand."

"Yeah, whatever. Are you the secondary or the primary?"

His eyebrows lifted. "You mean: Which came first, the bishop or the spy?"

"Something like that."

"It's more like we're both secondary. He's dominant unless I'm triggered—but I get all his memories, and he doesn't have a clue I exist."

"Huh. Creepy."

"It's not so bad. They say they can reintegrate me when I rotate out. Besides, I'm used to it by now."

"Seems a little extreme."

"You think it's easy running an Eyes of God post where the unfriendlies have truthsense?" He pulled a mournful face. "The Knights of Khryl don't do diplomatic immunity, and they are not to be fucked with."

"I've heard rumors."

"Rumors. Right." He grimaced and shook his head. "Our last undoubled station chief got his arms pulled off."

He finished laying out the items from the hutch: a flat leather pack the size of his palm, four matte-black knives—two guardless diamond-blade throwers and two of the Cold Steel Peacekeeper XXs that had been brought to Home by the Social Police Expeditionary Force that had invaded Ankhana three years before—a spring-loaded telescopic baton, a garrotte of thin black cable wrapped around grip-molded steel skeleton handles fixed to either end, and a huge stainless 12mm Automag with a custom barrel screw-fitted to receive the large black silencer beside it.

I checked the edge of each knife and scanned the garrotte's cable for any signs of raveling. I picked up the Automag, popped the clip to eyeball the caseless tristack shatterslug rounds, then dropped the two spare clips into my purse before I tucked the gun into the leather holster patch sewn inside the rear waistband of my pants.

Tourann picked up the silencer. "What about this?"

"Keep it. Then when I miss, at least they duck."

"We can blue the finish for you—"

"I like it bright. Nobody has to squint to figure out I've got a handful of Big Fucking Gun. Who else knows I was coming here?"

"I'm sorry?"

I picked up the throwing knives, rechecked the edges briefly, and slipped them into their holsters in my boots. "How do you make reports? Artan Mirror to Ankhana, right?"

"That's need-to-know information—"

"So on this end, there's you and the Mirror Speaker, at least; anybody else?"

"No—no, no, of course not—"

"Then there's the Speaker on the other end. Reports with my name on them go straight to the Duke of Public Safety, right?"

"I, ah, I'm not allowed—"

"Don't worry about it. So at least somebody's told Deliann by now, I'm guessing."

Tourann licked sweat off his upper lip. "I—what the Emperor may or may not know is beyond my—"

"Look, it's all right. It's not exactly a secret. Except from the Khryllians."

"Purthin Khlaylock. Sure." The bishop nodded wisely. "Want to bet he still remembers you?"

"Only when he looks in the mirror."

"Um, yeah. Um. No wonder you're incognito." He coughed. "What about that nonrecognition magick of yours? It worked on me, and I am far from undefended—"

"It's called the Eternal Forgetting, and it's—complicated. It doesn't erase personal experience. He'll remember me, and what I did to him. And maybe to the Black Knives. He just won't be able to put that Caine together with, say, the hero of Ceraeno—"

Tourann nodded. "Or the Prince of Chaos, or the Hand of Ma'elKoth—"

"Yeah, yeah. Drop it."

"Nice."

"Mostly useful in places where I don't run into old friends."

"Friends?"

"Or whatever."

"What'd you get on Orbek?"

"Not a lot." He looked like his stomach hurt. "Uh, I have some bad news about that—"

"I heard."

"You did?"

"I guess it was some size of deal."

"You could say that." Tourann pulled some pages of handwritten notes from a hutch drawer, and passed them over. "Orbek Black Knife: Taykarget. Hit town three months ago, give or take. Maybe two or two and a half."

"You're not sure?"

"He came in illegally. No customs records, no employment documents, nothing. Nothing official until the, uh, incident."

"You let these cock-knockers detain an Ankhanan freeman? What the fuck are you doing?"

"My job. Gathering information. Filing reports."

"Shit."

Tourann spread his hands. "No diplomatic relations, Caine."

"Shade."

"Yes. The Knights recognize no government beyond the Laws of Khryl. Break their Law and nobody cares if you're the queen of Lipke. They were going to question him on another matter, but he refused submission. Then he just berserked and opened up."

"Another matter?"

"A murder. A grill, up in Hell. Shot."

I only grunted, reading ahead.

"You don't look surprised."

"You're not my only source," I muttered, still reading. "The Knight Accusor—Angvasse Khlaylock—"

"Niece."

"I heard. What do you have on her?"

Tourann lowered himself back into the swivel chair. "I'd stay clear if I were you."

"It's not up to me."

"No?"

I didn't explain.

The bishop shrugged. "She's the old man all over again. Doubled. Only twenty-seven, and Khryl's Champion for three years now."

"First since Pintelle, right?"

"Odds-on to be the first female Justiciar since Pintelle, too, when the old man cashes out. The grills call her Vasse Khrylget, and it's only half a joke."

"Any leverage?"

"Leverage. Sure." The bishop snorted. "She's so clean you have to brush your teeth before you kiss her ass. Incorruptible. Which I know because we've been trying for about ten years."

"Yeah?"

"Each new chief takes a swing at her. It's like a rite of passage. I wouldn't mind landing one on her myself."

"You better have long fucking arms. What's Orbek doing up here in the first place?"

Tourann shrugged again. "At a guess? He might have been in with Freedom's Face—they smuggle the worst kinds of Ankhanan thugs over the mountains—"

"Thug, shit. He's just a kid."

"A kid who managed to compost two Knights of Khryl. You have any idea how hard it is to kill a Knight of Khryl?"

I looked up from the page. Just looked.

"Oh, right." The bishop reddened. "Right. Sorry."

"What the fuck is Freedom's Face, really?"

"Officially? Renegade Folk terrorists. Ruthless, bloodthirsty psychotics out to destroy the worship of Khryl."

"I said *really*."

He shrugged. "They're mostly Ankhanan kids who thought it'd be a thrill to ride over the mountains and Strike a Blow for Ogrillo Freedom. Mixed in with a few pretty hard-core Warrens and Alientown operatives supplied by an old friend of yours from the safety of her—"

"We're not friends," I muttered. "Why haven't you stepped on these idiots?"

"It's not exactly our job. And the Empire isn't exactly anti-Ogrillo-Freedom, either, when you get to the bone."

"What's this got to do with Orbek?"

"Maybe nothing. It's also possible he was in with the Smoke Hunt."

I nodded. "Talk to me about the Smoke Hunt."

Tourann gave me a sidelong look. "What's your interest?"

"It was the reason for a major ass-whipping I took today," I said evenly, "and might be the reason for a couple I might deliver."

Tourann flinched, just a little. "Bad news is what it is. Every so often some ogrilloi get cracked on booze and rith and go wilding. Just fist and claw stuff, but that's serious enough."

"I remember."

"People get hurt; a lot of them die. Including the grills. The Knights see to that. That's the official story."

"All right, sure. And unofficially?"

"They're organized. And it's getting out of hand. The activity jumped roughly the same time Orbek hit town. The Knights are trying to keep a lid on it, but they're starting to see Smoke Hunters once or twice a week. Even a solo can do serious damage before he's put down, and often it's a pack. Sometimes more than one. And there's a handful of Knights Attendant—nine so far—who have supposedly been promoted and gone On Venture—"

"Supposedly."

"Two confirmed kills, three more probable. Maybe all of them."

"Nine *dead? Nine?* Without firearms? Shit, even *with* guns . . ." I shook my head blankly. "The name?"

"They shout, '*Dizhrati golzinn Ekk.*' It's like their motto or something."

"Sure. A fucking hint, huh?"

"You don't speak Etk Dag?"

"In my day nobody did. Nobody human."

"Huh. I suppose not." Tourann rolled a hand a couple times. "Translates as 'I am the Smoke Hunt.' "

"What's that supposed to mean?"

"How should I know?"

"You could try maybe asking a grill."

"Caine, come on; you know what it's like with slave culture." The bishop affected a thick Boedecken accent. "N'buddy know nudd'n. Nevva do."

"Slave culture," I echoed, chewing the inside of my lip. Again. "Great."

"You say that like you disapprove."

"Not my business." I bit down hard enough to make an eyelid flicker. "What's the connection to Orbek?"

"More than the coincidence of timing? We're looking into it, but I can't make any promises. This past month or so, all my tame sources have dried up and blown away. And I might not have gotten much regardless; the Smoke Hunters all seem to be intacts."

"Intacts—?"

"You know, unaltered." The bishop rolled that hand a couple more times. "Ungelded."

I tasted blood.

"Don't look like that." Tourann shifted as though the swivel chair hurt his ass. "It's not what you think. The Knights don't just go around clipping balls. It's voluntary."

"Voluntary."

"Sure. Geldings and fem neuters are eligible for better jobs down here in the city. Jobs with human contact. Jobs that require social skills, a little education, learning to read, that kind of stuff. Intacts are pretty much stuck with stoop labor on the estates, maybe some dock work or light hauling if they're lucky. Or in the mines. You'd be surprised how many volunteer."

"No, I wouldn't." The smart ones. The ambitious ones. Negative selection: breeding out dangerous traits.

I bit down and swallowed. "So?"

"So my sources were all eligibles. Intacts and eligibles are almost like separate cultures. Like, I don't know, castes—"

"I get how it works." I looked back out the window, up at the fat bitch lolling in the sunset, high on the parapet. "That's what they're all whipped up about, huh? These Freedom's Face cocksmokes?"

"In the Empire, grills're full citizens." Tourann turned a hand toward the view. "Here, they're—"

"Tame." I stared toward the fat bitch on the parapet, but it was other bitches I was really seeing. Dancing in firelight below my cross. Again.

I'll be seeing that for the rest of my life.

"Ask me if it breaks my fucking heart."

"Hey, I'm not political. I gather information and I write reports, and a year and a half from now I'll be one person again. In Ankhana. Where Knights of Khryl are the ones who are tame."

"Sure they are." I tossed the papers back on the desk and started gathering up the rest of my equipment. The spring-loaded baton came in a small holster; I pushed up my left sleeve and laid it along the outside of my forearm. "What about Disciples?"

"You mean Cainists?"

I made a face. "Whatever."

"Outlawed. You can probably understand why."

"I can guess."

"The Khryllians wouldn't tolerate the Church itself if Ma'elKoth hadn't reaffirmed Toa-Phelathon's land grant after the First Succession War. And, y'know, there's the Spire—"

"Yeah."

"So, y'know, they *like* elKothans here. But even so, we have to play by their rules, if you see what I mean. The Cainists, though—they have, ahh, what you might call a, ah, *complex relationship*, I suppose, with the whole concept of *rules . . .*"

"Tell me about it," I said, fastening the last buckle on the baton's holster straps.

"Frankly speaking, they're a major embarrassment."

"Huh." I shook out my sleeve and squinted down at its drape along my arm. "You should try it from my side."

"If you don't mind my asking—" Tourann wheeled the chair over to the grate and fed the papers one at a time to the flames. "—what's the Emperor's interest in this Orbek?"

I slid the knives, one at a time, each into its own sheath sewn within my clothing. "I don't work for the Emperor."

"You don't? But—I, uh—I mean, everybody knows—"

"We're friends. Maybe even family. That's all." I untied the thong on the leather pouch and inspected its contents: an array of spring-steel lockpicks and tension bars. "He doesn't tell me what to do."

"This is personal?"

"Everything's personal." I retied the pack and slid it into the same purse with the spare clips, then tucked the wrapped-up garrotte into the top of my boot.

Tourann's frown gathered toward a scowl. "I would not be happy to risk exposure of this post just because somebody owes you a favor."

"This is plenty official. Your better half'd think so, anyway." I made one last check, seating knives and gun securely in their places, shifting and twisting to make sure the tunic draped without binding.

"He would?"

"Yeah. I'm on a mission from God."

"Oh, sure. Very funny."

"Not to me."

"You—" The bishop blinked, and blinked again. "You're serious? You're working for—" He rolled his eyes significantly. "What does He want you to do?"

"If you find out, be sure you let me know."

Tourann cocked his head. "I don't get it."

"He doesn't tell people what to do. He might as well take on an Aspect and do it Himself, which starts the kinds of problems the Covenant of Pirichanthe was designed to prevent. And He sure as screaming fuck wouldn't tell *me* anyway."

"No?"

"We have history. Some of which your better half would call gospel." I scratched at the lattice of scar and callus that padded my knuckles. "So I make my own plans, and if He doesn't like them, He should stay the fuck out of my head."

"Uh."

I flexed my hands to flush the scars white and then red again. Here I was, being an asshole. Again. As usual. It wasn't Tourann's fault that the god he served had murdered my wife, and my father, mind-raped my daughter, and made my best friend into His immortal zombie meatpuppet. Gods are like that.

And what the hell: He's my god too.

I sighed. "He told me once I have a gift for breaking things in useful ways. So sometimes He pushes me toward things He thinks need breaking."

"What needs breaking here?"

"Shit, what *doesn't*?" I waved us toward a new subject. "What do you have on the Artans?"

"Please, my lor—er, Caine—"

"Shade."

"We really don't need any of your kind of—are you *certain* that Our Beloved Father has sent you *here*—?"

"I'll find out soon enough anyway."

Tourann sighed. "Does the name Simon Faller strike any sparks?"

A shake of my head. "Sounds Artan, though."

"Transdeian papers. Rolled into town about ten months after the Assumption. Rolled literally: on his own private train."

"You have rail?"

"We do now. Faller came complete with two hundred stonebenders and a pair of rockmagi laying track ahead of him."

"Money."

"Plenty. He bought BlackStone Mining, and he could afford to operate at a loss for almost two years."

"Knights soft on him?"

"They'd bear his children. Faller's connected in Transdeia. Where do you think the Khryllians get those fancy guns?"

I frowned. "Diamondwell?"

"Show a stonebender a machine and he'll come back the next day with one that works twice as well and is ten times as pretty."

"They don't do autoloaders? All I saw was pump-lever stuff."

"They're Khryllians. They're not interested in a gun unless it can double as a mace in hand-to-hand. Anyway, Faller made the deal for them. He's a sharp operator."

"All he's got going is this mining company?"

"BlackStone's not just mining. Some precious metals, but primarily it's a griffinstone producer. These past few months they've moved serious weight. Low-end stuff—mostly bled out—but a lot of it, and he seems to be making money now. Uses grills for the labor, but his managers and overseers are human. Probably Artan. Forty-two, all told."

"Forty-*two*? Holy crap. What're they really after?"

Tourann shrugged. "Besides money and power? You tell me."

I rubbed my eyes. The headache was coming back. "Let me give it to you in small words. This whole bloody continent—shit, probably the world—is lousy with Aktiri and Overworld Company goons stranded here on Assumption Day. Most of them are kind of like me: we don't play well with others. Now you're telling me there's more than *forty* of them, all together in one place at one time. Something fucking serious is going on here, and I don't feel like getting my ass shot off while I'm trying to figure out what."

"Well—" Tourann shifted his weight uncomfortably. "—this is strictly conjectural, based on an . . . unreliable resource we have inside Freedom's Face. This resource is, well, Folk—you know how they are; might be true, and it might just be a funny story—"

"Yeah, spare me. Give."

"There's supposed to be a *dil* to the Quiet Land here in the Battleground. In Hell, actually—somewhere back inside the bluff. The story is that Black-Stone's looking for it."

My eyes drifted closed. One hand came up, fell again, reached for the edge of the desk, and missed. I lurched drunkenly.

"Caine? Caine, are you unwell?"

By the time I opened my eyes again, Tourann was half out of his chair. I waved him back into it. "I'm all right. I'm all right, I just—wow. Just—this has been a kinda rough day. Shit, I gotta sit down."

I took a faltering step and half fell into the horseshoe chair in front of the fire.

"Caine—seriously, I don't wield the full range of Ule-Tourann's powers, but if you're sick, Our Beloved Father does grant me—"

"Nothing that'll help."

I shoved myself forward and from somewhere found the strength to hold my head up and look the bishop in the eye. "That story's not a story, that's all. You need to get on your Artan Mirror tonight. Now. You need to tell Ankhana. There really is a *dil*, and BlackStone's not just looking for it. They've found it."

"Really? Well, that's certainly interesting, if true, but it's hardly urgent, is it? It's not like they'll ever be able to open it, after all."

"They have. More than once."

"Impossible. Even the power of Our Beloved Father—"

"You need to get a message to the Duke *right now*. The Emperor needs to know the *dil T'llan* has been breached again, probably from our side."

"But it's not *possible*—"

"Fuck not possible."

"Please—you must understand—communications of this type are out of policy, and without a very good reason. . . . I mean, you didn't even *know* about the *dil* until I brought it up—"

The headache chiseled gouges along the inside of my temple. My hand went to my eyes again. "Know about it?"

*—darkness stinking of shit and fear and human breath, naked and hot and cold and slime-wet until shivers ripple like shockwaves from flesh to clinging flesh, rune-carved rose quartz shimmering in the blue nonlight of the blade-wand—*

My hand came away from my eyes and my mind leaped twenty-five years in a single bound. "Know about it?" I said again. "I've *been* there."

"Caine—"

"Tell them I saw it in a fucking dream."

"What?"

"Just do it, huh?"

"Really, Caine, consider: the Emperor is also the Mithondionne, after all. Adopted grandson of the bloody elf-king who magicked up the *dil T'llan* and closed them all however many centuries ago. If there were a *dil* in Purthin's Ford, don't you think he'd have mentioned it?"

"Unless he had good reason not to."

I looked down at my hands. I spend a lot of time staring at my hands.

"You know why I was up here in the first place? I was covert for the Monasteries, working an exoteric identity as a Boedecken scout and ogrillo expert for a half-private expedition. They were after a magickal artifact—this giant fucking runecut blush diamond, big as my head. A Legendary artifact, ramping up on True Relic. If they found it, my job was to backdoor an Esoteric strike team. If it was what the partners thought it was, the Monasteries were fucking sure gonna swallow it at one bite no matter who got chewed up."

"So?"

"So it was the Tear of Panchasell."

"Panchasell—?"

I nodded. "That bloody elf-king you were talking about."

"But—but—the Tear of Panchasell—that's just a *legend*—"

"Or something."

"It was never found—"

"It was never recovered." My lips curled under. I couldn't fit that many teeth into a smile.

"Well, I—still, I wouldn't give it too much thought. Even if these Artans manage to find a *dil*, it's not like they can open it; even the power of Our Beloved Father is barely—"

"Will you shut up about Our Beloved Fucking Father? What do you have on the BlackStone compound and operations?"

"Not much. Just what we've been able to bribe out of a couple ellie delivery grills."

"No scry on them, either? You've never even had an Eye inside?"

"Caine, BlackStone's a *griffinstone* producer. They don't want us to know what's going on in there, and they have power to burn."

"Yeah, whatever. Write another fucking report, will you?" I lurched to my feet and dragged my sorry butt back over to the window.

Hell stared back at me. "Son of a fuck-my-ass bitch. They already know I'm here, too."

"They do?" Tourann sounded more surprised than skeptical.

"Faller will have had somebody over in Riverdock, watching the steamers unload."

"How do you figure?"

"It's what I'd do. Not that he's expecting me—though he might be, shit, I hadn't even *thought* of that—but on general principle. He'll want to know who's coming and going." I shook my head and tried to unclench my jaw. "Any Artan would recognize me. Any. I'm amazed the fucker didn't buttonhole me for an autograph."

I swung back around toward Tourann. "What do you have for resources on the ground here?"

"I don't have authority to talk to you about that." He shifted uncomfortably again. "I will tell you it's not a lot."

I waved a hand. "Never mind. I haven't even been here a day and I know more than you mopes already."

"More of what?"

"Don't bother mirroring the Duke. It's a waste of time."

Tourann blinked. "I—what?"

"Forget about it. They already know. Deliann does, anyway. Son of a bitch."

"He does?"

"Listen, this Khlaylock girl—three years is a long damn time to be Champion, isn't it?"

"That's part of why they call her Khrylget."

"*Three* years, though. . . . She stand for Champion before the Assumption? Or after?"

Tourann coughed, frowning. "You mean *the* Assumption, right?"

"Yeah. The one your better half doesn't like to talk about much. The one where I cut Our Beloved Fucking Father in half and jammed a foot of sword through His Beloved Fucking Brain."

Tourann coughed hard enough that he had to wipe spit off his chin. "I don't actually know—I could look it up for you, but I don't have the records handy—"

"Make a note to check it out. Because if she never stepped up till after the Assumption, well . . . it might be significant."

"I don't see it."

"It has to do with the Covenant of Pirichanthe, and Ma'elKoth and Assumption Day, and it's . . . complicated."

I found myself staring at the scars on my hands again. "Just find out."

It was all I could say.

"There's a cold-post board in Weaver's Square. The date'll be posted in numerics on a note that says, 'Rod, here's your box number.' You have that?"

"Yeah. Rod here's your box." I rubbed my eyes. "Yeah, I got it. All right, last thing before I get out of your station. I need some eyeball with the Monastic agent-in-place."

"I don't have any official—"

"But you know who it is. You have to. Give."

Tourann took a deep breath. "You know the Monasteries are decidedly unwelcome on the Battleground."

"Yeah, I heard. And there's no way in any given variety of Hell the Council of Brothers would let a whole nation of Khryllians go unmonitored."

"Well, yes. So—" The bishop tilted his head with a sort of preparatory flinch. "—sometimes the best way to hide a *really* illegal activity is inside a *mildly* illegal activity, you follow?"

"Why do I get the feeling you're warming me up for something I'm not gonna like?"

"Remember what I told you about the Cainists?"

"Oh." I rubbed my eyes again; this couldn't be good. "Oh, for fuck's sake."

"It gets worse."

"Worse than that?"

"I'm afraid so." Tourann nodded sympathetically. "You know her."

I stopped rubbing my eyes; if I kept going, I just might jam my fingers into the sockets up to the second knuckle. "You have *got* to be motherfucking *kidding* me—"

"If only I were. I've had to deal with her myself once or twice."

He wrote an address on a scrap of paper and passed it to me. I crumpled it in my fist. "Fuck me inside out."

"I'm sorry. I truly am."

"Not as sorry as I am." I sighed and let my fist fall. Out the window, the fat bitch lolled in the firelight on the ledge. I took a deep breath, sighed it out, then turned back to Tourann and began, "The chalice with the palace—"

He held up a hand. "I'll put myself away, if you don't mind. I'm usually out only after midnight." He made a half-apologetic wave toward the window. "It's been a year since I could have a brandy and watch the evenfires."

"What about the Bishop?"

"He'll remember a perfectly ordinary Rite of Atonement." He produced an earthenware jug and a pair of cordials. "Care to join me? It's Tinnaran."

"Another time."

As I turned to go, Tourann said, "It must be a, erm, peculiar feeling . . ."

I stopped. "Yeah?"

Tourann waved the jug in a little circle. "This. All this. Being here."

"Peculiar is one word for it."

"I mean, *you* did this. If not for you, none of this would be here."

"It wasn't just me. Lots of people—"

"Lots of people, sure." Tourann splashed a cordial full of brandy. "Any of them still alive?"

I took that without a blink. "Purthin Khlaylock."

"Sure, sure. The city's called Purthin's Ford, but it's the river that makes all this possible; it changed this whole corner of the continent into a garden. You know what they call the river, up here?"

I looked down at my hands while I tried to breathe past the brick in my guts. "The Caineway."

"That's right. The Caineway. I can't imagine how that must feel."

"Me neither," I said, and left.

Night had swallowed the vertical city.

By the time I dragged my exhausted ass down the steps of the cathedral, the streets of Purthin's Ford were buried already in the horizon's shadow; the sinking sun had levered darkness upward to erase each tier of Hell in turn. The cliffs and the city reflected enough firelight that the street I walked shimmered with blood-colored gloom.

*if not for you, none of this would be here*

I sagged into a polished stone bench and let my head hang.

Slave culture. Intacts and eligibles.

*turned this whole corner of the continent into a garden*

I had to look sometime. I was fresh out of excuses to wait.

*black knives don't kneel*

I lifted my head and opened the eye of my mind.

Twists of night knotted around me: vast braided cables of interstellar black frayed into strands that tied me to the river, to the Spire, to Hell above and every breath of the damned and their masters: a fractal arterial network pumping shadow from all this place had been to all I was, from all I had been to what it was.

The night smeared and writhed and wrapped itself around me, swallowing me, entering me, oozing like oil into eyes and mouth and nose and ears. I shook my head. A humorless chuckle rattled in my throat. This was what I'd been avoiding? This had had me running scared? It didn't seem possible.

Since when am I afraid of the dark?

# FOREVER AND AMEN

## RETREAT FROM THE BOEDECKEN (partial)
### You are **CAINE** (featured Actor: Pfnl. Hari Michaelson)
#### MASTER: NOT FOR DISTRIBUTION, UNDER PENALTY OF LAW.

*S*ffrins a lxry. Heerz manser.
     Here.
Is my.
Answer.
Maxmum bad.
Snot nough.
Not.
*Enough.*
Hav topen meyes.
Have to.
Fuh kk kk k—
Fuck.
Me.
God.
Hrrr.
Air. Air is all.
Air's everything but—
So . . .
Tired . . .
But.
Don't need air to talk to *you.*
Technology is a wonderful fucking thing.

I just—

Need.

To *hurt* more.

It's night.

Must be night. No sun on my skin.

I can open my eyes. I can. And I will. Pretty soon.

I will.

Keep . . . *breathing.*

Motherfucker.

Wind . . .'s still shifting. Cookfire smoke . . . mulch of rotten blood and gamy meat high and soft and blue . . . funerary platforms west of camp . . . staked out their dead for the buzzards and the crows . . .

Just.

Breathe.

Out.

In's no problem.

Breathe.

*Out.*

It took J—ahh, hrr. Hrrgh . . . conditioning . . .

Still can't—

Here, then. Here. I can do this.

Control Disciplines.

I can.

I can.

I can do this.

I can.

Okay.

This is what I mean.

The son of that old-fashioned god back home, where you are, took all day to die. Not sure how long it's been for me. Guess I'm in a little better shape.

Or maybe it's because I'm up here for my *own* sins . . .

Or—

Grunting, alien words, the creak of rope and greased wood and yes, and yes, it's me, they are, yes.

Yes.

My scaffold of timber reclines, rotating slow as the wheel of stars that must be somewhere above, angling backward on its horizontal axle like an easy chair until my overstrained diaphragm spasms out of muscle failure and gasps and wheezes and pumps my starving lungs again: this is the real reason I'm outlasting the son of that old-fashioned god.

Because they won't let me die. Not yet.

Oxygen whispers away the shadows in my head.

I open my eyes.

My hand—that's *my* hand, above on the weather-greyed arm of the Y-shaped cross. Looks like I've got a cramp: fingers twisted into talons of somebody else's agony. I can see the cramp. I can't feel it. My hands and feet are gone: blocks of wood. Lumps of stone. Maybe my pain center's finally burned out.

Maybe the rusty spikes through my wrists and ankles severed the nerves.

The blood that wells around the spike is dark in the orange light of the bonfires. It gathers brighter rose as it trickles thick and cooling down crusted channels to my shoulder.

Not hanging from the spikes. Grill-size cross: wrist shackles beyond my fingertips. Not worth a custom job. Tied me on. Spikes're just to keep me from slipping the rope.

The Y to which I am nailed eventually rotates far enough back to take some of the pressure off the spikes they drove between my Achilles tendon and ankle joint. Now my struggle is to hold up my head. To look upon our torturers. Their half-assed let's-pretend sorcerors.

Bitches.

Would have guessed it would be bitches. Would have known. Even if I never seconded the Barand. Would have known.

Dad showed me that story—was it horsemen out of the far eastern steppes? was it nomads I cannot name in a desert I cannot name?—how they took as an article of faith that a man's only proper role is war; that to inflict pain upon the helpless will ruin a warrior for battle. So when they had taken someone they despised so much that only infinite suffering could answer the ache in their blood—

They'd give him to the women.

Bitches dance around me in their gloss-black feathers and blood-brown paint and swinging swollen dugs, and they pinch me and pull my hair and talon-flick my balls and tease my shrinking flesh with any petty insult they can imagine. And when they get bored, they offer me spit and urine in a wooden ladle, and the thirst that consumes me is stronger than my disgust.

And that's exactly the problem. Suffering is a luxury. I don't hurt enough. Haven't hurt enough.

Not yet.

Far below us, a vast field of bonfires paints the badlands with pools of sunset. Down among them Black Knives pursue their Black Knife lives: cooking and washing and eating and drinking, telling jokes and dancing, lying and singing and wrestling and fucking and doing whatever else ogrilloi do when nothing special is going on.

Very few even give us a glance.

Fuckers.

They were not real to me before. Even the ones I fought hand-to-hand. They were abstract. Impersonal. A natural disaster. A flood, a fire, an avalanche. Something to deal with.

Things are different, now.

Now I see them. I smell them.

I *know* them.

And if I can just hurt *enough* . . .

But that's the problem. Suffering is a luxury.

This is different from the Barand. A whole different world. He and his boys were taken far out in the Waste; they were used, and used up, on the spot. That was just a clutch of them, long-range raiders. This is a whole different world.

This is some kind of fucking Althing.

More than that.

They didn't need us for this party. It's BYOV. The screams and whimpers that are their favorite dinner music come mostly from other ogrilloi. Criminals. Cowards. Captives from other clans. Who gives a shit? The point—the sharp end of the fuckstick—

This wasn't something staged just for us. This was what they came here for.

This. Not us. It was never about us. It was about being *here*.

Shit, y'know—?

Shit.

We might've got away after all.

Ahh, there it is. There. Now I'm starting to hurt.

Good. Good. I *need* to hurt. Because some things are starting to make sense to me.

Because this Althing of theirs is more than an Althing—it's some kind of mass combined  baptism-confirmation-bar-and-bat-mitzvah-rite-of-fucking-passage. The walled bowl against the perimeter, where we paddocked the horses . . . see how crowded it is?

Those are cubs. Can you see them? Their children. Baby Black Knives. Hundreds of them. Some kind of crèche: all in there together, from blood-wet infants to half-grown juvie bucks, walled away from the rest of the camp.

Kiddie prison. Or something.

And on the line of crosses below me, the ones hung with ogrilloi . . . shit, there they go again: another handful of juvenile bitches—they look about the same age as the ones who have been looking after the cubs in the kiddie prison—come trailing out behind that big fat cunt in the glossy headdress like a mane of crow feathers, the one who acts like she owns the fucking planet. They spread themselves out obediently, turn their backs and bend over to present like baboons in heat, and Crowmane goes up to the crucified prisoners one at a time to jab her blood-crusted thumb-talon up their butts . . .

Yeah. Here's one for you science geeks out there: ogrillo males carry their prostates the same place humans do.

And as she manually collects each one, she lifts each handful to the night and howls something in the local babble before she jams it up the snatch of the next juvenile bitch, which is the exact point in the process of Black Knife ritual-exogamy-by-manual-insemination where this whole deal jumps the sword from revolting to downright fascinating.

How fascinating? It's holding *my* attention, and I'm dying on a fucking cross.

Funny thing is, you probably can't see it. Not even with my eyes.

If I'd stayed in Battle Magick, I could show it to you: I'd have learned to turn visualization into vision, imagination into hallucination. But if I'd stayed in Battle Magick, I wouldn't understand what it *means*.

That's the thing, here. I know what it means. That's my edge. The difference between me and Mick Barand.

A Monastic education.

This is what you can't see with my eyes:

Crowmane raises her fistful of goblin jizz and hacks out her hairball invocation, and around her hand—around her head, her mane of glossy feathers, around her rows of nipples dangling like boneless thumbs, around her mounded rolls of asscheek—there gathers a significance, a *realness*, a vivid lucid-dream intensity that makes everything else in the screaming bloody night fade like it's barely even here.

I mean *everything*.

The crucified ogrilloi. The juvie bitches. The Black Knife camp, and the shackled rows of captives waiting their turns. Even Kess, who's still twitching and struggling where he hangs from meathooks through his jaw while ants and nightflies chew the coils of his guts that trail in the dirt around the scrabbling balls of his feet . . .

Even me. Even the new pain I've found.

We don't count right now.

Right now, we're only details. We don't matter. All that matters is that Crowmane's fistful of jizz is gonna grow up to be a Black Knife superhero. Fast. Strong. Physically flawless. Completely without fear. The perfect warrior.

How do I know? I know the way you know things in your dreams. I just *know*. That's the *real* that makes the rest of us into a dream. That's what she's paying for with our pain.

It's exactly like a dream. Because it *is* a dream. But it's not *my* dream.

That's why I need to suffer. I need to get the attention of the dreamer.

And I can. That's the kicker. That's the punchline. That's what'd make me laugh if I could laugh. That's why suffering is a luxury.

Because their demon isn't Bound. Not by them, anyway.

Now, like an answer to my silent prayer, they bring out the next two.

It's Marade and Tizarre.

Streaked and stained with filth and blood. They both are gagged with thick mouth-jamming knots of rope. Tizarre's lips are smashed and her eyes swollen near to shut with bruise. Marade's golden skin is flawless beneath the crust of clot and muck, for Khryl still loves her. She must have fought them even here, even after she awoke within their camp: she is shackled with chains that could bind a dragon, where Tizarre is tied only with rope, cruelly tight; her hands are as swollen as her eyes and shading toward the same necrotic black.

The bitches kick their knees from under them and cast them to the stone before me.

I have figured out what it is. Why they have put me where I am. Why they make me do what they make me do. Did I tell you? Did I say it inside my throat, or only in my mind? I can't remember.

It's because I showed brave the way a grill stud might show brave. Because I went out against them alone. Because even now they cannot make me beg for death.

It is possible they intend this as an honor.

So I will be the last. I will watch the others. Their infinite pain. Their unimaginably ugly deaths. I could close my eyes, but I won't.

I will not.

To be their witness is the only penance I can offer.

This is how I pay for making myself the star of the Caine Show.

And now it's time to choose.

The final refinement, one that some remotely clinical part of my mind can even appreciate: the bitches remove their gags. So I have to hear them beg.

And because it's them, because it's Marade and Tizarre, because they are both heroes in a way I can barely imagine, each of them begs me to choose her, to spare her partner.

To let her partner live one more day. One more hour.

Their begging turns to shouts as they try to drown each other's voice. Their shouts become desperate screams and finally wordless siren wails.

And I will make the choice.

It is what I do, now.

I will send one of them to a deeper circle of Hell, and the screaming of the chosen and the curses of the spared will rain as fire upon my head.

Should be grateful. Isn't this what I wanted? Isn't this what I asked for? Swallowed by dark. Blind beyond the memory of day.

All the way down.

And—

I *am* grateful. This is what I wanted. This is what I asked for. Didn't know it was possible to hurt this much.

For this I thank You.

Make of this suffering a sacrament: a covenant between us.

Do this one thing, and there will be agony beyond Your imagination. Only grant my one small desire, and I promise You a universe of pain.

Just get me off this cross.

That's all. Get me down from here. So I can *hurt* them.

Get me down from here, and I will be Yours forever. We'll make our *own* Caine Show. Together.

A universe of pain. Everlasting. Forever and amen.

Just get me down from here.

*part two*

# PRINCE OF LIES

I sat on that bench outside the Cathedral for a long time.

I sat while night took the city. I sat while Khryllian lamplighters tromped by, kindling the hurricane lanterns that hung from tall wrought-iron hook-poles to mark each street corner: faint candles in the vast Boedecken dark. I sat while the night clogged up with rain again and barely visible people hurried past me with lowered heads and shoulders hunched against the chill, carrying shuttered lanterns that leaked strips of flickering yellow light. I sat long enough that my ass either warmed the bench's polished stone or went dead numb.

Finally I got up. "Fuck this for a joke; I'm freezing my balls off. I'm leaving."

*Don't. I feel safer here.*

I spun and the Automag found my hand.

Around me: rain and empty darkened streets, featureless looming bulk of the Cathedral and the face of Hell. I was entirely alone.

No surprise: that whisper had been a Whisper. Not an actual voice at all, but a minor TK variant directly manipulating my eardrums. Makes the slithery breathy nondescript almost-voice sound like it's coming from everywhere at once.

I safetied the Automag and put it away. "Come on out. If I meant you harm, I would've come looking."

*You have been known to change your mind.*

I didn't deny it. "At least tell me which direction I should face."

*It matters not. I'm well out of range of your pistol, and I can hear what you say no matter where you say it.*

"Yeah?" I settled back onto the bench. It had been my ass going numb after all; the stone was cold as a bitch. "How long have you been watching?"

*Since you walked out of the Cathedral. Straight to the Eyes post; you're so predictable.*

"Sure." Doing my dark-adaption trick, I scanned the sightlines of ghostly windows in buildings around the little plaza, checking for ones that overlooked both my bench and the Cathedral steps. There were only two: one on the face of a third-floor gable, and the other a picture window at the front of a one-story shop. "And it tickles the fuck out of you to sit up there in your little garret room and watch me shiver."

*Caine, please. You insult me. Nor am I in the bootmaker's. Unlike you, I'm not that easy to locate.*

"Whatever." It wasn't worth pushing. "All right, I'm listening."

*You were the one who wanted to see me.*

"That'd be nice."

*Oh, ha. You see? I pretend to appreciate your wit. You pretend not to hate me. Can we do business now? This must be important—or, I imagine, poor dim Tyrkilld would be dead already.*

She'd been smack on about me changing my mind; right then I'd have cheerfully slapped the points off her ears for being a condescending elvish cunt. There's only so much talking-down-to I can take, and I've had about five lives' worth from Kierendal.

"I guess he told you I took a job for the Champion."

*I had hoped Tyrkilld's welcome might leave you disinclined to help the Khryl-lians. You were supposed to come into this on our side.*

"Whose side is that?"

*Ours. The good guys. You know: truth, justice and the Ankhanan Way.*

I made a face. "Since when do truth and justice have anything to do with the Ankhanan Way?"

She laughed at me: that elfin titter that sounds like somebody dropped a handful of glass bells off a cliff. *Since Assumption Day, of course. You arranged it so yourself, didn't you?*

"Sure, funny. Now let's talk about side of what, and why you dragged Orbek into it."

*Dragged? Me?*

"Orbek went to Ankhana to visit friends—friends who are half-made Faces, just like he used to be. Three months later he's shooting Knights of Khryl and playing Black Knife *kwatcharr*."

*Not playing, Caine.* I could hear a shrug in her Whisper. *A clever little feral like you shouldn't have much difficulty figuring it out.*

"I just want to hear you say it."

*Deliann doesn't want you involved. Our Sainted Emperor feels you've done enough.*

"He's sentimental that way."

*Not sentimental, Caine. Squeamish. Our Sainted Emperor knows what happens when you get busy. Three years later we're still rebuilding Ankhana.*

"I've heard. So Orbek was just bait after all. Because you knew I'd come."

*I'm not squeamish.*

"I remember. Tyrkilld will too."

*Oh?*

"Must have come as a bit of a surprise that he lived long enough to report in this afternoon."

*It's not the first time you've disappointed me.*

"You sure he's outlived his usefulness? He's smarter than he plays, and he's got a good heart."

*A fatal virtue, in this place and these times.*

A tilt of my head: not quite ready to agree. "You were willing enough to use his heart when it suited you."

*So are you, I think.*

"I quit playing good guy a long time ago."

Her Whisper chipped sharp as an obsidian scalpel. *Have you seen how you feral scum treat Folk here? They're* slavers, *Caine.*

"Some of them."

*No one ordered you here. No one even asked you. Especially not me. Let Deliann flash on me all year long. This is your choice. Nobody else's.*

"That's what people keep telling me."

*How much do you know about what's really going on?*

"It's what *you* know that worries me. What you don't."

*This is your war I'm fighting, Caine. Don't you understand that yet? Do you know what this place is?*

"Yeah."

*We are the First Folk, Caine. I stood in this place when Panchasell Mithondionne carved it from the gutrock of this escarpment more than a thousand years ago. Do you know what your Artans have here? This is not just a* dil—*not just a gate to your hellworld—*

"I told you: I know."

*Then you know why I need you here, Caine. This is the task I have been given by our Emperor. By* your *Emperor. To defend the* dil T'llan *against your people—*

"Yeah, I get it."

*They're your enemies too.*

"Uh-huh. I say again: So? What's your offer?"

Silence.

Hush of rain and the beat of my heart.

"Come on, Kier. What do you want me to do about it?"

Without hesitation: *Kill the Champion. Kill Angvasse Khlaylock.*

I laughed at her. It wasn't easy; she's not exactly funny. But I could fake it.

*I can make it worth your while.*

"No, you can't."

*You don't think you can do it?*

"For starters."

*And the rest?*

"I don't *want* to."

Silence.

She said, *Really.*

"Really."

Silence.

Eventually: *Why not?*

"Reasons are for peasants."

Silence.

*I'd settle for Purthin.*

"Oh, right. He *knows* me—"

*So did Ma'elKoth.*

My turn to fall silent. Eventually: "I thought you said you were fighting my war. Sounds like you want me to fight yours."

*BlackStone is under Khryllian protection. Before I can touch the Artans, we have to—*

"Yeah, yeah, sure. Keep it up, Kier."

A hush like a breath of wind: a sigh, maybe. *What does the Champion want you to do?*

"Is that your business?"

*If I say it is.*

"Leave the Artans to me. When I'm done, they won't be a problem."

*How does that get me what I want?*

"Didn't say it would." I let air leak out between my teeth. "Does Deliann know you don't give a shit about this supposed mission of yours?"

*Our Sainted Emperor and I have an understanding.*

"He wants the *dil T'llan* protected. You want ogrilloi free in the Boedecken."

*Like I said.*

"Because that's what the Black Knives were in the first place. Part of Panchasell's defense of the *dil T'llan.* I mean, ogrilloi were your dogs, right? Hunting dogs. Guard dogs. Isn't that what you bred them for?"

*We did better with them than we did with you.*

"You *are* sentimental."

*There is no way in which ogrilloi are not superior to humanity. Stronger. Faster. More loyal, more faithful. More honest and more courageous. True always to their own nature—*

"Yeah, so are horses. Except horses don't eat people."

*Nor do ogrilloi. Not anymore.*

"Tell that to the Smoke Hunt."

*If only I had the chance.*

My teeth found that raw spot on the inside of my lip. "The Smoke Hunt isn't yours?"

*Mine? How would you think it mine? Random slaughter is your style.*

I couldn't argue. If shit were gonna be simple, God would've called somebody else.

*The Smoke Hunt is the worst thing that has happened to our operation. Pointless, useless, wasteful bloodshed. They accomplish only the spread of terror; they keep the Khryllians on the highest alert, and ensure the constant vigilance and militarization of the entire population. They are the enemy of the ogrilloi as much as they are of the Khryllians—the Smoke Hunt justifies the oppression of Hell. Not that they wouldn't have their uses, if properly directed—*

That spot on the inside of my lip was getting way too goddamn sore. "Orbek."

*Yes.*

"It wasn't *just* about me—Smoke Hunters carry the Black Knife clan sign—"

*He was my best hope to get inside. After all, you trained him.*

"Since you sicced Orbek on the Smoke Hunt, are Hunts up or down?"

*Why?*

"Just answer."

*Up.*

"Nine Knights down—how many were yours? Or sympathizers?"

*Four. Where are you going with this?*

It was my turn to laugh. It didn't come out sounding real humorous. "They're *Black Knives,* you dumb cunt. You were using him. You think he wasn't using you? Like you said: I trained him."

*We're not going to get along until you start telling me what you know.*

"Sometimes shit isn't complicated," I said. "You just have to be willing to accept the absolute fucking corruption of everybody involved."

Silence.

Eventually: *So where does this leave us?*

I shrugged. "Let's deal."

*Deal how?*

"Play Cainist for a minute. Talk about what you want. Not what you told Deliann you'd do. What you really want."

*Why would I do that?*

"You ever read Deliann's book on me?"

*I'm not literary.*

"He has Ma'elKoth say that the only way to beat me is to keep me running in so many different directions I can't focus. That to give me a clear view of my enemy is to hand me victory."

*So why would I give you a clear view?*

"Because we're not enemies."

*It warms me to hear you say so.*

"Play straight with me and you maybe get something for it. Take the chance, Kier."

*I have trusted you before.*

"And the truth of it is you came out pretty good. It's not my fault shit went bad in the middle." Which truth might have been stretched around a corner or two, but she let it go.

Slowly, like it hurt her to say: *I want the Knights of Khryl and the rest of your vile feral slavers broken like you broke the Black Knives.*

I nodded. "And you don't care what happens to anybody else around here."

*Do any of them care about Folk?*

"Some do. Some don't. That's not what we're talking about."

*What are we talking about?*

"I can help you. But you have to help me."

*There are limits to what I am willing to do.*

"I'm not asking a lot."

*I'm listening.*

"I know shit's about to blow up here; what do we have, a week?"

*Less. A revolution is an avalanche. Once you crack the crust, you can only ride it out or let it roll you under.*

"Yeah. It's more than just the grills and your local agents, right?"

*Caine, please. However much we may pretend to trust each other, you can't expect me to give you anything you can take to the Champion.*

"Fair enough. But let me play clever little feral for a minute, huh? Your people have something going that'll trigger a major crackdown on Hell— maybe even a minor massacre—which will make a really swell excuse for the full-scale invasion by, say, several divisions of the Ankhanan Army that Deliann has in concealed positions on the border, because he's already been talking with the Lipkan Court about the Poor Oppressed Ogrilloi and the Nasty Oppressing Khryllians and how the Ankhanans Have No Territorial Ambitions, and after all Lipke's still moderately cheesed with the Order for bailing on the Plains War, which means that Deliann can have this place fully invested on maybe two weeks' notice." I spread my hands. "How am I doing?"

*Two weeks? You forget we have rail now. And steamboats.*

"Yeah. I'm still not used to that. I bet the Khryllians aren't, either."

*We're counting on it. What price your help?*

"Lay off the Smoke Hunt."

The Whisper ratcheted down tighter. *Ask for something else.*

"That's what I want."

*Aren't you the man who used to say you can't make a revolution without breaking heads?*

"No," I said. "I'm not. And I didn't come here for your revolution."

*I thought freedom was a kind of religion with you —*

"That's the Cainists. Don't confuse gospel with reality."

*What is the reality?*

"A lot of people ask me that."

*I want you on my side, Caine. I have gone to considerable trouble —*

"My heart's pumping pisswater for your fucking trouble."

Frustration twisted the Whisper into a hiss. *Why is this so important to you?*

I shrugged. "Orbek's my brother. The Black Knives are my clan."

*Oh, please. Since when?*

"I was adopted."

*You are the most preposterous, self-aggrandizing excuse for a —*

"I'm serious about this, Kier. Remember what happens to people who hurt my family."

A whole river of glass bells cascaded off that cliff. *Your adopted ogrillo family!*

"Kier."

Glass kept tinkling. *What?*

"Faith is adopted."

The river of bells flash-froze in midair.

When she finally spoke, her Whisper was very soft, and very slow, and very, very flat, soothing, the way a cautious trainer might speak to an escaped bear. A big, hungry, angry bear.

*Let's say I agree. Let's say I change my plans, shift my resources, and take the risk. What do I get?*

I stood up. "Exactly what you asked for."

The discreetly fist-shaped brass knocker on the reinforced door produced no results, but a knuckle-size rock against the shutter of the lone lamplit window on the second floor produced a voice that was clearly female though in no way recognizably feminine. "Don't do that again. You won't like it if I have to come down."

"You'll like it even less if I have to come up."

The shutter swung open. The silhouette of a squarish head on squarish shoulders appeared just long enough to deliver a nod and a hand-wave toward a black shoulder-breadth archway three steps down from street level. "I've been expecting you. Use the kitchen door."

The sunken walkway led between the townhouses to the garden alley behind. The garden gate was reinforced as well, but I heard the *clack-chank* of a heavy bolt being drawn. The gate swung open.

Nobody there. Nobody visible, anyway.

A head-high panel in the kitchen door stood open, spilling pale lamplight into the back garden's clutter: random weeds dying among rocks, from pea gravel to fragments of boulders the size of chairs. I picked my way through the gloom, nodding thoughtfully at the unavoidable crunch of my footsteps.

The kitchen door swung open. I said to the squarish silhouette, "I thought you quit."

"I resigned my Exoteric post, for which I was cast forth in disgrace into the outer darkness. Disgrace, as you well know, is often useful to the Esoteric Service." The silhouette retreated from the doorway. "Come in. I have a chair for you by the stove."

The kitchen was modest, barely large enough to fit the small coal-fired stove, iron washbasin, and tiny breakfast table with its two leather-upholstered chairs. Another chair, of plain wood, stood near the stove, and it was to this one that she pointed her thick straight cane.

"Sit there until you dry. My front room holds a variety of valuable documents, and I will not have them damaged. Take off your boots if you like."

Instead I stood just inside the doorway. "I'm surprised the Esoterics took you."

"Took me?" T'Passe of Narnen Hill, one-time vice-Ambassador to the Infinite Court, lately the self-appointed apostle of the gospel of Cainism and queen of that permanent hornet's nest in my buttcrack, leaned heavily on her cane for the step or two it took her to reach the table. "It was not a matter of taking me. It was a matter of getting the best use from me."

"You were always—?"

She pointed at a lamp. Its wick flared to life. "Chief of post for Ankhana. Oh, yes—Toa-Sytell's men chose well when they arrested me."

I nodded, frowning, remembering. "I guess . . . you never were afraid. Not even in the Pit. Facing down Serpents. Facing down Orbek."

She shrugged. "Neither were you."

"That's different. I was looking to die."

"Die in the manner of your own choosing. I, conversely, sought to live . . . in the manner of my own choosing. The results were identical because the *fact of choice* was identical; the commitment to absolute freedom. As we Cainists say: *My Will, or I Won't.*"

"Oh, for fuck's sake, don't start, huh?"

She chuckled and waved another lamp alight. "Our Abbey schools do a terrible thing when they teach us to think, eh?"

Her hair had been shaved to a salted stubble over the rumple of scar that swept up and back from her cheekbone across the ruin of her right ear. She lowered herself into the breakfast chair with care that bespoke chronic pain, and sat with her right leg extended while she stripped a sheet of bleached paper from a stack on the table in front of her, then found a pen, an inkwell, and a small sand shaker.

I said, "You've looked better."

She grunted. "You, of course, haven't. Sit."

I shook my head, shrugged, and did as I was told. "That all from Assumption Day?"

She gave me a sidelong look. "And I am so grateful for your concern—though one might be forgiven for wondering, given such concern, why you did not, say, visit me in the embassy's infirmary."

"I did. Before you woke up. You're a lot easier to take when I don't have to listen to you yap."

"We have that in common, then." She dipped the pen and began scratching on the paper. Her head down, not looking at me, she said softly, "The hip is Assumption Day. The ear . . . my most recently previous assignment was . . . difficult. Not everything is about you, my friend."

I made a face. "Since when are we friends?"

"My last assignment was likely the reason Ambassador Raithe was amenable to my request to be transferred here: in the expectation that it would be a quiet posting, where I might recuperate in peace."

"You can give that shit up right now."

"I never held that illusion." Her doughy face came up. I had forgotten how bright and hard her eyes could be. "I knew exactly what I was getting into."

"You're a genius."

"What I am," she said, "is the world's leading authority on *you.*"

I scowled at her. "You said you've been expecting me."

"Yes. Ever since I arrived. What name are you using?"

"Huh?"

"You had been going by Jonathan Fist, yes?" She shuffled through the pages in front of her, frowning, squinting at the rows of close-crabbed writing on them. "At least, that is the name I have for you when you went south, when you instigated that border war along with Orbek and the horse-witch—"

"We didn't instigate anything, we—and how do you *know* that?"

"The name. Some reference to an Artan legend, isn't it?"

I shrugged. "He made a deal he couldn't get out of."

"Ah." She tapped the pen to the end of her nose, smiling. "I should very much like to meet the horse-witch. Did you bring her with you?"

"Will you *stop?*"

"No, of course you wouldn't—primitive masculine-warrior complex— you'd never willingly bring her into danger. You rarely even fight women, let alone kill them—it's clear you've always found it distasteful at best, if not outright intolerable . . . unless they're a different species, of course, which doesn't exactly count, does it? In fact, I believe of all your murders, women account for only—"

"I might add one more if you don't shut up a minute."

She turned a raised eyebrow toward me. "Oh, please. Now: What name are you using?"

"I am very tired," I said. "I am dripping fucking wet and the last meal I managed to eat got spewed all over a cell floor while a Khryllian Knight played handball with my head. You've got a serious problem in this town. All I want to do is dump it on you so I can go get a hot meal and some goddamn sleep, all right?"

"And I am *very* interested in what you have to say. But we will do this in an organized fashion, or we will not do it at all. The name?"

I sighed. "Dominic Shade."

"Ah." She held the pen folded between her hands, but I could glimpse movement on the tabletop: letters scratching themselves into view upon the paper. "Both names by which you have been actually known—during your novitiate and in Kirisch-Nar. You don't think that's a risk?"

I shrugged. "It seemed like less of a risk than lying to Knights of Khryl, magick or not."

"And you are using magickal nonrecognition?"

"A variant on the Eternal Forgetting."

"That was the magick devised by Konnos the Artificer, yes? Used by your late wife in her Simon Jester identity?"

I nodded. "It's supposed to make people unable to connect separate facts about me. That's why I figured to use real names. But I'm not sure it's working very fucking well." I waved a hand at her. "You're evidence of that."

"As you should have expected; thaumaturgic magick is uncertain through-

out the Battleground, the more so in closer proximity to Hell. However—"
She checked her papers again. "As I recall . . . yes, here it is. The Eternal Forgetting is vulnerable to those whose core image of the subject transcends op-
erant identity."

"What the fuck does *that* mean?"

"It's not important. Let's continue. Why did you abandon the Jonathan Fist
identity?"

I'm not going to belt her, I told myself. I'm not. "What are you, writing a
fucking book?"

"Why, yes." She gave me a smile so warmly smug I almost changed my
mind. "Yes, I am."

I dropped my face into my hands instead. "Oh, sweet shivering fuck. I hate
you. Do you have any idea how much I hate you?"

I heard her chuckle. "Stop. You'll hurt my feelings."

"There's *already* a goddamn book on me—"

"I've read it. But it's not really about you; to my reading, it's more about the
damage you inflict on the lives of those around you. My book is to be far more
than his; no mere history, no simple-minded biography, but instead the defin-
itive treatise on your *phenomenon,* rather than your life: you as more than
merely you."

"Oh, god."

"The essence of what makes you *you:* the quintessential spirit of the Caine
in us all. Which is, after all, my sole interest. Cainism will never be a pure phi-
losophy, a truly useful and universal moral compass, until that essence can be
carved free of your unfortunately messy reality."

"It'd be a better moral compass if you fuckers had named it after somebody
else."

She didn't seem to hear. "Why do you think I requested Purthin's Ford?
This was the site, after all, of your functional apotheosis. This was where
you—"

"How much have you got on this book?"

"Well—I'm still compiling my notes—"

"So I don't have to kill you *tonight.*"

"Oh, please. You don't kill—nor harm, nor even hurt—merely to protect
your vanity. You never have."

"I'm trying to outgrow that. What the hell is a 'functional apotheosis'?—ah,
forget I asked. I don't want to know." I jerked myself upright and tracked wet
footprints across the kitchen floor. I picked up one of the lamps and weighed
it in my hand.

When I drifted behind her toward the inner door, her cane thumped horizontally into the wall across my path. A subtle spin of her forefinger—and the wick wheel of the lamp in my hand turned exactly the same amount. Down. The lamp went out.

"My mistake," she said. "I should never have mentioned the documents in my front room—though you see I can anticipate, and easily thwart, your attempt to dominate our conversation by threatening my work."

I sighed down at the curl of smoke rising up the lamp's glass chimney. "I ought to just crack your goddamn skull with it."

"And how, exactly, will that persuade me to use Monastic resources to help you rescue Orbek?"

I stared at her.

"That is why you're here tonight. Don't trouble to deny it."

"I'm talking to you," I said heavily, "because the Council of Brothers needs to know what's going on in this fucking town."

"Horseshit."

"What?"

"Horse," she repeated precisely. "Shit. I repeat: I am the world's leading authority on you. I *know* Orbek—know him well, as you'll recall. I know you. And I know that there is nothing you will not say or do to save the life of someone you care about. It's a matter of principle, isn't it?"

"Which is why the Council needs to hear this from you. Because nobody believes a sonofabitching word I say anymore."

"And why will *I* believe you?"

"Because," I said, "you're the world's leading authority on me."

She frowned. I could see gears clicking behind her face.

I had her. I just needed to set the hook.

"So I'm a liar," I said. "You're the expert: Talk to me about my lies."

"Ah . . ." She sat up, her eyes brightening. "Ah, yes . . . the lies you fed the King of Cant to trigger the riots that led to the Second Ankhanan Succession War—that you would show Ma'elKoth to be an Aktir before the entire city . . ."

"Yeah."

"The lies you told us in the Pit, to build the morale of the condemned before Assumption Day . . . even as you were being taken to your death in the Shaft, *still* you lied . . . and yet . . . and yet—"

"Yeah. And yet."

"And Ambassador Raithe—his account of your accord with the Ascended Ma'elKoth is in the Embassy Archives in Ankhana—when you agreed, *falsely* agreed to surrender . . ."

"Yeah."

"And in every case," she murmured, her eyes alight with distant awe, "your lies became truth . . ."

"It makes me a little careful about what I say to people, you know what I mean?"

"Caine, I—" Her brittle voice had gone breathless. She sounded very, very young, and I caught a glimpse of the girl she must have been forty years ago, before the world had crushed the best of her dreams. "*Caine . . .*"

It sounded like a prayer.

I had to turn away. "Look, don't get on your knees or anything. Just keep your goddamn magick ink thing going so you can read this back when you make your report. You know how I got jobbed here in the first place?"

Her brows contracted. "You approached the Abbot of—I could look up the exact details in only a moment—ah, Tremaine Vale, yes, with intelligence on a semi-private expedition out of Prethrainnaig. Partially funded by the Kannithan Legion. In search of some primal Relic—something to do with Panchasell Mithondionne—"

"It was this big-ass gem called the Tear of Panchasell. According to the *Lay of the Twilight King,* it was formed of Panchasell's weeping for the Folk trapped behind in the Quiet Land when he sealed the *dil T'llan* against the Blind God."

"The oral histories of the First Folk are notoriously—"

"Yeah, I know. Call it a metaphor."

"Yes. A pity we cannot examine the Tear itself." She coughed delicately. "I do recall, now, reading your report . . ."

I waved that off. "You know what the *dil T'llan* is?"

She shrugged. "Primal is a tricky tongue; nearly every word has a variety of related meanings, depending on context. *Dil* can mean path, or maze, or gate, or wall. *T'llan* is the Primal for the moon. It's also a proper name for the moon, which they consider a person. It's also the name of their goddess who takes the moon as Her Aspect. It's also a descriptive modifier for anything that undergoes regular phase changes, or that is seen mostly but not always at night, or is related to tidal effects, or—"

"Yeah, yeah. In simple terms: the *dillin* are gateways to the Quiet Land. What the Primals call the Quiet Land is what you call Arta."

Her eyes widened. "Your world. The Aktiri world. Yes: as I said, I've read Deliann's book."

"In my home language it's called *Earth.* The Khryllians call it the True Hell, and that's as good a name for it as any. You might remember the last time my people decided to show up in force. We call it Assumption Day."

She lifted her cane and grimaced. "I was there."

"Yeah, well, sometime around a thousand years ago, this Panchasell started to understand what my people were going to be capable of. That's when he decided to close the *dillin*. That's what he did with the *dil T'llan*. Shut them. Shut them all."

"Impossible."

"No, it isn't."

"The primals may be the greatest spellcasters of Home, but no mortal could wield power of that magnitude—not even Ma'elKoth, prior to His Assumption. Across the *world*? Overload would have incinerated even Him like one of His own Firebolts. To close the *dillin* for even a moment, let alone a thousand years—eight hundred years after Panchasell's *death*—"

"You said it. No one mortal."

"Ah." Her eyes narrowed, then widened again. "A Power?"

"Yeah. An Outside Power." Knots that I hadn't noticed tying themselves in my guts started to wrench tighter. "*The* Outside Power. The god of the Black Knives."

"But even so—were It Bound to the Tear, to channel so much—"

"No. The Tear was . . . just a device. The Tear gave It control over the river. Let It control the local weather, start the odd wildfire, whatever. The Tear was what let It make the Boedecken into the Boedecken Waste."

She was looking off into the distance, now, far beyond the walls.

"Outside Powers feed on anguish," I said. "Not just human anguish. Panchasell made It master of the Waste, letting things grow here just enough to suffer. And when the Black Knives would offer it, well, snacks—extra power— it could pay them with power in return."

I looked out the kitchen window, out over the garden toward the face of Hell. "It still does."

"You're saying it's still here."

"I'm saying here is what it is." I waved a hand out her window into the darkness. "This is it. *That's* it. The *dil T'llan*. Right there."

"How do you *know* all this?" Her voice was hushed, but with awe, not disbelief.

"You said you read my report."

"But—but for all these years—"

"Shit, t'Passe, I was a kid. I didn't know what I knew. It wasn't until three years ago that anybody other than Ma'elKoth and my dad knew that the Quiet Land was Earth—y'know, Arta—and my dad was fucking crazy. It's not like the Outside Power understands what it's doing; it's not even really sentient, as near as I could or can comprehend. It's just a bundle of bizarre fucking tropisms that exists on the far side of reality. That's how the Black Knife bitches could use It without Binding It: It was already Bound here. With the right kind of attunement, the part of It that made contact with a bitch's mind would automatically resonate with her intention. Goddamn reverse theurgy."

"But even so—how is this the concern of the Monasteries?"

"It's not. Not directly. It's the concern of the Empire. Because BlackStone Mining is an Artan operation—run, most likely, by Aktiri and Overworld Company goons trapped here on Assumption Day—that has found a way to control the *dil T'llan*."

"How do you know *this*?"

"Not important. The point is: there's an Ankhanan insurgency already operating in Purthin's Ford."

"This Smoke Hunt?"

"Freedom's Face."

"Oh, please, Caine—we know all about—"

"You think you do. Among all those idealistic starry-eyed middle-class Ankhanan kids are hard-core covert operatives—most of them probably primal, concealed under different types of Illusion, but maybe humans too. Thaumaturgic Corps adepts, Grey Cats, I don't even know what. They're here to take out the Artans and regain control of the *dil T'llan*, but the Artans are under Khryllian protection. And nobody knows how much the Khryllians know about what the Artans are up to. One thing I know for sure is that this whole city's about to go up in flames."

"And how do you know this?"

I looked her right in the eye. "Because *I'm* here."

Her answering stare went thoughtful.

"You need to get this in a report to the Council of Brothers right away, and they need to get—at the very least—a reinforced strike team inserted into Purthin's Ford just as fast as the fuckers can friarpace. This may be the our only opportunity."

"Opportunity?"

I took a deep breath. "The Order of Khryl has at least one, probably two, True Relics."

The pen in her hands snapped with a sound like a breaking finger. "You cannot be serious."

"I could be wrong. But I don't think so."

"Caine, it's impossible. We would know."

"Sure you would. They're here, in Purthin's Ford, and they're in use. Regular, everyday ritual practice."

"But they—" She let the fragments of her pen drop to the floor and passed a hand over her eyes. After a moment, she said softly, "What sort of ritual?"

"Some kind of Atonement. It seems to be something that is a guaranteed privilege of any ordained Knight. Beyond that, I'm not sure."

I held out my right hand, opening and closing my fingers meditatively. With just the faintest breath of mindview, I could see the power of Khryl's Blood shining there. "The True Relic I think they have—one I can't confirm, but I'm pretty sure—is Khryl's Hand."

Her face was white as the bleached sheet on the table beside her. "The Butcher's Fist . . ."

"They call it the Hand of Peace."

"They would."

"I think they've had it all along; I think Ma'elKoth built it into the Spire for them. I think it's the only reason the Spire can stand at all."

"You *think*?"

I shrugged. "Ma'elKoth and I are not on speaking terms these days. There's some source of power holding that fucking monstrosity up. I can't imagine anything less than a True Relic would be reliable."

"The fortress of their faith," t'Passe murmured. Her bloodless lips quirked toward a smile but missed it on the twitchy side. "That would suit Ma'elKoth's, mmm, I suppose one might call it His sense of humor. Or artistic irony, perhaps: to build the Order of Khryl an impregnable keep founded upon a True Relic of their god—their worship itself upholding their Eternal Vault . . ."

"Yeah. Look at me laughing. The other True Relic is one the Council's gonna be even more interested in. You better tell Ambassador Raithe too. This one I can personally confirm; I was close enough to touch it. They've got the hilt to what they call the Accursèd Blade."

I dropped back into the chair by the stove and tried to swallow the sick twist in my stomach. "It's the Sword of Man."

T'Passe's cane thumped on the floor. Both hands on its head, she shoved herself upright. "This—this would not be a Relic—Jereth was no god—"

"It's a Relic. Whatever the Godslaughterer might have been—whatever his sword might have been—it's for motherfucking sure a True Relic *now*."

"How—?"

"How should I know? Let the giant brains at the Monasteries figure it out; what the hell else are you good for?"

"Well . . . I suppose," she murmured, frowning, "having struck the defining wound to their god would Fetishize it for them considerably . . ."

"They're not the only ones who Fetishize the goddamn thing. We call it the Sword of fucking *Man*, for shit's sake."

She stopped and turned to squint at me. "This is more than your reflexive hostility. You are *angry*. What has you angry about this?"

I found myself panting through clenched teeth. "Here's another one for you giant brains," I said. "This is what I think you better share with Raithe. I'm telling you: I was *this* close to that fucking thing. It's *old*. It's easily the five-hundred-plus years old it'd have to be. And it's been in the Knights' possession a long damned time, maybe all five hundred years. And they don't show it to Incommunicants. But I've seen it before. I've held it in my *hand*. So has Raithe."

"I don't understand."

"Me neither." I stared into the flames within the stove. "I had that fucking thing sticking out of my guts eleven years ago. Three years ago I jammed it through Ma'elKoth's face."

"Caine, what are you talking about?"

"The Sword of Man, the Accursèd Blade, whateverthefuck you want to call it." I met her eyes, and my voice emptied out.

I said, "I'm pretty sure it's Kosall."

# *CAULDRON*

*W*et

cool wet sting lips tongue throat

water fuck me it's *water*

hakHAKH

fuck that hurts

fuck hurts just breathe

breathe

a pinhole star in the void bright and brightening and going red and wind hushing to a roar and the star screams toward me and yawns beyond the universe—

And I'm awake. And it wasn't a dream.

I'm still on the cross.

Tilted back so I can breathe. Must be some—

It's Crowmane. Cold yellow eyes framed with gloss feathers gleaming black-red in the light from the bonfires. Looking in her face feeds the furnace in my chest with dreams of fist-fucking her eye sockets.

She lifts a dipper to my lips and I take a mouthful of cool clean water—fuck me, it *is* water, it *is*—and I spit it on her anyway.

Try to.

My gut just won't push that hard right now.

Water dribbles down my chin and neck and chest and some of it goes down my throat, and y'know, if she'd bring that dipper up again I'd just fucking *drink* it, but instead her raw-liver lips peel back around her tusks and she says something to me, waving down at the lower tier with the dipper, splashing carelessly the water that is my sole hope of heaven, painting the retaining wall with little black wet dustballs that I would gladly lick off her asshole just to get that moisture past my lips . . .

Down where she points, the other bitches have Pretornio.

Shit, they haven't even stripped him yet. I couldn't have been out more than a couple of minutes.

Shit.

I wanted to miss this one.

Next to where the bitches hold him rises a pole seven feet tall, blunt as a knuckle and big around as my wrist. It's fixed on a sprawling iron stand so it won't tip over when he starts to struggle. I wish I could look away. I have, y'know, some, what you might call, issues with anal penetration. In general. And this will be, y'know —

Overly specific.

I *really* wanted to sleep through this.

I wish there were some way I could stop myself from imagining how it'll feel.

The bitches go to work on his clothing, cutting it off so they can strip him without opening his shackles, and he's still staring up at me — I mean, it *looks* like he's staring up at me, kind of, in a sick way — with that same stupid dreamy smile he had when he begged me to pick him for this. Which is bone-fucking creepy on a face with only clot-crusted holes where eyes used to be.

Well, this is what you asked for, man. You can fuck me if I have a clue why.

Under his robes he's all soft and white. It's hard to look. I mean, sure, priests don't have to be athletes, even Kannithan priests, but shit he's got these little saggy man-tits . . . and when they cut away his pants, his crotch is just a thatch of mud-colored hair.

Huh. Since when is Dal'kannith one of those, y'know, those full-castration type of—

Oh.

Holy shit. I get it. I get it now. Those aren't *man*-tits.

Pretornio—

He's a chick.

## >>scanning fwd>>

When the world comes all the way back the smell is still turd-smoke and old meat; the feel is still easterly breeze on my face and my chest and my balls but not on arms and legs that are numb as the wood they're nailed to. The sound on the wind is still Pretornio's voice, gone high and ragged, still chanting away in Old High Lipkan, and when my eyes fall open she's still impaled on the pole like a trout on a fish spear.

Doesn't wriggle, though.

Me, I'd be thrashing with everything I've got. Drive my weight down onto the blunt end of the pole. *Make* it rip through me. End it fast.

She's perfectly still. Must be holding out for something from Dal'kannith.

Good fucking luck.

Moon's out, way over in the west. The top bitches are back up here. I catch Crowmane's voice behind me, and Dugsacks leans on the retaining wall and chews wood-roasted meat off what looks a little like it could be half a giant chicken wing but is actually the forearm of somebody I know.

Knew.

Maybe somebody who died in the fight. Stalton. Rababàl. Maybe somebody who's died since. Somebody I chose. Maybe Kess, or Nollo.

Maybe Tizarre.

Dugsacks sees me watching her eat and tosses the arm to Cornholes, who gives me a friendly snort that sounds like a lion's cough because each of her nostrils is bigger around than my dick. Teasingly, mockingly, she lifts the arm up within reach of my teeth.

So I take a bite.

Why not? Better than a sop of vinegar. Tastes good too.

The ridges of flesh that serve her for eyebrows pop wide. While I chew, she chuckles and says something to the other bitches and they hoot and when she turns back and lifts her head to laugh up at me, I figure my gut's recovered some. I make an experiment: I spit the hunk of somebody-I-know in her eye.

Dammit. Wanted it up her nose.

She starts for me and Crowmane stops her with an authoritative bark. Dugsacks says something that gets a laugh from the other bitches and Cornholes' eyes bulge and she whaps Dugsacks a good one with the roasted arm and they go for each other and Crowmane has to wade in personally, and while they're all still hooting and clawing and shrieking and struggling—

This place is suddenly getting *light* . . .

Shadows sharpen and stone glares and what exactly the hell is going on here? Not dawn. Can't be. Dawn here is vermillion dust. This light's yellow as a lamp and it's coming from—

It's coming from—

Hot staggering fuck. Pretornio's on *fire*.

A crown of flames fans the night from her skull, lightning-blue where it springs from naked bone, rising to a sunflower spray, and across the badland camp Black Knives turn and stand and stare, and the world goes quiet except for the night wind's whisper and the harsh spit of flame. Flesh has burned off her spine, and the exposed bone spits a column of blue blaze up to join her crown, bright as an arc-welder. Bright as a star.

Shit, she's in overload.

And she's still chanting . . .

Guess Dal'kannith's coming through for her after all. With something Old fucking Testament.

The bitches have forgotten about me now. They've forgotten about each other. They line the retaining wall, staring down in brain-dead stupefaction at their homemade fusion torchsicle.

Crowmane recovers first. She roars something into the camp, where awed Black Knives have stopped eating and fucking and gambling and everything else to stand and stare with stupid looks scorching into their warthog faces. Crowmane roars again, and a couple of bucks grab a water barrel and run at Pretornio. This tickle in my guts might be the pre-echo of an oncoming laugh. They're gonna be sorry.

The bucks skid to a stop at the base of the impale-o-matic and heave the barrel. A gout of water splashes up onto her and power explodes through it like a fuel-air bomb. The shockwave blasts cook fires into showers of burning shit and shreds tents and sends ogrilloi tumbling. What's left of the two bucks looks like Daffy Duck after the dynamite goes off in his beak.

And Pretornio chants on.

Another roar from Crowmane. Bucks scramble to string their bows, and four-foot arrows as big around as my thumb zip out of the night and smack into her unresisting flesh with a stutter of flat whaps like bored applause.

Every one of them bursts aflame: instant torches fed with her melting body fat. And I finally manage that laugh.

The laugh shakes me. It rocks me. It rips barb-wire chunks off my ass-boned-to-Neverland diaphragm. I don't mind.

It always did hurt.

"Hey . . ." Dead crows wheeze better than that, if they're fresh enough. Nobody even looks around. "Hey . . . dumb cunts . . ."

Gahh. Throat's worse'n my gut.

Fuck it anyway.

I suck a fold of lip between my teeth and bite down and thick salt-black metal syrup slides down into my throat before I give myself time to think about drowning in my own blood.

"*Hey*, you stupid goddamn *cows*—"

Dugsacks turns and gives me the fisheye. I gasp strength back into my lungs. "Tell your head shit-suck over there that you have maybe two minutes. Maybe three. Then it's fucking *over* for you."

Next to Crowmane at the retaining wall, Cornholes snarls something savage over her shoulder at Dugsacks, who snarls something back and Cornholes raises a fist that'd stun a buffalo but Crowmane's all over them again and one of her hands has gathered unto itself all the reality there is to be had here on the parapet, and I simply and purely dream-certain *know* that if they get seriously into it right now, she'll make them seriously dead before either of them can seriously blink.

They know it too. Cornholes shuts the hell up. Dugsacks mutters something, and Crowmane barks at her. Dugsacks flinches, and says whatever it was again, louder.

Now Crowmane looks at me. The hyper-real shimmer around her hand swells toward my face, and when she growls something that sounds like *nerroll pagganik torrin nezz, paggtakkuni*, the eldritch dream-knowing tells me that she means *What do you whimper, little rabbit?*

I lift my head enough to give her a look at my teeth. "I know what she's doing. I can tell you about it. Maybe in time."

She swivels her swinging tits toward me and gives me a toss of the crowfeather headdress. *Nershrannik pagannol. Pelshragikk laggan?*

*Why do you tell me? Why do I listen?*

"Because I want off this fucking cross." More panting brings enough strength to go on. "Because you know it."

One pace closer. The other bitches cluster instinctively at her shoulders. Those yellow eyes never flicker. *Pagallo nezziokk. Burshraggikko ymik treyy, paggtakkuni. Ymik.*

*Talk now. Later I take you down, little rabbit. Later.*

"I got your little rabbit for you right here, you stupid fucking cunt. You want to play games? Fine. I'll die up here. Laughing." I cough a wad of blood out of my throat and manage a spit that sprays it across her face. "Because I get to watch *you* die down *there*."

She doesn't flinch at my blood. She doesn't even blink. The flarelight from Pretornio's overload has gone stark white, crowning Crowmane with a halo of starfire. *Pagallo nezziokk.*

*Talk now.*

Out of the west come the low skirling whispers of storm winds spinning up over gravel-scoured badlands, rising into the hush where I can still hear the hiss and snap of the lightning-blue corona of flame and the high, thin sound of Pretornio's voice, still chanting, still screaming her invocation to her god while His power burns away her breasts and her fingers and her cheeks and her eyebrows and her scream loses words and spirals upon itself into the simple shriek of superheated gases that opens into an end-of-the-world thunderclap.

A whipcrack shock blasts out and over us and the camp and the vertical city and the badlands. Every bonfire and torch and hurricane lamp and even fucking *candle* flares into instant firestorms that claw for the stars—

And go out.

Darkness. Only a sliver of moon, and embers swirling toward the sky.

And near-to-silence, while night-blind Black Knives pick themselves up and try to discover just how badly hurt they all might be.

Shapes moving in the ink pool below my cross: Crowmane and her bitches. One of them murmurs, and a parapet stone casts sickly green light enough to let them find their feet.

Out in the camp, all that's left of Pretornio is a smoldering ember on the end of half the impale-o-matic.

Three feet of vertical cigar.

Crowmane's a little singed, but by the time she's on her feet she's pulled herself together and is already shouting orders down into the camp, getting torches relit, bonfires rekindled, burns tended.

To the west, the storm winds whisper themselves up to moans.

And I just hang here. And watch.

I watch Crowmane and Dugsacks and Cornholes and Thumbnipples and Turdcrotch and all the rest of them look around and check themselves out and chuckle at each other and convince themselves that they were never really scared in the first place. That the stupid Lipkan bitch-on-a-stick just didn't have the juice, when the balls hit the butthole. I watch them get their party going again with an extra kicker because they had a little thrill but it's all over now.

I watch Crowmane giving her orders, wielding her handful of Reality, striding back and forth on the parapet doing her Cinerama Tits-to-the-Wind Napoleon thing without even turning me one more glance.

I only watch. I don't say a word.

Because I was just, y'know, making that shit up. About knowing what Pretornio was doing. It was just a story to get me off this cross long enough to get my teeth into Crowmane's throat. That's all it was. But that's not all it *is*.

Here's a nifty thing about my Monastic education—

It tells me, for one thing, that we have time right now for a history lesson, if I make it quick.

The Monasteries were founded by Jantho of Tyrnall at the end of what people here call the Deomachy—the God War. When gods go to war, it's an ugly thing—that whole Armageddon Rag, Ragnarok'n'Roll shit. It's never really over till everybody's dead. That's what got Jantho Ironhand's brother Jereth up in arms; he decided to make the God War as ugly for the gods as it was for the poor bastards who worshipped them, which brought the Deomachy to a relatively swift and bloody end. Bloody on all sides. Though Jereth didn't survive the war, he is reputed, before his death, to have kicked substantial deific butt.

His epithet is "the Godslaughterer."

The Deomachy is why Our Founder, Jantho Ironhand, was of the considered opinion that the greatest threat to humanity's survival on Home was our unfortunate tendency to murder people for bowing down to the wrong gods, and the gods' unfortunate tendency to take advantage of *our* unfortunate tendencies, to play power games just because they can.

The whole murdering-people-because-we-like-their-land—and murdering them as an oh-well-what-the-hell side effect of making money and murdering them because, y'know, it's the kind of fun you just can't get anywhere else—those were all side issues for ol' Jantho, so the Monasteries didn't start worrying about any of that shit till later on. Of course, most religions get into those businesses eventually, too.

So a lot of what the Monasteries do is keep an eye on the gods, and on their worshippers; a lot of what we in the Esoteric Service do is get ourselves bloody when some of these religions look to start running a little wild.

So we have to know the gods. All of them. And their religions—which, of course, often don't have a whole lot to do with their particular gods, but let that go. We're encouraged to be consecrated to some god's worship and rise in their service, even their priesthood. So Monastics know a lot of, well, esoteric shit, if you'll pardon the expression, about every major religion. Including some of the splinter sects that follow Dal'kannith Wargod.

This is why I'm sounding kind of fucking cheerful right now.

When I said I knew what Pretornio was up to, yeah, I was lying . . . but, y'know, funny fucking thing. I was also telling the truth. Just took me a while to remember.

Probably that dying-on-a-cross thing screwing with my concentration a little.

And maybe it was because I was still thinking she was praying to Dal'Kannith . . .

They were supposed to have died out or been suppressed—I can't remember—something like two hundred years ago. That might be another reason. The *trehv'Dhalleig Jzranapal*, if my memory can be trusted, something like that anyway—the Silent Pure, more or less. Reluctant hostage-sacrifices from Chi'iannon to her son/husband/master Dal'Kannith, so the story runs—but really they were more like Home-grown Joans of Arc, strapping down their tits and stuffing fake codpieces and becoming, before the world, full Kannithan battle-priests. Often the most powerful Kannithan priests, in fact, so long as their secret was never exposed. And so long as they stayed virgins.

Surrendering virginity surrendered power. But surrendering virginity's one thing. Rape is something else.

The Great Mother of the Lipkan pantheon rules the dead as well as the unborn—because, y'know, they're the same, right?—and there is one tale in the Monastic Record, one fucking scary one, of an incident in Paquli's Western Marches some three hundred and change years ago, in the Vale of the Dead, when one of the Silent Pure called upon Chi'iannon, instead of Dal'Kannith, while being murdered by sexual mutilation. Want to know why it's called Vale of the Dead?

Wait—

Hear that?

Those low swirling storm wind moans from the west? I know you can hear them. You're using my ears. Hear them ramping up toward the howls of a full gale? The question is, how long before those storm winds catch the attention of Crowmane and her bitches?

How long will it take them to notice that the wind they can feel is only a medium breeze? And it's coming from the *east*. And then, sooner or later, eventually, maybe, one of them's gonna remember that all there is *west* of the camp . . .

Is the funerary platforms.

Those winds you're hearing with my ears—I bet you guessed it already. That's not wind. It's howls of mindless insatiate hunger.

The voices of the dead.

There's a storm coming out of the west all right, but it ain't fuckin' *weather*.

### >>scanning fwd>>

"—your ass till it comes out your ears. Had your chance." I'd need the voice of a civil defense siren to be heard over the screams and howling from the horror show in the camp, but I'm pretty sure Crowmane catches my meaning anyway.

I laugh down into her smoking yellow stare. "I'm comfortable right here."

My instructor in Applied Legendry at Garthan Hold—Brother Clement, his name was—I remember him bloviating about the Vale of the Dead story: *How minor incidents become exaggerated to preposterous degrees over only a few years. . . . Clearly impossible for a single individual, no matter how com-*

*plete her attunement, to channel power sufficient for* yammana yammana yammana bullshit. Pompous old fuck.

Wish he could be down in that camp right now.

The rest of the top bitches have joined the final defense perimeter, a thick wall of wide-eyed, flared-nostril, clenched-jaw fight-to-the-death determination between the howling chaos of the camp and the corral area where they've got all their cubs and juvies. Their last line of defense, with all the power they've got left. Dunno how much it is. Down in the camp, Black Knife bucks have given up on arrows and spears to use whatever heavy cleaving shit they can lay hands on to hack desperately at the arms and legs of writhing howling shadows that are all teeth and claws and hunger.

I think the bucks might be winning, might have a pretty good chance of containing the corpses and chopping them down. It's hard to tell.

Goddamn shame so many of 'em we killed went down sliced in half by my bladewand, or with spines or legs crushed by Marade's morningstar or arms severed or legs hamstrung by Pretornio's porters. If we'd left their dead in better shape, this would have been a shitload more entertaining. But, y'know . . .

It's still not bad.

From the foot of my cross, Crowmane shows me her age-greyed tusks and sends a wave of dream-Real threat up to close over my head.

*You think it can't be worse for you. I tell you it can.*

I show her my own teeth. Probably pretty fucking grey by this time, too. "Now you're just flirting."

She snarls up at me and squeezes her ball of Reality—

—and my days of death on the scaffold rewind within my head in a harlequin whirl of white-noon blaze and black-ice midnight until the dead cold carved-oak tree limbs that are nailed to the arms of the cross and connected still somehow to my shoulders and hips spasm and jerk—

Hang on to your balls, kids. My arms and legs . . .

She's bringing them back.

Ligaments twist barbwire through acid-etched joints. Muscle fibers ripped in handfuls like hair from my head, steelclamped around the spikes—

I can *feel* the *spikes* again . . .

Iron on naked bone scraping blossoms of screaming midnight off my arms—ankles—

Gahh.

Gahhhh.

Fucking pain center . . . got *that* going again too . . . betcha . . . *noticed,* huh . . . ?

huhh—

the spasms and the twisting and the spurt of tears into the blood that trails from my lips—

tellya . . . secret . . .

secret to—

—*gahhhhh*—

The secret to great Acting.

Huh.

Huh fuck huh.

Here's the, the, the secret to great Acting—

*give the people what they want.*

So I finally let it out: the howling and the sobbing and shit, sure, she's seen me cry already and she's heard me moan and sob but here it is: I finally let it all hang out.

All the the begging for mercy.

All the pleading that she just fucking *end* it I don't *care* anymore just make it *stop*—

All the weak sad shit I've been sucking back and swallowing ever since I first saw that buck stand up in the badlands.

I give it up. I give it all up.

"I'll *tell* you I *swear* I'll tell you *anything*—it's the Cauldron of *Chi'iannon*, all right? I know about it! I *know*! *Please*—just get me *down*—! Just make it stop . . ."

Fading now: a broken whisper.

Broken like me.

". . . *just get me down. I'll tell you everything . . . please . . .*"

And because she wields a piece of Reality in her right hand, she knows my pain is real. She knows my break is real.

She knows I'm telling the truth.

She goes to the big wheel-crank that controls the angle of my scaffold and turns it until my cross becomes a timber bed. A curl of contempt twists her lips around her tusks. She slashes the ropes that tie me to the cross with the filed-sharp fighting claw below her left hand. She leans across my face, and with the same hand she yanks on the spike through my right arm. The wood squeals as it comes free, and my arm comes with it and my shoulder's silent roar is loud enough to grey out the universe.

Annnnnd . . .

When the world comes to life, I'm off the cross.

Under my back—

—night-cold *stone*—

Oh god—

Oh god oh god I *made* it. I'm off the fucking cross.

I made it.

Thank you. Oh, thank you.

The night gathers force in my ears: roars and screams. Smell of burning shit and hair and rotten meat.

Pressure on my chest crushes my sobbing down to thick gasps, then to a choked hush. I open my eyes. It's Crowmane's foot.

Long as my forearm. Wide as my hand span. Toenails hooked enough to draw blood from my chest. Her eyes smoke yellow into the stars around her head. Reality pulses around her right hand. *Talk now, little rabbit. Talk of this Chi'iannon's Cauldron. Tell me how I stop it.*

Shit.

Gahh. She left—

Fucking spikes're *still* in my wrists—

And—ahh, fuck me, fuck me, she left my *ankles* nailed together, ahh, fuck—

Guess I can give right the hell up on that quick getaway.

*Talk now, little rabbit.*

So I meet her eyes and give her the truth I promised. "You can't stop it."

Without transition her huge foot is on my throat—so goddamn *wide* she's breaking my sonofabitching *neck*—

*Tell this again, little rabbit. Tell this for the last time.*

If she weren't crushing my throat right now, I'd tell her I love her.

With weakly trembling hands, I scrabble at her ankle, then let my arms fall back, right thrown across my face to mask what she's got to think is despair.

Hands work. So do arms. Maybe even legs, if I can take the pain.

She did this for me. And I'm off the cross. She did that for me too.

I love her very, very much.

I don't need Control Disciplines. The singing in my ears makes the night a wonderland of shimmer and fades the screams and roaring into a distant melody of blood.

Darling . . . they're playing our *song* . . .

From behind my right elbow I manage some whimpering gasps around her huge clawed foot on my neck. "Y'can't . . . *stop the spell—'s done—all y'can do . . . 's chop 'm up and burn 'm . . .*"

She leans over me, shifting weight onto the foot-wide paw on my neck. My cervical vertebrae pop and crackle as the ligaments stretch. Her drool drips down across my face. It smells of rot. *Been too gentle with you, little rabbit.*

I shift my left hand three inches. Her eyes never flicker. She didn't pick up

the motion. The heel of my left hand is now against the head of the spike
through my right wrist.

Oh, my god, how I love this bitch.

*Some ideas I save. Something special.*

I love her so much, I'm going to fuck her.

*Special just for little—*

Right swinging backhand from my left armpit, left jamming like a short
shovel-hook and I can't get much on them but together I don't need a whole
hell of a lot. The spike through my right wrist spears deep into the side of her
knee.

It grates on bone and I can't tell if it's mine or hers but I'm balls-up
adrenoamped far beyond feeling any fucking pain.

She jerks like I clamped a high-tension line to her nipples and says—

"...*hurkk*..."

—and I give the head of the spike another good whack with the heel of my
left hand, and this time the bone it grates on is the inside of her kneecap because when she yanks back her leg, the spike rips down and jams behind her
patellar tendon, so her yank of the leg yanks me with it by the spike, which sits
me up and plants her foot within the loop of my pinned-together legs and
slams my battered nervous system hard enough to grey the world down by better than half—

But there is a fundamental difference between her and me. On the street, in
the ring, on Adventure—so many times I've been half out or better, so greyed I
didn't know where my fucking legs were, hurt, cut, bleeding, having to use one
hand to hang onto my guts while I try to cover my head with the other—

I can deal.

Crowmane, though—what is she? She's no Marade, no Pretornio. She's
not even a Tizarre. When you carve all the way to nuts and guts, Crowmane's
just a bitch with a shitty attitude, playing games with somebody else's power.

Which is why when some of the world is slipping back into focus she's still
screaming like a brain-damaged howler monkey and trying to shake me off her
leg.

It's only now that she remembers she's got better than a hundred pounds on
me and a razor-sharp fighting claw curving around the fist that is directly over
my head.

All I can do is bring up my left as her right comes down and in the last in-
finitesimal fraction of a second I register the relationship between her fist and
my forearm and an image blossoms and my forearm adjusts its angle without
interference from my brain.

Her fist comes down. Her fighting claw spears into my trapezius and scrapes my collarbone but goes no deeper because my block braced my left forearm across my head which set the spike in that forearm against my skull like a spear grounded to receive a horseman's charge.

The horseman, in this case, is Crowmane's fist.

She takes the spike between the second and third knuckle and she jerks again, rearing up, yowling—

Which is when we both remember that the fist she just punched me with, the fist I just spiked, was her right.

The one holding that ball of Reality—

whiteout

The world darkens back into existence . . .

Still pinned together—my forearm to her knee—

Not pinned forearm to fist anymore. She doesn't have a fist. Just a stump of charred bone.

A snap of my left arm whips the white-hot remnant of the spike out of my charring flesh, and there is a bleak red light shining up on her and from the smell and the pain I'm guessing that my hair's on fire, and I don't give half a mouthful of shit. That spike was grounded against my skull.

We've been joined by the Outside Power.

She's looking down at me, and in those yellow eyes now is the greatest gift she will ever give me.

Fear.

Because we Know each other now. And the punkass bleeding heart who said "To understand all is to forgive all" wasn't from my fucking neighborhood.

I grin up at her. "Shaikkak Nerutch'khaitan . . ."

I roll her name around in my mouth.

"Skaikkak Nerutch'khaitan—" My left hand spasms with nerve shock from the burn through my forearm; I let the spasm beckon to her. "I believe this is my dance."

Her stump and her left hand make an off-balance pinwheel when she tries to backstroke into the night sky. I throw my weight forward when her heel hits my nailed-together ankles, and my forearm spike comes free from behind her kneecap and I keep the momentum going forward so that I can roll up onto one shrieking foot and shove myself up her leg and hook my left arm behind her neck. My weight captures her balance, and she keeps on staggering backward.

Behind her is the perimeter wall and beyond that there is nothing but coils of black turd smoke spinning toward the sky.

Guess this is my star exit.

Finally.

Good-bye, fuckers. Good-bye all of you sacks of shit who're watching at home with your dicks in your hand or a thumb up your snatch.

Hope you had a good time, and kiss my ass.

The perimeter wall hits her above the knees, crushing my nailed ankles into a snarling white flare inside my head, and the wall's just barely high enough to hold her, so I crook my arm behind her neck and croon lovingly into her rumpled mass of ear—

"When you wake up in Hell, you festering slab of rat cunt, I'll already be killing you *again*."

—and I backhand the point of my forearm spike at her right eye.

Nothing wrong with her reflexes: she jerks her head back and away from the point—

—and so the spike—

—which I hadn't really expected to get her eye with, y'know, anyway, so there's no point in shitcanning my follow-through—

—takes her just under the cheekbone, above her upper jaw, into what on a human would be a savagely sensitive nerve cluster around the trigeminal—

—triggering a transcendently satisfying airhorn shriek and instant stiff hyperarch of her back—

Guess ogrilloi keep a nerve cluster there, too.

—and we topple over the wall.

With a kick that's half convulsion I yank my ankles apart as we start our long slow tumble into the darkness.

Why not? Like our Garthan Hold personal combat Brother used to say—

Hurts now. Be over soon.

Gahh—

—'d like to hear that fucker say it *again* with a fifty-penny *nail* behind his motherfucking Achilles tendon—

But I still swing my legs around and wrench her thrashing underneath me as we fall free, because I am for ass-raping sure gonna land on—

*Wham.*

—tumbling flailing clawing—

WHAMWHAMWHAM

. . . .

. . .

. .

.

stars in the dust
breathe
—*whoop*—
breathe goddammit *breathe*
—*whoop*—
stars
*hrakchakh*
stars come out like a window
dusty sand settles around me and
on me
into my eyes and up my nose and
fuck my bleeding ass I'm still
*alive*
One minor—
*hrakchakh*
—minor flaw . . . in the whole sonofabitching plan . . .

The vertical city isn't exactly vertical, exactly.

More of a steep slope.

I'm in one of the houses . . . still has walls . . . hasn't had a roof in a thousand years or so . . .

With the kind of effort that would have gotten Sisyphus to the top of his motherfucking hill, I roll my head sideways.

The city above catches enough of the firelight from the camp that I can pick out Crowmane's body crumpled on the rubble maybe ten feet away.

She looks worse than I feel.

That is to say: dead.

I figure that between my two half-working hands, I oughta be able to chopstick a big enough piece of rock to make sure. And I will.

I will.

Just—

Just as soon as I get my breath . . .

Yeah.

Someday this week.

All right, fuck breathing. I'll go . . . I'll go—

Just as soon as I can make my eyes work.

Because I can't blink away those haloes—migraine-aura prismatic splinters of starlight crystallizing over the rubble, crawling Crowmane's bloody face, shimmering along my hands and arms—

That's not my eyes. That's the fucking *universe* slipping *out of focus* . . .

This isn't happening.

This isn't *happening* . . .

But no denial can keep the stars in the sky.

No denial can stop the freefall sideways-inside-out

*yank*

that puts a ceiling of acoustic tile and recessed fluorescent tubing over my staring eyes—

—that replaces the rubble under my back with a Winston Transfer platform—

—and the crumbling millennial walls of the abandoned city with the white latex gloves and surgical masks and blue antimicrobial cap-and-gowns of Studio EMTs—

—who heave me onto a crash cart in a bone-wrenching hurricane of *stat this* and *amp of epi* and *no narco, no narco, adrenocorts only* and thunder me out into some corridor of anonymously sterile tile, and there's only one guy among them with a real face, and I reach over to him and grab his arm with my right hand.

"Am I—is this for real—? I've been having this dream—on the cross, I don't know how many times—this dream where you pull me—"

The guy with the face—a mid-thirtyish flabby pale kind of guy, with colorless eyes and too-fleshy lips, already losing his hair—can barely keep up with the EMTs pushing my crash cart while he stares down at the bloody spike through my wrist with a creepy revolted fascination, like it sickens him and gives him a hard-on at the same time. "Oh, oh, no, Entertainer Michaelson," he says, "oh, this is entirely, ah, *for real*, I assure you. Really."

"I'm home . . . ?" The new tears that find the crusted trails down my cheeks are hot enough to burn me. "You brought me, brought me *home* . . ."

"I've been in touch with your, er, Patron, that is, mm, Businessman Vilo," he says, jogging alongside the cart, already going breathless. "He underwrote your emergency transfer, and he has, mmm, authorized me to, ah, renegotiate your contract—once you've been stabilized, of course . . ."

"I don't care," I tell him, "I don't care. Just . . . thank you, that's all . . . thank you. Oh, god. Oh, god, thank you. I don't even know your name . . ."

"Oh, I am . . . ah." He surrenders trying to keep up and stops with a little wave.

"Kollberg," he calls after me. "Administrator Arturo Kollberg, Entertainer. Get yourself patched up. We have a, ah, great deal to talk about . . ."

He waves again. "A *great* deal."

# PRATT AND REDHORN

The Pratt & Redhorn was a small but well-appointed hostelry of three floors and maybe twenty-odd rooms that occupied a lively corner of the River-dock parish not far from the vigilry. I paid off the cartboy and tracked rain through the foyer.

A sign on the table in the tiny lobby advised me in three languages to ring the bell for service, so I did. Tobacco and meat smoke and considerable noise—voices raised in drunken song, accompanied by the planking of tune-less metallic percussion—billowed through a half-doored archway, which was blocked by a sign that advised, with apologies in the same three languages, that the dining hall was reserved for a private function. My sigh was more than half growl when I rang the bell again, louder.

I was in no mood. For anything.

I don't know what reaction I'd been expecting out of t'Passe. It sure as hell wasn't a gleam in her hard bright eyes and a nod and a brisk *I've been wondering how it might turn out.*

I didn't make a hassle over it at first; after all, she'd been still unconscious in the Monastic Embassy infirmary on the day I'd driven Kosall into the stone at the upstream tip of Old Town and let Ma'elKoth's flame flow through my hands to destroy that fucking blade forever. But when I reminded the World's Greatest Living Expert On Me of this detail of trivia, she just shrugged. "Destroyed? Not while you live, I suspect."

She was making my stomach hurt. "You better explain what you mean by that."

"It is so intimately linked with your legend that the two of you are inextricable. Think: this is the blade that *killed* you, Caine, on Assumption Day, and thus plowed the field for your rebirth into—"

"Except I wasn't exactly dead."

She shrugged again. "Seven years in what our hosts name the True Hell?

Argue semantics if you like. This is also the weapon that slaughtered the goddess Pallas Ril—"

"Except she's not exactly dead either."

"We speak of legend. Of what is known. It is known that you used this same blade to bring her back from beyond even Hell, and on the Day of the True Assumption you—again with the sword—unbound the Ascendant Ma'elKoth to make Him Master of Home. Kosall and you are virtually one and the same. Even its name—I've done a bit of research on that—"

"Of course you have."

"Do you want to hear it?"

"Would it matter if I don't?"

" 'Kosall,' " she'd said with a slightly malicious smile, "turns out to be a Westerlicized corruption of the Lipkan *Kh'Hohtsanjanell*, which means, in their usual straightforward fashion, Blade That Cuts Everything."

I'm not ashamed to say that I actually flinched. "Deliann—Deliann once called *me* that—"

"I know." The malice in that smile had faded back behind the smug. "I was there."

"But—that's just a name—those are just stories—"

"You," she said severely, "are fighting the hook. Are you—you of all men—trying to claim that names do not signify? That there is such a thing as *just a story*?"

I had plenty of wriggle left in me. "Are *you* claiming that stories count for more than what actually happened?"

"What 'actually happened' depends on whom one asks, doesn't it?" She grinned at me. "And once you explain what 'actually happened,' aren't you merely replacing their story with yours?"

"*Fuck* that." I was getting angry all over again. "No story is gonna make something *unhappen*. No story is gonna turn a fucking pile of slag at the tip of Old Town back into a magick sword and drop it five hundred years in the past—"

"Unless," she said, all seriousness now, shading into grim, "a god is telling it."

I didn't answer. She poked her goddamn cane at my chest. "You know it's true. That's what's really been on your mind. That's what has you at a rolling boil."

"This is exactly the kind of shit Jereth and Jantho started killing gods over," I said.

She nodded. "Using, if your intuition is correct, a sword that had already been and would someday be used to slay three gods anew."

"Three—?"

"Pallas Ril, Ma'elKoth, and—"

I interrupted her with a maybe unnecessarily forceful "Oh, for fuck's sake."

"Still . . ." She got up and limped toward a stack of books on the floor by the inner doorway. "Are you certain it was Kosall? Could it not have been the black runeblade?"

"The what?"

"The one you found in the chamber . . ." She opened one of the volumes and started leafing through it. "It was in your report . . . I have notes on it, let's see—"

"What the fuck are you *talking* about?"

She looked up from the book. "The one you used to unleash the river."

I shook my head, uncomprehending. "I used the bladewand."

"No. Here it is: a hand and a half blade, polished blue-black, chased with silver runes—"

"I'm telling you, I used the *bladewand*. It's the only reason I lived through it—through any kind of material weapon, feedback would have killed me—"

"Apparently not."

"Let me see that—"

"The original report is at Garthan Hold, of course. But I have read it, and my memory is, I believe, flawless. You came across the blade in the chamber of the Tear of Panchasell—"

"Your memory is fucked."

She cocked her head. "Though it *is* a curious coincidence—a black blade with silver runes—Kosall was a *silver* blade, and were the runes on it not *black*—?"

"Will you *stop*?"

But of course she wouldn't, and the harder I argued the less sure I got, because pretty soon I discovered that I just couldn't really remember if I *had* used the bladewand or if I'd found some motherfucking reversed-color image of Kosall, and my head was pounding like something was alive in there and chipping its way out with a ten-pound hammer and a railroad spike, so I just left.

Which is how I ended up in the foyer of the Pratt & Redhorn in a dripping-wet foul mood, jamming my hand down on the service bell like it was the top of t'Passe's pointy fucking head.

After a moment a thin, pale, tired-looking man with a few scraps of hair plastered sideways over his sweat-dripping scalp slipped around the sign. He was drying his hands on a brown apron, which then went up to mop clean a swath across his face as he came forward, shaking his head. "I wish I could offer you welcome, my friend." His accent was Ankhanan. "We're full up for the night, and I'm afraid—"

"Why does everybody around here want to be my friend?"

The thin, pale man stopped, blinking. "Why, I—I don't mean anything by it, goodman—"

"Forget about it. It's not goodman, it's freeman. I'm Dominic Shade. Somebody delivered my trunk."

The man's face cleared. "Oh, Freeman *Shade*! Welcome! I'm Lasser Pratt. Always good to welcome a countryman. Oh, this *is* fine. I'd become afraid you might'n't make it. Lord Tarkanen's order—and your trunk—got here just in time for us to get you into our last room tonight—it's on the top floor, I hope you don't—"

"As long as it's dry." I nodded toward the raucous dining hall. "Look, I can see you're busy with the party. You think I can just get a plate of something hot to take up to my room?"

"Oh, not at all, no no no, not at all. Please, Freeman Shade, you're *welcome* at the party—"

"I am?"

Pratt gave a nod that was half shake of his head. "Oh, yes, very much so— and not only because you are a guest of Lord Tarkanen. They, ah—customs on the Battleground—are . . . well, I'm Ankhanan by birth myself, y'know, from New Bend, d'you know it? Just three days downriver—"

"Yeah, I've been there. Skip the blowjob, huh? I just want some dry clothes and a hot meal."

"I, ah, well . . ." Pratt's grin deflated. He rubbed his eyes. "Sorry. Force of habit."

"Forget it. I know what it's like to work for a living."

"But you really *are* invited to the party—"

"Maybe later. I have to go right out again."

"On a night like this? You have business that won't wait till morning?"

"You wouldn't happen to know if that Tyrkilld character spends his nights in the vigilry, would you?"

"Knight Aedharr?" Pratt nodded toward the smoke billowing through the dining-hall door. "He's right in there."

"You're putting me on."

"If only I were," he sighed. "My eldest went Khryllian—he's an armsman of this very parish, still has hopes of Knighthood some day. One of the fingers in his own fist was killed this morning. Braehew, his name was."

"Yeah." My too-empty stomach suddenly knotted, and a phantom stab brought my hand to my right side. "I was there."

"I know you were." Pratt made ushering gestures toward the doorway. "That's why you're invited."

I stared.

Pratt spread his palms. "Like I was saying: On the Battleground, customs are . . . different."

I went to the half door and looked in.

The party must have been going on for a while already.

Tables and chairs had been shoved aside from half the dining hall's floor, to make room for what looked like some cross between square-dancing and jujitsu. Other tables were piled with meats and bread and loaves of cheese, and everywhere were steel cups and tankards and schooners, most lying empty, tumbled and forgotten on tabletop or chair seat or kicked out of the way of the dancers.

"They don't look too broken up about it."

Pratt was at my shoulder now, looking past me into the dining hall. "It's a celebration. A victory party."

"Come again?"

The hosteler shrugged. "Braehew was killed in battle, discharging the lawful command of his superior. Falling with honor, he goes to join Khryl's Own. From the Khryllian point of view, what greater victory can he hope for?"

I cocked my head. "Living through it?"

Pratt chuckled. "And that's why Ankhanans never quite fit in around here. Well, from my angle, I'm told you played no more than the part Khryl wrote for you, if you know what I mean. They'll be happy to make you welcome."

"I'll bet."

Customs are customs—but the laughter was too loud and too sharp, the singing was too hoarse, and the smiles on too many lips left too many eyes too blank. Looked like there had been too many of these victory parties lately. I stared over the half door and let the loudest and sharpest of the laughter and the hoarsest of the singing draw my eye.

Dimly through the smoke I could make out the barrel shape of Tyrkilld, Knight Aeddhar, seated in the far corner on a vast chair set atop a table like a mockery of a throne. He was out of uniform for the second time that day, wearing only the wool-woven vest-over-belted-sweater, sheepskin breeches and boots of a Jheledi shepherd. In one hand he held a vast bucket of a cup, big enough he could have worn it as a helmet; the other hand was occupied by keeping a giggling twenty-something redheaded girl firmly attached to his knee. She was the only woman in the room not wearing the Khryllian crewcut and armsman colors; she had a slightly-too-short-for-modesty print dress gathered around trim thighs, and a somewhat longer apron belted too tightly around an also-trim waist.

"Pretty waitress. Jheledi?" I said sidelong. "Should know better than to turn her loose around Tyrkilld."

"As if I have a choice," Pratt said sourly. "She's my wife."

"Really? And you have a kid old enough to be an—oh, I get it. Married the serving girl, huh?" I glanced over my shoulder. "No wonder you look tired."

The hosteler sighed. "It's a long story."

"They all are, buddy."

Pratt snorted half a laugh. "Now *you're* the one who wants to be friends."

I chuckled. "Fair enough. Listen, I need to talk with Tyrkilld, but I really don't want to walk into that party. Is there any place here where he and I can sit down and have a quiet drink?"

"Well—" Pratt frowned. "There's the grill side—I closed it down for the night—"

"Grill side? You serve ogrilloi here?" I blinked. "Is that legal?"

Pratt's tired face took on a flush of red. "I may *live* on the Battleground, but I'm still Ankhanan—I'm no damned bigot, and if you—"

"Easy. I'm just asking."

"I—uh. Sorry." He passed a hand over his face and used the sweat from his forehead to slick back his thinning hair. "Long night. Sorry. Yes, it's legal. We do very good trade among the eligibles, especially at daymeal. We just have to keep the dining areas separate." He waved a hand toward a door under the stairs. "We can set a table for you on the grill side. It won't be anything fancy."

"As long as it's quiet."

"Oh, I can guarantee that. Give us a moment or two—"

"No problem. I need a chance to get into some dry clothes and warm up a little. Set me a plate of something hot, huh? I don't care what, so long as there's meat and a lot of it. I'll make it worth your trouble."

"Don't think of it. Really. It's no trouble at all."

"You're a goddamn liar."

"Truth is flexible in this line of work," Pratt said easily. "Oh, and—it won't be a problem for you to be served by an ogrillo, will it?"

"Why would it?" I smiled faintly. "Aren't I Ankhanan too?"

The meal turned out to be half a roast duckling with black cherry sauce and glazed walnuts over duck sausage dressing, and a peppered baked apple stuffed with pulled-pork confit. The ogrillo server turned out to also be the head cook and kitchen manager, an immense pudding-waisted eligible named Kravmik Red Horn: Lazzevget.

The junior partner.

Seemed Pratt took his Ankhanan principles seriously.

"Good man, good as they get," Kravmik proudly proclaimed in a voice deep enough to vibrate the tabletop as he spun a steel cup of water and a mug of his own iced homebrew into place around the plate. "And I'm not talking flavor, either, hrk!"

"Mm-mmm." I was too busy chewing to give a civil answer. There was a smoky tang to the limpid crust of fat under the skin of the duck breast that twisted my heart with unexpected, entirely astonishing longing for something I couldn't quite recall . . . something in the beer, too . . . something dark, burnt-chocolate on the nose but fading and dry on the tongue . . .

Gods, it was good. My eyes stung. What *was* that flavor . . . ?

Kravmik was more than capable of holding up both ends of the conversation. Before the half duckling was half gone, he had roughed out the highlights of the Pratt & Redhorn's history, including thumbnail sketches of the more colorful members of the staff, the notables who'd stayed there, the luminaries who made a point of dining there, and, of course, the ongoing kitchen-sink romance of Lasser Pratt and his wild young Jheledi bride, even wilder now that she'd stopped nursing their infant twins and had a bit of freedom and got herself a pair of respectable tits in the bargain, not to mention the inappropriate amount of attention she was receiving from the Younger Pratt, who had a new bride of his own, y'know, and a child soon to be along as well—

Finally I stopped chewing long enough to stem the flood with a raised hand and a thoughtful "You speak better Westerling than any ogrillo I've ever met. Better than the Ankhanan ones, in fact."

Kravmik opened hands the size of saucepans. "Want to get ahead, you gotta talk the talk, that's what Pratt always says. He works with me. Helps me be presentable. Pratt says pretty soon my Westerling will be good as his. Good as yours."

"Huh. In Ankhana, grills talk different on purpose. They're proud of it."

Kravmik nodded. "Pratt says that too. And he says they're mostly thugs. Best jobs they can get is strongarm stuff, and they mostly die young. Me, I got stuff to live for." He swung one of those hands at the kitchen. "Sure, I'm eligible, but I got staff here, they're my family—ellie, human, whatever. Cubs ain't everything in the world, y'know. Just bein' alive's worth something. Worth a lot."

"Yeah." I stared down at my plate. "I have a friend I'm hoping I can convince of that."

"Hey, you're not eatin'—it's all right? That stuffing get cold?"

"No—no, it's great. I just ran out of appetite." I pushed the plate away, picked up the water cup, set it down again, and shoved aside the mug of iced beer. "Got anything to drink? I mean *drink*."

"We do a little freeze-wine, from last winter—crack off the water-ice, and what's left is—"

I made a face. "Real drink."

Kravmik shook his head dolefully. "Can't make fortified stuff. Nobody does—brandy's illegal. And the import duty's just impossible."

"Shit. I'd start a revolution too." I waved a hand. "All right. More of the beer, then. And ask Pratt if he can tell Tyrkilld I'm over here now."

"Knight Aeddhar?" Astonishment tinged with suspicion flickered across the huge ogrillo's face. "What's he got to do with you? Why would he care you're here?"

"He'll care. That beer, huh?"

Kravmik's professionalism overcame his skepticism enough that he only ducked his head and cleared away the remains of the meal. The beer arrived shortly before Tyrkilld did.

The Jheledi Knight moved around the empty tables in the gloom with the slow, dignified zags of a three-master tacking into the wind, one vast fist still wrapped around the stem of the bucket-size flagon. When he got to the table, he blinked down at the grease stains on the wadded napkin beside the mug of iced beer.

"*You*," he said with ponderous precision. "Are not *here*. For the *party*."

"Got that right. Sit down before you fall down."

"While I *am* indebted. To *you*, master Monassbite Esoterassbite assassass-assbite, for your *kind* hospitassitude. I would prefer to *stand*, fuck you very *much*." Tyrkilld blinked again. "What *are* you doing here?"

"Your buddy Markham got me a room. By no fucking coincidence at all. Quite a sense of humor, that sonofabitch."

"While I freely *admit*. To a catalogue of sins *innumerable*. Mortal, venial, and merely *cheerful*." He swayed, and swung the flagon in a violent circle that managed to spill not a drop. "Accuse me but *once more* of being *friend* to Lord *Tarkanen*, sir, and we shall again. Make trial. Of Khryl's *Justice*."

He unleashed a belch that rattled the windows and seemed to unstring his knees, and he delicately settled the flagon on the tabletop and himself into the waiting chair. "A room, you say? Perhaps I may assay your Monassbite hospitassitude after all—a scrap of floor makes bed enow betimes—"

"I thought you had a call to make tonight—the Widow Braehew—?"

"And from whence gather'st thou requisite testicle to lecture a Knight of House Aeddhar upon the obligations of—"

"Yeah, yeah, ring of dog's piss, goatherd and a sling, you told me already." I squinted at him. For Khryllians, the obligations of command are absolute . . . though there may be certain details of some obligations which no one could blame him for failing to fulfill, should the failure arise of incapacity due to doing a bit too much honor to the memory of a departed liegeman . . . "All right, goddammit. What's in the flagon?"

Tyrkilld blinked. "Your pardon?"

I leaned forward. "There is no possible way in Home or Hell you got completely pisseyed just on this crapass beer. I want to know what you're drinking, and I want some."

Tyrkilld's face took on the sly cast of a man who's drunk so much he thinks he's sober, and he leaned far enough backward that he was in danger of toppling over. "First you share this issue of such. Staggering import that it warrants. Coming between a poor thirsty Knight and his much-deserved imbibulation. Then perhaps the matter of the contents of my flagon might arise, as it were, willy-nilly."

He was bringing back my headache. "Do any *other* Jheledi talk like you, or is this just something you put on to aggravate people?"

Tyrkilld lifted the flagon and took such a long, slow sip that the studded steel rim of the cup strategically covered what might have otherwise looked like a long, slow wink. "And is that a matter of any great import at this dire hour?"

"Since when do Jheledi nobility go Khryllian, anyway? Last I heard, the noble houses of Jheled considered Lipke an occupying power up until Ankhana took you away from them in the Plains War, thousand years or not."

Tyrkilld made another expansive whirl of the flagon. "There is not a blessed thing wrong with the service of Khryl, my lad. Saving only the company."

"Yeah." The iced beer in my hand got real interesting all of a sudden. "I talked with the lady in question. Thanks for delivering my message."

He assayed what he undoubtedly thought was a subtle glance around the empty dining hall. "And no harm it did me. Thus far, as it were."

I nodded. "We were going to talk about how I spotted you."

He held up one of those hands that I was still too overly familiar with. "Nay, that I have determined. 'Twas my amateurish questioning, was it not? That I started with Freedom's Face, and my foolish reference to elven magicks foiling Khryllian truthsense, and moving on too easily once I found you might have knowledge enough to do damage . . ."

"So you're not quite an idiot."

"In my own defense, Master Monassbite, let me aver that your estimable self was to be loaded in pieces back onto the afternoon steamboat and sent south to heal over the course of some months. Or years. In which case my minor slips would have signified not at all."

I nodded into my beer. "Shit just never quite goes the way we plan, though, huh?"

"Never quite, my lad. Never quite."

"You and I need to talk about what Our Mutual Slag is really up to, here. And what we're gonna do about it."

"Do we now?" He unleashed another window-rattling belch. "That is to say: now? You'd be hard put to argue this as the best time for such news."

"There's never a good time." I pushed my chair back from the sagging table and leaned on my knees. I picked at the ridges of callus across my knuckles. "Shit never happens when you're ready for it. When you're healthy and full of beans and spoiling to take on the world, the world leaves you the fuck alone. It always waits till you've got the flu and your dog's sick and the mortgage is late and y'know, whatever. That's when it gets you up the ass."

Tyrkilld nodded, his sloppy grin fading to half a faint smile. "You speak with the air of a man having some small experience of planetary buggery."

I tried for a smile and missed. "Funny thing is, before all this started, I was pretty goddamn close to happy. Happier than I think I've ever been. I was free. Really free, for I think the first time ever. I had the whole world open in front of me. I was happy. And now I've jumped into this shitpool with both feet."

"Happy men," Tyrkilld said, leaning forward to lay a brick of a hand on my arm, "are only half alive."

I decided not to tell him my life could be read as a chain of evidence establishing exactly that. "I figure you're a decent guy, Tyrkilld. As low-rent cocksucking thugs go, y'know."

"Gracious as ever."

"I figure you wouldn't really be in this if you had the faintest fucking clue what was really going on. Freeing enslaved ogrilloi doesn't have shit to do with it. Freeing ogrilloi is only a means to an end."

Tyrkilld swayed a bit. "And—? You'll have to help me, lad; I'm no master of the mental arts even when sober."

"Freedom's Face is a cover for an Ankhanan insurgency. Because even now, nobody wants to fight the Knights of Khryl straight up. Not even the Empire."

The Knight's eyes went round. "*Fight* us? Ankhana?"

"If they have to."

"For what? What do we have that they could possibly want?"

"This." I waved a hand. "Everything. All of it."

"The *Battleground*?" He looked dazed. "The vast Ankhanan Empire covets our poor scrap of a corner of the Boedecken Waste—? What *for*? Hasn't your bloody elven sorceror of an Emperor land enough already?"

"It's not about the land. It's about what's *here*. It's about your Artan guests and BlackStone Mining. It's—complicated."

"Are we so short of time?"

"Maybe. And I'm not sure I could make you understand why they want it anyway. And you're sure as hell short of brains right now. No offense."

"None taken; freely admitted, my lad. Freely admitted. And how do you come by this sudden trove of intelligence that Khryl Himself avowed you lacked only this morning?"

"People tell me things. When I ask them nicely. You should give it a fucking try someday."

Tyrkilld's wariness evaporated into a sudden chuckle. "Red Horn! A flagon! And one for the freeman!" He pounded the table with the flat of his hand. It cracked, and sagged in the middle.

He blinked at it, then shrugged. "And so pray, Master Monassbite, if it would please your Imperial Lordliness to impart to a poor humble hedge Knight one last pittance of your Shining Verity . . . why bring'st you this news to *my* insufficiently sober self? I can barely hope to remember it, much less take action . . ."

"Nobody told you to get pisseyed."

He leaned back again and favored me with a long, slow, alchoholically deliberate scrutiny. "If what you've told me is true, you understand that what you've just done is . . . well, for want of a kinder word, one can only call it *treason.*"

I shrugged. "I've done worse."

Tyrkilld blinked, blinked again, and then unleashed a roar of laughter. "I'll drink to that!" He peered around. "Or I would . . . Red Horn! Where's my *swill?*"

He slapped the cracked table. It split with a groan and collapsed. The kitchen doors banged open again and Kravmik lumbered in, another bucket-size flagon in one hand and a civilized cup in the other. "And here we go— *grk.* For love of—Tyrkilld, you break another my table!"

"Bring on the swill," said the Knight with a lordly wave. "Put the table on my account."

"Bet I will," the ogrillo grumbled as he set the flagon and the cup on the edge of the nearest undamaged table. "Be more careful, you, hey?"

"So you two know each other, huh?"

Ogrillo and Knight looked at each other before looking at me with expressions of mildly inquisitive innocence.

"No taking a knee. Not even a 'the Knight thisandthat.' Not to mention your own private barrel of whateverthefuck this is."

Tyrkilld yawned and smacked his lips. "I'm not in Khryl's Battledress, and thus informality is no insult. As for the barrel—"

"'S just grillswill," Kravmik said. He hung his head a little. "The Knight Aeddhar's gotten a taste for it, that's all. So I keep a barrel topped up for him.

And in exchange, he makes sure the parish armsmen don't bust up my pot still."

"Pot still?" I sat up straighter. "Pot still as in *distill*?"

"And a nasty vile fluid it dispenses, too," Tyrkilld sighed, reaching for the flagon. "He boils the alchohol off his beer, capturing the spirit in a long coiled tube of—"

"Wait. Stop. Both of you. Hot staggering *fuck*." I lurched to my feet. "Grill-swill is distilled *beer*?"

"Not so *loud*," Kravmik muttered. "I know we're alone here, but it's not completely legal, you understand?"

"Or even at all," Tyrkilld said, taking a long draught. "And for good reason too."

"*Give* me that." I snatched the cup off the table. Inside was a very pale, almost colorless liquid . . . with that dark, burnt-chocolate scent . . . but also some heather, and honey, and exotic spice . . .

That was the smell. The taste that had brought tears to my eyes.

I remembered now: Orbek recounting the boogeyman stories his father used to tell him. About marsh ghouls in the Boedecken, who'd lure you out into the bogs and suck out your eyeballs and pull you down . . . into the bogs.

The bogs that were full of—

"Peat." Wonder kindled within me like summer dawn. "It's sonofabitching *peat*."

Kravmik frowned at me. "It's bogearth. We cut it for the cook fires—wood's too expensive to burn here, coal ruins the food, and turds . . . well, humans get funny about turd smoke."

"You're making beer out of malted barley. That you're drying over *peat* fires," I murmured reverently. "Bogearth, whatever. And you're distilling the beer to make, uh, *grillswill*."

"Well, yeah."

"Oh, my sweet and generous gods." I took a sip. It was liquid fire. Too young. Too harsh. Unfiltered. Yeast and fermentation esters.

It was fucking *magnificent*.

I said, "Kravmik Red Horn: Lazzevget, will you marry me?"

"Come again?"

"How much for my own barrel? Shit, how much for *all* the barrels? How much grillswill can you *make* without getting arrested?"

Kravmik nodded at Tyrkilld. "Ask him."

Tyrkilld shrugged up at me. "You can stomach this disgusting brew?"

"Oh, Tyrkilld—" I took another sip. It lit up my brain. "Oh, it's pretty hairy, I'll give you that—"

"'S just grillswill," Kravmik muttered. "What d'you expect?"

"But that's because you're holding it in beer barrels for, what, a few days? Weeks? Listen, I can ship barrels of Tinnaran oak up here—new oak, and some already used to age their brandy—if you barrel it for *years*, instead of days—three years in the new oak, macerate some tannin into it, then finish it in the—"

"He's gone entirely mad," Tyrkilld said in wonder. "Kravmik, take his cup. Two sips and the poor lad's mind is gone."

"Reach for this cup and I'll break your fucking arm."

I took another sip, a long one, and held it in my mouth until my tongue burned. Must have been a hundred forty proof or better. Amazing he could distill it without blowing the roof off the building.

But after a moment I remembered where I was. And why.

I swallowed the swill and set down the cup.

"Son of a bitch." Sweat had prickled out across my forehead. I swiped my sleeve upward over my face. "Talk about shit happening at the wrong time . . ."

Tyrkilld and Kravmik were still staring at me. I shrugged at the huge ogrillo. "Thanks, Kravmik. I mean it. And thanks for sharing your barrel, Tyrkilld. You'll never know how much it meant to me. But I have to go to bed now. Tomorrow's gonna be a busy day."

Kravmik shook his head and turned away. "Ankhanans," he muttered, lumbering back toward the kitchen. "Can never tell with those people . . ."

Without a table to lean on, Tyrkilld had some difficulty regaining his feet. Once upright, he frowned down into his flagon. "And amongst all this still rests concealed, Master Monassbite," he murmured, "the truth of why you have brought your tale to *me*."

I cycled a dozen different lies; a couple almost made it into my mouth.

But—

"You're the only one to bring this to, Tyrkilld. I'm putting this on you for the same reason that Kierendal decided she wanted you dead: because you're the one who knows shit—you've been on the inside. You're the one who can hurt her, when she starts to make her real moves, and . . . ah, fuck it anyway." I reached for the cup again. "It's because I don't *like* you."

"You'll have to favor the ignorance of a poor parish Knight; I've averred already that I'm no great mind, even sober. Which it might serve you well to remember I am currently *not*."

A one-shoulder shrug brought the cup to my lips; swillfire lit up the inside of my skull. "I figured you'd only half believe me. So instead of, say, going to Angvasse and mounting a full-scale sweep—which you can't really do anyway, without telling her more than you can afford for her to know about your, y'know, compromised position—you'd go and snoop around a little, pick up some Faces, and pound 'em to check out my story."

Tyrkilld nodded somewhat more vigorously than entirely necessary. "As would any prudent Knight who'd had experience of your dishonest self."

"Sure. The punch line, though, is that I'm telling the truth." I took another shot of the swill. "And Kierendal is no one to be fucked with. Which is also the truth. About the time that you found out it was all true, you'd be in the middle of being violently dead."

"Ah."

"Which would set off a full-scale round-up of Freedom's Face—which is what I want—and would leave you in bloody chunks that even Khryl couldn't put back together. Which was also what I wanted."

Tyrkilld rocked onto the balls of his feet and stuck his chin out as though that might help him keep his balance. "And yet now you have revealed this nefarious plan entire."

A swirl of the cup set the grillswill in motion enough to sharpen the air with the sizzle of raw alcohol.

"Maybe I'm just not the hard-ass I used to be," I said. "It's one thing to figure out how to get a guy killed. It's another to do it cold while you look him in the face."

I raised the cup.

"And it's something entirely else to do it to a man who's just bought you—when you thought you'd never see another for the rest of your pathetic suffering life—a big damn mug of scotch."


Already on the edge of the bed, tunic hanging on the post, baton unstrapped and pistol unholstered, I was pulling off one of my boots when I sagged and let my foot fall back to the floor. "Goddammit."

I flopped backward onto the bed and threw my arm over my eyes. It didn't help.

Pretty soon I moved my arm. Stars stared at me through the skylight. A winding crack in the plaster spread crooked winter stain from the casement toward the door.

Somehow it looked like the Caineway.

"Son of a bitch." I heaved myself upright and put my tunic back on.

Downstairs, the dining hall was a shipwreck of post-party debris. A couple of listless eligibles drifted among the wreckage, righting tables and performing triage on the chairs and benches. Young Mistress Pratt had her hair bound up now, and a sheen of sweat to match the pretty flush on her cheeks as she shouldered a massive tray piled high with tankards and half-empty platters toward the kitchen doors, while a sullen teenage human boy swept spillage toward the alley door.

Pratt was piling more trays with tankards and platters, but he stopped willingly enough when my wave from the doorway caught his eye.

"Freeman Shade?" He wiped his hands on his apron as he came over. "Is there a problem? What'd you say to Knight Aeddhar? He came back and walked through the crowd, and the party just melted away . . . not that I'm complaining—flat-rate event, y'know; the less they drink, the better we do—but from the look on his face—"

"Out here, Pratt, huh?"

"Oh, sure, sure, freeman." He chuckled tiredly as he slipped through the half door. "No harm in letting Yttrall do some of the work—not that she doesn't pull her weight. D'you know how much it's worth to this establishment just to let her sit on Knight Aeddhar's knee and laugh at his jokes? Which is a job in and of—"

"Pratt."

The hosteler met my eyes and seemed to see me for the first time. Sudden wariness pinched the fatigue-lines deeper down his thin cheeks. "Something's wrong, isn't it?" His voice had gone quiet. "Really wrong."

"Pratt, you need to get your family out of town."

The hosteler's feathery, almost invisible brows drew together. "What?"

"I mean it."

"I don't understand."

"I know. And I don't think I can explain."

Pratt took a step back. The apron fell forgotten from his opening fingers. "Are—are you *threatening* me—?"

"Listen to me. You have to go. All of you. Forget about cleaning up. You can do that later. If there is a later. Things are in motion here—I've started things in motion—"

I shook my head, and my teeth found the sore spot on the inside of my lip. "It's about to get bad here. I don't know how bad. Maybe worse than it's ever been. If you don't go now . . ." I sighed. "You may not get the chance. You could be dead. You and your pretty wife. And your baby twins. Dead *ugly*."

"What—" Pratt's mouth was slack, and what little color his cheeks had ever had was now somewhere south of his collar. "I don't *understand*—what are you *talking* about?"

"I'm trying to save your life."

Pratt was pleading now. "Why are you saying these things to me?"

"That's the funny part." My laugh didn't sound amused, even to me. "It's because I like you."

Pratt only looked helpless.

"I like your place. You do a good thing here at a fair price, and you treat people better than you have to. You're the kind of guy the world needs more of."

"So you're—so you're scaring the *crap* out of me—?"

"Take a fucking vacation, Pratt. Take your pretty wife and your new kids south on the first steamer tomorrow. Go someplace nice. Here will *not* be nice. Here could get you all dead."

"But I can't—I can't just—"

"I'm not kidding, Pratt."

Pratt gave himself a little shake and managed an unsteady laugh. He swiped the thinning hair sideways across his scalp. "I . . . appreciate the—uh, the warning, Freeman Shade. I do. But really, the Battleground is the safest place on Home—"

"Not anymore."

"Well." He sighed. "It's the middle of the night, and my place is a wreck. I can't make any moves until tomorrow, can I? And meanwhile, there's still work to do, so if you don't mind excusing me, freeman—"

I hung my head. I hate this part.

"Freeman?"

*Hate* it.

"Er, Freeman Shade, if you don't mind, I really do have—"

My hand seized Pratt's shirtfront faster than he could blink. The hosteler had just barely enough time to draw breath for a shout of alarm before my other hand flicked out to lay my palm gently along his cheek.

"You know me."

Pratt's shout of alarm died in his throat. His mouth worked. His eyes stared wildly for an instant, then squeezed shut, and he clapped his hands over his face and his legs buckled. He threw himself to his knees at my feet.

"Forgive me—forgive me, Lord, I did not *know* thee—!"

"Get up."

Shivering on the floor, face pressed into his knees, Pratt moaned. "*Ma'elKoth is Lord of Gods and Master of Home, and Caine is His One True Hand. . . . Ma'elKoth is Lord of Gods and Master of Home, and Caine is His One True Hand . . .*"

"Get *up*. Don't grovel. I *hate* groveling."

Pratt lifted a face transfigured by terror and awe. "My Lord?"

"And those bloody Psalms. They're *so* depressing." I pressed a hand to my head, blinking. How much of that damned grillswill had I drunk, anyway? "Just get up, huh?"

"As the Prince of Chaos commands—"

"And *stop* it with that shit."

"As the—"

"Shut *up*."

Pratt stood in a half crouch, cringing away from me.

"So take it as coming from Ma'elmotherfuckingKoth Himself, all right? Get thee fucking *hence* from this *place*, goddammit."

Pratt barely allowed himself to whisper, "*As the Prince of Chaos commands* . . ."

I left Pratt shaking on the foyer rug and stomped up the stairs toward my room.

*Christ*, I hate that shit.

# BAD GUY

*I* linger upon this moment, as I have a thousand times, or a million, or only once forever; no number can signify, because times have no more meaning than does Time. All of you is present here: your painful birth and your blasted childhood, your criminal youth and murderous manhood, your sad slipping-down maturity and all your many deaths —

And yet none of you is here now, too.

In this moment, for this moment, you have erased yourself. No longer an Actor, a man, Hari Michaelson, Caine.

You vanish into the legend you are still creating.

The conference room is institutional green. The conference table is faux-granite grey. The conference chairs are mauve.

Do they look comfortable to you?

Do you somehow sense the quantum smear of futures in which you'll someday sit in them — when you'll have conversations too much like this one with other, younger Actors?

This question will hang suspended without answer until I have voice to ask.

For now, I focus on the hum of the motorbed under your ass, on the saline drip streaming drool into your strapped-down left arm, and on the salt I taste on the back of your tongue.

The vast curving screen that fills the far wall of the conference room shows a glowing skeletonized schematic of the vertical city. The schematic rotates slowly, displaying differently colored pinpoints of light: a virtual orrery of four-teen planets.

"I, ah, must say, Michaelson," muses the doughy troll that you call Administrator Kollberg, "you are taking all this rather, mmm, well . . ."

You roll your head to the right, and without the slightest twist of emotion regard the nine inches of iron nail still jammed through your wrist. "It wasn't exactly a surprise."

And I love how your voice sounds inside your head, even at a dull flat hum . . .

"Well, yes. When you pull the spike *yourself*, online—oh, that will be *very* dramatic."

"I can hardly wait."

"Don't let it concern you. You'll get another round of injections before the retransfer. You'll barely feel a thing. We dial down the dolorimetrics on the cube recordings anyway; no one wants to *really* feel your pain—the public wants to savor your suffering, not share it."

"Yeah."

"So think of this as an opportunity to do some real acting for a change. Make it convincing and move on. Staggering off into the darkness—"

"I want to talk to Marc Vilo."

"I beg your pardon?"

"My Patron. I want to talk to him."

Kollberg shifts his weight backward in the comfortable-looking chair and lets his thick lips flap their way through a long, slow sigh. "I'll take that tone from you once, Michaelson. But you're not on Overworld now. Mind your place."

You close eyes that burn and sting. *From the air,* you tell yourself in silent monologue. *Something in the air.*

Already you narrate your life.

"Sorry, Administrator. Sorry. It was the meds talking. But please, sir, if you would only let me—"

"Entertainer." The plump Administrator rises and folds his soft pale hands in front of his crotch. "As I have explained, Businessman Vilo has already signed off on your new contract. He's a very busy man."

"*Please* put a call through, Administrator. Please. He'll take it. He will."

"He may. But he won't change anything. He can't; Studio operations are sacrosanct. Now. Here's your escape." Kollberg takes a few steps toward the head of the table. One of those soft pale hands unhitches itself from his crotch and clicks a pen-size control.

The schematic of the vertical city dissolves into a new view, from the upland plateau side. One bright red star shines well away from the exit tunnel.

"This is where you will retransfer. Once you have removed the spikes from your arm and your ankle—"

"How am I supposed to have gotten all the way up *there?*"

Kollberg looks at you.

You swallow, and drop your eyes—a conditioned reflex? Or is the empty malice in his colorless gaze too much for the nerves of a mere Hari Michaelson? "Sorry. Sorry, I don't mean to interrupt. Please, Administrator. Continue."

"Well." Kollberg clears his throat: a cough delicately indulgent as a cautious pedophile's. "Actually, it's a fair enough question. After you retransfer, you'll cover the continuity gap in your Soliloquy. It doesn't take much—just a phrase or two about the struggle to crawl all that way, and something about the confusion of the battle against Pretornio's zombies covering your escape—"

"But—" You shake your head, your face twisting to mirror the twist of sick anticipation in your stomach. "—but, well, I mean, first they're not zombies—"

"Oh, whatever, Michaelson, *please* don't quibble—"

"And there's just no way I could have crawled that far in that kind of shape. Hell, I don't think I could crawl that far *now*, meds or not—I don't think I could crawl that far if I were *healthy*—"

"It's a silly objection, Michaelson. No one will care. After all, that ogrillo bitch practically healed you on the spot, didn't she?"

"Not exactly healed; I mean, *look* at me—"

"Now, as you struggle away from the city, you'll find a saddlebag just *here*—"

He clicks the control again, and a new pinpoint lights up a few hundred virtual meters from the first.

"—which you will theorize must have fallen from one of the horses during Kess Raman's abortive attempt to flee—"

"Are you serious?"

"In that saddlebag are four canteens of water, as well as jerky and flatbread. There are also several vials of a cream which you will identify as a medicinal salve; when you rub it on your wounds, this will cover the effects of the intradermal time-dissolve antibiotic and steroid capsules we've injected along your spine. They'll release over the next seven days, though you'll hardly need them that long, as you shall see."

The twist on your face becomes a full wince; nausea thickens below your throat, and it can hardly all be from the antibiotics and steroid injections, can it? "Um, Administrator—?"

Kollberg again clicks the control, and the virtual city shrinks into a vanishing perspective; a new star appears virtual kilometers away. "Roughly here— where you can easily arrive before daybreak—you'll find two horses, which you will identify in Soliloquy as from the company's remuda and theorize that they must have escaped from the others during the raid. Make up whatever names you like; it's not important. One will be fully tacked and will have saddlebags of its own, also containing filled canteens and provisions, as well as some spare clothing and boots, so that you can dress yourself and bandage your wounds. Don't worry about having to find them—we'll transfer them in near enough your location that you'll be able to hear their tack jingle—"

"Administrator, please." You duck as though you would bob and weave if you weren't strapped to the motorbed. "Isn't that a little . . . *convenient?* I mean, come on, sir—finding the saddlebag with exactly what I need—then a horse, with clothes and boots—not to mention that ogrilloi *don't* let horses just wander off; horsemeat tastes like—"

"Michaelson, this is a *fantasy.*" Kollberg sighs with exaggerated patience. "No one expects it to make sense. It's not *supposed* to be realistic."

He clicks the control again, and the wall view dissolves to a colorfully illuminated map of the eastern Boedecken. "Now. You're only seven days' ride from the Khryllian outpost at North Rahnding; by switching horses and sleeping on horseback, you could make it in less than five—"

"Five *days?* Sir, please—if you'll only make the call to Businessman Vilo—"

"Wait, wait; you haven't heard the best of it, Michaelson." Kollberg's voice heats up, and a sheen of sweat slickens his upper lip. His eyes go squirrel-bright. "We will arrange for a Khryllian reconnaissance-in-force to be moving out into the fringes of the Boedecken; though I cannot guarantee the actual makeup, there is a strong chance that you should see at least five Knights, possibly as many as ten, and up to one hundred fifty armsmen—"

"What good does that do anybody?"

"You'll encounter them less than three days out from the vertical city. You'll tell them that the Black Knives have a *captive* Knight of *Khryl* . . ."

Kollberg leans closer. His breath smells of lavender and orange mints. "Imagine the rescue, Michaelson. *Imagine.* Ten Knights. One hundred fifty lancers. Falling upon the Black Knives like a steel thunderbolt . . . with *you* as the advance scout, having received a Khryllian Healing for all your wounds. With *you* penetrating the camp to locate the prisoners, to prepare them for rescue. With *you* finally using all the skills of the Monastic assassin you are, to eliminate pickets and preserve the element of surprise . . ."

"I can see why you like it."

"And this is why *you'll* like it, Michaelson. This is why I went to Businessman Vilo; this is why I risk my career on an emergency transfer for an unknown Actor. A never-was."

Kollberg leans even closer. Under the sick-sweet pastilles, you can smell on his breath the blood-sugar problems that are bringing on his type 2 diabetes. "Can you say: *first-handers?*"

And now you can't breathe at all, and I'm sure it's not from the smell. "Are you serious?"

"Oh, yes. Oh, I am. I've been showing clips of your Adventure to a few . . . select connossieurs . . . already. As soon as you make contact with the Khryllians, we'll be putting you on *live*. For the whole rest of the Adventure. Live."

"Live . . ." you echo. Your lips hang. You can no longer feel your toes, or your fingertips.

"Because I see something in you, Michaelson. I saw it from the moment that buck stood up on the badlands. I know star power. You have it. And I saw it *first*."

As you stare at him, all you see now is the sweat beginning to collect in droplets on his face. "If you only knew how long I've been waiting to hear somebody tell me that."

If he only knew how what should have been the sweetest moment of your life somehow leaves your mouth full of dust and bitter ash.

"I'm going to *make* you, Michaelson. I'm going to make Caine the star you deserve to be. And in the process, I'm going to make myself into the top Administrator in the whole damned Studio System. It all starts right here. But you have to play, Michaelson. I can make you go back, but I can't make you *be* the Caine you *need* to be to make this *work*."

You lower your head and stare again at the spike. And I can only guess what you are thinking.

Are you remembering that the whole time you've been back in the Studio—the whole time you've been back on Earth—from the tiny Winston Transfer chamber to the emergency infirmary to the recovery room to here, you have been given not so much as a glance outside? Because this is all you say here: all you have ever said: all you will ever say:

*Not one window.*

No glimpse of the world you were born into. The universe you had left, and to which you have been returned.

It is at this moment that something within you unlocks. I feel it in your chest: as though an iron band fastened around your heart snaps open at the touch of a key in your mind. "I get it," you say slowly. "When you rescued me, you weren't saving my life. You were saving your career."

Kollberg actually grins. "Michaelson, you died the day you passed your Boards. If you'd given yourself up for dead back then, you'd *already* be a star."

You do not answer, for truth requires no reply.

"All right," you say after a moment. "All right."

Your left hand can make a fist. Your right can, too, and though the nerve-block handles the pain well enough, the slide of your wrist tendons around the nail twists you full of nausea.

That is the nausea's source.

Isn't it?

"All right. It is what it is."

Kollberg offers a moist chuckle. "Most things are."

You nod toward the screen. "Give me back the vertical city, will you?"

Kollberg clicks, and the schematic grows itself around the constellation of fourteen stars.

"Those are the surviving humans?"

"Mmm."

"How do you track them?"

"By their thoughtmitters, of course."

You only stare.

Kollberg's lower lip bulges. "I'm sorry—was this a mystery?"

Again you can't quite manage a deep breath. "They're all *Actors*? *All* of them? The porters—*everybody*?"

"Oh, yes."

"Pretornio?"

"Livia Murphy, out of New York." Kollberg manipulates his control, and the screen flares with a view of the Black Knife camp seen through a veil of blue-white flame, while hidden speakers burst to life with the crackle and spit of burning fat and the bone-conducted distortion of Pretornio's voice, chanting her Old High Lipkan.

Another twist of the control cancels the audio, and Kollberg sighs. "Quite the pity, actually. Had any of her own Studio's Administrators a hint she was capable of such power, she may have had a more . . . extensive career."

"Holy crap . . ." You lie motionless on the bed, cold and once again numb. "It *is* a snuffer . . ."

"Oh, please." Kollberg looks disgusted. "Grow up, Michaelson. The Studio doesn't produce snuffers. That's an urban legend."

"All Actors," you murmur. "Every one of them . . ."

"Of course. How do you think your bloody expedition was organized? You think it's easy to place Actors on *real* treasure hunts?"

"Why didn't—but we didn't *know*—"

"Because you're *Actors*." Kollberg flicks a piece of imaginary lint off the sleeve of his Administrator's chlamys. "Even with unbreakable conditioning-blocks and the most expensive training in the history of Earth, you just can't *stay* in bloody *character*. Look at you and Bergmann—the instant you're alone together, you're reminiscing about your damned *school days*. I mean, really. Do you have any idea how much editing we'll have to do in that sequence?"

"Bergmann? You mean Marade?"

He nods. "Olga Bergmann, out of Vienna. By the way, the sex was superb; we're keeping that. Very nicely played, on your part; you have an eye for neurotic weakness. If she lives through the rescue—and you do, of course—we'll slot you for some team-up Adventures. Banging the big Nordic blondes always goes down well. Oh, and speaking of going down—next time, make sure she gives you head. I'll speak to Vienna about it. You can sixty-nine if you want, but really it's better if she just does you. You've heard of the sexual position sixty-eight? 'Give me a blowjob, and I'll owe you one.' Ha-hrm. Especially if she's on her knees. That's nuclear when it's a powerful woman; the more submissive, the—"

"Administrator, for Christ's *sake*—"

"*Entertainer.*" Kollberg leans on the word. His little piggy eyes have receded into his face. "The proper response to a direct order is 'Yes, Administrator,' or, informally, 'Yes, sir.' "

He waits.

Vomit burns the back of your throat.

Kollberg says, "Let's give a try, shall we? Entertainer?"

Your jaw locks down so hard your teeth ache. Your throat clamps shut. You manage to say, "Yes, Administrator," anyway.

You've done harder things. Can you remember any right now?

Your gaze goes from the spike through your wrist to the fleshy curve of Kollberg's cheek and back again. *The real difference between him and Crowmane,* you monologue, *is he's too fucking smart to give me a free shot.*

And, of course, that Kollberg has offered you something to lose. "Yes, Administrator." It's easier the second time. It gets easier every time. "All right, Administrator."

"Now. Let's start again."

You grind words out between your teeth. "I still need to talk to Marc Vilo. *Please*, sir."

Kollberg shakes his head. "I thought I explained—"

"You did. But you don't understand, Administrator. I'm not trying to get out of this. I'm not trying to get out of *anything*."

Kollberg settles back into his chair and folds his hands over the soft curve of his belly. "I'm listening."

"We're on the same side here, Administrator. You want Caine to be a star. I want Caine to be a star. More than anything. More than being *alive*. Being an Actor—that's all I've lived for since I was ten years old. And you—well, I don't know you. But you're what, forty? And you're still putting together crapass straight-to-cube Adventures with packs of no-names? Your career's not going exactly the way you hoped either, I bet."

Kollberg's only response is a squint that seems to suck his eyeballs all the way to the back of his skull.

"I'm guessing this Adventure's the biggest you've ever done. It is, isn't it? And sometime before we all got bagged—maybe back when I went walking out that gate—you saw a whole new future open up in front of you."

You can't get your teeth to come apart, but you can unleash a facsimile of Caine's grin. "I'm reading your fucking mind, aren't I?"

Kollberg's lips squeeze themselves into a liver-colored asshole.

"Pulling me was the biggest chance you've ever taken. That's why you're down here. That's why you're bullying me into this horseshit escape thing. You bet that brand-new future on me."

Words squirt through those lips like a fart. "If I did?"

"You're gonna lose."

Kollberg lurches forward, red flush climbing his face. "The difference between us, Michaelson, is that I can lose and *live*. Remember I can put you back right where I *found* you."

And this, My Love, is where you *become* My Love. This is where I know you are truly Mine. When you let the grin fade. When you let your eyes go soft, and you let your voice drop like a lover's. When you say, "That's what I *want*."

"Eh?"

"Administrator, you're not a real Studio man. Not really."

"I *beg* your pardon?"

"I'm not trying to be impertinent, please, Administrator, but—where did you come from? What branch of Service?"

"Health care," Kollberg admits reluctantly. "I ran St. Luke's Ecumenical, in Chicago. But I've always enjoyed—"

"Yeah. Everybody does. But listen: popping in a cube now and then isn't the same. It doesn't mean shit. Adventures Unlimited is my whole *life*, Administrator. I have breathed Adventures in and breathed them out since I was old enough to work secondhander gear. Before I was an Actor, I was a student of Acting. Before I was a student, I was a fan. A *real* fan. Do you have any idea what that *means*? What it *is* to be a fan?"

"Well, I hardly think—"

"*Fan* is short for *fanatic*. You get it? This isn't just a hobby for me. Or a career path. This is my fucking *religion*."

"Religion." That liver-colored asshole drops the echo like a soft turd.

You let passion rise in your voice: the iron band that had unfastened within your chest goes red, then white, then melts and burns away. "When you're a fan, it eats your life. There's nothing *else* for you, you get it? Administrator, everything I *know* came from Adventures—shit, the only reason I learned to *read* was that there just aren't enough good *real* Adventures, so I started reading ones people just made up—then I started reading the shit they based those Adventures on, and—well, I just never stopped. It's all I ever *thought* about. It's *still* all I think about."

You turned your face up toward the joining where the ivory ceiling meets the green wall, but you are looking at something I cannot see with your eyes.

"When I was twelve I got in a knife fight with an older kid. All we had were homemade shanks, all point, y'know? I wasn't even *scared*; I'd cubed *White Fire, Black Steel* maybe twenty times, so I let him slash me over the ribs because I knew it'd only hurt but wouldn't kill me, and I stabbed him in the thigh—just like Jonathan Mkembe, get it? And he ran away. Jesus Christ, Administrator, when I lost my goddamn *virginity*, you know what I was thinking? I was thinking we were both decent fucks, doing pretty good, considering neither one of us were, y'know, Actors, and I was using pro technique, y'know, because I'd already fucked maybe seventy or eighty women secondhand—and she'd done more than that. . . . The biggest thing that ever happened to me? When I was maybe ten or eleven years old, I met Nathan Mast. You know who he was?"

Kollberg shakes his head. "I don't see where you're going with this, Michaelson."

"Doesn't matter. He used to be famous, back before I was born. He was one of Mkembe's sidekicks for a while. The point is, he was living in the Mission District Sorrows—the Single Room Occupancy Temp flops. He was a brokedown old ragface."

"Pathetic."

"Not for me. It was the greatest day of my life. You know why? He was just an *ordinary fucking guy.* You get it? He wasn't a god. He wasn't Superman. He was just like any other Temp ragface. Just another loser."

"So?"

"So he was just like me."

Kollberg squints. "Ah."

"Yeah."

"And so—"

"And so that was the day I discovered I had a shot at this. I've been getting ready for it ever since. I'm not going to fuck it up."

"Fine, then. I'm very glad to hear it. Now, the garrison commander at North Rahnding is a Knight Captain by the name of Purthin Khlaylock—"

"Administrator, you're hearing me, but you're not *hearing* me. What I'm trying to get through to you—without any disrespect at all—is that I *know more about this shit than you do.* Than you possibly *can.* That's nothing against you, Administrator. Adventures are just your job. They're my whole life. There is nothing in my life I care about more than *story.* There is nothing I know more about than the difference between a good one and a bad one. You're betting my life and your future on what happens in the next day or two. Let's go balls-out to make it the Greatest Fucking Show on Overworld. Come *on,* Administrator. What do you say?"

Kollberg's lips go back to asshole. "Are you trying to tell me you have a better idea?"

You draw a long, deep breath. The word *inspiration* has never been so appropriate on so many levels, for with the air comes your true spirit. Your power.

My Power.

"What I'm telling you is that Caine can't run away."

"Eh?"

"I know you've gone to a lot of trouble to set up this escape, and I appreciate it—"

"It's not an escape, Michaelson. It's a *rescue.* That's why you're not going first-hand until you make contact with the Khryllians—"

"Yes, sir. And if you can get the Khryllians coming, you can have them coming all the way to the city, right? Why bother leaving at all?"

"I'm sorry?"

"What if—instead of supposedly crawling out of the vertical city—I were to supposedly crawl *into* the city? *Deep* into the city?"

"I don't follow."

"I'm with you on the *nobody cares about continuity.* You're right. Fuck logic. It's fantasy; who gives a shit as long as it juices your shorts, right? So: what if I were to crawl into, say, where the Black Knives stashed all our *weapons* . . . ?"

Again you bring your voice down like a lover's. "Think about it, Administrator—think about Caine alone in the dark, surrounded by ogrilloi, yanking out these spikes—then finding the *bladewand* . . ."

Kollberg's eyes light up. "I can see it. I can *see* it!"

"So a few extra things could have been stashed among the gear as well, huh? You could manage that, right? Another magick weapon or two, maybe some real Healing salve instead of the fake crap . . . a few things that nobody told anybody else they had. Now Caine's got them all."

"Right . . . right . . ." Kollberg frowns. "No, wait, it won't work—the Black Knives have already distributed your belongings. They're all over the camp."

You shake your head in crisp dismissal. You have him now, and you know it; the battle is won. The rest, as you will come to enjoy saying, is mop-up.

"Doesn't matter. Look, we were after the Tear of Panchasell, right? So *other* people must have been looking for it *too*—so I've crawled in someplace and passed out among the bones of some centuries-dead treasure-hunters. You can manage some dusty old bones, can't you? Now I'm armed. Shit, with the Winston scanners, you could locate the Tear itself, can't you?"

Kollberg's sideways half-shrug half-nod is a shade too noncommittal.

"Oh." Your lips might make a smile if they weren't so thin and flat against your teeth. "You already have."

"Well—"

"It's really there? It's not just a legend?"

Kollberg sighs. "It's really there."

"Cool. You can drop me in right on *top* of it—how's *that* for dramatic? Semiconscious, I've crawled in and passed out right next to the legendary treasure that we've given our lives to find?"

Kollberg's lower lip sucks in between his teeth. "It's . . . not *bad* . . ."

"So there I am among the bones, next to the Tear of Panchasell . . . maybe with a hot-shit magick weapon, or something else to give me an edge, huh? I can move okay, even wounded, but if I can get close to Marade, I can get Healed too. Or drop some Healing shit in among the bones—whatever you've got on hand; I don't care. I'll make it work. All I need is hard intel on where everybody is and how to creep their positions—you can do that through their POVs—and Winston scans can get me the layout of the camp, with guards and whatever. I need to know where the top bitches are, and I want to know who's got the fucking bladewand, and we can work out the rest of the details as we go along. Whatever else I need, you can just kinda slip in there, where I can be conveniently surprised to find it . . . just exactly when I need it most . . ."

Kollberg's nodding along with you, his gaze directed inward, at visions of monitors lit with an imaginary Adventure. "Audience," he mutters. "Audience. We can sell cubes, but you should really have first-handers for this—"

"*That's* why I want you to call Marc Vilo for me."

Kollberg's eyes narrow to fleshy slits. "Eh?"

"Businessman Vilo *knows* people, Administrator. Lots of people. People with what you call *exotic tastes*."

"I don't get what you mean."

"You've heard of him, right? You know how he makes his living?"

"Well—Vilo Intercontinental—"

"Is a front for organized motherfucking *crime*, Administrator. He can probably fill your first-hander booths just out of his own top boys."

"Really?" Again, the light in Kollberg's eyes fades to a frown. "Well—this will be exciting, to be sure, but I hardly think a rescue, even single-handed, can be called *exotic*—"

"Rescue?" Your laugh is dark as night on the cross. "Fuck rescue. Those people died when they passed their Boards."

"Michaelson, really—" Kollberg tries to hold onto a disapproving frown while a smile fights for control of his mouth. "I mean, even Marade? Your promise—"

"Guys say lots of shit when their dicks get hard."

Kollberg's mouth opens. Then it closes again.

"I learned a lot about myself out there. I learned I'm not who I thought I was. I'm not who I wanted to be."

Lips peel off your teeth. "Who I am is *better*."

Kollberg blinks. "Michaelson—"

"This is the question, Administrator. You don't have to answer. Don't answer. Just think about it. What was the part that made you decide to pull me? To take this chance on me? What got your dick hard?"

Kollberg's lips vanish altogether, and his eyes nearly do the same.

"I bet I can tell you what it *wasn't*. It wasn't when I was making that speech about being legends. It wasn't when I sold everybody on the *die fighting* crap. It wasn't even when I went out alone and fought Spearboy. None of that hero shit."

"Heroes *sell*, Michaelson—"

"Sure they do. Hell, I like 'em too. What's not to like? You can't piss without splashing a hero in this business." More of your teeth appear. "But you weren't out pimping *Marade's* clips, were you?"

Kollberg looks thoughtful.

"I'm not one of the good guys, Administrator. I am what I am."

"This—" Kollberg still looks thoughtful. "—is not necessarily a problem."

"That's what I'm trying to tell you."

"I believe," Kollberg murmurs, "that I am beginning to understand."

"That's what's wrong with the whole escape-and-rescue thing. Getting your friends out, saving lives, all that shit. That's good-guy crap."

"And you . . ."

"I don't care if they live through it. I don't care if I live through it."

Kollberg gives you a half-believing smile. "What *do* you care about?"

"I care about *story*." The heat in your chest boils into your throat, but your voice stays low and hard.

Because now it's your voice. Not Hari Michaelson's.

"Remember what I said about story? I'm gonna teach those shit-rotten rat cunts a fundamental principle of *real* story."

"Ah?"

"When you fuck with the *bad* guy—" Your true grin unfolds like a butterfly knife. "—the bad guy fucks you *back*."

And I, as I did, as I do, as I will forever, say—

Yes, My Love. Yes.

Fuck.

## RETREAT FROM THE BOEDECKEN (partial)

You are **CAINE** (featured Actor: Pfnl. Hari Michaelson)

MASTER: NOT FOR DISTRIBUTION, UNDER PENALTY OF LAW.

I take my time unwrapping the wire from the dagger's hilt, smoothing each kink, stroking it long and straight. It's good wire, flexible, copper maybe, eight feet or so; I double it, slip the dagger through the loop, and wrap off the ends to the dagger's naked tang just below the guard. And that's it.

Time to go.

I unfold myself from the Warrior's Seat. Undoubling my legs brings a red snarl from the crusted spike-holes in my ankles. It makes me smile.

The blue sparkle has faded from the mud, and it has dried now, and I scrape it from my arms and chest and back with the dagger's blade, shaving with it fear, and doubt, and the memory of pain.

I have no need to check the belts, or the gear I have taken from these ancient bones. Each piece is in its place, as I am in mine.

The mud falls away, and the blade touches scars I bear.

*This is the axe from Kor.*

*This is the arrow from the Teranese floodplain.*

*This is the spike from the cross, and this the burn from Crowmane's god.*

*This is the alley knife from home, and this the brick, and this my father's fist.*

There are scars the blade cannot touch, but I don't need them. The ones on the outside are enough to tell me who I am.

I am strong. I am relentless. I am invincible.

I bend now and lift from among the dusty armored bones the spikes I pulled from wrist and ankle. Dirt has caked my blood upon them. In the rose-pale glow cast by Panchasell's Tear, I weigh them in my hand. Then I stick them behind my belt.

I grin at the runecut rose diamond the size of my head on its pedestal of gold, and the vast shadows of the cavern echo my black chuckle. "Think you're the biggest tear ever shed?"

I thread the dagger through its doubled loop of wire. "That'll change."

## >>scanning fwd>>

He hunches away from his partners and shuffles along the shadowed alley-way. At the ass end, he leans his spear into the corner so he can use both hands to unwrap his breechclout, and he squats.

Ogrilloi and humans aren't that different. They're pack hunters, we're op-portunistic scavengers, but the behaviors overlap enough that our evolution-ary adaptations have a lot in common. Like, say, we both prefer a little privacy when we crap.

Has to do with diets heavy in protein and aromatic fats. We evolved using the undeniably fierce smell of our feces to mark off territory. And being top predators—or, in our case, smart enough to be dangerous to top predators—we don't worry about fresh fecal reek attracting the wrong kind of attention.

Our shit says *better keep the fuck off.*

Loudly.

And it's a hell of a lot louder to a scent-hunter like an ogrillo than it is to us poor nose-challenged humans.

Steam from one hard turd rises faintly into the slanting moonlight. Which is why that squatting buck over there has no idea I'm slipping over the lip of this ruined wall. He leans on the shaft of his grounded spear, grunting low in his throat, waggling his hips, trying to work the next turd out. Poor bastard's crapping diamonds. Too much rich food.

But, y'know, I'm about to help him with that.

I slide through the moonshadow along the crumbled wall, bare feet feeling each step before I shift weight forward.

There are two contrasting styles of garrotte. The more popular is the cheese-cutter style: a single strand of thin flexible wire between a pair of han-dles. It's pretty damned foolproof. Slices the external jugulars, crushes the tra-chea, and with the right kind of takedown there's not much struggle either. The downside is that it takes a long damned time; a determined man can keep fighting quite a while with no fresh oxygen to his brain, and if you get a little careless on his back he can still kill you before he bleeds out. And if the wire's too thin it can cut the trachea instead of crushing it, and then you've got a *real* fucking fight on your hands.

I favor the strangler's noose.

Squatting, he's put his head just at my chest height; the doubled loop of the dagger's hilt wire slips down past his eyes, his snout, his tusks—the loop's extra-wide; if it snags I'm a dead man—and in the nightshadow he can't see it. The first he even knows it's there is when my two-handed yank on the dagger snaps the noose tight under his chin. He jerks up standing, and I ride his rise, doubling my knees to put my weight into his shoulder blades.

One one thousand.

My weight captures his balance; we go staggering backward. He drops his spear to claw at his throat, and his cry of alarm doesn't even make a hiss past the two strands of hilt wire that clamp shut his trachea.

Two one thousand.

His backward stumble takes us to the ruined wall. He hits it just above his knees and we topple over it. His weight crushes me into the rubble and flares splash the inside of my head and I don't care.

Three one thousand.

He kicks and flails and rolls and tries to reach back over his shoulders to get at me with his fighting claws, but his own massive musculature betrays him; his arms won't bend that way.

Four one thousand.

And now he finally remembers the spear he left on the ground over by his steaming turd, and he struggles to his knees and pulls himself over the wall again.

Five one thousand.

And he takes one step, and my weight drives him to his knees. He keeps trying—the bastard's no quitter—but this is the thing about the strangler's noose: properly applied, it doesn't cut the jugular veins, it only squeezes them shut—and it doesn't close the carotid arteries. Which is to say: it doesn't stop blood from going to your brain. It stops blood from coming *out*.

The whole thing takes only a little more than twice as long as it takes to say *massive cerebral hemorrhage.*

He makes it to the spear at seven seconds, but his hand will no longer close upon it. At eight seconds, his will can no longer drive his collapsing body, and he crumples, twitching.

He keeps twitching for a while. Even after he's basically dead. His sphincter never does let go. Poor bastard.

I take the wire off his neck before I skin him. I leave the flesh on his head, except for the musk glands under his jaw, which I have use for.

Last, before I go: I take from behind my belt one of the nails that had fixed me to my cross. I use the pommel of the dagger to pound it into his forehead.

Because they're scent hunters. Because I want them to know.

Caine is here.

Caine is coming for them.

# *I Am the Smoke Hunt*

I woke with the taste of raw human flesh still fresh and bloody on my tongue.

I rolled over and scrubbed at my face with one hand while my other groped for the pitcher on its stand beside the bed. I rinsed my mouth with stale water, then made a face and spat it on the floor. Fucking water tasted worse than the blood.

I hacked goo up the back of my throat and muttered, "Now, that was a *party* . . ."

I poured water into a shallow terra-cotta bowl and splashed it on my face, softening the sleep gunk at the corners of my eyes before scraping it away with my fingernails. Dawn had paled the stars above the room's slanted skylight. I sighed and shook myself till my ears rang. It'd probably be an hour before I could get breakfast. Or even coffee. After a soggy minute or two, I remembered ordering the Pratts out of town.

My head got too heavy to hold up. It sank into my hands. "Oh, for fuck's sake."

I pulled the chamber pot from under the bed and opened the lid, reflecting that somebody on this planet really ought to invent twenty-four-hour room service. As I settled my bare ass onto the night-chilled steel, I decided I could live without the room service. What Home really needed was a couple million union plumbers.

And plastic goddamn toilet seats. With heaters.

I spent a while staring at my hands. Soft and pink and small. Far too small: flimsy fingernails barely thick enough to crack a flea. Forearms smooth and bare where I still vaguely sensed that fighting claws should be. And clean. Too clean. No crust of drying blood, no shreds of ripped manskin —

It could have been just a dream.

Sure it could. Really. It was possible.

I finished with the chamber pot, flipped the lid shut and shoved it over by the door. The day porter'd take it from there. If there still was a day porter. I sat on the bed and laced up my breeches. Left in its holster patch overnight, the Automag jabbed into the small of my back. I was about to yank it out and toss it on the bed, but I stopped with my hand on its butt.

A dream-echo of the drumming pounded inside my head.

This hadn't been like the vision of being Orbek. That had been real as waking life. This was the gradual leakback of memory after a bad drunk.

But maybe just as real. I hadn't been that drunk.

Some kind of ritual. I couldn't quite tease it up to the surface of my sleep-fogged mind. Flames in a cave. Leaping and stomping and whirling. Chanting. A house-size bonfire and the savory tang of burning rith. A stone chalice, filled with blood.

Kaleidoscopic. Hallucinatory. The three D's: drums, drugs, and dance—

Dad, wearing his anthropologist hat, would have called it *ritual frenzy*: a deliberate, systematic breakdown of self, of the ego's defenses of recursive inhibition, shredding self-awareness to open a religious communicant's mind to the infinite. Unreserved, unconstrained, enthusiastic pursuit of transcendant union with—

What?

I had a sick feeling that I knew.

The textbook answer was *a higher power*. But this hadn't felt like transcendance. Not like emptying myself into the infinite. Just the opposite.

It had felt like summoning.

*I am the Smoke Hunt.*

I still had that nagging *presqué vu*. This should remind me of something. The Wild Hunt, maybe. I've always had warm shorts for the mythology of the Wild Hunt: a storm of chaos sweeping across the land, destroying all in its path. What's not to like?

Reminds me of my Acting career.

But the Wild Hunt wasn't it. At least not all of it. This was a different kind of hunt.

The dream or vision or whatever hadn't stopped with the drumming and the dancing but had flowered into an effortless lope through moonlit streets filled with scents of piss and rainwater, spilled wine and human sweat—

A sense of connection . . . like the Meld the primals do, a sense of being more than one person . . . or being one person spread through different bodies, all the bodies, so that in my pack I could look at myself through different eyes at the same time, and see myselves wreathed in flickering scarlet flames that cast no light, and the flame was the connection, and the connection throbbed thick and hot with shared werewolf lust.

Hitting a building. A door ripped from its hinges. Lamps shattering, flames licking wide: real flames here, crackling and scorching flesh. A casual punch splintering through a wall. Burying my jaws in soft screaming pink-fleshed humans tangled in bedsheets that leaked bright sweet blood into shredded mattress ticking.

More flames, and more terror, and more sweet copper blood.

Grey-fleshed fists crushing meat and bone with the same wet ripping crunch as the seven-bladed morningstars in the hands of men in chainmail that bore the sunburst of Khryl, the thunder of their long guns, the *shirr* of buckshot and the *shree* of rifle slugs, the clatter of steel-shod hooves on cobbled streets and no fear, no pain, just impact: blows given, blows received.

And draped over a crumple of ruined wall, shreds of corpse so battered it could have been ogrillo or human or pieces of both, freshly dead, sharp-slanting moonlight catching wisps of steam curling up from open gleaming meat—

Steam from the wounds . . .

My dad, maybe forty years ago, had told me an anthropologist's theory about the origin of the myth of the human soul: that water vapor rising from deep wounds might have been mistaken by ancient humans for the soul escaping from the body. Probably the origin of ghosts, too. The word *spirit* comes from a root meaning *breath*; in most traditions, ghosts resemble the curling fog you see from your own mouth on a chilly day. All the crap about the afterlife, about Heaven being in the sky . . . all from nothing more than wisps of condensing vapor, coiling upward like smoke—

Like *smoke*.

I said, "Son of a bitch. Son of a *bitch*."

Sure. That was it. Had to be. *Had* to be. Drummming. Dancing. Mind-altering substances. Ecstatic union with a higher power . . . no fear, no pain—

Even bullets can't hurt you. They can only kill you.

Take a pacifist Earth-human millennial religious movement, filter it through the consciousness of sentient pack-hunting carnivores, and what do you get?

The Smoke Hunt.

"They're *Ghost Dancers*, for shit's sake. Fucking ogrillo Ghost Dancers. Crazy fuck my ass Horse and Jesus stinking bloody Christ on a *stick*."

I ground my face harder into my hands. "Orbek—what the fuck have you gotten your stupid dog ass into?"

It was a rhetorical question. Because there had been more to the dream. There had been her.

Armor like a mannequin of convex mirrors. Out from the shadows of a street's mouth across the plaza, a massive two-handed morningstar propped casually over one shoulder. Reflected firelight dancing on façades. Three of me sprinting across the flagstones to meet her, smeared with the blood of the finest soldiers of Home. Casually removing her helm, shaking loose her hair. On her face, no fear. No anger. Only a reserved, remote sadness.

Her scent: human, female, thick with death. Red-smeared mirror-curves of armor rumpled with fist-shaped dents and pocked with bullet holes. Hair caked black with clotted blood. A morningstar rising with mechanical precision, falling in steel thunderbolts. Shreds of meat plastering cheekbones and forehead into unhuman texture around her vivid eyes.

Vasse Khrylget, they called her. I had a pretty good idea why.

"Yeah, okay," I muttered. "What d'you want me to do about it?"

Not that I really expected an answer. Or needed one.

I scowled at the pulse of orange dawnglow on the frame of the skylight. Too early for coffee for sure. Maybe I could snag some beans from the kitchen, chew them like aspirin . . . which was another goddamn thing this world could use—the pounding in my head was turning out to be less drums than migraine again . . .

Still only half awake, I had already pulled on my boots and was looking around for my tunic when it finally occurred to me that dawnglow doesn't pulse. "Oh," I said. "Oh, crap."

And what was that noise? Voices?

I stood on the bed and shoved the lower edge of the skylight until it squealed loose from the rust on its rim.

Yeah: voices. Faint, empty with distance, but clear—

*Dizhrati golzinn Ekk!*

Okay: not a dream. Not a vision.

Prophecy.

I sagged, hanging from the skylight's lower rim. "Son of a bitch."

Did I have to deal with this before I even got coffee? "Son of a *bitch*." I rubbed my stinging eyes. "Yeah, okay. Whatever."

Fixing the prop to hold the skylight open, I turned around and grabbed the rim underhand; with a groan of middle-aged morning, I heaved my legs up through the opening and back over the lip. As I slid through the skylight belly-down, I collected a soot-greased scrape on the stomach from a sharp slate and a bang on the skull from the lead-framed pane, so when I pushed myself up to my knees I was already pissed as hell, rubbing the back of my head and looking around for somebody to take it out on.

A distant surf of ogrilloid roaring half-drowned shrieks of terror and agony and rage. Human shrieks. Probably.

There: three or four blocks over, toward the voices; that was the glow I'd thought was dawn.

Buildings on fire.

My breath smoked. Splashes of the water I'd wiped from my face trickled goosebumps across my bare chest. I glanced longingly back down through the skylight at my warm rumpled bed—but the false dawn caught my eye again. Looked warm enough over there.

I was already backing up to get a running start for the leap across the alley to the rooftop beyond when I finally thought, *What in the name of sweet shivering fuck am I doing?*

I was *fifty years old*, for shit's sake. Fifty years old and about to run the rooftops toward some kind of goddamn free-for-all massacre. For no reason. Just because it was there.

Without even a shirt on.

I shook my head and lifted a hand as though telling some pushy asshole to back the hell off. "Not my business."

I didn't sound convinced, or convincing.

"Not my *business*." That was better. Good enough.

Now the shouts and screams picked up a soggy kettledrum backbeat. Gunfire. Full-throated: heavy-caliber stuff. The Khryllians had arrived.

Anything I needed to know, I could find out in the morning. After the shooting was over.

*You want me to stuff my aging ass into* that *meat grinder?* I monologued to my audience of one. *Make me a fucking offer.*

God did not reply.

I shrugged. "Have it your way," I said aloud. "I'm going back to bed."

Sitting on the edge of the bed. Leaning on my knees. Staring at the floor. At the splotch where I'd spat that mouthful of water. Just a blot now, about the size of my hand, darker in spots where water had soaked into wood through worn-down varnish.

It had tasted like blood . . .

Now, in the dim pulse of fireglow through the skylight, it looked like blood, too.

Gunfire and screams.

*Dizhrati golzinn Ekk!*

And bubbling up out of that soggy black swamp of that dream: stone walls crumbling beneath my fists and two of me leaping into a bedroom full of screams and blood—

A thin pale human dying across the body of a young trim redhead—

And the saliva that pumped along my tusks when both of me heard howls coming from the twin bassinets beside their bed.

This prophecy thing pretty much sucked dog ass.

I put my shirt on. After a second's thought, I added the rest of my clothes: my knives, the spring-loaded baton, the garrote, and the spare clips for the Automag. Even the flatpack of picks. Because you just never fucking know. Then I headed for the stairs.

At the landing below the second floor, I heard Pratt's voice. He didn't sound happy. He sounded like he was trying not to crap himself.

"I'm *sorry*, goodmen. *Please*, the hostelry is *closed*, you'll have to come— no, Kravmik, *don't*—!"

A stranger's voice drawled, "Yeah, Kravmik. Don't."

The period on the sentence was the cold double-click of a single-action hammer going to full cock.

The stranger had an Ankhanan accent.

Somebody else said calmly, "Go sit down. Both of you. Next to the girl."

On the landing above the lobby, I stopped and muttered, "Shit."

There was a window at the far end of the hallway behind me. I was already turning for it, already seeing myself dropping the four, maybe five meters to the alley, when I heard "But he's not even *here*."

Pratt sounded desperate. "He ate, changed his clothes, and went right *out* again—he had something to do with Knight Aeddharr—I don't know what it was—"

"Put it away, Hawk," the calm voice said. "There's no need for that. Yet. Whistler?"

"I've got him."

"What are you doing? What is that thing?"

"Don't worry about it."

The voice of Whistler: "Now. Did Freeman Shade really go out?"

"No, not really," Pratt said sheepishly. "I just made that up, because I was afraid you guys might want to hurt him or something."

"Pratt?" Kravmik's rumble sounded blankly astonished, and a woman's voice said, "Lasser, what are you *doing*?"

"Oh, it's all right," Pratt told them. "These are good people. Really."

"That's right," said the voice of Hawk. "We're good people. Now shut up, both of you."

"Hey—" Pratt lowered his voice conspiratorially. "Hey, do you know who he really is? I mean *really*?"

"Yeah," Calm Guy answered. "We know. We're friends of his."

"Oh, good. Everything's better when everybody's friends."

Up on the landing, I wasn't feeling friendly.

A professionally laid-in Charm. At least one handgun. Three in the lobby, one a thaumaturge. That meant probably one in reserve on the street out front and two more covering the alley. That's where they'd have the heavy stuff. And the Smoke Hunt was on its way.

"Pratt, let's take a walk up to his room. Whistler, on me. Hawk, watch the grill and the girl."

"By myself?" Hawk sounded bemused rather than worried. "This could get interesting."

"If he slips us, use them. Use the girl."

"He'll give a shit?"

"Sometimes he gets sentimental. Especially when they're pretty."

"I'm feeling a little sentimental, myself . . ."

"Keep your pants on. She won't live that long."

"I can be *real* fast—"

"Yeah. If there's time we'll all get a turn. But I'm *first*, get me? Whistler. Come on."

I pulled up the rear of my tunic, drew the Automag and very gently racked the slide. Holding the big pistol tight against the back of my right leg, I started down the stairs.

Sometimes I do get sentimental. Especially about people who work for a living. Pretty or not.

To my left, through the posts of the bannister: Kravmik sat half hunched across Yttrall Pratt next to the dining-hall door, shielding most of her tiny figure with his huge curve of shoulder. In front of them slouched a nightclub-pale junior featherweight with glossy black hair, his compact efficient-looking frame loaded into a slashed-velvet doublet and hose under a loose knee-length cape. Hands empty. Loose.

Hawk. The gunman.

Middle of the lobby: Pratt, hurricane lamp in one hand, turning toward the stairs, catching sight of me, face lighting with a smile of pure uncomplicated welcome. At his side another smallish man, thin, long-faced, balding, folds of flesh sagging under eyes mournful as a bloodhound's, wearing a thigh-length hunter's vest, all pockets, a twist of thread between thumb and little finger on which spun gemstone flashes.

Whistler. The thaumaturge.

And half-turned toward the stairs, left hand extended to usher Pratt and Whistler past, bigger, solidly into cruiserweight, head shaved and polished the color of tea-stained mahogany, also doing the slashed-velvet doublet thing but his worn open like a jacket, no hose here—the pants would look normal enough on a darkened street, but even in Pratt's lamplight they jumped up and bit: close-fitting heavy leather, flapped at the ankle to overlap instep and heel tendon, jointed at the knee, thick boiled panels over hamstring and quads joined by heavy wire, not much against a bullet or a Khryllian morningstar, but they'd turn most blades—and it was a good bet the jerkin under that open doublet was made the same way because that's what Grey Cats favor when going out for red work. Or ex-Cats gone merc.

No-name. Calm Guy. Giver of orders. Whose right hand was out of sight.

This might turn out to be a bit of a trick.

Another step down the stairs and Pratt's pure uncomplicated welcome burst out with pure good nature. "Hey, here he is now!"

"Hey, here I am now." The Automag was cold through the thin cotton of my breeches. "Let's nobody get stupid."

"Sounds like a plan." Calm Guy didn't move. Didn't even blink. "You first."

Another step down the stairs. "Civilians can walk, huh?"

"Maybe they could have," Calm Guy allowed, "if it had been my idea. Since it was yours, I like them where they are. At least until I see both your hands."

"You first."

A shrug. "I'm easy."

Calm Guy turned and spread empty hands. The ruffled cuffs of his doublet draped his wrists and half his palms. The drape along the insides of his fore-arms was just exactly the wrong shape.

"Those blades up your sleeves'll get you pounded by a Knight."

Another shrug, and a tilt of the head at the kettledrum backbeat of gunfire in the night streets beyond the lobby's lamplight. "Knights are busy."

"Yeah. That's exactly the problem." I took another step. "We can still get out of this with nobody dying."

"Dying?" Pratt looked from me to Calm Guy in growing distress. "What exactly is going—?"

Whistler said, "Shut up. Don't worry about it."

Pratt relaxed. "Oh. Oh, sure. I forgot: you guys are all friends."

"Yes," Whistler said, spinning his gemstone. "Yes, we are friends."

Calm Guy squinted up the stairs. "Still haven't seen your hand."

"Yeah. I appreciate the invitation, but—"

"You think this is an invitation?"

"If you were here to kill me, we wouldn't be talking."

"Killing you's Plan B. Moving up toward Plan A-and-a-Half. You're coming with us. Peacefully. Peacefully in our company or peacefully in a bag."

"I like peacefully." I can play nice, when I have to. "Peacefully works for me just fine."

"Come on, then."

I didn't move. "Where we going?"

"Simon Faller has requested the pleasure of your company. Forcefully."

"Faller?" I tried them in English. "Y'know, I've been wanting a word or two with Mr. Faller myself—"

He gave me a *what the fuck?* smirk, and spread it around to his friends. "You talk too much already," he said. In English. He had a Brooklyn accent. "We're not here to talk." He chuckled and made a slight, ironic bow. "Just guys with a job to do, you get it? Deliverymen."

I went back to Westerling. "I'll make you a deal."

He did too. "I don't think so." I guess he was used to Westerling enough that he didn't really care.

I did, though.

"The Smoke Hunt's outside," I said. "We don't want to be on the street anyway, right? We'll wait here. All of us. Once the Knights take care of the Smoke Hunt, I'll go with you to BlackStone and see Faller. Peacefully."

And when those amped-on-God fuckers break in here and find, instead of some sleepy hostelers, an assload of heavily armed Actors, it'll make me a shitty prophet, but a happy one.

Not to mention that it wouldn't exactly break my heart to have Tyrkilld and Kierendal—and, say, Angvasse Khlaylock—know I'd been hauled at gunpoint off to see the Wizard. But nobody ever wants to do things the easy way.

Calm Guy shook his head. "We're on a schedule. Once the Knights take care of the Smoke Hunt, it'll be too late."

"Too late? For what?"

"For you'll find out, smart guy."

"I made a good offer. Think it over."

"Don't have to."

I sighed. "Is your fucking schedule worth more than your life?"

"Maybe not." Calm Guy grinned up at me. "But it's worth more than *their* lives. Hawk—?"

"Hey." A glossy white grin unfolded under the gunman's glossy black hair. "Wanna see a trick?"

"Not really."

Hawk's right hand and arm became a blur that in less than an eyeblink resolved into a big black pistol leveled at arm's length on Ytrrall Pratt's pretty red head.

Kravmik growled wordlessly and tried to pull her closer.

"Go right on," Hawk told him easily. "I'll just shoot you first."

I sagged. "That's a pretty good trick."

"Ain't it just?"

"You're fast, kid."

"Fastest you'll ever see."

"Fastest I ever saw was Berne. Saint Berne, they call him now. Maybe you heard what happened to him." I nodded toward Calm Guy: the ex-Cat. "Or you could ask him. He'll know. He might even have been there."

"Ancient history, old man. A whole different world ago."

I looked down at this grinning killer who'd been in short pants then. Who had maybe just been born when Black Knives ruled here. But only maybe. Ancient history. "I guess it was."

"Let's see that hand," Calm Guy said.

"Yeah, whatever." I showed them the Automag. Nobody looked impressed.

"Put it on the stairs behind you and keep coming."

I didn't move.

"You said you know things about me." Half a shrug half lifted the Automag. Not enough to get anybody tense. "Most of what you know about me is wrong."

"Let's find out," Calm Guy said. "Hawk: the grill. Leg first. Then the head. Then the girl."

"The leg?" Hawk sighed. "I hate when they yowl."

"Wait." I scowled down at the blur of my reflection in the Automag's chromed slide, tilting it like I wasn't entirely sure what I was seeing. And I wasn't. Not really.

I was trying to decide exactly who I was right then.

"Hawk." I rolled the nickname around my mouth. "Hawk. Ever study at an abbey, Hawk?"

"Hey—" Calm Guy began.

"I'm talking to Hawk. I'll talk to you again when I'm done with him."

The words came out slower and slower, like my spring was winding down. Slower and flatter and colder. "Ever do any Esoteric training?"

Those glossy white teeth showed up again. He had a lot of them in that soft red mouth. "What's it to you?"

"I'm gonna ask you a riddle, Hawk. An Esoteric riddle."

"Do I give a shit?"

"If you know the answer, *Hawk*," I said, dead slow, dead flat, "I might let you live."

A dead cold silence.

Calm Guy and Whistler exchanged a look like they were asking each other if either of them liked Hawk well enough to get in the way of whatever was about to happen without knowing what the fuck it was about to be. They each saw the same answer.

Hawk saw those answers too. His pale cheeks flamed. "*Screw* this—"

"What—" The riddle came out soft, gentle, quizzical, like I really wanted to know. "—is the sound of one hand clapping?"

Hawk's eyes narrowed, then widened, and then his extended arm and hand and pistol became again a blur, now in a quarter arc toward the stairs, but even that blur had to cover a meter and a half while the muzzle of my Automag had to twitch only a couple inches.

Both pistols blasted flame. Hawk's blasted once. Mine blasted three times: an autoburst, which is an accommodation for crappy shooters, which I am. The autoburst fired three of its caseless tristacks—a total of nine shatterslugs— in a brief sequence that kicked its muzzle through a short arc up and to the right. A couple of brief shrieks came from over by the dining hall door: Mrs. Pratt, maybe. Maybe Kravmik.

Splinters burst from the bannister in line with my navel: Hawk's round. A great shot, that kid—ten times the shooter I'll ever be. For all the good it did him.

Splinters also burst from the floorboards past Hawk's right knee. As well as from his right thigh, right hip, spine, and the left side of his rib cage. A different kind of splinter.

Shatterslugs break into tumbling needles after impact: full kinetic transfer and a shitload of internal shredding. Hawk went down like a sack of hamburger. He didn't bounce when he hit the floor. It was more of a splat.

He lay there making dying-fish popping noises, and his eyes stared beyond the world.

"Good guess, kid. Too bad you can't take a bow."

And that told me who I was. For now.

I turned the Automag on Calm Guy. Calm Guy was backed off in a crouch, the snarl on his face distorted through what appeared to be a semisubstantial curve of shimmering glass that had sprung out of nowhere to enclose him and Whistler, along with the preternaturally calm Pratt.

A Shield.

"Hey, nice. You're fast too." I nodded a smile toward Whistler. "Was that on a trigger? Set on the first gunfire, I bet."

"Hawk—*Hawk!*" Calm Guy's calm had evaporated.

I shrugged down at them. "I was just kidding about letting him live."

I thumbed the Automag to single shot and squeezed off a tristack against the Shield. The three shatterslugs burst into flares of sparks that crawled over the half-real curve of energy. Whistler grunted like he'd been punched.

"Feedback's a bitch, huh? Think your Shield'll hold against my whole clip?"

"*Take* him, Whistler!" Calm Guy had become Pretty Fucking Nervous Guy. "Take him *now*—!"

"I've got him." Fast, smooth, professionally nerveless, Whistler reached into one of the pockets on his hunting vest. His other hand was busy keeping his gemstones spinning, and Pretty Fucking Nervous Guy had a knife in one hand and a pistol in the other and both eyes on the muzzle of the Automag and Lasser Pratt, without a word, a preparatory breath or so much as a flicker on his utterly serene expression, lifted the hurricane lamp and smashed it over Whistler's head.

Whistler's face went blank. The shield went down.

The lobby darkened.

The Automag roared but only floorboards splintered because Pretty Fucking Nervous Guy was quicker than a cat and had already thrown himself sideways into a shoulder roll that brought him to his feet on the far side of Pratt and the lobby was brightening again now because Whistler had fallen to his knees and the lamp oil had wicked his vest and caught fire, and Whistler went down on his face, burning on the floor, and Pretty Fucking Nervous Guy smacked Pratt on the temple with the pommel of his knife and caught his sagging body under the arm with the same hand, so that he had a knife in front at the notch of Pratt's collarbone and a pistol under Pratt's jaw at the rear, and he snarled, "*Drop* it! Drop it *now!*"

I walked down the stairs.

"I'll cut his fucking head off! Drop your *weapon!*"

I said, "Why should I?"

Blood trickled along Pratt's cheekbone. "Fuck this guy. He told that cocksucker to kill my wife. Shoot him."

"Shut *up!*" Pretty Fucking Nervous Guy jabbed the muzzle up into Pratt's jaw hard enough to make the hosteler grunt. "Didn't you *hear* me?"

"I thought," I said, "you know who I am."

"After I kill him—" His eyes were bright and hard and slick: gemstones wet with spit. "—we'll move on to the grill and the woman. And the kids."

"Why don't we talk it over by the light of your burning spellbitch?"

Pratt said through teeth forced shut by the pressure of the muzzle under his chin, "Shoot this fucker."

"*Shut up!*"

"When you get back to Faller, tell him I said there's more going on here than he knows. More than he can guess. Tell him I said it's Caine's Law, here. Ask him if he knows Rule Three."

"What the fuck are you *talking*—"

"You let Pratt go." I gestured at the flames on Whistler's back. "We put out your spellbitch while he's still breathing. Then you go out that door and I never change my mind about letting you two live."

"I don't like this deal."

I lifted the Automag. "You think Pratt's life means more to me than yours does to you?"

Pretty Fucking Nervous Guy considered that. Not for very long.

This is a perk of being me.

He licked his lips. "Put him out first."

"Kravmik. The tablecloth."

The huge ogrillo reluctantly let go of Yttrall, pulled the tablecloth out from under the remaining lamp on the small lamp stand, and spread it over Whistler. The lobby darkened again.

Pretty Fucking Nervous Guy started backing for the door, yanking Pratt along with him. "You can't protect them, old man."

Old man. I felt every day of it. "Don't forget to tell Faller what I said."

At the doorway, Pretty Fucking Nervous Guy shoved Pratt stumbling back into the lobby. "I'll tell your *mother*," he snarled from the shadows beyond. "I'll tell her that you—"

The Automag blasted another autoburst. From the night-shadowed street came another shredded-body splat.

I watched a wisp of smoke curl back along the Automag's muzzle. "Guess I'll tell him myself."

I walked without hurry across the lobby. I thumbed the Automag again to single shot and put a tristack into the back of Whistler's head as I passed. Whistler's transition from man to corpse was marked by a single whiplash buck and a halo-splash of blood and bone splinters into the carpet.

At the doorway I kept close beside the jamb, where the dim lamplight wouldn't line me to the street outside. I looked down into the shadows off the boardwalk at the crumpled mess of Pretty Fucking Nervous Guy, who had now become Writhing and Struggling to Breathe as He Bleeds to Death Guy.

"You—you said . . ."

"I said—" I lifted the hem of my tunic and reholstered the Automag. "—I wasn't gonna change my mind."

"You . . . you . . . don't let me just . . . for the love of God . . ."

"Which god?"

I stood there and watched him die. It didn't take long.

I raised my head and called out into the night. Not loud. They'd be close enough to hear me. "Hey. You seeing this? Hawk and Whistler are dead too."

The night answered with echoes of distant gunfire.

"Think you can do better? Take your best fucking shot. I'll be right out."

When I turned back from the doorway, pale faces were peering down from the second-floor landing: other hostelry guests, clutching half-closed clothing around themselves and rubbing sleep from fearful eyes.

"Get everybody up and anybody Armed, get armed," I said. "The Smoke Hunt's outside, bandits and looters are everywhere, and the Knights can't protect you because they've got bigger problems. Get every weapon you can lay your hands on and get ready to fight for your fucking lives."

The faces stared blankly down at me. I pointed at Hawk and Whistler. "You want to be dead like them? Go!"

The faces disappeared.

I went back across the lobby. Whistler smelled like bad barbeque. Hawk smelled like roadkill.

Kravmik was trembling all over. "You—the Knights—have to go to the parish—"

I picked up Hawk's pistol. "Can you shoot?"

Kravmik's face twisted doubtfully. "Never have."

"Hold it tight and keep your wrist locked. The safety's here. Aim it like a handbow. Can you manage?"

The pistol nearly disappeared inside his vast fist. "It's a weapon. I'm an ogrillo," he said with a deep breath. "I'll manage."

Pratt was half crumpled in his wife's arms, shaking with adrenaline collapse. "Got 'em—we got 'em, didn't we?"

"You hurt?"

"I, ah—I dunno, I—"

Yttrall shook her head without looking up. She stroked his thin sweat-damp hair. "He's well as can be hoped, my lord. No harm beyond the shaking, I think. Though I feared much for my brave Lasser lad—"

"No need, no need—they had me right where we wanted 'em," Pratt said with a shaky laugh.

"Yeah. How'd you slip the Charm?"

"*You* should know," his wife said.

"I should?"

"Wouldn't be real successful here if every ass-mandrake and his buttsister could Charm me out of their bill, would I?" Pratt fished inside his blouse and pulled out a coin-size medal on a chain. "Proof against all forms of magickal compulsion."

I reached for the medal and turned it over in my hand. It was damp with the touch of Pratt's skin, and of a warm pale metal, maybe white gold. On one side was stamped a representation of a pair of hands, both holding daggers; the forearms crossed at the wrists and were pinned together by the blade of a sword that stuck up between the angled dagger blades to bisect the angle they made. The opposite side was plain except for a phrase inscribed in simple Westerling script.

*My Will, or I Won't.*

"Son of a *bitch*." I dropped it like it had burned me and jerked to my feet. "Didn't I tell you to get out of town?"

"We—well . . ." He made a faint backhanded wave around the small lobby, which I only now registered was lined with baggage piled along the walls. "We can't just go, not all at once, my lord—"

"I'm not your lord."

"—I mean, please, you must understand, we have staff here, they're family—and they have families of their own—"

"Oh, for fuck's sake."

"And our guests . . ."

"What about them?"

Pratt cast a *help me* glance at Kravmik, who just shrugged and shambled over Whistler's corpse toward the door, already holding Hawk's pistol like he'd been born with it in his hand.

Pratt gently disengaged himself from Ytrall's arms. "It's not that easy to explain."

"Nor so hard either," his wife said. "A guest in our house has a claim on us, begging your lordship's pardon. We'll not be leaving while there's danger they must face within our walls, or without. It's a duty, your lordship. Not unlike your own."

I wasn't going to debate my duty. Whatever the fuck it might be, which is something I've never been able to get entirely straight. "It's worth more than your life?"

Pratt shrugged helplessly. "It *is* our life."

"Then get them out of here *too*."

"That we shall," Ytrall said. "When it may be done. Which is not this instant, begging your lordship's pardon."

"Well—" I locked a snarl behind my teeth and stifled a sudden lust to slap the snot out of both of them. "—*do* it, that's all. As soon as shit calms down enough that you can hit the street."

"Not this street. Not anytime soon." Kravmik turned back from the door. His eyes were empty yellow saucers. "We got Hunters outside. I think they're coming this way."

From the front of Kravmik's massive shoulder, the street looked empty.

"I don't see them."

"Me neither." With the muzzle of Hawk's pistol, Kravmik tapped his snout alongside one age-greyed tusk. "But they're out there. And not far."

"Any idea how many?"

I felt him shrug. "Thirty years ago, maybe I coulda. No stalker, these days."

"Don't smell Tyrkilld anywhere, do you?"

"Not if I don't have to." But he couldn't even force a smile.

I leaned into the doorway. "Hey," I said, louder. "Hey, fuckers. Still there? Talk to me."

Blank storefronts and boardwalk for fifty yards to the river. The other way, just a long straight gloom, half-lit orange by fireglow reflected from low clouds.

Indigo shadows still and sharp as the gaps between stars.

"We got a mutual problem that can have a mutual solution," I called. "Come on, fuckers. You want to be out there with the Smoke Hunt?"

Nothing. Maybe I was wrong about the backup. Or maybe their nerves were just really, really good. One way to find out.

I stepped through the door and bent over Calm Guy's corpse to pry the gun out of his dead hand. Nobody shot at me.

The weapon was Earth-make, not stonebender: a Smith & Wesson select-fire, loading thirty hypervee steel-tail aluminum tumblers in a double-stack extended clip. Old-fashioned, but these rounds could pick a lock at a hundred meters and body armor doesn't even slow them down. Not that Smoke Hunters would be wearing any.

It fit my right hand just fine.

From out on the boardwalk, the street looked even more deserted. Shuttered storefronts stared back at me. A puddle left from last night's rain rippled burnt orange in the breeze. And the gunfire sounded to be moving the other way.

How good was Kravmik's nose anyway?

I mean, that breeze was on the back of my neck . . . the firefight was fading beyond the shadows down the street . . . any Hunters that would be coming this way must have slipped the armsmen somehow, because the Khryllians sure as hell weren't chasing them . . . was Kravmik's nose good enough to scent them from blocks off? Downwind?

Which was when a tiny voice inside my head whispered, *that's right, dumb-ass, the breeze is on the* back *of your neck.*

I turned.

Six were already in the river. Faint shimmering haloes of scarlet witchfire around their heads evoked corpse-lanterns on the Great Chambaygen—except they were coming at us across the current, and at a pretty good clip. Two more right behind, slipping silently down into the black water. One last on the far quay. Standing. Staring at me.

Naked. Rippling with flames of power.

He spread arms like the thighs of bulls, and drew air into a chest like a bargeload of boulders—

And I, for roughly the duration of my entire lifetime in reverse, froze.

Sort of.

I didn't so much freeze as I froze about freezing.

I was hanging from a wire an arm's length over my own head: a psychic Sword of Damocles. Because I really didn't know how I was going to take this. I've been having this dream half my life.

Back in the Boedecken . . .

The details are different every time, so it doesn't matter who's with me or how the place looks, how I'm armed, none of that, all that mattered was that I was back in the Boedecken but I was old and slow and tired with killing.

And Black Knives were coming for me. Again.

It felt like some kind of justice. This was where I really started—everything before was prologue—so this was where I ought to end. There was a bitter po-etry to it: after all the spectacularly fraudulent mock heroics that had made me a legend, I freeze on a dark street in front of people who'd fallen for that leg-end so hard that they worship it. That might be the only way to pay for being me. To make my end not a storied, gloried song but the punch line to the bad joke I've always been. To go out like a punk.

Stalton's eyes . . . opal stars of slivered moon—

You don't decide to freeze, or to break, or to crumple in a corner and crap yourself any more than you decide to black out when somebody cracks your head with a pipe. It's something your brain does without your cooperation. When the demons asleep in the back of your skull wake up hungry.

Crowmane's smoking stump and Stalton's eyes and Purthin Khlaylock, lifting his morningstar to pray—

So I hung there over my own head, dangling from a golden thread of *I think maybe but how am I supposed to know and when the fuck, exactly, does my wave function collapse and leave Whiskers' corpse rotting in my skull?*

But in the same instant I was remembering—as my dead wife used to remind me, way too fucking often—not everything is about me.

Kravmik and the Pratt family and a house full of ordinary damn people bobbing downstream toward the fecal falls were counting on me to be the closest thing they had to a canoe, and justice for me wasn't gonna do them any goddamn good at all, so for a decade-long blink of an eye I saw myself starring in *Beau Geste* again, this time for real, making a stand here in the hostelry, trying to hold off the Smoke Hunt with a grand total of three guns, two balls, and no brains at all. Which wouldn't end up doing Pratt & Co. an assload of good either. It'd just make me feel better about dying ugly.

Which, because in my heart I'll always be an Actor, made me think of Edmund Kean's last words, *Dying is easy—comedy is hard*, and I found myself muttering, "You think so? Just watch how fucking funny *this* is gonna be."

And it had all started and finished in an Ox-Bow Incident half-second, because by the time that buck across the river unleashed the roar he'd been drawing breath for, I had already snapped back into my body and was turning to Kravmik in the doorway. "Forget what I said about fighting them. Get the Pratts and the staff and all the guests up to the roof and have them scatter over the alleys to the surrounding buildings. I mean *scatter*. Anybody who can't make the jump? *Throw* 'em. And give me back that gun."

He scowled down at me. "But you say—"

"Forget what I said. You're not gonna fight them. Get people going and go with them. I'll lead the Hunters off—slow 'em down till Tyrkilld and the Riverdock armsmen can get back here—"

The big chef squinted toward the river. "Maybe I can talk to them—grills are grills. Smoke Hunt's got no reason to hook red with—"

"Kravmik."

He heard it in my voice. That doubtful scowl crawled back down his crown ridge. "What?"

Kravmik had to be pushing my age—maybe from the wrong side—which meant he was old enough that this was one of those happy accidents where I could just tell the truth. "Those are Black Knives."

His eyes popped to about the size of my hands, and he made a noise like he'd swallowed his tongue. When he could finally get out a word, that word was a half whispered, "No . . ."

"Yes."

His mouth hung slack for a second or two, then his lower lip started to flap. "But—b-but—n-n-no clan sign—"

"Not where you can see it. Don't believe me? Go over there and ask Pratt who I am. But give me the gun first." Because, y'know, ever since I made sure the Khulan Horde went down at Ceraeno, Black Knives aren't the only grills who have reason to hold maybe a bit of a grudge, and I wasn't in the mood to take a round or two in the back for being a fucking wise guy.

"Who you *are*—?"

"Just do it. Go on, move!"

He frowned like he'd found a rat turd in his almondine, but he put the gun in my outstretched left and jogged heavily back around Whistler's corpse toward the Pratts.

A couple of the Smoke Hunters were already out of the river. One loped toward me along the street, slow and easy, trotting on all fours, and the other reared up and spread his arms and expanded a steamer-trunk chest to unleash a contrabasso blast of—

"*Dizhrati golzinn Ekk!*"

—which somehow, on its twisty cart ride through the funhouse I use for a brain, didn't do anything like start a freeze; a toasty red glow kindled somewhere around my balls and spread up through my chest and down my legs and into my arms, and when it finally reached my head, what the buck had roared ended up translating *Welcome back to the Boedecken, Skinwalker.*

And I felt a whole lot better.

I nodded a smile back at him as I leaned my left forearm against the board-walk post in front of me and wedged my right hand down hard on top of it with Calm Guy's Smith & Wesson braced against the post on the side, because steadied like that with a gun like this, even a crappy shooter like myself can get medium-range accuracy on the order of a carbine, and so my reply to his welcome was a cheerfully warm *Thanks; it's good to be home,* which was delivered in a three-round burst to the heart that slapped him down flat and wet and floppy.

I swung the sights onto the one trotting toward me—who hadn't even broken stride—and let him have his own burst into the upper lip. His head exploded like a meat grenade.

Four more were up out of the water and the other three were behind them and I was coolly taking aim, y'know, *two down, seven to go; hey, honey, watch me turn* Rover *into* Spot, and generally feeling pretty snappy about myself until the first one got up.

So I shot him again. More than shot him. I hosed him down—at least ten rounds. Big wet chunks of Smoke Hunter ripped loose and plopped onto the puddled street. Including his right arm.

Which was when he bent down, picked up his own severed goddamn arm by his own severed goddamn wrist, and swung it around his head.

"*DIZHRATI GOLZINN EKK!*"

He wasn't even *bleeding.*

And I wasn't feeling all that snappy anymore.

I remember blinking stupidly until I could finally make my mouth work. "Fuck *this* for a joke—"

It got even less funny when the one with only a gooey mess of raw sausage where his head should be rolled to his feet and loped over to join the others.

The dream-vision-prophecy . . . that Meld thing . . . how I had spread my mind though different bodies . . . seeing through each other's eyes . . . plus a sick twist on the Ghost Dancer bullets-cannot-harm-us thing . . .

Somebody had learned a new trick. No. An old one.

*—the Black Knife camp below my cross alive in the night with shadows leaping, howling, teeth and claws and hunger—*

Somebody learned *Pretornio's* trick.

No wonder the Hunt could ring up Khryllians wholesale. I'd watched reanimated corpses of Pretornio's porters rip Black Knives limb from limb— reanimated ogrilloi would be proportionally stronger—

From the dream: that fantasy of power, stone walls shattering under a blow of my grey-leather fist . . .

. . . a fantasy of being stronger than a Knight of Khryl.

*Now* there's *a new kind of suicide bomber* . . . I monologued to my audience of one.

Now they were all down to all fours, coming at that ground-eating lope, not in any hurry so I had maybe all of three seconds, and across the street an alley mouth yawned darkness, and I remembered another alley up around the corner, and in that two-seconds-left I decided to bet my life that they were connected.

I ran out into the street, holding down the Smith & Wesson's trigger, not aiming, spraying low to empty the clip and hope for a boneshot to a leg or two to slow a couple down. The slide racked open before I hit the opposite boardwalk and I dropped it and stopped at the alley mouth to empty Hawk's pistol at them too before I fell back into the shadows and that's when shit went *really* weird.

Because one of Smoke Hunters said, "Hey, check it out—did you guys *see* that? I think that was *Caine!*"

And another said "No fucking way," and a third said, "No, man, I think he's *right*—"

They were speaking English.

"Do we kill him?"

"*Kill* him? Before I get his *autograph?*"

So there, in the alley, back against the cold wet brick wall, two-handing the Automag up by my cheek, I did freeze. I didn't have the faintest fucking ghost of a clue what could possibly be going on, or what I should be doing about it. Which led me to do maybe the only really smart thing I'd managed since I got off the boat yesterday morning.

I called out in English, "Hey—what the fuck, huh?"

All eight of them clustered at the alley mouth, slowly, squinting into the moonshadow. The one carrying his own left arm let it dangle forgotten by his leg. "Holy *shit*—it's you, isn't it? You're really you?"

I replied, "Back the fuck off. All of you."

They didn't.

I swung the pistol down into line. "You can see well enough to see this gun, right?"

They all kind of shrugged and nodded to me and each other—except the one with no head—but kept inching tentatively closer. "Yeah—yeah, Caine . . . yeah, it's not even really dark out here, not for us."

"This isn't one of the civvie pieces I shot you with before," I told them. "This is a Social Police Automag."

They stopped.

"Hey, no, shit, no—Caine, we're not after *you*—" One-Arm said. "I mean, Jesus Christ, this is *so* fucking *awesome*, you're like my *hero*—"

"Oh, he is *not*," another one said.

"He *is*. You *are*," One-Arm assured me earnestly. "You're the *greatest*—I always said so—"

"Packard, you are *such* a *buttsuck.*" The second one cocked his head toward me confidentially. "He never bought a cube of yours in his life—his whole collection is like some K'Trann and Jhubbar, and some old Pallas softcores from before she met you that he beats off to—"

"Shut *up*—!" One-Arm backhanded him with his severed arm hard enough to knock him sprawling. "It's not my *fault*—my *parents*—"

One of the others snickered in my direction. "Ass-Packard's mommy won't let him have your shit because you say fuck all the time and stuff. Doing it's one thing, but she gets weird when you say it—"

"Will you *drop* it? Jesus *Christ*—!"

I found myself sagging against the alley's wall. "Who are you fuckers?"

They told me. Their names were a roll call of Earth's Leisure Congress. Packard, Rand, Windsor, two Sauds, a Walton, a Bush, and—the one whose head I'd shot off—a Turner.

"Turner?" I said, blinking at the headless hulk of ogrillo. "You're one of Wes Turner's kids?" Back in the day, Westfield Turner had been the president of Adventures Unlimited.

My former boss.

The headless one waved this off and pointed at One-Arm—Packard. Packard said, "Leisureman Turner's his *grandfather*. Little Turner's the one who gets us the berths, y'know. Usually he plays really well—it's hysterical you blew his face off like first thing—you should see how it looks when your eyes explode, it's *so* awesome—"

I let the Automag fall to my side. "How old are you?"

"Fifteen."

The one he'd knocked down—Bush—snickered. "You are not. He's not."

"I will be in two weeks."

"Two weeks makes you a lying sack of fourteen-year-old shit."

"I am *so* gonna beat your ass."

"Oh, sure." Bush got up. "*Try* it, Lefty."

"I mean after. I am gonna fly down to your broke-ass daddy's dinky little white-trash island and I am gonna *pound* you."

"You're kids . . ." My brain had somehow turned into a wet wool blanket stuffed inside my skull. "You're all kids."

"Well, sure," one of the Sauds said. "This is still in beta, and they need play-testers, and Turner's really pretty all right, you know, he set us up, it's a real party, even though everything's virtual. The simichair hookup cost my dad a bundle, and he's itching to play, too. Maybe once they smoke the bugs out and get this ready for release. This is *way* sweeter than even firsthanding, because, you know, first off, the Studio hasn't even *done* that in like forever, and even then, if we were like firsthanding you, we'd just be riding along while you kill people. This way we get to kill them *ourselves*—"

"And *eat* them." Bush's tusks gleamed pale and wet in the moonlight. "We get to kill them and eat them. This is *way* harder core than even *your* stuff—no offense, y'know; I'm a real fan, not like Ass-Packard. I have your Collector's Platinum Edition box-set, plus I've got a bootleg master of *Servant of the Empire*—"

"Just 'cause your mom sucked Turner's wrinkled old grampadick for it," Packard sneered.

I shook my head. "You little shits understand that these are real *people?* You get it? This isn't just a fucking *game*—"

"Sure it is," Packard said. "Our pack gets points for every civilian we take out before the Knights knock us to pieces. We get extra points for taking out armsmen, and killing a Knight's an automatic win, unless another pack gets a Knight too, and they've got more civilian kills than—"

"And you get points too just for duration, you know?" Bush nodded enthusiastically. "We're short on kills, but just standing here talking to you we're racking our score, and that's bone grippy, because we get to meet you and everything, and we can still do our mission objective, because we came down the river—these grills we're piloting are already dead, y'know, they don't have to breathe—and the Knights aren't here yet—"

I couldn't get my mind around it. "You're just sonofabitching *kids*—"

Packard smirked at me. "Yeah, right. How old were you the first time *you* killed somebody?"

"The first time I killed somebody I was fighting for my *life*, you little bastard." Which was a damn lie, but what the hell. "You're a pack of spoiled Leisure brats sitting in simichairs a universe away—"

"Well, sure," the other Saud said, shaking his head at me like I was a goddamn idiot, which was exactly how I felt. "You think our parents would let us do this if we could actually get *hurt?* I mean, check it out—" He lifted his loincloth to show a ragged stump where the Smoke Hunter's cock had been severed at the root. "We can't even fuck. What are we supposed to do except kill people?"

"I never killed *anybody* just for *fun*—"

"No, you killed 'em for *our* fun." Bush's smirk was almost identical to Packard's. "You were good at it too. The best. You know you're still in the Top Ten? Sure, the Studio hasn't released anything fresh from anybody in about forever now, but you'd probably hang in there even against the new guys, they're such pussies—"

"Shut up. Everybody fucking shut *up* a minute."

I was *not* going to have this argument with goddamn Leisure brats who were playing at being Black Knives in a virtual sonofabitching *game*.

Especially since this was an argument I'd lose.

I came to Overworld—became an Actor in the first place—to taste the kind of power I could never have on Earth. Sure, wealth. Sure, fame. Adulation, and even some political influence. But all that was just perks, y'know? The real prize was power: to ignore the laws that circumscribe the lives of Earth's undercastes. To live without law altogether. To bow to no law except my own will. But that's more abstract than it really was; when you get right to the bone, it was about being a god.

To kill without consequence.

It's never been a mystery to me that I'm more than a little crazy. It's also never been a mystery that if I hadn't been an Actor, I'd have died in prison. So I got myself to a place where bloodlust is power, and casual murder is the point of the game.

Same as them.

They were starting out from a place of power already, that's all. They get to have everything I busted ass for without putting their butts on the line.

But y'know, my butt was never all that much on the line either. Half the scars I carry are from wounds that should have killed or crippled me—*would* have killed or crippled anyone who's not an Actor. Unlimited access to the most cutting-edge medical treatment in the world, plus the occasional use of flat-out magick: the best health plan in the history of both universes.

So what's the difference between me and them? The real difference? They were in it for fun. I got paid. That's about it.

It's an old joke at the Studio Conservatory, and not a funny one: If you kill for money, you're a soldier. If you kill for fun, you're a psychopath. If you kill for money *and* for fun, you're an Actor.

*Dizhrati golzinn* motherfucking *ekk.*

My headache thundered in my ears. "You said you had a mission objective."

"Sure." Bush swung his talons toward the Pratt & Redhorn. "It's a sander. On that hotel."

"Sander?"

"Search and destroy. Nobody left alive. And we burn the place down. Five hundred points. Fuck, don't you know *anything*?"

"I know some things."

Search and destroy. I would have vanished without a trace—missing, presumed dead in the fire. . . . This Faller character was going about things in a very organized way. Looked like he always did. He had a setup twice as nifty as the Khryllian trick of using grill hostages as draft animals. Ten times as nifty.

Let's say you're an Overworld Company goon trapped here on Assumption Day, and you want to get home. If you know enough folklore, you know about the *dillin*, and you might even remember the references in my dad's book, *Tales of the First Folk*, where he suggested that the Quiet Land—the place the *dillin* are supposed to lead to—might be Earth. You might also remember cubing *Retreat from the Boedecken* and the story behind the Tear of Panchasell, and when you get to Purthin's Ford, you start mining griffinstones. But not for money.

For power.

And when you find out about this Smoke Hunt business—that some enterprising ogrilloi have managed to find a way to tap into the Outside Power that was both the *dil T'llan* and the onetime God of the Black Knives—you discover that animating the Smoke Hunters draws enough energy off the Outside Power that you can force open the *dil*.

Well and good. You can get to Earth. But you don't *go* to Earth . . . because you're smart enough to know you're sitting on the only working gate between Earth and Home.

I discovered that I was kind of looking forward to meeting this fucker.

I squinted past them at the bloody corpse of Calm Guy on the boardwalk, then up over the skyline of the hostelry's roof. "I know some things," I repeated. "I know you fuckers aren't going in there. And you're not gonna burn it down, either."

"Aw, come on," one of them—I think it was the Windsor, but it was dark, and really, when you come right down to it all dead grills look pretty much alike to me—said, "You're gonna cost us the *game*—"

"A little over five minutes ago I killed three men to protect that place. Three real men, who really died." I looked deep into the Windsor's piss-yellow eyes. "What do you think I'll do to *you?*"

The Windsor blinked. "Whoa—for real? Would you really? I mean, that'd be so fucking *cool*—*way* better than an autograph!"

"I'll torture the fuck out of you, if it makes you happy. Just don't burn my shit."

Bush sniggered. "What, were you in there? We could have killed *you?* Hot fuck, how awesome would *that* be? To be the guys who killed *Caine?*"

Packard nodded slowly. "Y'know . . ." He looked around at the others. "We still *could* . . ."

"Settle down—"

Bush looked suddenly thoughtful. "All you've got is that gun, right?"

I said, "Let me explain," and put a tristack into his kneecap.

The impact spun him, and when he tried to catch himself, his leg bent backward and folded in half and toppled him sideways, because the shatter-slugs had chopped his knee joint into ogrillo scrapple.

"Hey . . ." he said, aggrieved. "Hey, come on. What'd you do *that* for?"

I hefted the Automag. "Anybody else?"

"This *sucks*," Bush said as he struggled to get back to his feet. Er, foot. "I haven't got to kill *anybody* yet!"

"Cry me a fucking river." I shrugged down at the ogrillo body he was wearing. "You should be grateful. Other people who make that mistake with me don't live through it."

"It was *Packard's* idea—why don't you shoot *his* leg off?"

"And it's still a good one," Packard said. "Everybody spread out. When he opens fire on me, rush him. I don't know how many points he's worth, but who gives a shit? This is *Caine*. How cool are we?"

"Sure, ice cold, you are." I took a step backward into the alley. If I could get deep enough, I could enfilade them as they came at me. Which wouldn't likely be enough to save my life, but I didn't have any better ideas.

A slight noise from behind me in the alley—a metallic rustle, like a sleepy silver rattlesnake—and I risked a quick glance over my shoulder in time to see the shadows transform into a straight, severe man in straight, severe armor, plain and functional except for the golden Sunburst upon the open electrum Palm on the breast of the cuirass, and I said, "Holy crap—I never thought I'd be saying this, but I am *really* glad to see you right now—"

Markham, Lord Tarkanen, replied simply, "*Pynhall.*" He was faster than Tyrkilld.

I never saw it coming.

# THE CAINE WAY

**RETREAT FROM THE BOEDECKEN** (partial)
You are **CAINE** (featured Actor: Pfnl. Hari Michaelson)
MASTER: NOT FOR DISTRIBUTION, UNDER PENALTY OF LAW.

"*T izarre*—!" I hiss as loud as I dare. "Tizarre, goddammit . . ."

The next flare of summer lightning shows only the back of her neck and the strings of her mouse-brown hair. She hasn't moved. Not even a twitch from her limp-fingered hands, corpse-pale above the knotted rope that holds her arms and head and shoulders above the half-liquid muck of rotting flesh and marrow-sucked bones, scraps of unidentifiable vegetables, old puke and softening turds.

While the rumble of thunder rolls past the camp, I scratch up a fistful of sand and gravel. No point in calling anymore; any louder and it might not matter how good my improvised ghillie suit is. Some alert Black Knife buck might start to wonder why a pile of scrub and rock near the edge of the slop pit is suddenly stage-whispering in a human voice.

Pretty soon somebody's gonna notice there's one too many piles anyway.

I push my fist out from under the ghillie's rope fringe and drop some gravel into the the slop pit's darkness. Onto my best guess at the back of her neck. "*Tizarre*—!"

The night gives me a long, cold wait for the next flash of lightning. If she's dead, I'm completely fucked. I can't do this without her. Maybe I can still run. Maybe. Maybe if I hadn't taken out so many pickets and gotten the fuckers thousand-amped about their perimeter, I would have had a shot.

God damn you worthless weak fucking whiny sack of shit whore, you better not be—

When the lightning finally comes, it shows my fondest hope: a flicker of white above the slop pit's muck: one of Tizarre's eyes, turned up toward the ragged rim of night sky.

"Who . . . z'there?" Her voice is as dead as her hands. "How d'you know m'name?"

"Keep it down, for fuck's sake," I hiss at her. "It's Caine. We need to—"

"Caine?" Blank and dull. Not even a spark. "How—?"

"Never mind that. We need to get you out of there."

Silence.

"Tizarre?"

"I—don't, Caine. I can't. Don't make me. Just let me die."

Not fucking likely. "Don't quit on me now, Tizarre. Not now. I need you. *Marade* needs you."

A whisper from the darkness: "I can't . . . feel my legs, Caine. I can't feel anything. They . . . they *cut* me before they hung me in here. . . . Storm's coming. I can end it. I can drown . . ."

Huh. If she wanted to drown in other people's shit, she could've just stayed home.

"I can *help* you. I found stuff, Tizarre—"

Fuck it anyway. "Stuff from *home*, Tizarre."

Another flash of summer lightning.

Both her eyes are open now. "Home?"

"Yeah. I've been home. You get it?"

"Marade—before they took her, she said—she said you *promised*—if they took you home—"

"Yeah, I promised."

I let the thunder roll past before I go on.

People who have moral qualms with bald fucking lies don't become Esoterics in the first place. What I am about to say won't give me the slightest twinge.

"And here I am. I came back for her. I came back for *you*. Because she'll never leave you behind."

Another flash—and her eyes are wide now, and they seem to hold the light. Her voice is still a whisper, but its hush is no longer lifeless. "You—you came back *here*—to save us . . ."

"I can't do it alone, Tizarre. I need you. We can save Marade."

Thunder rolls by. Louder.

Some god sounds angry.

"We can save *everybody*."

The next flash of lightning gives me the answer on her filth-crusted face, and that answer gives me a brief sick twist just below my heart.

Maybe I was lying about that *not the slightest twinge* part, too.

## >>scanning fwd>>

The thunder crashes before the flare of lightning fades, and the cloudburst roar almost covers her half-strangled snarls as her hands twitch and shudder and spasm themselves back to life.

"... nahh ... *shit*—" The rain erases any tears before they reach her cheeks. The cords bulging from her jaw to her collarbone pick up faerie-fire highlights from the faint blue glow of the gluey mud that packs the bandages on her legs. "Never thought I'd be *happy* to hurt this bad . . ."

I shrug at her from the doorway. "Pain's just God's way of reminding you you're alive."

"Then . . . gahhh . . . maybe I need a kinder god . . ."

"We all do." I come out of my squat. "That's enough. Get too clean, you'll smell human again."

"All right." She nods and wipes a smear of snot from her nose onto the back of one shaky forearm. "All right, help me in."

I pull her back into the dry and settle her against a wall while I smear her bare feet with one of the last of the glands.

"What are you doing?"

"They can still track us if they try hard enough, but this way we at least won't draw their noses unless they already know we're here."

"Those are—"

"Scent glands. Grills carry them under their jaws, in the palms of their hands and the soles of their feet. A subtler way of marking territory than just pissing around."

"You—cut them out? Out of their—"

"What do you think keeps me ahead of these fuckers? Good looks and charm? Come on." I pick her up, sling her arm over my shoulder, and half carry her into the winding dark.

"Where are we going?"

The one safe place in the entire fucking Boedecken. "Somewhere you can't get to until you've already been there."

Deep into the black. I count steps, listening for rainfall ahead, landmarks where the ceilings have caved in. Up and up, and up some more, and she's gasping against my shoulder. "How do you—don't they search?"

"Not on foot. Not anymore." Her weight turns my chuckle into a grunt. "I guess they decided that's a bad idea."

"But—magick? They have magick—"

"It's not—" Shit, she's getting heavier. "—thaumaturgy. It's theurgy. They have to petition their god for power."

"So?"

"So I killed their high fucking priestess. The big bitch with the headdress of black feathers."

"You—how could you *possibly*—?"

"Easier than you think. You could say it was luck, but I don't think so."

Now I do manage a low laugh. A real one, dark as the storm outside. "I'm pretty sure their god's on my side."

## >>scanning fwd>>

She huddles against the dust-dry rock, arms crossed over her breasts, dripping dirty rain into the sand. The rose-pale glow from the Tear puts a blush on her bare skin that could make her look healthy, if not for the shivering, if not for the pain and bleak horror in her eyes.

"It was really here," she keeps murmuring while I dig through the pile of old bones and armor and weapons and shit for a tunic and pants and boots. "It was really here, all this time . . ."

"Yeah."

"And we never would have found it."

"Yeah. That's the magick on it. If I'd been looking for it, I couldn't have found it either."

Her eyes are wide. I wish it could be wonder. "This is . . . all this gear . . . it's from home?"

"Nah." I give her an apologetic shake of the head. "That was . . . well, this is mostly shit I found here. We're not the first people in the last thousand years to come hunting the Tear. Some of them died here for reasons other than Black Knives."

"But—"

"And some of it's our shit. Some of it's stuff I took off Black Knives this past day. They were carrying useful things besides their scent-mark glands."

Awe wipes the pain-twist from her face. "You're the skinwalker."

"The what?"

"A monster—a shapeshifter—kind of the ogrillo boogeyman." She smears wet hair back from her eyes. "I heard them talking about it—about *you*—"

"You understand them? You speak their language?"

"No, nothing like that—it's magick, kind of a limited telepathy—just something I'd do when they'd be close enough to hear—to, to take my mind off—"

"Yeah."

"They said you'd gotten off the scaffold, but—they said you were dead. You had to be. Some of the bucks were saying a skinwalker's stalking the camp—it can walk through walls, turn invisible, read minds, and it can look like anyone it kills—it takes their skins and wears them, and it becomes them on the outside, but inside it's a monster . . ."

"A skinwalker." Huh. I like it. Must be why they stopped stalking me—a little superstitious terror goes a long way. And there I was, skinning the bastards only because it makes the bodies look like hell on a stick.

Just lucky, I guess.

"Yeah." I flex my hands. I like the way they feel. "Yeah, that was me."

"But you—you *have* been home, though? You're going to take us *home*— you said . . . you said you'd take us . . ."

"I said what I had to say to get you out of that fucking pit."

Air squeezes from her chest. "You . . ."

"I need you alive and fighting, Tizarre. I've got shit here that can clean out your infections and give you back some strength. I've got food and weapons and some armor and some magick stuff that I'm not even sure what it is. But none of it would've done you any good down there. None of it'll do you any good up here if you're not game to use it."

"I . . ." She wraps her arms over her tiny breasts and can't look at me. "Down . . . down in that *hole* . . ."

"Yeah." I squat next to her and lay the tunic over her chest. "I'm not gonna pretend to know what it was like for you down there. But I went through some shit these last few days myself, y'know?"

Her fingers are working well enough to grasp the tunic and draw it around her like a blanket. "Yes. Yes, I know. But you—you were always strong . . ."

"Nah. Just dirt mean."

Now she can look at me again. Now I can see the tears.

"This is what I figure," I tell her. "I've been through some shit before this, too. Nothing this bad. Nothing as bad as what they did to you. Nothing as bad as what they're doing to Marade right now."

"Marade . . ." she echoes, hollow and distant and sad. "What are they doing to her?"

"It's . . . bad. Worse than what they did to me. Worse than what they did to you."

"Oh . . . oh, gods." Fresh tears now. "Oh, gods, I can't stand it . . ."

"She can."

Mouse-brown brows draw together.

"That's the thing about Khryllians. That's the gift of Khryl. It's a rough fucking gift, but it's there. She can survive anything except giving up."

"She won't. She'll never give up—"

"She will when she finds out you're dead."

"Oh . . ." Her eyes widen again, and her mouth goes slack. "But, but I'm—"

"That's why you have to pull your shit together. Now. When this storm stops and they look into that slop pit and all they see above the surface is that pair of dead arms I hung in that rope—"

Her shaking's getting worse.

"I can't do it for you, Tizarre. It's your power. You're the thaumaturge. You can do Cloak. You can walk right into the middle of that fucking camp."

"You—you want me to—go back *in there*—?"

"You have to."

"I—can't. Caine, I *can't*—"

"You can. That's the thing. That's what I'm trying to get through to you. You're stronger than you think you are. I've seen other people go through shit. Some of it worse than this. I know something about how people survive. How people live with it. It's not complicated. It's just hard, that's all."

"Hard." She laughs now, and there's a bright brittle edge to it. "*Hard?*"

"Yeah. You just keep fighting. No matter what. You just have to not quit."

"Caine—"

"It's the same for regular people as it is for Khryllians. We can survive anything except giving up. Sure, for them it works for their bodies too—but screw that anyway. As long as you don't quit, all these fuckers can do is kill you."

Maim you, blind you, cripple you, leave you brain-damaged and drooling, whatever . . . but a good lie trumps a bad truth every time. I put a hand on her arm. "Dying's not the worst that can happen."

That's true enough, anyway.

"You don't understand." Her shivering's getting worse, despite the tunic. Guess it doesn't have anything to do with cold. "I did quit. I gave up. I was screaming . . . begging . . ."

"Yeah, me too."

Once again, white appears around the rims of her irises.

I shrug at her. "They broke me like a rotten fucking stick. So what? They break everybody. It's what they do."

"But—but—"

"But that was then." I stand up. "Fuck *then*. Then is over. Fight *now*."

"I—I don't know if I—"

"They have Marade chained facedown over a pile of rocks. Naked. In the middle of the camp. So the whole clan can watch while the bucks take turns on her."

"Caine—Caine, don't—"

"You know why she's still alive? It's not just because she's Khryllian, Tizarre. Yeah, her god Heals her, because she fights. Every time. She fights every time. But you know *why* she fights every time?"

I shift my squat in front of her and take her arms, so she can't look away from me. "It's because I'm not on that cross anymore."

"Caine—"

"It's because *you* might still need her."

"I—"

"Are you gonna *leave* her there?" I give her a shake. "*Are* you?"

"How can you—how can you put this on *me*?"

"Because it *is* on you. It's on both of us. Because there's nobody else."

I show her some teeth.

"Because I have a plan."

### >>scanning fwd>>

The rush of rain becomes a sizzle. Then a hush. Fading thunder rolls away to the east.

Time to go.

I lean into the rope harness hard enough to scrape bloody hemp-burns up my chest and over my shoulders. The sledge lurches into motion, and I drag it out toward the night.

My night.

It's a good night to die, fuckers.

The Black Knife camp spreads rain-smoking watch fires across the badlands, three hundred feet below.

Out along the parapet . . .

There's still enough hush in the misting drizzle to cover the grind of the sledge through sand and over wet stone, and I am taking no chances because night and hard stone can play tricks with sound. The weight of the sledge counterbalances me only a couple hand spans off the rock. One of the skids catches on a corner of crumbled wall, and a couple of the barrels tip loose of my half-assed lashings and tumble off. I scramble out of the harness and dive for them before they can roll out a gap in the retaining wall.

Not yet. Not here.

My hands shiver and jerk while I struggle to get the barrels secured back onto the sledge. For sure this time.

Details. It's always the little fucking details that kill you.

Come *on*, goddammit. My fingers just won't for shit's sake cooperate, and the stress floods out my Control-enhanced nightsight until I'm fumbling blind and I am *not* going to bitch this up. I'm not. Not this time.

When the barrels are finally back in place, I check the lashing on the chest that holds the bottles, and the rags that wrap and wick them. If I lose *those* . . .

Solid. Solid. All right. Keep breathing. It's all right.

Back in the harness. A few breaths brings the parapet back to a ghostly grey-blush shimmer in my peripheral vision. Good enough. Let's go.

And I go.

But—

Fuck.

Taking too long. Too much scraping. And I just don't have the strength. Without the pain to remind me, I keep forgetting how fucked up I still am.

Should've dry-run this thing. But how could I? Too late now anyway.

Just push.

I lean deeper into the harness. Rope grinds through skin and muscle and burns into bone okay not really but still it feels like hot staggering *fuck*—

Fucking *push*.

It's too loud the rain's stopped they can't hear me but they can, I know they can hear me and I can't go any faster but I just can't *get* there push goddammit *push*—

I make the point just as my knees give out. I slip the harness and throw myself into the point's muddy sand and let the blood from my chest and shoulders mix with the puddles while I try to figure out how I'm ever gonna get my breath.

"Caine—"

I jerk and spasm onto my back and roll to my feet by reflex with knives in my hands before I register that it was Tizarre's voice. I fade from the lip of the point and get my back to a wall.

"Shit," I mutter through my teeth as I put away the knives. "Might as well, y'know, slap my balls or something. Be nicer."

A hand I cannot see attached to an arm I cannot see lands lightly on my shoulder, and a shuddering wave of dream-wakening twists through my mind because I *can* see her, and now that I can, I know I always could . . . but only with my eyes. Not with my brain.

Until she decided to let me.

Thaumaturges creep the shit out of me, and Cloak is one of the reasons why.

"Everyone's as ready as I can make them." She has the bladewand, and she offers it to me butt-first. "Any fucker close to Marade when the show starts is in for a hell of a surprise."

I take the bladewand. "I'll bet."

"You have no idea." Her face is still bleak, but now a grim fire glimmers deep in her eyes. "Instead of the shackles on her wrists, she had me half cut the staples that fix the chains to the stone."

"Um."

The image is vivid: Marade rising naked from that pile of rubble while from each hand three feet of chain as thick as my wrist screams into a lethal iron blur—

*Hell of a surprise* is one way to put it, I guess.

Makes me wish I could be there to watch.

I stick the bladewand in the top of my boot and extend my hands. "Dawn's coming. Set me up."

She takes my left hand in one of hers. I get a faint half-orange image of her licking her lips, frowning. "It should really be, y'know, copper or silver paint—"

"Blood'll be fine. Do it."

"You do it."

I pull a dagger and gash the base of my thumb; she catches my blood in the cup of her palm. "Have you ever done this before? Used a Shout?"

"I know how it works."

She nods. "Don't forget to cover your ears."

"Yeah."

"This'll take a little bit. Go ahead with the oil barrels now. After I do your hands, you can't use them for anything else."

I put the dagger away and draw the bladewand out of my boot. "Get on it."

She stares down at the pool of blood in her palm and starts taking the deep, slow, regular breaths that will drop her into mindview. The blood begins to shimmer with a faint alcohol-flame glow that casts no light.

A twist of intention sends a blue plane of force flickering out from the tip of the bladewand; the lashings on the barrels fall away, and the tops of the barrels themselves slip sideways on glass-smooth cuts. I slap the top off the first one and just tip it over. Oil floods out onto the point, oozing and rolling and twisting over the water-soaked sand, flowing thick and sluggish down toward the apex, where the wall has fallen away. I kick the second one off the other side of the sledge and let it spill there, then lift the third and the fourth carefully to the gap in the retaining wall and set them there as the spilled oil begins to roll over the lip and drain along branching channels below.

"Caine—" Her voice has that spooky emptiness; she's still in mindview. "Now."

I scrub oil and grit from my palms onto my breeches, then give her my hands. She dips a forefinger into my blue-shimmering blood.

Humming under her breath, she paints sigils in blood on my palms. Pretty soon she lets my hands drop and brings her finger to my face, painting around my mouth and up onto my cheeks. After a few seconds of this, she sighs, and full consciousness swims back up to the surface of her eyes.

"All right." She gives herself a little shake. "Whenever you're ready."

My breath goes short, whistling faintly through my clamped-tight throat. "Get in position."

"Caine—" She squints against a half-strangled cough. "We won't live through this, will we?"

"Hard to say." I shrug to cover the shakes that are starting to ripple along my arms. "A couple days ago, I would have said no way. But my luck's been running good lately."

"When I—" Another cough, choked, with maybe a little bit of sob behind it. "When I was telling Marade the plan, Whispering to her—y'know, the diversion, the rendezvous, everything—she started to cry. It's the—I've never *seen* her cry, Caine. I don't think . . . what they did to her . . . But she started to cry when I told her the plan, and I asked her—well, she just said she was grateful, that's all. She kept saying thanks. But not for the, y'know, the escape. The rescue."

She swallows. "For the chance to hit back."

My eyes burn. Not with tears. "Yeah."

"That's what I want to say too. Thanks. For the chance to hit back."

"It's more than a chance," I tell her. "You remember what I said the night they took us, how the Black Knives would remember us for a thousand years?"

"But that was just—"

"Yeah, it was. Then."

Storm clouds part. Stars wink into being.

"You and I, Tizarre, right here, right now—"

Can she see my teeth?

"—we just might make it true."

### >>scanning fwd>>

Even the wind goes still. Rich fruity fumes steam up from the oil on the point.

From the apex, the Black Knife camp is a clutter of cinders and ash and smolder like a kicked-out campfire. The cinders are the hide tents, the ashes are knots of bachelor males sleeping out under the stars and the rain, and the smolder is the remains of watch fires burning down now with the approach of dawn.

*I'm in place. Go.*

I don't bother to signal her that I heard.

She'll figure it out.

Vengeance is mine saith the Lord but this morning He's gonna fucking well have to share.

I press my painted palms to my painted cheeks. I draw as deep a breath as I can and open my mouth as far as it'll go, then clap my hands once, crisp and sharp, in front of my open mouth.

It makes a sound like most of the Boedecken just exploded.

The magick of the Shout directs the sound away from me, but still the blast is physical, staggering me, buckling my knees and smacking stars into my eyes.

Cover my fucking ears too fucking *right*—!

Like I have any hearing left to lose.

I can't even imagine what it must have sounded like to the Black Knives, but that sleepy kicked-through campfire just became a kicked-over anthill as ogrilloi jump up and rush out of their tents and spin around and fumble for weapons and probably shout and howl and squeal, if I could hear them, and I'm not even started yet.

Now I do cover my ears, and I Shout:

YOU
WERE
WARNED

The sound is too vast to be called speech: it is as though the escarpment itself roars at them. The anthill of Black Knives slows, and stops. Dim smears of ogrillo faces turn toward the sky.

THIS PLACE
IS MINE

With a foot, I tip one of the remaining oil barrels carefully, so that it pours over the lip of the point into the branching stone channels that drain down the face of the vertical city.

I SAID
I WOULD FEED YOU
YOUR FUTURE

On cue, the spill of oil running down the channels catches fire.

Good girl.

Rivers of flame cascade across the face of the vertical city, spreading through a delta of absolute darkness. And fire licks back up the channels as well, climbing, converging into a giant burning arrow.

Pointing exactly at where I stand.

BUT I AM
A MERCIFUL GOD

I tip over the final barrel of oil and skip back away from the point as the flames claw through the gap and the whole point becomes a pillar of fire fifty feet tall.

I WON'T MAKE YOU
EAT IT
RAW

I'm still chuckling as I get the first of the bottles out of the chest and ignite the wicks at the burning trickle where I tipped the first oil barrel. Even there it's hot enough that I have to shield my face with my arm and I can smell my hair starting to crisp, but I don't care, I'm chuckling anyway. It sounds like God playing dice with planets.

Didn't think that was funny? Watch this.

I heave a burning bottle high out off the parapet and follow it with another, little specks of whippy flame snapping through long arcs down into the fading night, and turn back to the chest for a couple more before those two hit the ground. I don't need to watch them land. I know where they're going to hit.

I may be a crappy shot, but I throw really, really well.

At the retaining wall with two more lit in my hands, I wind up—

*Caine—what are you* doing?

Not really a Whisper. Is there a spell called Snarl?

I launch the bottle anyway before I look down at her red-lit form a level below.

WHY THE FUCK
ARE YOU STILL THERE?

The Shout makes my head ring. She flinches and covers her ears, but a second later she's back at the wall down there waving an arm down at the Black Knife camp. Down at the flames spreading from where my oil bombs landed. Down at the crowded crèche. Crowded with screaming cubs.

Screaming burning cubs. Burning juvie bucks. Burning juvie bitches.

The pregnant ones.

*That's not the plan! Those are—those are* children—!

GET MOVING
GODDAMMIT

*But they're only children—babies—they never did anything—*

I fling the other bottle. It shatters against stone ten feet from where she's standing.

She has to skip back along her parapet to avoid the splash of flame, and in the brighter light down there now, I can see the horror and loathing on her face, and I don't give half a squirt of runny fucking shit.

MOVE
OR YOU GET THE NEXT ONE
IN THE FACE

With one last look of pure outraged betrayal, she turns and runs.

Down below, somebody's already unbarring the gate of the crèche, and the whole camp is alive. Arrows clatter around me. Everybody who's not scrambling to save the cubs is either shooting at me or sprinting up into the vertical city.

Works for me.

I turn back to the chest of bottles. If I really want to roast the little shits, I better get busy.

### >>scanning fwd>>

"Tizarre, goddammit—!" How many times have I said that today?

I whip into a spin-kick that slams my right heel into the Shield hard enough to rattle my own damn teeth, but beyond the shimmering curve, the rose-pale glow of the Tear shows nothing but a tightening in the white pinch around her eyes. This is a hell of a time for her to discover she's got real power.

Not to mention a conscience.

Standing among the shreds of bone and armor beyond the Tear of Panchasell, arms wrapped around her narrow chest to squeeze down her shivers, she looks like she's ready to just stand there and watch. "You never said anything about killing their *cubs*."

She has completely bone-my-ass cracked. "I'm *sorry*, all right? I promise I'll fucking *suffer* for it the rest of my *life* if you'll just fucking *let me in*—"

"Those were *children*, Caine—you never said you were—"

"If I *had*," I snarl at her, "would you have *helped*?"

"Of *course* not!"

"There's your fucking *answer*, then."

Here they come on my trail now. Hear those howls echoing along the empty cavernways? Hear that blind ravening rage? Hear that pain? Sounds to me like they want to rip open their own guts with their bare hands and claw the pain out so they can stuff it down my throat till I strangle.

I probably shouldn't let her see my grin.

Tizarre can hear their pain too: I can see it on her face, in her pinching-down eyes and the white smears where her lips should be.

"What are you gonna do? Leave me out here? With them?"

"I *should*—"

I slide a hand around to the back of my belt, onto the butt of the blade-wand. "The only thing you *should* do is make up your fucking mind before they make it up for you."

"What am I going to tell *Marade*?"

Oh, for shit's sake. "*Tell* her? She's *watching* it right *now*—don't be such a fucking *baby*—"

"Don't say that to me—*you* don't get to *say* that to me—"

Yeah, fair enough, not the best image, I'll apologize if I live through this but right now those howls are close enough that they're raising hairs on the back of my neck, and I'm starting to hear feet on stone and screw this anyway.

I pull out the bladewand and jam its business end against her Shield and necessity triggers a surge of intention that sends shearing force out from the tip. The Shield collapses in a cascade of sparks and she staggers and I spring into the chamber and just barely stop myself from stabbing her in the eye for being a whining weak-ass cunt.

Instead I keep on going past her toward the Tear. "Get that fucking Shield back up!"

"Caine—"

"No time for your shit. Do it!"

The Tear of Panchasell shimmers at me from its pedestal of solid gold, a private sunset the size of my head. Runic cirrus-ripples curve and twist across its surface and sink beneath as well, sucking my gaze into its rose-diamond depths.

I lift my own slice of sky: the electric sizzle of the bladewand's edge.

"*Caine*—"

A thousand years ago, if the stories are true: Panchasell Mithondionne, near-immortal High King of the First Folk, weeping as he labored over his masterwork, an aeon of Primal lore guiding the hand of the greatest adept in the history of the race—the history of the world—to create a Thing of Power that is also a thing of beauty, a song in crystal, a dream of peace made solid to defend his people and this world . . .

And here I am, a vicious little ghetto punk whose whole life wouldn't be an eyeblink to the least of the First Folk, about to cut the fucking thing in half. Because somebody they never heard of pissed me off.

That, my friends, is a deep lesson about how the world works.

Which is when Tizarre finally does get my attention, not by calling my name but with an ear-shattering blast that sucks all the air in the chamber into a whirl that follows the sideways column of flame roaring from her hands out into the cavernway I just came from, and she's got the black iron head of an ogrillo arrow sticking a span out from her left kidney and that is exactly the down payment on what we might both have to pay for me being too fucking sentimental to pull the trigger, because a flight of arrows they got off just in time comes bursting through the ass end of her Firebolt trailing flames of their own, and one's coming straight for my face and I'm already falling into a shoulder roll and it just clips my forehead and I take the roll backward over something on the cavern floor that rams into my own kidney hard enough that I can't even make it all the way back to my feet because my knees have gone to cloth—

And the bladewand's off.

From the floor I point it at the Tear and call upon my will and all I get is a scorch on my palm from the eggbutt and that hiss of blue static discharge from the tip.

"Caine—"

Now her voice is a half-strangled gurgle. She's got a sickly smile behind blood on her mouth, and both hands wrapped around the arrow shaft sticking out of her belly. She retches more blood. "Sorry—I'm sorry—"

"Don't be sorry. Just fucking *stop* them till I make this thing *work*, then we can get out of here—"

"*Stop* them? There are *thousands*—you made sure they'll *never* stop—"

Goddamn right.

I try for my feet, but again my knees buckle, and I catch myself with a hand on the knob of rock that jammed my kidney—

Huh—huh—did you—

Did you *see* that?

Was that my eyes, or just in my head?

When I touched the rock, there was—

A severed hand—I was—she was—he and me and she—pinned through the spine—staring into the sky, taking the hand of a kneeling man, cut in half and the waterfall's spray falling into my open, staring eyes, my own face above among the buildings and the blade driving toward my forehead and—

And where my hand is on the rock, the rock isn't rock. Not anymore. It's the hilt of a sword.

And where I touch, this hilt sings with the high humming whine of Power . . .

I look up at Tizarre. She blinks at me. "What—what's happening—?"

"What always happens," I say, because that is what I always say now.

She nods, because she understands. "What happens next? *Is* there a next?"

"You already know."

She nods again.

I toss her the bladewand. It hangs eternally in the air. It is in her hand before it ever leaves mine. Before she catches it, she has turned away, though she still faces me and will forever.

"Keep it," I tell her. "It's yours. I don't need it anymore."

I stand, and the Sword cuts free of the rock. It shrieks in my hand.

I hold it poised above the Tear of Panchasell.

Long and straight and heavy, its blade is the color of mirror-polished tungsten. The runes deep-graven from forte to tip are graceful and smooth as brushtrokes, and they burn with fire so black that my eye cannot hold them; they shift and twist and shimmer and crawl along the blade, sucking light from the air . . .

I have never seen anything like the Sword. I have known the Sword for lifetimes.

When it destroys the Tear, it will break the Power's hold upon the river. A river choked for a thousand years will shatter this place and burst free through these chambers. Will crash from the face of the vertical city upon the camp below.

In my hand is the death of the Black Knives, and their rebirth.

Their death is today.

When the edge carves into the Tear, it screams like I'm murdering the world.

And maybe I am.

### >>scanning fwd>>

Dawn at my back ignites the rainbow.

Beyond huge . . . solid as Bifrost in the billows of my waterfall's spray . . .

One foot stretches out from the face of what was the city's fifth tier, high above; the other is grounded somewhere out in the vast mist-shrouded sea wrack that used to be the Black Knife camp.

That's my pot of gold. Right there. In the endless earth-shaking thunder of my waterfall, I can imagine the echoes of Black Knife screams.

Somewhere to the south, a new river rolls down the Boedecken Waste, black with mud and shreds of tent, shattered wagons and broken bodies.

I look upon the work of my hand, and it is good.

Only one flaw in the plan so far: the rendezvous is far enough away from the waterfall's thunder that I can still hear the idiots argue. About me.

I lean against the wall outside the shattered gape of what used to be a window, where the nine survivors are dressing themselves in the clothing I brought for them, treating whatever wounds Marade can't Heal with supplies I gave them, and eating and drinking food and water I provided for them, while they all talk about how they just can't trust me.

"—it doesn't make *sense*." Marade's still standing up for me, at least. Sounds like she's the only one. "If his sole need was revenge, why risk the rescue at all? He could as easily have left me—left me—"

Even from out here, I can hear the choke. She can't say it.

"Where we were," she finishes lamely. "He could have done what has been done without even *your* help, though unleashing the river would have cost his life—"

That much is true.

"You weren't there," Tizarre says. "None of you. You didn't see him. You didn't hear him."

"And the cubs—I mean, so what?" This from Jashe the Otter. "How many would have lived through the river thing, anyway?"

"That's my *point*," Tizarre says. "Why . . . do that? Why the *show*?"

"Diversion," Marade says, but she doesn't sound too sure of it.

"That's what he *said*. That's what he *told* me it was about. To make sure they'd chase him up into the city. To thin them out on the ground and give you all a better chance to escape—but then he hit their *children*. So more of them *stayed*. To *protect* the children."

"Well, I don't care," somebody else says. "I'm just damn grateful to be alive."

"You say that now," Tizarre insists darkly. "But he's not done with us. That's why the rescue. He still has a *use* for us. That's the only reason. Just wait. You'll see."

Another man might be offended. I probably would be, if she were wrong. But, y'know, some Black Knives can probably swim.

I stare out at my waterfall. At my rainbow. The rainbow is a promise from God that there will never be another Flood.

I don't plan to need one.

Fuck punishment. This is about *extinction*.

# KHRYL'S JUSTICE

t wasn't a good dream.

I couldn't make it make sense, even as a nightmare: it should have been a net over my face, not a burlap sack. Chunks of puke shouldn't be flopping around my head. I was sure of that.

The next time awareness knocked a hole in my skull, I started to worry that I was naked, when I should have been suited up in my black leathers. And this wad of cloth tied into my mouth with what felt like rope? Where the fuck had *that* come from?

It did, however, explain why the chunks of puke were pretty much all small enough to have come out of my nose.

Later, a dimly foggy realization chewed into my forehead that the shoulder I was facedown over should have been flesh instead of metal.

The last worst part: it wasn't rope on my wrists and ankles. Forget that I didn't have the throwing knife that was supposed to be in the concealed sheath behind the collar of my missing tunic; not only would that knife have been useless against the armor on this particular back but it wouldn't have cut what was binding my wrists anyway, which I could recognize because I still had some feeling in my fingers, because he hadn't put them on as tight as the Los Angeles Social Police had a few years back when they pinched me for Forcible Contact Upcaste.

Stripcuffs.

I puked into the sack again.

Then I fell back down the black hole.

I've been lucky enough to make it through my life so far with less than my share of major head trauma. Sure, I've been knocked around, bashed with sticks and stones, quarterstaves and iron-bound clubs, warhammers and friggin' morningstars, even a brick or two; stabbed with stilettos, daggers, knives, and smallswords; taken a broadsword through the liver and an axe into the thigh; been variously shot with arrows, sling stones, bullets and motherfucking *blowgun* darts—not to mention being once or twice hurled from high places—but I've mostly managed to avoid being whacked on the head hard enough to produce more than a few seconds of unconsciousness.

Now, even those few seconds are serious enough; that's a concussion right there, and anybody who thinks an untreated concussion isn't serious should go recheck the mortality figures. Still, though, it's something you generally live through. You wake up with a bad headache and persistent dizziness and nausea, general weakness and shit, and you need some bed rest—or, say, a Khryllian Healing, like the one I got after Tyrkilld slapped me up—to get over it, but you do. Eventually.

When those seconds stretch into minutes, you go from bad headache into the territory of, say, subdural hematoma, which is a fancy way of saying that your brain's bleeding and starting to swell, which means that you're not gonna just open your eyes and shake it off and go beat up the bad guys. It means it's a roll of God's dice whether you're gonna open your eyes at all, and if you do it'll probably be a lot like it was for me: a fucking nightmare.

This is not just a metaphor.

The bleeding-brain kind of unconsciousness is a fall across an event horizon of oblivion: an infinitely instant shredding of everything you are as psychic tidal forces smear you into an eternal scream. Waking up is no treat, either; it doesn't happen all at once, but in little flickers and flashes that start out as needles and graduate to razors in the eye and the grip of God Himself upon your balls, and it involves a lot of vomit and choking and wishing you could go back to falling into that black hole, because the eternal scream is a helluva lot more fun.

That's how it is for me, anyway.

Maybe it's because it seems like every time it happens to me, I start that whole razors-in-the-eyes waking-up crap in a bag over somebody's shoulder while the sonofabitch is out for a jog.

The only way I can reconstruct roughly how long I must have been out before I started twilighting up from semiconsciousness is to guess how fast Markham could haul my twitching ass from the Pratt & Redhorn to the jitney ramp up Hell while making a wide circle around the Spire, because he wouldn't exactly want to bump into any inquisitive Khryllians on the way.

Did I not mention that part?

Turns out I wasn't wrong about Calm Guy's backup. I wasn't even wrong about the really, really good nerves. My only mistake was assuming that the backup in question would have reason to be afraid of the Smoke Hunt.

Well, okay. That wasn't my only mistake.

There are ways in which I think really, really fast. Like how to kill people. There are ways in which I don't think really, really fast. Like working out that the only way Faller's gunmen could have known I was at the Pratt & Redhorn was if they found out from Kierendal & Tyrkilld & Co.—not fucking likely— or if they found out from, say, the all-too-conveniently lurking-in-an-alley- across-the-street Lipkan ass-cob who booked me the room in the first place.

At the time I was playing sack of meat potatoes, I didn't have any idea of any of this. There were some inexplicable images swimming around the brimstone swamp inside my head, of Boedecken badlands covered in grain and vineyards and a river dividing a city of neat whitewashed brick tangled up with headless ogrilloi burning with a red fire that cast no light. And that was about it.

I don't remember much of the early part of my visit to BlackStone. Some- body must have taken the sack off me, because I remember somebody saying *good lord, clean him up*, and sometime after that I was wet and there was a blinding-bright haze pumping in through my eyeballs that was overinflating my head until I could feel the bones of my skull grinding against each other along jagged fissures as they began to separate and a distantly familiar voice said from the top of the well I'd fallen down—

*lord tarkanen—you hit him too hard*

Then another distantly familiar voice, not Markham's—like the voices of Actors from Adventures I'd cubed a few times when I was a kid, I always had a good ear for voices—

*or perhaps not hard enough—were you not once the practicing necromancer, simon faller? a shade will answer honestly where a man may not—*

Which I tried to laugh about, y'know, because of the pun, but I'm pretty sure I only managed a dull moan.

*no no no, he has to be alive—my orders—a healing—do a healing—*

*Nay.* This voice *was* Markham's. I could even make out a strict grey cloud among the bright haze that filled my universe. *This hurt was not taken in bat- tle. Khryl's Love will not avail.*

A round pale shadow in the bright haze began to resolve toward the blur of a face.

*Michaelson? Michaelson, can you understand me at all? Do you know where you are? Caine, talk to me.*

I remember, here, trying to answer.

*Dead . . .* I was trying to say. *Dead . . .*

*Simon Faller*, said that familiar voice which wasn't Markham's, *he raves. Let him die. If he lives, we will all come to regret it. This I know from bitter experi- ence.*

Here I would have laughed again, if I could laugh. Somehow thinking how many people could honestly say the same made me giggly.

*It's not up to me,* the blur of a face replied. *And it's not up to you, either. We'll turn him over as is. Let them deal with him however they want; then if he dies, it's their problem.*

*Are Artan Healing magicks superior to Khryl's?*

*Just—ah, different, that's all. Let them in.*

That face-blur leaned down closer, and more details came into focus: grey cream-plastered wisps of comb-over, a crisp salt-and-pepper beard giving shape to soft jowls . . .

It was Rababàl.

*Michaelson—maybe you can't hear me, but—I know you always say that everything's personal, but this really is business. Really. I got over hating you a long time ago. This is just business.*

"Dead . . ." This time I did manage to get the word out past my teeth, instead of bouncing around inside my fractured skull. "You're *dead* . . ."

*Even when he cannot move, can barely speak, still he threatens you—*

*It's not a threat.* The dead man retreated to a blur, then to a cloud. *As far as he knows, it's simple fact.*

And before I could summon anything like sense to the surface of my scrambled brain, things got even weirder.

*In accordance with the treaty between our peoples,* Markham was saying, *I now deliver this fugitive into your custody and your care.*

Then a couple of new shadows loomed in my personal haze. When they leaned down to pick me up, both of them wore on their inhumanly rounded heads these sickeningly familiar funhouse-smeared leers that were still unmistakably me.

My own face.

I knew me. Them. I grew up in a San Francisco Labor slum. Anybody Labor would have to be six days dead to not recognize the Social Police.

*Administrator Hari Michaelson.* The electronic digitizer in the soapy's mirror-masked helmet didn't work in Home physics; he just sounded like he was talking with one hand over his mouth. *You are under arrest for the crime of capital Forcible Contact Upcaste, in the murder of Leisureman Marcus Anthony Vilo.*

It's funny, y'know—

Life has a way of sticking a knife in my eye at just the right time.

Being handed over to the Social Police was a dull knife. Rusty. Serrated too. I guess I'm lucky that way.

It went in my left eye socket and sawed around inside my sinus cavity until the scrape of rusty serrated metaphoric steel on metaphoric bone cranked me up across my personal event horizon, and though I could not summon any ghost of a clue where this might be happening or why, through the pain and general mystery I was able to dimly recognize that this situation boded ill for my immediate future.

So I thought, *Fuck it. Let's fight.*

This may seem like an unusual decision from a semiconscious middle-aged naked guy with a skull fracture who's bound hand and foot in unbreakable high-tech police restraints, but I have this rule of thumb, one that I've practiced so long—ever since I was a kid running wild on Mission District streets—that it's become hard-wired instinct. When bad guys try to take you somewhere by force, fight.

Fight *now.*

Because they're taking you into their comfort zone. That's why they're not killing you where you are: because wherever you are, you still have a chance. For whatever reason. Witnesses. Police. Weapons. Escape routes. Something. That's why they want to take you somewhere else. And once you get where they're taking you, it's over.

Or it's not over. Not for a long time.

Fighting might get you killed. But it's better than whatever's waiting for you where they can take time to enjoy themselves.

It happened to some of the street kids I knew back in the District. They'd disappear. And their bodies would turn up later. Sometimes you could tell they'd been kept alive for weeks. Or months. By how many of the wounds had scarred over. Even some of the amputations. And castrations and vaginal mutilations and you don't want to know.

So—

Fuck it.

*Fight.*

But, as people who know me will have heard before, there is fighting and there is fighting.

"Rababàl . . ." I managed to say, or thought I did, blinking toward the dead man. "Rababàl, you *need* me . . ."

The dead man leaned back into the fog. *Rababàl died twenty-five years ago. You didn't help him, and I need no help from you.*

"You can't . . ." The words seemed to be sticking in the haze inside my head. I worked harder to push them out into the air. "Turn me over . . . this place . . . gone . . . a few days, that's all . . . war—war with *Ankhana—*"

That made some kind of impression; the grey-fringed face recoiled into a deeper blur. *Is he—could that be true—?*

The almost-familiar voice answered, *I learned long ago that from this man's mouth, not even Khryl can hear truth.*

Ah . . .

So *that's* who Almost Familiar was.

Even to my splintered consciousness, finding him here made everything make sense. I'm just fucking intuitive that way.

*Khryl's friends within the Infinite Court assure me that his position in Church and Empire is purely symbolic. If war is to come, it will not come on his behalf.*

I tried to shake some use into my brain, and my mouth. "Not . . . about *me*, dumbass . . . make a deal—we need to *deal*—"

*Michaelson, I'm sorry.* The grey-fringed blur didn't sound sorry. *It's done.*

"No—no you *can't*—can't send me back . . . can't give me to them . . . please—"

*I already have. Officers? Time is short. If you'll bring him this way, please.*

"Stop, goddammit . . . stop—"

Hanging from the wire-laced gloves of the Social Police, hands stripcuffed behind me, ankles bound together with the same wire-reinforced plastic, naked, retching, unable to stand, unable to see, I still somehow snarled myself an internal sword of sunfire to cut through the fog inside my head and burn it away. No matter how broken I am, somehow I can always get pissed enough to kill somebody.

Because, y'know, I've never been the type to go gentle into that et cetera.

The room snapped into focus. It looked like the hideout of a half-successful caravan raider. Expensive furniture that didn't match, delicately carved where it wasn't notched and starting to splinter, upholstered in beautiful leathers and crushed velvets and brocades that couldn't hide the stains and wear of careless overuse. The rug that filled the whole room had once been fine as anything I'd put in the Abbey, my San Francisco mansion back when I was a star, but now it bore a grey-brown smear of ground-in wear track between the door and the overlarge, overcarved big-dick I'm The Boss desk in overstained cherry. And there were wall hangings and shit that framed silver hookstands holding blackened glass lamps, but the silver was tarnished and the tapestries smudged with lampblack and the walls they hung on were cheap whitewashed plaster tracked with blue-grey mildew. The whole place looked impermanent, half-abandoned already, like this Faller guy had boosted the best of Duke Kithin's furnishings before he'd left Thorncleft, then had just stashed the shit in some shack so he could piss on it like a bear before leaving it behind.

In that raider's cave of a room—besides me and the Social Police and Markham Lord Situational Fucking Ethics and the middle sixties–looking guy who was Rababàl's ghost or twin brother or identical goddamn cousin or whateverthefuck that I didn't care about right then because he was a problem for another time—stood a magnificent man in magnificent armor, the kind of Radiant Mantle of Kingship sonofabitch that doesn't really exist outside of stories and songs; you know, Arthur, Charlemagne, Frederick Barbarossa, Richard Cour de Lion, all those blood-drunk thugs with good enough press agents to somehow end up heroes to way too many gullible losers.

Not unlike me, I guess. But let that go.

The armor was chrome steel, curves and angles of mirror that gleamed like dawn's own rhodos goddamn dactylos in the lamplight. The guy inside was your basic snow-topped mountain of Biblical Patriarch, but in the blossom of mature strength—y'know, like that white brow and beard salted his face only to give the calm certainty in his eye a translucent shimmer of Revealed Truth.

When I say *eye*, by the way, that's literal.

Half his face had that carved-from-God's-Own-Granite agelessly rugged beauty that well befits said legendary king. The other half, well . . .

His left eye socket was a crumpled ruin of empty scar above a deep ragged dent that once had been nobly jutting cheekbone; it looked a lot like some vicious ghetto punk had, about twenty-five years ago, say, sneak-punched him with his own morningstar.

This appearance was not, as smart people might have guessed already, coincidental.

With all the mental and physical clarity my internal sunblade could bring me, I managed to gasp, "I was *never* his *prisoner* . . ."

"All that matters," the soapy on my left said in very credible Westerling, "is that you're our prisoner now," and he and his partner kept on hauling me toward where Rababàl's ghost twin cousin was holding the door for us until six foot nine of chrome steel and Biblical Patriarch moved into our way with the reluctantly majestic unstoppability of an entire glacier cracking free of a mountainside to slide into an arctic sea.

The Social Police, wisely, stopped. So did I, perforce.

Purthin, Lord Khlaylock, Justiciar Impeccable of the Order of the Knights of Khryl, turned that Revealed Truth glare on Markham, Lord Tarkanen, Lord Righteous in service to the Champion of Khryl. "Is this truth?"

Markham didn't so much as blink, let alone flush. "I was tasked by My Lord Justiciar to deliver this man without fail," he said simply. "I did not fail."

"Ambushed me . . ." I slurred. "Abducted . . . while I w's *tryin' t' save* people . . ."

Now Markham did have the grace to flush, just a little bit. So I twisted the knife. It's what I do. "While I was doing *his* duty . . . defending the Civility of the Battleground . . ."

It was more than moderately gratifying to watch color rise through the face of that supercilious Lipkan asscob all the way to the roots of his crewcut.

"A direct order—my duty is to the—"

"Everybody's got . . . a fucking *excuse* . . ." Adrenaline sang in my ears. I didn't know the words but I could sure as hell hum the goddamn tune. "You abandoned your people to danger . . . you swore an oath to Khryl H'mself . . . the word's *recreant*, yeah? You *ambushed* me . . . without warning or Challenge— makes you, ah—*craven*—"

The red in Markham's face had gone white around the eyes. He wheeled on Khlaylock. "My Lord Justiciar—this *abuse*, my Lord—"

His niece's jaw had looked like it could split logs; his could crack rocks. "You need not suffer it."

"He seeks only to cheat the carnifex."

"It is never wise," Purthin Khlaylock murmured mordantly around that rock-breaker jaw, "to assume that one knows this man's intention."

He didn't actually lift a gauntlet to the ruin of his empty eye socket, but I'll bet my nuts he was thinking about it.

Markham aimed that Lipkan nose toward my face like a blade at garde, then waved a mailed hand as he turned away. "I see no reason to allow a personal affair of honor to interfere with the course of justice."

"Personal . . . ?" I forced out. "I'm an Armed Motherfucking *Combatant* . . ."

Markham went still. So did Khlaylock.

"'S *your* fucking Law . . ."

"It is Khryl's Law," Mount Khlaylock rumbled above me, "and you would do well to mind your—"

"Yeah . . . sure. Whatever." My shrug made my head hurt worse, which helped me grin and kept the haze at bay for a few seconds so my mouth could work. "I did not Yield, and I was not defeated in Combat. Markham, Lord Tarkanen, is no true Knight, but is a whatthefuck—a recreant craven ambusher and common criminal, yeah—and I call upon Khryl and His Justiciar to Witness the truth of my charge. I swear by your God and His Law, I am by right a free man."

This looks on the page a lot more impressive than it sounded drooling out of the smashed-up mouth of a middle-aged blood- and puke-smeared naked guy with stripcuffed wrists and ankles who was hanging from the grips of a pair of homicidal supercops in high-tech body armor, but it worked.

Markham stared like I'd invited him to bend over and lube his asshole. Rababàl—Faller—dropped his face into one hand with an English "Ohhh, for Christ's God damn sake." The soapies tilted their mirrors at each other, then pointed them back at Khlaylock.

"Legality is moot," one said. "Administrator Michaelson is our prisoner now."

"No." If the stone tablets on which God carved the Ten Commandents could talk, they would have sounded a lot like Khlaylock's voice did then. "Khryl is Lord of Justice. If Our Lord affirms his charge, this man is free. It is the Law."

He faced Markham. "Lord Tarkanen, will you Answer?"

Markham looked appalled. "My Lord, he is but grade six—hardly more than an armsman—and his injury . . . I misdoubt he can so much as stand—"

"If the Lord refuses my Challenge, I'll do more than stand." I tried to sound like I believed it. "I'll walk right the fuck out of here, and it's your goddamn duty to make sure I—"

"Do not presume to instruct me on Khryl's Law." Khlaylock's stare never wavered from Markham. Maybe he didn't want to dirty his eyes with the image of my face. Deliberate as the planet's turn, and as relentless, he said, "Will you Answer?"

Markham sighed. "My Lord, I will."

Khlaylock lowered his head. "So let it be. I will Witness."

"You were here—you'll tell them, you have to *tell* them—" Rababàl was babbling at the soapies, who were again pointing the mirror-masks of those helmets at each other. "He was alive when I delivered him to you—this is *not* my fault—"

"And he will be alive when we deliver him to Social Court," Soapy One said.

"That remains to be seen." Khlaylock paused at Markham's side and set his gauntlet across the top curve of the Lord Righteous's pauldron. "Markham— entertain no assumptions, and cherish no confidence of victory. He would not make such Challenge had he no stratagem to defeat you."

This was true, but hardly sporting of him to bring up right then.

Markham's bleak grey stare settled on my presumably short future. "My Lord, your words are heard."

"Nor depend upon Our Lord, even with truth on your side. This man uses the Law only to serve his ends. He knows nothing of honor."

This, on the other hand, was a damn lie; I know plenty about honor. It just happens to be a luxury I can't fucking afford.

He had good enough reason to dislike and distrust me. Twenty-five years ago, when he was still the Knight Captain commanding the Khryllian garrison at North Rahndhing, just outside the southeastern fringe of the Boedecken, and I was nearing the end of the Adventure that was making me a star, we had a minor disagreement about the tactical approach we should take in dealing with the remnants of the Black Knife Nation. This disagreement became a dispute, which I settled in a less-than-strictly-honorable fashion—because in a straight fight he would have killed me before I could blink—and our working relationship ended with me leaving him for dead in the hands of the surviving Black Knives.

Regardless that it turned out pretty well for him in the end, I admit this was a rotten thing to do. I was a very bad man in those days. I'm not much of a good man now.

Which is not an excuse.

I'm not trying to rationalize anything, or even to explain anything. Actions justify themselves, or they don't. Words can't make them right or wrong. Dad used to say, "If you need to justify something, you shouldn't have done it." Like I said when I started this: it's about what happened. Not why.

So this is what happened.


I met Purthin Khlaylock at the end of the actual retreat part of *Retreat from the Boedecken*. By my best count—because I don't make a habit of reviewing my old Adventures, especially that one—it was thirty-four days, give or take, after I destroyed the Tear of Panchasell and unleashed the Caineway.

I still can't remember how many people were in Rababàl's original expedition—thirty-nine or forty, something like that. Ten of us got out of Hell alive.

Not counting Rababàl himself. But let that go.

The cook, Nollo, supposedly of Mallantrin; his lover, also supposedly of Mallantrin, Jashe, the guy everybody called the Otter; three "brothers" from Hrothnant, Tarpin, Matrin, and Karthran; a pair of surly "Jheledi" bondsmen, Kynndall and Wralltagg; and Marade and Tizarre.

And me.

By the time we made contact with the Khryllian outpost at North Rahndhing, there was Marade and Tizarre, and there was me.

It was the best month of my life.

In a straight ride—with water and spare horses—it was seven days from Hell to North Rahndhing. In friarpace—a semimagickal meditative form of running I'd trained in at Garthan Hold—I could have made it alone in five, if I'd been in top form. About as fast as a healthy ogrillo warrior, again assuming I could find water along the way.

But if we'd gone straight anywhere, they would have run us down and killed us ugly.

It's hard to say how many Black Knives died when I unleashed the river, because nobody I've talked to really knows how many there were to start with. Some estimates say there were as few as seven thousand in the clan. Some put the number closer to fifteen thousand or even eighteen thousand. I can tell you this, though: those who survived that night were not the old, or the very young, or the weak, or the slow.

And there were about three thousand of them.

Three thousand of the toughest, meanest, fastest, strongest bitches and bucks of the Black Knife Nation pulled themselves out of the wreckage of their most sacred holy ground to find themselves standing among the broken corpses of their brothers and sisters. Their parents. Their children.

The remnants of the Black Knife Nation were, as one might imagine, immoderately pissed at me.

I was top of my entire novitiate in Smallgroup Tactics at Garthan Hold, but I barely even needed my training. Every one of the seven surviving "porters" had graduated from the Studio Conservatory's Combat School, so even though none of them were superstar material—except maybe Jashe—they knew their business inside and out. And Tizarre, whose Cloaks could make us more or less invisible, and we had the bladewand, and a shitload of other stuff Kollberg had strategically placed for us . . . not to mention Marade, who was a homicidal Wonder Woman and kinda immoderately pissed herself.

Screw tactics.

All I needed was to remember some of those books Dad used to make me read. Such as *War and Peace*.

According to Tolstoy, Kutuzov beat Napoleon on the French retreat from Moscow by refusing to do battle. He kept their armies in contact, so Napoleon could never relax—he had to keep his army in battle order at all times—but every time Napoleon would march out to fight, Kutuzov would retire. When Napoleon would go back to his camp, Kutuzov would advance: the military version of Push Hands.

I combined this principle with some basic concepts of guerrilla warfare I'd picked up from *The Life of Geronimo*. So when the Black Knives would come out in force, we'd circle behind and murder wounded in their camps. When they'd send out single-pack scouting parties, at least one entire pack, sometimes two or three if they weren't too far apart, would vanish . . . and be found later as skinned corpses, missing their scent glands. If they posted pickets, we killed the pickets. If they picketed whole packs, well . . .

Ogrilloi bunch up when threatened. It's instinctive. So when spooky noises would start coming from the darkness, they'd drift together—then one swipe of the bladewand . . .

We'd drag the bodies around before we skinned them and piled them up, to make it look to the Black Knives like we'd been able to kill the pack because we'd caught them spread too far apart. Get it?

And, y'know, the corpses wouldn't be only skinned, either. They'd be partially eaten.

This was not just for effect.

I could pretend it was simple pragmatism. We had to be mobile. Our lives depended on it. So none of us carried supplies other than water skins. We lived on what we took off Black Knife corpses. And on the corpses themselves. Sure, blood's thicker than water. But you get used to it.

Tastes good, too.

I'm not into pretending, though. Not anymore. The real reason everyone was eating Black Knife meat and drinking Black Knife blood is because I made them do it.

Partly it was my innate sense of justice.

Yes, *justice*, goddammit. If they want to kill and eat me, I will kill them, and I will eat them.

Period.

This was not the argument I made to the rest. I didn't make an argument. Our first day out, I came back into our cold night camp with a skinned ogrillo leg over my shoulder and told Tizarre to take the bladewand and start carving off chops.

They weren't real excited about this idea.

After all, the only differences between ogrilloi and humans are some details of phenotype; the two species are closely related enough to even be cross-fertile, to a limited extent, kind of like horses and donkeys. Eating ogrilloi was close enough to cannibalism to make everybody but me more than a little queasy.

I won't go into the details of the scene, who said what and all, because that's not what this story is about. Let's just leave it at this: It started with me telling everybody that we'd be eating ogrilloi because it'd make us all smell more like ogrilloi—we'd be sweating their proteins and crapping their fats, y'know?— which was starting to work until somebody, Jashe, I think, pointed out that it wouldn't make us smell like grills, it'd make us smell like humans who are eating grills, which was when things started to turn ugly.

I ended up explaining in a very calm, very quiet voice that we didn't have enough supplies to survive, and we couldn't carry people who weren't pulling their weight, and anyone who wasn't willing to go all the way with this should just trot on back and give themselves to the Black Knives right fucking now.

This was not the real reason I made everyone eat ogrilloi either. The reason was another of those books Dad made me read.

*Heart of Darkness.*

There was one thing I never understood about that book: why people think Kurtz went crazy out there. The way I saw it—the way I still see it—Marlow was the crazy one. When Kurtz was murmuring *the horror, the horror,* I always figured he was talking about having to go back to Europe.

I guess it's because, y'know, I grew up in the jungle. My jungle had gutters and alleys and CID prowl cars circling just below the cloud deck, but it was a jungle just the same. That was why when the Black Knives showed up was when I started to get happy for the first time since I graduated from the Conservatory. Who says you can't go home again?

And that's what I had to do for the others. I had to bring them over to *my* yard: make them understand that they were in the jungle now. That everything they thought they knew about Who They Were and How Things Are Done and What the World Is All About had been fucked up the ass with a live grenade. That the trick to the jungle is to be top predator.

To eat *everybody.*

After what we'd been through, they didn't need a lot of convincing. Oh, there were some token protests about holding the line between us and them and that kind of moral-high-ground bullshit, but the real lesson of *Heart of Darkness* is that the jungle is always there, inside even the most civilized of us. It whispers shadow love in the twilit corners of our minds, and no matter how deaf we pretend to be, we can't help but listen.

Don't believe me? Check the rental figures for my Adventures.

The only survivor with the moral authority to stand up to me would have been Marade, who not only had that parfit gentil Khryllian Knight of Renown thing going but also had been through so much worse at the hands—and otherwise—of the Black Knives than any of the rest of us that if she'd said no, I probably couldn't have made anybody else say yes without holding knives to their throats. But Marade, for all her power, for all her certain knowledge of Khryl's Love for her, was not to the manor born; underneath all that Armor of Proof and Morning Star in Her Hand and the rest of it was still just an Actress after all, and I . . . well—

I've done a lot of things I'm not proud of.

Saying she was not to the manor born doesn't say enough. She wasn't really Marade, not the way I'm Caine. Marade was just a character she was playing. She was still really Olga Bergmann, third daughter of a failing Business family from the Swedish southland who had turned to Acting because her two older sisters' marriages hadn't managed to revive the family fortunes. Nothing in her privileged upbringing had remotely prepared her for the brutalization she suffered from the Black Knives; hell, I don't think anything could prepare anyone to go through something like that. I doubt a Home-born Knight could have survived it any better. I know I wouldn't have.

She put a good face on it; as long as we were running and fighting, the pressure we were under held her together. But once she was safely at North Rahndhing . . .

Her breakdown isn't really part of this story either. Let's just say that when the Knights of Khryl came out to face the Khulan Horde at Ceraeno a year and change later, Marade wasn't with them. She was undergoing drug therapy in the inpatient unit of the Vienna Institute for Social Wellness. She never did recover enough that she could enjoy sex; she'd do it—when it was in her contract—but she'd freeze up and start to shake, and it was always pretty ugly. Which, though nobody ever actually said so, was maybe mostly my fault.

I've always had an eye for weakness. It's a little late to start apologizing for it now.

Then a while after that, down in Yalitrayya during *Race for the Crown of Dal'kannith*, I'm pretty sure it was at least partly her lingering issues with me that made her get stupid with Berne, which I know for damn sure made her and Tizarre both wish they'd died back with the Black Knives. I've second-handed their final cubes. I owed it to them.

Remember what I said about *Saving people is not among my gifts?*

Anyway, here's the thing—

As entertaining as it was to kill dozens, maybe hundreds, of Black Knife bucks, I never kidded myself that we were actually accomplishing anything. Except making me, Marade, and Tizarre into overnight superstars. We never forgot that we were there to entertain people; half the battle was coming up with ever-more-inventive ways to slaughter bucks, and the other half was to make sure we never actually escaped.

No fear of that, anyway.

The bucks weren't our enemies, though, not really; probably starting with Spearboy all the way back outside the gate of Hell, they kept coming at us because they were more afraid of their bitches than they were of dying. For good reason.

So the goal wasn't to kill bucks (except to amuse the folks back home—who, as it turned out, never got tired of it). And Marade seemed to enjoy herself, but y'know, she had different issues.

All I was trying to do was lead the surviving bucks as close as possible to

North Rahndhing, because I had it on, ahem, reliable authority, that there were between five and ten Knights posted there, and one of the few creatures on Home that can outpace a friar or an ogrillo over the long haul is a Knight of Khryl. It's why they don't ride. Khryl doesn't approve of it; Knights bear their arms and armor with their own strength—actually His Own Strength, but let that go. So they run in full armor, and they run like hell. With armsman cavalry to engage the bucks, I could lead Knights on foot to their rear and take out the bitches.

All of them.

I had gotten enough out of that weird-ass three-way I'd had with their god and their top bitch, one I'd nicknamed Crowmane, to understand who was really in charge. Only females entered their fucked-up priesthood of the Outside Power. So once the bitches were gone, we'd have not only wiped out the next generation of Black Knives, we'd also have cut them off from the thing that really made them Black Knives in the first place. Simple, yes?

Simple no.

Try explaining this to Knight Captain Purthin Soldiers-of-the-Lord-of-Battles-Do-Not-Make-War-Upon-Women-and-Children Khlaylock.

So I didn't bother. Explaining, that is.

His attitude was no mystery to me; it was the institutional attitude of the Order of Khryl, which—as the most militant cult of the Lipkan pantheon—was not exactly unknown to the Monasteries. They all felt that way, and I knew it going in, and timing, as they say, is everything.

Back in the day, it seems that the chance to take a chunk out of the Black Knives was the kind of thing that'd make any Knight Officer of Khryl cream his surcoat. Five hours after Marade had a chance to tell our story, Purthin Khlaylock strode forth from the white gates of North Rahndhing at the head of a column of seven Knights Venturer, a Knight Attendant, and three hundred mounted armsmen, which seemed like a ridiculously small number to head-on a couple thousand-odd Black Knife warriors. Until I saw them in action.

There was only a single engagement in the field, before the big one that ended it, back at Hell. It wasn't much of a contest.

Khryllian armsmen are the finest soldiers on Home. Lacking the spiritual gifts that would qualify them as full-fledged Knights of Khryl, they compensate by obsessively developing their physical skills, and by their absolute devotion to a code of honor that does not permit even the thought of defeat.

One hundred brilliantly coordinated heavy cavalry with superior armor, razor-barbed lances, and the devastating seven-bladed morningstar, supported by two hundred disciplined, starkly courageous mounted arbalestiers who also carried short billhooks for close work, against a mass of lightly armed ogrilloi who, for all their advantages of size, strength, and speed, had a concept of warfare dependent upon the sort of personal heroics that went out of style at Troy.

To handle any necessary personal heroics of our own, we had nine Knights of Khryl.

I don't know how many bucks we expedition survivors had killed during the *Retreat*. It was a lot. I mean a *lot*. Over a hundred, anyway. Maybe one-fifty. In thirty-four days. So the Black Knives were not exactly pussies, y'know, because they just kept coming, no matter how many we took out. But they ran from the Khryllians.

They had reason.

By the time the grills broke and ran and the Khryllians finished riding down the stragglers that afternoon, the Black Knives had lost roughly *seven hundred* warriors. In a little over two hours. The Khryllian dead numbered, I seem to recall, a couple dozen. Armsmen.

There were no casualties among the Knights.

Khlaylock wanted to harry them on their retreat. I told him to save his horses. I knew where they were going.

They were running home for Mommy.

We caught up with them four days later. They were dug in on the far side of what is now called the Caineway, using that half of the vertical city as a defensive emplacement and the river as the world's biggest moat. They still had thirteen hundred or fourteen hundred warriors over there, and almost all of them had bows, and even though the river was no more than chest deep now that it had spread across the badlands, wading through it into a storm of those five-foot-long thumb-thick arrows was nobody's idea of fun.

And even if Khlaylock had made the swing south and found a crossing a few miles downstream, what the hell were he and his armsman cavalry supposed to do against thirteen hundred Black Knife bucks and maybe eight hundred–odd bitches dug in among the streets and alleys and ruined buildings of the vertical city?

On the other hand, the Black Knives weren't in such a good position either, because if they set foot out of the city the Khryllians could cut them to shit on the plains, and they knew it. So Khlaylock decided to send a couple riders back toward North Rahndhing to alert the Order that he had the entire Black Knife Nation bottled up; then he could settle in to wait a few weeks for the six thousand or so heavy infantry it'd take to clean them out house to house. Nice and neat and safe.

Nice and neat and safe, however, was emphatically *not* what I was getting paid for.

Besides, I knew how Khryllians operate. Once the battle was over, they'd release the bitches and the cubs and just castrate any bucks who'd make submission.

I considered this an unacceptable outcome.

I was back in my cover, y'know, scout and resident ogrillo expert, so I didn't have any authority or standing to argue with a Knight Captain of the Order of Khryl. All I had was a tip from Marade that her Khryllian truthsense had never worked on me at all.

And, y'know, that eye for weakness.

So early in the evening after he'd sent off the riders, I stopped by Khlaylock's tent to commiserate.

The Knight Attendant had just finished preparing Khaylock's dinner, and the Great Man was relaxing on his camp stool in front of a small turd fire. I ambled over and squatted on my heels across from him without waiting for permission. "That was a fine thing you did today, Knight Khlaylock," I told him. "I admire you for it. Not many Khryllian commanders would have the courage to put the lives of their men above their own honor."

He didn't even blink. "Have a care, Caine Lackland. Think twice before suggesting dishonor to a Knight of Khryl."

This *Lackland* moniker was something he'd hung on me, believe it or not, as a sign of respect. Knights all have House names and carry the name of their lands, or the lands they are sworn to; Marade, for example, was formally Marade, Knight Tarthell of Kavlin's Leap. In the Lipkan Empire, only serfs have a single name—like, say, Caine. So, in deference to my actions in freeing Marade and Tizarre and escaping the Black Knives, he did me the honor of nicknaming me Lackland, as though my not having lands and a surname was some kind of oversight.

"Oh, shit no, I'm sorry. Didn't mean it like that. No disrespect intended." I shook my head like your average amiable dumbass. "I was talking about—what d'you Khryllians call it? Your Legend, right? The story Knights and armsmen and all the Soldiers of Khryl will tell each other about your life, for as long as the Order survives. Everything good or bad about who you are that might help another Khryllian face a tough situation, right?"

He nodded at me over the top of a steel mug of wine. "It is in our Legends that Knights continue to serve Our Lord of Valor, even long after we fall in His Service."

"Well, yeah. That's what I'm talking about. I mean, a few days ago you fought what will probably go down in your Legend as one of the greatest cavalry engagements in Khryllian history. Maybe in the history of the world. Now today, though . . ."

He squinted at me. "You find fault with my orders?"

"No, no, no. Not at all. That's my *point*. I think it's great that you have so much compassion for your men. Rather than lose any more, you're willing to be remembered as the Knight who let the Black Knives slip away."

He set his mug on the ground beside his boot, and sighed. "I am no fool, Caine Lackland, and a fool you must be not to have discovered so before now. The Order of Khryl does not exist to serve your private vengeance."

*Tell me that again tomorrow*, I thought, but I said, "All right, look, sure, I can't play you. I get that. But now lend me half an ear, huh? The Black Knives are settled in over there, and they're spoiling for a fight. On their terms, right? Because you made them fight on your terms four days ago, and they want some payback. But when they find out you're not gonna attack—when they find out it's a siege instead of a battle—things are gonna change. Especially when their food starts to run short. It'll be more than a month before your infantry can get here. I know for a fact they don't have supplies to last that long."

Khlaylock leaned into the firelight. "Then fight they must, and we can—"

"No. Run they will, and you can't."

He scowled at me.

"They'll leave just enough bucks behind to keep some fires lit and shit to make it look like they're still there, while the rest of them slip away. Once they're gone, they'll scatter. And the Order will never catch them together again. Not in your lifetime, anyway."

He turned that scowl toward the darkness beyond the Khryllian camp. He was seeing the badlands inside his head, the way any good cavalry commander could: the way they had looked at sunset, the way they would look from any vantage points he could reach, from any scouting arcs he could order.

The way they would look from the vertical city, once it was empty.

He murmured, "You are saying there is another way out."

"Yeah. But better than that—better for you, and for that Legend of yours," I told him. "I'm saying there's another way *in*."

He brought his gaze back across the fire and spoke the two words that if I were a more demonstrative guy I might have kissed him on the mouth for. "Show me."

Which is how, a couple hours later, Khlaylock and I found ourselves in that tactical dispute I mentioned earlier.

We were on the plateau overlooking the vertical city, next to the topside access tunnel. Getting up there wasn't a problem; the cliffs were limestone, which made sedimentary layers that I could go up better than most men climb stairs. I towed a light cord attached to hemp rope that I pulled up and tied off to an outcropping, and Khlaylock, with Khryl's Strength, just hand-over-handed himself straight up the rope without raising a sweat. The prairie grass on the plateau was waist-high by then and there was a night breeze from the west, which put us downwind from the access tunnel and covered our motion. Sound was not an issue, because my waterfall was roaring out from the escarpment only thirty-odd feet below the lip, which made it an easy sneak, even for Khlaylock, who was less than ideally stealthy, despite leaving his armor behind and carrying only a long knife and his morningstar.

The Black Knives had posted a couple of sentries up there, but the sentries got lazy, as sentries do, and when one of them went back down the access tunnel for something, I got the other with my garrotte. He made enough noise—thrashing around, trying to get me off his back—to draw the attention of the other one, who poked his head up the access tunnel to see what was going on, which news was delivered to him by Khaylock's morningstar at something like lightspeed.

The medium, as they say, was the message.

And sure, the lightspeed thing is hyperbole, but not as much as you think. That particular strike graphically demonstrated the distinction between a Knight Venturer, like Marade, and a Knight Captain; whereas a shot from Marade could lift a full-grown ogrillo from his feet and hurl his corpse a yard or two, when Khlaylock hit that buck in the face, the poor bastard's head just fucking vaporized.

Which almost made me reconsider. But only almost. Like somebody I used to know had liked to say: I died the day I passed my Boards.

From the lip of the escarpment, the vertical city fanned out below us in a spray of pinprick campfires fogged by the waterfall's spray. A gibbous moon hanging in the southeast whitened the peeled-back levels while I laid out my half-fake plan. I pointed out the downramp from the vault and explained how easy it'd be for Khlaylock to lead his Knights down the tunnel to take the Black Knives from the rear.

Khlaylock, unsurprisingly, was having some difficulty seeing the tactical advantage in this. His scowl kept getting deeper the longer he looked down at the city. "In the best case, our surprise attack turns the Black Knife line long enough for my cavalry to ford the river. Which leaves my Knights and me inside the city with two thousand Black Knives and my cavalry—again at best—funnelled into narrow streetways as they strike inward to join us, forced to fight Black Knife warriors on the worst possible ground."

I shook my head. "You do this the way I tell you, you won't have to fight them. They don't *want* to fight you—"

"Black Knives are the fiercest warriors of the Boedecken—"

"That's because what their—uh—priesthood does to cowards is far, far worse than dying in battle."

He turned that scowl on me.

I nodded down into the scatter of spray-fogged campfires. "You know the Black Knives practice sorcery. What you don't know is that it's not just sorcery, it's their *religion*. And this is their most holy place. It's the seat of their god. I killed their . . . high priest, I guess you'd say—" Because I sure as hell wasn't going to tell Knight Captain Khryllians Do Not Make War On Et Cetera that I had murdered a female noncombatant. "—and I know where the rest of their priesthood will be. I can take you straight to them. Once you wipe them out, the warriors will crumble. Shit, they'll be *grateful*."

Well, maybe. I had a feeling they wouldn't be lining up for a chorus of "Ding Dong, the Bitches're Dead," though even if my conditioning would have let me tell him that, he wouldn't have gotten the joke.

His scowl vanished into a pale stone stare colder than the moonlight. "Knights of Khryl are warriors, not assassins."

"Oh, grow up, for shit's sake. What's more important to you: Playing fair? or *winning*?"

"To act with Honor at all times is the absolute obligation of every Knight. Maintain the Honor of your Person, the Order, and Our Lord. Speak the Truth, though it mean your Death. Defend all those who cannot—"

"Yeah, yeah, yeah, I've heard it before."

He was already turning back toward the topside access stair. "And there is no need for attack, nor to fear escape of the Black Knives below. Two Knights alone—three perhaps at most, given resupply up the rope we have ourselves lately employed—might hold this shaftway 'gainst the Black Knife Nation entire."

He was right, of course, which was the problem. Well . . . not exactly a *problem* . . .

The only reason I was arguing with him in the first place was that I kind of liked the guy. I had a soft spot for the true-blue Honor-and-Justice types. Still do, a little.

When I was a kid, second-handing pirated Adventures bootlegged off the Net, I was as big a Jhubbar fan as the next guy—even though I couldn't admit it, exactly. Or even at all. Not in my neighborhood. In the Mission District, you pretty much had to worship Mkembe, though he was long dead; Jhubbar—Raymond Story—was too goody-goody, y'know, noble and coura-geous, defend the weak and Show the Power of Truth through Righteous Action and all that shit. I was a sucker for it. Though I couldn't tell anybody—not even Dad—I even wanted to *be* him when I grew up. He was a Knight of Khryl.

Sometimes I still want to be him.

Sometimes I wonder how much of the stupid shit I've done was just to punish myself for not growing up to be Jhubbar Tekkanal. I wonder sometimes if that's why I married my late wife: because, down deep, we both despised the man I really am. It was the only thing we had in common.

I got over hating myself. Mostly. She didn't. But let that go.

The point is, I hadn't brought Khlaylock up there to sell him the plan. My plan wasn't my plan. My plan was to bring him up there and kill him so I could tell the rest of the Knights he'd been taken by the Black Knives, and then I could lead them in a "rescue" raid; basically, to con the Knights into killing the Black Knife priest-bitches before they found out Khlaylock was dead. Liking the guy was giving me a little trouble pulling the trigger, that's all.

And that wasn't the only issue; I had my audience to consider.

We were close enough to the lip of the escarpment that a grab of his arm and a drop to my back for a simple *tomenage* would have done the trick—and that's exactly how I'd have handled it, later in my career. But this was early days, and I had no idea just how popular *Retreat from the Boedecken* had become.

Kollberg was a genius at marketing; he was selling first-hander seats on a per-day basis, with discounts for multiple-day purchase and an option to re-up for extra days if the audience member processed the credit request before he or she left the building. He was also licensing the Adventure to other Studios across Earth, along with a cut-down second-hander cube of highlights starting when I spotted the Black Knives coming across the badlands, so new first-handers could get up to speed on the story arc. Every Studio in the world ended up splitting out some excess capacity; the Studio system hadn't seen an extended Adventure with this level of nonstop slaughter since Mkembe and Mast in *Westmarch Raiders*.

By the time I was standing on the escarpment next to Khlaylock, I was already an international star; I just didn't know it yet. So I was still looking to turn the High Drama volume knob up to eleven.

Which is why I said, "Wow. So Khryl loves cowards now?"

There are lots of clichés for how he took it—pillar of salt, turned to stone, that kind of shit—but none of them capture his eerily explosive stillness; he was locked down like a vault around a bomb. Somebody took the millisecond pause between triggering the detonator and the blast and stretched it into a long, long silence empty of everything but the waterfall's roar. It really kinda gave me a shiver.

A hot black shiver, just above my balls.

I took that shiver in both fists of my Control Disciplines and jammed it into my adrenals. The night went bright and sharp and loud. Electric jolts along my arms and legs whispered that if I needed to, I could fly . . .

When he finally spoke I could barely pick out his voice; it sounded like boulders grinding together in the river beneath our feet.

"You are no Knight, Caine Lackland, and I am not in Khryl's Battledress—"

"I know a coward when I see one. Khryl does too."

The look he sent over his shoulder shot those hot black jolts all the way up to the top of my skull. "Were you Armed—"

"Fuck Armed." I pulled the knives out of my sleeves. A sharp flip of my wrists shot them both hilt-deep into the earth. "You have Khryl's Strength. I have the truth. You think I'm wrong, prove it."

"A Challenge? With *you?*" He stared, morning star hanging slack as his mouth. "Are you mad?"

"Yeah. Crazy too."

He finally turned toward me, slowly, considering, rolling it over in his head to get a good look at the angles. "You claim Khryl favors your plan—?"

"I claim," I said, "you're a gutless butt-weasel. You're a Knight *Captain*, for shit's sake. Even if you didn't have Khryl's Strength and Khryl's Speed and Khryl's Farts and who knows what else, you're twice my fucking size. What are you afraid of?"

"My reluctance," he said slowly, "arises of the debt you are owed by the Order, in the rescue of Knight Tarthell, and your aid against the Black Knife Nation. Do you understand that should I choose to Challenge and you Answer, your health, limb, and life itself are at peril? That even should Khryl favor your cause, you may be injured beyond the capacity of His Love to repair?"

I grinned. "Likewise."

He stared a moment longer. "Will you not retract? You cannot hope to stand against me, Caine Lackland, and I would not willingly do you harm."

"Sacrilege along with cowardice." I wasn't even talking anymore. It was the black jolt working my lips and tongue and throat. "*Khryl* decides who wins, doesn't he? Unless you're gonna pile on apostasy."

He lowered his head with a resigned sigh. "Very well. Make peace with whatever god favors you, little man; you will have no further chance. Challenge."

"Accepted," I said. "I will Answer."

So there we stood, on the lip of the escarpment, in billows of mist curling back from the waterfall. My back to the brink. His to the access tunnel. The moon, almost full and almost overhead, bleached the ten feet of softly damp pairie grass between us pale as a charcoal sketch on sheepskin. He lifted his morningstar in both hands; with the sun down, he could aim the weapon's head only at the sun's reflected light—y'know, the moon—and he composed himself for the prayer that would sanctify the coming Combat.

He drew himself up to his full height and lifted his head to Khryl's light— the last time a Khryllian Knight ever kneels is when he takes his Orders, un- less he's defeated and Yields in Combat—and when he slipped into the Old High Lipkan *Ammare Khryl Tyrhaalv'Dhalleig*, the head of his morningstar took on that St. Elmo's fire glow that began to creep down the haft toward his hands and I took one long skipping step for momentum and leaped.

In those days—years before Berne put Kosall through my spine—I could leap really well.

My Control Disciplines had my legs so amped that I might as well have been on the moon; when the arc of my leap reached him, I was still as high as his head and descending and I had to shoot the side kick down at an angle to catch the haft of his morningstar just below its centerpoint.

Now, sure, in those days I maybe weighed all of seventy-five kilos dripping wet—Khlaylock would have gone around one-fifteen buck naked—and I would have needed both hands to even lift his morningstar without popping a ball, and I could forget swinging it effectively in a fight. But I wasn't swing- ing it.

I was falling on it.

With my entire seventy-five kilos, plus all the kinetic energy I could cram into an exceedingly well-trained side kick, which made his two-handed grip into a fulcrum, the haft into a lever, and the seven-bladed head into Archimedes' Earth.

It caught him full on the left temple. This would have killed any ordinary man. Khlaylock didn't even fall down. The effect was pretty spectacular nonetheless.

A wet ripping crunch splintered his eye socket and cheekbone and fanned black blood spray into the mist; the impact turned his head and sent the morn- ingstar on past, taking most of the side of his face with it. The weapon flipped out of his slackening hands and he staggered, trying to turn toward me as I landed, trying to get his hands up—even stunned into next year he was trying to fight back—but his left eye dangled out of its shattered socket by his optic nerve, flopping against black-smeared teeth left exposed because his upper lip was lying on the grass somewhere still hooked to the head of his morningstar, and that had to fuck with his targeting, because he was waving his head around like he couldn't decide which eye he should be seeing with. Before he could figure it out, I threw my hip into a Thai roundhouse that slammed my right shin across his kidneys hard enough to capture his unsteady balance and send him stumbling toward the lip of the escarpment. I sprang after him, digging in my feet and jamming both hands into his spine to send him even faster, and y'know, if he'd been somebody else, somebody less the Legendary Warrior than Purthin Khlaylock, he still might have taken me, because another Knight would have fallen, and had a chance to get up again. Khlaylock, though, staggered to the very brink, caught his balance, and wheeled to face me.

Just in time to catch both feet of my old-fashioned flying dropkick in the middle of his chest.

He sailed out over the long, long drop with a curiously calm, flat look in his good eye, a look that bespoke absolute certainty that *this is not yet over, little man.*

The hundred-meter fall to the highest of the Black Knife campfires below disagreed with him.

I hit ground at the lip and just lay there for a while, letting the black jolts drain away into the wet and the grass.

The waterfall was too loud for me to hear him land.

After I stopped shaking, I dragged the two Black Knife sentries to the edge and shoved them over after him. I picked up my knives and stuck them back into their sleeve sheaths, then went over and shook the shreds of Khlaylock's face off his morningstar.

I held it in both hands, staring down at it until my arms started to ache. Not just a weapon. A symbol. The Morning Star. Enlightenment. The Dawn of Truth and Justice that Destroys the Night of Ignorance and Sin. I remember wondering if Khlaylock had lived long enough to appreciate the irony; must have been like getting pimp-slapped by Khryl Himself.

Then I shrugged and threw it off the cliff too.

I've had twenty-five years to think about the business on the escarpment that night, and I'm still not sure which one of us it makes looks worse. Yeah: I was an asshole. Pushing his buttons to pump up some drama. To jazz my career. Not to mention the whole premeditated murder thing. But I wasn't kidding anybody. Including myself.

And looking back on it, I can see the leading edge of a running theme of my career. I don't remember making a conscious choice in tactics when I picked the fight with Khlaylock; it just felt right. I could just as easily—*more* easily—have made the Challenge about our tactical dispute; by Khryl's Law, I could have Challenged Khlaylock to let Khryl decide between us. Strictly business. But I made it personal. Because it *was* personal. At the bone, it'd be him and me, no matter what we were pretending to be fighting about. To bring the other shit into it would have been . . . well . . .

Dishonest.

Which is a peculiar word from anyone who's done what I've done and been who I've been, but there it is. There I am.

Here's the truth of Purthin Khlaylock, under all his Truth and Honor and Devotion to Justice and Noble Reluctance to whatever: when you get to the bone, why exactly was he getting ready to kill me?

For calling him names.

Yes: I am a bad man. But I've never been *that* bad.

Purthin Khlaylock, the perfect Knight: one more blood-drunk thug.

And yeah, fine, *Blood-Drunk Thug* should be carved on my headstone. I don't claim to be better than him . . . but it does still chap my ass a little that everybody claims he's better than me.

I have my own vanity. I don't kill for it, that's all.

The rest of my plan went pretty much the way most of my plans do: just fine, right up to the point where it spectacularly exploded.

That point was dawn-ish, a few seconds after a handful of Knights Venturer and I had fallen on the Black Knife priest-bitches like an old building. I was, in fact, in the middle of pinning Cornholes' mouth shut with a knife through the soft tissue under her jaw when a roar went up from the Black Knives that was answered by the Khryllians across the river, and it got real fucking bright real fast, blue-white-star bright like Pretornio in the last stage of overload, and I looked down from the second level of Hell and thought, *Fuck my ass like a chicken pot pie*, because the blue-white star in question turned out to be a butt-naked Purthin Khlaylock, balls-deep in my river while he fought off the entire motherfucking Black Knife Nation. Single-handed.

They poured into the water after him like a black tide, a storm of locusts, a school of giant screaming piranhas, like a whatthefuckdoesitmatter because he wasn't running away, he was holding his ground inside a ring of sunfire that was the arc of his morningstar.

If you're ever in Seven Wells and you have a chance to stop by the Halls of Glory in the Great Holding of Dal'Kannith, you can see a really nice depiction by Rhathkinnan, the greatest living painter of Lipke: a fresco fifty feet high and three hundred feet long, *Khlaylock's Stand at the Ford*. It's got it all: the first spray of dawn on the vast shadow-pocked face of the vertical city, swarms of uncountable thousands of Black Knives, Khlaylock doing a reasonable facsimile of Khryl Morning Goddamn Star Himself at the center of a rising hurricane of raggedly severed ogrillo body parts while on the opposite bank his cavalry shouts itself into battle order.

I do not, by the way, appear in that painting.

This is only partly because Rhathkhinnan—and the rest of the Order of Khryl—would kind of like to forget I was there at all. It's mostly because I spent that battle learning the value of intellectual flexibility and improvisation under pressure.

My Knights, naturally enough, were about half a second shy of breaking for the river; they'd come to rescue Khlaylock, not to slaughter priest-bitches. Slaughtering bitches was my thing. So in that half second while they were all looking down the face of the vertical city instead of chasing the bitches who were scampering off upslope, I shouted, "It's *working*! Come on!"

Polished helmets swung my way.

"What do you think is keeping him *alive* down there? Pure thoughts?" I snarled at them. "If those bitches get away long enough to raise their god and their power, he's *dead* and we are *too*, so get your armored butts *moving!*" Then I turned and went after the bitches without looking back. Hell, for all I knew I might even have been telling the truth. In a second or two I could hear them on my tail, and I let myself smile into the dawn.

We killed every one of them. All we could find, anyway. Cornholes and Dugsacks and Turdcrotch and Thumbnipples, and when I couldn't remember if we'd missed any or not, we just went ahead and killed whatever other bitches we came across. It was fun, making them scream and bleed and beg. It was more than fun. Whoever said "Revenge is a dish best served cold" never tasted it hot.

It was so much fun, in fact, that I completely forgot to pack it in and slip away while I had the chance.

Pretty soon—too soon—it was all over. The surviving bucks and juvies had scattered to the Boedecken winds, and there weren't even close to enough Khryllians to run them all down; some were taken into other clans, but ogrillo solidarity in general didn't really extend as far as Black Knives. Most of them ended up ditching the Boedecken altogether for human cities, slipping into the Folk slums of towns all over Lipke and the Ankhanan Empire to try and live out their days pretending they'd never even heard of Black Knives.

Broken Knives, the other clans call them now. Limp Dicks.

All that came later, though; at the time, while the cavalry was still merrily slaughtering whatever fleeing bucks they could catch, I was getting a swift boot up the ass on my way out of the Khryllian camp.

Which is not the worst that could have happened. When a couple of the Knights Venturer caught my elbows in their gentle-but-firm too-bad-for-your-punk-ass way and and let me know they were hauling me off to where Knight Captain Khlaylock was waiting outside camp, all the *Holy shit, I actually fucking pulled it off* euphoria in my chest transubstantiated into a couple yards of ice-cold concrete because, y'know, in all the excitement I had just plain forgotten that Khlaylock was still alive. And that he might find himself inclined to be a little stern with me.

I kept seeing the cloud of bloody mist that had once been the head of a Black Knife after its close encounter with Khlaylock's morningstar. This image became considerably more vivid when we reached Khlaylock and I saw the ruin of his face. Khryl's Love had Healed it as it was, fusing bone and flesh into a rumpled crater of scar.

Imagine my surprise, then, when Khlaylock waved away the Venturers and led me down a nearby wadi, where I found a fully tacked saddle horse peacefully cropping scrub in the morning sun.

"Take him and go," Khlaylock said. His voice sounded like somebody was scraping cinder blocks together in his throat. "Go and never return, Caine Lackland."

I stood there blinking into the sun. "Excuse me?"

"He is a fine gelding," Khlaylock grated. "He will bear you well."

"I, ah—I don't know what to say—"

"You have spoken overmuch already."

"I just—well, I don't want to seem ungrateful, but—I mean, this wasn't exactly what I was expecting . . ."

"Think of it as undeserved grace."

"I guess I sort of thought you'd want another crack at your Challenge—"

To which, by the way, I was fully planning to Yield and fess up in front of the whole mob about how I'd clocked him with a Sunday punch and sort of throw myself on his, and Khryl's, questionable mercies, but he just turned his remaining eye on me like his stare could nail me to the ground. "Go. Do not let another dawn find you within my sight. Ever."

I went.

I was only an hour outside the camp when the Studio pulled me. Two days later—before I even got out of the hospital—I finally realized why Khlaylock didn't re-Challenge. He'd Challenged me for calling him a coward. Get it?

He was afraid he'd lose. Again.

No wonder he was pissed. We can forgive any crime except the murder of our illusions.

Khlaylock lifted that gauntlet from Markham's shoulder and waved it negligently in my direction. "Release him."

"You don't understand," Soapy Two told him from my right. "Administrator Michaelson is in our custody—"

"The failure of understanding is yours." A single gleaming stride had Mount Khlaylock louring over Soapy Two like an unquiet volcano. "I am the guardian of Khryl's Law on His Battleground. Release this man."

Soapies are not known for unsteady nerves. That mirror-mask gave back only a smear of Justiciar and a quietly flat "And we are the Social Police. This is, by treaty, Earth land. Please step aside, sir."

This could have gotten interesting in an existentially satisfying way, but there was also the unfortunate possibility they might have come to some kind of civilized solution, and one of the problems with being a bad guy is that civilized solutions just never turn out well for you.

Besides, it would have been plain sloppy to let this opportunity slip away. Not likely I'd get another.

I squinted my one good eye up at Khlaylock's. "Sucks to live in fear, doesn't it?"

"What?" He knew better than to get into a conversation with me, but I guess he just couldn't help himself. "Were you not pledged to Combat, I would undertake to teach you the meaning of fear."

Remember that eye for weakness?

I sneered into the pretty half of his face. "Yeah, teach me. Might as well learn from the master."

Lightning flickered behind his bright-gleaming eye. I had him by his metaphorically empty nutsack.

He went for contempt. "How a villain as low and vile as you can question my heart—"

"For fuck's sake, Khlaylock, do we have to have this fight all over again? It doesn't take guts to smash some poor bastard's skull with a morningstar. If you had any stones at all you'd kill me right here, you punkass sack of shit. Or just let Soapy haul me off. I mean, they're taking me straight to True Hell. That's closer to justice than anything you'll get from Khryl."

He took a step so that he could tower over me even more than he had Soapy Two. "Is that what you'd prefer?"

"Some people really are upright and pure and the perfect Knight and all that shit. Marade was. More than you, anyway. I'm thinking Angvasse is. You? You just play the part because you're pissing your codpiece terrified that if you screw up, Khryl won't love you anymore."

He drew himself up and gathered dignity around himself like a mantle of righteousness; he had an answer to this one. "Fear of God is the beginning of wisdom."

I had an answer too. "Who said that? Some other nutless wonder?"

Markham shouldered forward. "The courage of the Justiciar is *legendary*—"

"Only compared with yours, ass-cob." I shook some pity into my sneer. "It's one thing to be a good guy because that's who you are. It's something else to be a good guy because you're too much a fucking pussy to break the rules."

Cords twisted across the undamaged half of Khlaylock's forehead. "Were you not already pledged to Combat—"

"Yeah, yeah. Bored with this. Let's fight."

Khlaylock fixed his good eye on Soapy One, who had me by the left arm. "Release him."

Soapy One might have been carved from the same rock as Mount Khlaylock. "I repeat: please step aside, sir. I won't ask you again."

"Do you *threaten* me?" Incredulity ratcheted Khlaylock's head another inch or two to his right, which was more or less what I'd been waiting for.

"Here, I'll settle it. *Ch'syavallanaig Khryllan'tai.*"

Social Police stripcuffs are designed with a shear-strength high enough to lift a passenger car, and will withstand not only knives but also bolt-cutters and cold chisels, blowtorches, and maybe even arc welders. Basically anything that doesn't send out the coded electronic pulse that triggers the doohicky to re-arrange the cuffs' long-chain molecules is pretty much useless. They are not, however, designed to bind the wrists of a guy whose right hand can suddenly become roughly as hot as the surface of the sun.

I admit that that's more hyperbole—which anyone reading this might guess by the general lack of setting the atmosphere on fire and wiping out all life on the planet—but the point is that the Holy Foreskin was a couple orders of magnitude beyond the heat tolerance of the stripcuffs, so in addition to burning the staggering fuck out of my left wrist and freeing my hands, I shocked a quart of living crap out of Soapy Two, good nerves or not, when his peripheral vision registered a handful of sunfire swinging upside his head.

Nothing wrong with his reflexes: he let go of my arm and twisted toward me with a smoothly professional bob-and-weave that cleared his helmet under my swing, which was okay because I wasn't aiming for him anyway.

Markham jerked back out of my reach with his gauntlets coming up like a boxer's guard and some Old High Lipkan trigger word burst from his mouth to drape his entire body in electric blue witchfire—also top-rate reflexes—which was also okay because I wasn't aiming for him either.

Purthin, Lord Khlaylock, Justiciar Et Cetera, Radiant Mantle of Whothe-fuckcaresanyway, had just barely time to blink his eye and begin to draw breath for his own Old High Lipkan trigger word when my handful of Holy Foreskin came up his blind side and caught him below his left ear.

There's an esoteric variant of the Southern Cobra style of *chi tao chu'an* called Python; it's based on wrist and open-palm strikes that lead into joint locks and strangles. It was in that Python spirit that my slap didn't follow through after impact; instead my open palm hooked around the back of his neck so that his reflexive jerk away drove the base of his skull hard against the Holy Foreskin, which was—though less hot than the surface of the sun— plenty hot enough to blast the water content of his skin and muscle into a burst of superheated steam. A shotgun fired beneath the surface of a bathtub filled with blood would make pretty much the same sound.

And nearly as much mess.

Being a minor expert on destruction of the human body, I could go through the technical details, such as how the blast vaporized his upper trapezius and most of his capitor group, crushing his cervical vertebrae into chunks that blew out through his levator scapulae, and so on and so forth— not to mention coming *way* too damn close to blowing my own damn hand off—but the actual significance of all this was the sum total effect: by the time the Holy Foreskin faded from my palm, Khlaylock's half-severed head had flopped onto his breastplate and dragged his balance forward over locked knees so that he toppled like a felled tree.

Soapy One, still holding my left arm, took a reflexive step away from the ar- terial blood spurting out the ragged remnants of Khlaylock's carotids, which is the only reason a hundred-forty-some-odd kilos of armored meat didn't actu- ally land on me.

Holy Foreskin–dazzle slowly faded from my eyes, and color slowly leached back into the lamplit room, and from the way Faller and Markham were blink- ing, they couldn't see any better than I could. We all stood there for a stretch- ing second or two, staring down at Khlaylock's corpse while the only sounds were the soft plopping as scorched shreds of his flesh peeled off the walls and dripped to the floor, the sizzle of the steam coming off my newborn-pink palm, and Fallerbàl's low psychotic-fugue moan of *oh god oh fuck me fuck me fuck me god . . .*

Looking back on it, I feel like I should have had some kind of flash then, a life-passing-before-my-eyes vision of all the things Purthin Khlaylock has meant to me in the last twenty-five years. Who he was and what I did to him are so intimately intertwined with everything I am that without having kicked his armored ass off the escarpment above Hell, I can't imagine ever becom- ing me.

Instead I just sighed. "Well. That's done."

Maybe I'm not so sentimental after all.

Markham stood in a half-jittering immobility, like the blue witchfire crawling over his armor was a few thousand volts AC. I nodded to him. "Hey, you win. Congratulations. Here's your prize: you get to explain all this to Angvasse Khlaylock. She'll probably be here in a minute or two; I'm surprised she's not here already."

Markham and Faller favored me with identical owl-eyed blinks. "What?"

"Did I not mention that part? Hey, sorry." Guess I didn't look sorry either. "Think about it, Markham—you took me out of an alley that's in the middle of the Riverdock parish. In full view of Tyrkilld Aeddhar's favorite bar. Where one of his best friends happens to be an ogrillo. You think those shadows were dark to *him*? What do you think's gonna happen when he tells Tyrkilld that you slapped me into a skull fracture and hauled me off? In the middle of a Smoke Hunt. With Smoke Hunters standing right in fucking front of you. You don't think Tyrkilld's gonna be kinda curious? You don't think Angvasse's gonna be, say, a little interested in what happened to her Invested Agent of Motherfucking Khryl?"

"I—I was—" Markham had to cough his throat clear before he could go on. "I was acting on the direct order of the Justiciar—"

"Sure, all right. Did you waste those Hunters? Or do they have some way to recognize you? So they don't, y'know, kill one of the guys who's on *their* side."

Markham's mouth snapped shut with an audible *clack*.

"What are you gonna tell Angvasse about why you're even here tonight? You gonna tell her you were never in her service at all? Gonna tell her you're a lying bastard whose main job is to babysit her so that she never finds out what's really going with the Smoke Hunt?"

"An order of the Justiciar," Markham said though locked teeth, "which still stands."

"Sure. Good luck with that, huh?" I swung my ton-and-a-half of head toward Faller. "Shit, man, you'll have to tell her yourself."

Faller just gave back the empty stare of a jacklighted deer.

I pointed my chin at Khlaylock's corpse. "That pile of meat was the local head of state, who just got himself murdered by an Earthman on Earth territory. And you're about to whisk his killer out of reach of Khryl's Justice. You get it? You're maybe five minutes away from war with the Order of Khryl. And because he's also the Lipkan viceroy, you can likely toss in war with Lipke on top."

"I—I—I can't—I mean, the Social Police—I—" Faller's eyes bugged out and his stammer dissolved into choking.

"Listen to me, Rababàl. I'm showing you the way out, get it? All you have to do is tell the truth."

"What? What truth?"

"Tell her I killed him. Tell her I said I was doing my job. My Invested Agent of Khryl gig. Remind her she knew going in that hiring me doesn't always work out how my bosses hope it will."

"Hiring—? Your *job*?"

I nodded. "She hired me to stop the Smoke Hunt."

"To—what makes you think—?"

"That was the tricky part of this job. It's usually easy enough to figure out who's in charge of shit—all you have to do is find out who's getting the most out of it, you follow? Who's gonna win if it goes all the way. But the Smoke Hunt? *Everybody* gets theirs. It's a stable system. Nobody *wants* it to change. The Smoke God gets an endless banquet of dread, fury, and terror. The Hunt's leadership gets political power—they've unified the Boedecken clans in a way this world hasn't seen since the Khulan Horde. The Khryllians get a permanent enemy that keeps the whole population militarized and obedient. Black-Stone gets an open *dil*, an exploding business in export griffinstones, not to mention a stable slave-labor supply because the toughest, most committed troublemakers get chopped piecemeal into each new round of Smoke Hunters. The Board of Governors gets new access to Home. Hell, even Khryl wins; as an Ideational Power, His Power is a function of the devotion of his worshippers. When shit goes bad, what do people do? They fucking well *pray*. Khryl's never been *happier*. That's how I knew. It wasn't one of you, or two or three. It's too neat. There's too much to go around. That's how I knew you'd made a deal. It's *all* of you. All you fuckers. Everybody wins."

My mouth was full of blood and acid bile. "Everybody except the ordinary grills, living in slave ghettoes, trading their balls for a chance at a better life. Everybody except the regular fucking folk getting ripped limb from fucking limb by the fucking Smoke Hunt. Christ, I hate you people. If you only knew how I hate you."

I spat the blood on the floor. I was panting. My breath felt hot enough to ignite the room. "And now I've fucked you, because there actually are a couple decent fucking people in this artesian shitspring of a town, and they're on their way here, and there's no way you're gonna talk your way out of this. Hell, you can't even *want* to. The truth's your only fucking *hope*."

"Perhaps," Markham murmured. "And perhaps not. Do you believe Khryl's Champion is likely to defy the expressed Will of the Lord of Battles?"

"Just bet my life on it, didn't I?"

Soapy One snorted. "What life?" he said, and his shock baton came up on my own blind side and blasted starshells across my brain.

On Home, the physics are wrong for the capacitors in the shock baton. So he had to hit me a couple more times. I remember saying, as I went down, "Tell her—tell her she owes me. Tell her I want to get *paid* . . ."

Then the event horizon surged out from inside my head and swallowed me whole.

*extroduction*

*now:* A DEAL WITH GOD

# A DEAL WITH GOD

Once I woke up, it didn't take long to figure out where I was. I'd been there before.

Too many times.

The plain cream-colored walls, blank, windowless, featureless except for the touchpad beside the door. The flat cream-colored door itself, also without window. Or handle. The simple desk and chair, injection-molded of a single piece with the floor. Nothing on them. No books. No screen and stylus, and certainly no pen or paper. The lo-flo crapper in the corner. The bed, with the padded wire-and-plastic straps to secure my arms to the cold round rails of brushed stainless steel. No straps for my legs, because they didn't need any, and they knew it.

This was Earth.

The computerized spinal bypass that let my legs work in this universe hadn't been reinitialized since I left three years ago; the mental trick that lets me walk on Home is magick. From the waist down I was just dead fucking meat. Like—as Deliann once wrote—having a couple dead dogs strapped to my ass. Except I can't eat 'em.

I had a tube coming out of my dick, and a big diaper, and I didn't have any self-consciousness about crapping all over myself. If they didn't feel like cleaning up my shit, they could fucking well unstrap an arm so I could use the bedpan—the one success of my literally half-assed spinal regeneration therapy had been bowel and bladder control. But nobody minded cleaning up my shit. They weren't capable of minding.

If I'd had any doubt about where I was being held, it would have vanished the first time my attendants came in to empty my urine bag, replace my IVs, and change my diaper. I could see the lobotomized vacancy in their eyes before I saw the neural yokes on their necks.

Workers.

I didn't bother to try to talk to them. With their higher cognitive function overridden by the yokes, Workers can't do anything beyond give simple answers to direct questions. These couldn't even do that. They were deaf. Stone fucking deaf.

Surgically deafened.

To make sure that an inmate here had no one to communicate with. That the inmate has absolutely no unapproved contact whatsoever with anyone beyond his cell. Which I knew because for about ten years, I used to regularly bribe my way into this place, to talk to my father.

I was in the Buke.

The Buchanan Social Camp is one of the places Geneva puts people who need to have their antisocial attitudes rectified, or at least interdicted from healthy society. Usually permanently.

It's hard to say how long I was there; time has little meaning in the Buke. Workers came and went. My relief bag and diaper got changed, as did my sheets and my IV. My headaches went away. I got stronger.

I had time to think.

Thinking—real thinking—is not something I do often, nor particularly well. I was never trained for it, and I sure as hell don't have any natural inclination.

Thinking gets in my way. In a fight it's fatal.

In the real world, instinct and experience are superior to thought; Tolstoy wrote that in a contest of cunning, the peasant consistently defeats the intellectual, and he was right. Not because the peasant is smarter but because he doesn't have the self-doubt and the second thoughts and all the other mind tricks that make the intellectual out-think himself.

I was born to be an intellectual. Before his illness and multiple breakdowns, my father was arguably the most famous anthropologist of the century; his book *Tales of the First Folk* is still the standard text on Primal oral culture. My mother, before her death, had been his brightest student. Even after the Social Police arrested him and busted us down to Labor, he was still trying to make me think like a Professional, teaching me out of books on the net. Even after my mother died. Even after the madness had him wholly in its grip; on his semilucid days, he would make me read and talk and read some more. But I did that only to keep him from beating me into bloody unconsciousness. Any real chance of growing up an intellectual was over for me by the time I was six. My real education was street school.

I might have been born an intellectual, but I was raised a peasant.

Which—along with what a number of people have described as lunatic self-confidence and a truly staggering degree of self-absorption—might explain why I wasn't really worried.

It was clear why they put me in the Buke. This was tactical. Because of all those years of visiting Dad here. They were expecting my presumed future to smother me in wet-wool layers of claustrophobia.

Dickheads.

I spent days hanging from a fucking *cross*. I spent fuck knows how long chained to the wall of the Shaft in Ankhana's Donjon, dying of gangrene in a river of other people's shit. Spending the rest of my life in a nice clean quiet cell is gonna scare me?

Oh, yeah. Sure.

One of the books that Dad made me read—one that I've read again a few times on my own, in fact—was *The Art of War*. Because, like a lot of those old-timey Chinese guys, Sun Tzu had a gift for metaphor. The book isn't just about war, it's about handling conflict. You could even say it's about how to live well in a dangerous world.

One of the things Master Sun wrote is that a general who knows his enemy and knows himself need not fear the outcomes of a thousand battles.

I knew my enemy. That was my edge.

When I finally got a visitor, he seemed a little surprised to find me smiling.

His Professional's suit and tie didn't really fit—looked like it was cut for a guy with twenty extra pounds on him—and he scuffed the soles of his brown wingtips along the floor when he came through the door, but maybe it wasn't the suit so much as it was my eyes.

My eyes kept wanting to see his hair in a brown comb-over instead of grey strings waxed flat across bare scalp, and a dirt-colored stubble on thicker jowls instead of the stiff salty beard neatly trimmed. Age suited him, really: he'd lost weight and gained gravity.

And he could walk straight in and just sit down and let me stare at him and get my mind around his existence, and he didn't even have to do his goddamn coin tricks with nervous hands. He just kept them folded in his lap.

I kept smiling. I didn't have anyplace I had to be.

Pretty soon he leaned forward. "You don't seem to understand how much trouble you're in."

My smile spread to an open grin. "And you're looking good for a guy I last saw raining in pieces down the face of Hell."

He brushed that off with an irritable nod. "Ancient history."

"Feels like fucking yesterday."

He flushed, and his gaze flicked down toward his folded hands. His fingers twitched. "That was—" He shook his head and looked back at me. "That's not what I'm here to talk about. I'm here to save your life."

I shrugged.

"Capital Forcible Contact Upcaste, Michaelson. Were you awake enough to remember that part? You're on full-sense log murdering a *Leisureman*—"

I laughed at him.

"You think this is *funny*?"

"What am I supposed to call you? Rababàl? Simon Faller? Gofer?"

He flushed darker. "Michaelson—"

"That's not my name."

His fingers twitched again. Missing that platinum coin, I bet. "What kind of game do you think you're playing?"

"Same as usual," I told him. "The kind I win."

He stared at me, then swung that stare to my wrists and my diaper and my dead legs, the featureless walls and the blank inside of the door, inviting me to stare with him, to take in the reality of my cell, of the Buke, of Earth. "You're out of your mind."

"There is," I admitted, not without a certain pride, "a history of insanity in my family."

"You have *one* hope of coming out of this alive, Michaelson. One. And that is *cooperation*—"

"I told you that's not my name."

He rolled his eyes. "What am I supposed to call you, then? Caine? Shade? Tell me."

"Last time I was on Earth," I said, "the proper mode of address from a Professional to an Administrator was *sir*."

He stared.

"Let's give it a try, shall we?"

His mouth had to work for a while before it could chew out some words. "You *are* insane."

"And you can kiss my upcaste ass, you lackey fuck."

His lips started flapping. "Do you—are—you don't—"

"I'm not the one in trouble, Faller. You are. If the Board of Governors wanted me dead, I'd be dead already. I'd have never woken up. Instead somebody invested serious coin in neurosurgery, and instead of being the star of a show trial for killing Vilo, I'm sequestered with political prisoners. And instead of Soapy interrogators, I've got good old Rababàl here to have a chat with me about *cooperation*. Which means shit's already going bad enough on Home that somebody thinks they need me to fix it. So start kissing my ass or kiss yours good-bye." I batted my eyelids at him. "You pick."

His lips stopped flapping long enough to peel back off his teeth. "It's not just you, Michaelson. We know about your daughter, and we know where she is—"

"Simon, Simon, Simon." I could peel lips too, and my teeth were bigger than his. "Do you really want to bring my family into this?"

His lower lip snuck back up a little.

I cocked my head toward him. "Not that I'm worried about her; Faith's defended in ways you can't imagine. But if you want to do the we'll-hurt-your-family thing just on principle, I'm into it. Maybe you never saw the cube of what happened to Vinson Garrette."

His brows drew together and those lips tried for a disbelieving smile. "Are you *threatening* me?"

"Nah. I was just thinking how, y'know, with these bedrails for leverage—having the bed anchored to the floor makes it a great platform, real stable, just perfect—from here I can kick your head right the fuck off your shoulders. Right off. Like a tee ball. Rrrip. Bounce bounce bounce."

His right eyelid flickered. Color drained down his cheeks into his beard. "I read your chart—your legs . . . your legs don't—"

"Yeah, Simon. That's right. My legs don't. You believe everything you read?"

A sharp *chuff*—an aspirated *ki-ya*—and a twist of my abdominals, which are real damn strong, snapped my diaper toward his face, and those nervous hands flew up like startled pigeons and he jerked away hard enough to slide sideways off the chair and dump himself ass-first on the floor, and he got up madder than a teargassed bear because of course neither of my dead legs even cleared the rail.

"Just kidding." I grinned at him. "And I was lying about your head coming off anyway. I'm an asshole like that."

He took a step toward me and one of those nervous hands made a fist that swung up by his shoulder. And paused. And hung there while rage-swollen veins writhed across his forehead.

Which told me everything I'd been pretending to know had actually been true after all.

My grin widened. "You can fuck off now, Faller. Don't come back until the Bog's ready to deal."

Those veins kept on writhing, but the fist opened, and the hand fell to his side.

He lowered his head. "I don't know what else I was expecting," he muttered. "Why should it be different now?"

He half sat, half fell back into the injection-molded chair and let himself slump against the edge of the desk. "You haven't changed at all, have you? Not one little bit. And why should you? Being exactly who you are has always gotten you exactly what you want."

What the hell was he playing at now? "I wouldn't go *that* far—"

"Probably work this time too." He sounded like he was talking more to himself than to me. He kept his head down, like there was something on his face he didn't want me to see. "Just tell me one thing, Michaelson. Caine. Whatever. Why is it only the bastards ever win?"

I didn't answer. I was pretty sure which bastard he was talking about. He just sat there with his head down and those once-nimble fingers laced together so he could twist them back and forth against each other, working them tight as his voice, and he went on.

"Why is it the people who play by the rules—the people who just do their jobs and mind their manners and save their pay and really don't want anything more out of life than *one goddamned break* end up working away their whole lives and every time it looks like one damned ray of sunshine might fall into their lives there's some bastard with a shovel to tell you *No, that's just the mouth of your grave* before he starts piling the dirt in on top of you." His fingers twisted tight enough that his knuckles crackled like stiff cellophane. "That's all I want to know, Michaelson. You explain it to me, then I'll go tell the Board, and you can go ahead and cut my damned throat. Again."

"Cut *your* throat—did you *play* that fucking Adventure?"

My voice came out thick, and so raw it surprised me. Twenty-five years later, and I here I was again, looking at his throat and wondering if he tasted like pork. "At least *you* lived through it, which is more than can be said for fucking near everybody else. What was the deal? You bird-dog us into there and get a free emergency transfer out when things get hairy? The Fireball fake-your-death bit was good, Rababàl. Smart. That's what stopped me from hunting your jiggling ass." Good thing I was strapped to the bed. Otherwise I'd have made a try for him, dead legs and all. "They hung me from a fucking *cross*. And Marade—"

"I know."

His voice was barely more than a whisper.

"I—have the cubes. All of them. They . . . didn't tell me about the Black Knives. You have to believe that, Caine. I didn't know, going in. I wouldn't have done it, not even for—"

"For what?" My breath had gone hot and harsh in my throat. "Not even for *what?*"

"It was my shot, Caine. The only one I ever got. I'd been a location scout— a bird dog, yes; we know what Actors call us—for *fifteen years*. Because the

Scheduling Board didn't think I could be marketable as a leading man, and I, well, yes, I knew it; I didn't have the sense of humor to be a funny sidekick. So I waited. And I worked. I put in my time. Paid my dues. And finally, at forty—when most Actors, the ones that live that long, are thinking of retirement . . ."

He lifted his head then but didn't look at me; he just shrugged and turned his face away. "That Adventure was my big break. It was my shot. What I'd been working toward for fifteen years. And then—and then you . . ."

"Yeah," I said. "And then me."

"I don't know what *you're* angry about—that Adventure *made* you. It gave you the career I should have had."

"Except you're not me."

"True." He sighed. "Too true. The funny part is, you're not you either."

"Oh, *that* makes sense."

He finally turned back to me and he was trying for an ironic smile but his lips were twisted like his fingers and his eyes were too bright and too wet. "Did you never figure this out? It wasn't you, Michaelson. It was never you. It was the demon. What do you Monastics call them? Outside Powers. The one that runs the *dil T'llan*—that *is* the *dil T'llan*. I mean, *Retreat from the Boedecken* was the foundation of more than your career. It's the foundation of your self-image. It made Caine into Caine. You think I didn't watch you? You think I didn't second-hand your adventures? How many times were you up against it and pulled yourself through by thinking of *Retreat*—how you'd been through worse and didn't buckle? *Retreat* let you fool yourself into believing you were the baddest of the bad. The toughest of the tough. The guy who could take anything. Who could suck it up and spit it back out. And it was all because the first time you were *really* tested, you had a demon *eating your fear*. That's what made you brave. It was eating your despair. That's what made you strong. It was an illusion. A con. You were never that strong. You were never that brave. You're no tougher than anybody else. Caine was a fake from the *start*—but you fooled *yourself* along with everybody else. You were just make-believe. That's all. Make-believe."

I nodded. "Funny how shit works out, huh?"

He stared at me with those wet eyes.

"You think this was a mystery? I was Monastic, Rababàl. I knew it *then*." I turned one of my strapped-down wrists so I could open a hand. "I take whatever edge I can find. That's who I am."

Those wet eyes threatened to spill tears. "But—but then *how* . . ."

I guess some things you never really get over.

I should know.

"If it hadn't been me, it would've been Marade," I said. Softly. Gently. Because, y'know, I felt for him. I really did. It was too easy to imagine how I could have ended up him. "Or Stalton. Even Pretornio."

He shrugged helplessly.

"It's not complicated." My open hand flexed and curled, once, like it belonged to somebody else. "Look, after you, uh, left, what happened? You went back to work, right?"

He turned his face away from me, but he nodded.

"So that's what you've been doing for the last twenty-five years? Bird-dogging?"

He shrugged. "Up till—well, you know. Assumption Day."

"Yeah." Assumption Day changed things for a lot of people. "You married?"

"Yes—thirty-three years—we'd celebrated our thirtieth anniversary just before—"

"Children?"

"Two. Five grandchildren . . ."

"And that's it," I said. "Right there."

He turned back to me then, and instead of tears on his face there was the start of a frown of comprehension, which was a relief. For both of us, I'm betting.

"You probably know how my marriage went. My daughter . . . well, our relationship is—complicated. The difference between you and me, Rababàl, is that I wanted to be a star more than I wanted to live. For you it was the other way around. We both got our wish. So even in the middle of those nights when we wake up and think about all the shit we wish we'd done, we both ought to shut the fuck up and just be grateful for what we got."

He shook his head. "And . . . that's it? It's that simple? If I'd *wanted* it more . . . ?"

I shrugged. "Who knows? The difference between me and Marade, me and Stalton or Pretornio . . . basically comes down to luck, as far as I've ever been able to see. They wanted it as much as me. They were as tough as I am, probably tougher—Marade sure as hell was—as smart or smarter. I was lucky. They weren't. Imponderables. Shit falls one way, you're a star. Shit falls another, you're dinner."

"Luck? Just luck?"

"That's why you don't see guys like me sitting around in our old age whining about what could have been. Because if we don't get what we want, we're not around to complain about it. We're fucking well dead."

He looked thoughtful.

"But you could say the same, y'know? You're one of the lucky ones too. You've had a forty-year career in some of the most exotic and exciting places that exist, and you still got to have a real marriage, a family, a home . . . how many men get all that?"

He nodded. "My wife says the same. I spend too much time thinking about what I don't have, and not enough being grateful for what I do . . ."

"Yeah, well," I said, "a guy I met the other day was telling me that happy men are only half alive."

"He sounds like another bastard."

"Yeah. I don't think you'd like him."

Abruptly he laughed, and then he was shaking his head again, but now in some kind of half-astonished amusement. "I came in here to—and then we're talking about my wife and my grandkids, and you're *cheering me up*—"

I shrugged. I could feel myself flush a little. Embarrassed, I guess, at being so easy. "As a tactic, being human works pretty well."

"That's not—it wasn't part of my—"

"You walked in doing the hard-on with pockets thing. Come at me like that, what do you think I'm gonna do? Swallow?"

He nodded. "I just—I didn't mean to dump my troubles on you, Michaelson. It's a funny thing, but after all these years, it's like I *know* you—"

I nodded back. "Don't take this wrong, Rababàl. Faller. I'm used to it."

He frowned at me.

I sighed. "People who followed my Adventures all those years—lots of times when I'd do public appearances, people would start talking to me like we're old friends. Kind of like you just did. Because Caine was part of their life. They'd known me so long, they just somehow figured—without ever really thinking about it—that I knew them too. It used to bug me. A lot. I hated it. Now I miss it."

He squinted at me. "Really?"

"Really. Doesn't happen on Home. Over there I'm, y'know, the Prophet of Ma'elKoth, or the hero of Ceraeno, or the Enemy or God or whateverthefuck. I'm a walking motherfucking Epic. People forget I'm a human being. I have to pretend to be somebody else just to have a normal goddamn conversation with a normal goddamn person."

"Be careful what you wish for, eh?"

"Got that right." I found myself chuckling. "Tan'elKoth—Ma'elKoth during his exile on Earth—he used to say, 'When the gods would punish us, they answer our prayers.'"

He leaned forward and rested his elbows on his knees. "This wasn't what I wished for."

I rolled my eyes around the cream-colored walls. "Not exactly the top of my Christmas list either."

"Michaelson—Caine—" He sighed. "What *should* I call you?"

"You can call me Jonathan Fist."

He frowned at me. "Jonathan Fist?"

"He made a deal too."

"I don't get it."

"That's because you're thinking in English. The original name is German."

He shook his head. "And?"

I just shook my head. "Nobody fucking reads anymore, you know that?

"Fist, then. Please understand. I'm sixty-six years old. I was trapped on Overworld three years ago when you cut off Studio operations on Assumption Day. Along with all the Actors and scouts and Overworld Company personnel and everybody else. I thought I would die there, finally, after all. I mean, we didn't know what you had done; all any of us knew was that we couldn't get home. I was near retirement, looking forward to watching my grandchildren grow up . . . and then—"

"Yeah."

"I was in Kor when it happened. All I could think to do was get to Thorncleft, to the Railhead . . . but when I got there, of course they were as trapped as I was—but they had a copy of, well, your recording . . ."

I knew which one. "Yeah."

"I *am* sorry—it was clear how much she meant to you—"

"It seems like a long time ago."

He cleared his throat. "Anyway—finding out that the *dillin* were actually gates to Earth . . . I remembered Hell, and the Tear of Panchasell, and there was one slim chance that we could see home again, if we could find a way to open the *dil* . . ."

"I get the picture."

"And that was all I wanted. To get *home*. That was all any of us wanted. But when we finally . . ." His voice trailed off.

"They made you an offer."

He nodded. "Do you have any idea what it's worth to the Board to have Overworld access again? Plus we're importing griffinstones—did you know that there are magickal effects possible here? Do you have any idea what can be done with the combination of magick and cybernetics?"

"Yeah."

"Some of your recovery, in fact—" He stopped. "You knew?"

"You'd be surprised what I know. Look, Rab—uh, I should call you Faller, huh?"

He nodded. "Rababàl died twenty-five years ago."

I shrugged. I shrug a lot these days. The more I know, the less I have to say.

He said, "I have a very, very good thing going on the Battleground right now. I am very close to a retirement that is a great deal more comfortable than I could have ever hoped for—and then *you* show up, and I thought—I mean, think about it. Think about our history. Or my history, if you want to put it that way."

"I get it."

"And it's not just that. Every Company man on Overworld has strict instructions to hand you over on contact, Caine."

"Fist."

"It would have meant my job at the very least. Possibly my life."

"I told you: I get it."

"It wasn't personal."

I nodded. "You probably won't believe this, but I didn't come to Purthin's Ford to pee in your soup."

He offered a tired-sounding chuckle. "Give me something I can take to the Board of Governors, Caine. That's all I want, you know. That's what I came here for. Just . . . something. Something to make them think I'm not completely useless."

"Tell them I'll play," I offered. "Tell them you convinced me. We can negotiate."

He stared at me. "You mean it?"

"Sure. We don't have to butt heads, Faller. Unless you want to. I know what it's like to have the Bog on my neck. I'm not gonna wreck you just for doing your job, man."

"You—" He blinked, closed his mouth, and tried again. "All I had to do was *ask?*"

"You know how rare it is that anybody *just asks?*" I nestled my head back into the pillow and stared at the blank cream ceiling. "When anyone wants anything from me, they're always trying to bully me or blackmail me or play on my guilt or shame or fucking beat me into submission. The best I get is a generous bribe. Nobody ever even suspects that I might so much as cross the fucking street just because I'm not one hundred percent pure shitbag."

"I can see how that must hurt. Poor misunderstood mass murderer."

He was laughing at me. I joined in. "They're off by at least a percent or two."

So we had our little chuckle. It didn't last.

He said, "Do you—do you really think you can make a deal with the Board? After everything you've done?"

"Depends. I need you to get some recording equipment in here. The Bog can do that for you, huh? All up-and-up."

"I don't get it."

"There's things about the situation over there that I'm pretty sure they don't know. There's things I can do for them that I'm damned sure they don't know."

He gives me a half up-and-down, half sideways seminod of noncommittal agreement. "I can . . . I suppose I could come back, well, online . . ."

"You can?"

He tapped his skull behind his left ear. "My thoughtmitter . . . I suppose— since you—they've decided it pays them to keep an eye on what all of us are doing over there."

"Works for me. How bad are things on Home? I mean, I'm guessing— because you're here and all—that Angvasse didn't go berserk and kill every-body."

He nodded. "She—is not your biggest fan."

"She's on board with your whole Smoke Hunt game?"

"I—don't know. After—well, I haven't seen her. No one has."

That couldn't be good news. "What about Markham?"

"Lord Tarkanen is . . . I suppose you'd call him Acting Justiciar. Pending confirmation by the Lords Legendary."

"Fuck me like a goat. Orbek?"

"The Justice never happened. She didn't show up."

"So? They let him go or what?"

He shook his head. "I've had—more pressing concerns."

"It's that bad?"

"I would never have dreamed everything could go so wrong so quickly."

"Good."

He frowned at me. "It is?"

"The worse shit gets, the better I do."

"If that's true"—he sighed and sagged forward until his chin rested on his hands—"you'll probably end up king."

Which brings us to more or less now.

Without my help, the best you can hope for is destruction of your Black-Stone operation, and permanent loss of your access to Home—that is, Over-world. I repeat: that's your *best*. Remember that Deliann truly believes that the fundamental purpose of the Ankhanan Empire is to defend Home against fuckers like you. Like us. Remember that it was his grandfather who forged the *dil T'llan* to keep us out. Remember that Deliann is also the head of House Mithondionne, which makes him king of the elves. Who are the greatest spell-casters of Home. Remember what happened to your invasion force three years ago. Remember that the entire Ankhanan Empire has spent these past three years preparing to make war on you.

Try to imagine what that war will be like. They won't be coming to conquer; we've got nothing they need. They'll be coming to *punish*, get it? You won't know what a scorched-earth policy really is until you see it executed by a conflagration of dragons. Think of Deliann as me with an army. Think of yourselves as the Black Knife Nation.

Between them and you, all you've got is me.

This is what I bring to the table:

The Smoke Hunt still exists, so I'm still an Agent of Khryl. No matter how much Markham hates me, he can't touch me publically. Pretty much every Khryllian I meet has to kiss my ass, and the Soldiers of Khryl are still the finest fighting force in the history of either world. I've got a Khryllian Knight in my pocket. I've got Kierendal believing I'm on her side. I've got an Esoteric strike team that's probably in place already, which is commanded by a woman who worships me as a god. I'm the goddamn boogeyman of the ogrilloi, my brother is *kwatcharr* of the Black Knives—unless, y'know, I am—and no one alive can match my understanding of the *dil T'llan*.

Not to mention that I am, all modesty aside, the Hand of Ma'elKoth.

I can get you out from under the Khryllians. When I'm done, you'll have *permanent access* to Overworld. Permanent.

I can stop the war. Or, y'know, win it.

This is what I want:

I want my job back.

Not Acting. I guess you could say I want Faller's job. Better yet: I want to be his boss. Call it Director of Overworld Operations. I want an iron-clad lifetime contract, along with a full wipe-the-fucking-record-clean pardon for any and all prior acts.

I know you don't trust me. The beauty is that you don't *have* to. Nothing I can possibly do will make shit any worse than it is already. Call it my gift to you: the gift of no tomorrow.

Think it over. Take your time.

I've got nowhere I have to be.

This story concludes in
Act of Atonement: Book Two:

*His Father's Fist*

MATTHEW STOVER believes that nearly everything worth knowing about his life can be found in his books.

ABOUT THE TYPE

This book was set in Electra, a typeface designed
for Linotype by W. A. Dwiggins, the renowned type
designer (1880–1956). Electra is a fluid typeface,
avoiding the contrasts of thick and thin strokes that
are prevalent in most modern typefaces.

Printed in the United States
by Baker & Taylor Publisher Services